D0029320

The Hounds of Sunset

Edith Pargeter

Being the third book in a sequence entitled
THE BROTHERS OF GWYNEDD

HEADLINE

Copyright © 1976 by Edith Pargeter

First published in Great Britain in 1976
by Macmillan London Ltd

Reprinted in paperback in 1988
by HEADLINE BOOK PUBLISHING PLC

British Library Cataloguing in Publication Data

Pargeter, Edith
  The hounds of sunset. – (The brothers of
  Gwynedd; 3)
  I. Title
  823'.912[F]   PS6031.A49

  ISBN 0 7472 0008 4
  ISBN 0 7472 3017 X Pbk

Printed and bound in Great Britain by
Collins, Glasgow

HEADLINE BOOK PUBLISHING PLC
Headline House
79 Great Titchfield Street
London W1P 7FN

CONTENTS

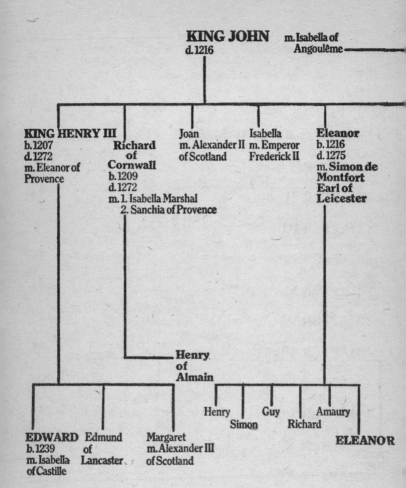

KING JOHN
d. 1216
m. Isabella of Angoulême

KING HENRY III
b. 1207
d. 1272
m. Eleanor of Provence

Richard of Cornwall
b. 1209
d. 1272
m. 1. Isabella Marshal
2. Sanchia of Provence

Joan
m. Alexander II of Scotland

Isabella
m. Emperor Frederick II

Eleanor
b. 1216
d. 1275
m. **Simon de Montfort Earl of Leicester**

Henry of Almain

EDWARD
b. 1239
m. Isabella of Castille

Edmund of Lancaster

Margaret
m. Alexander III of Scotland

Henry

Simon

Guy

Richard

Amaury

ELEANOR

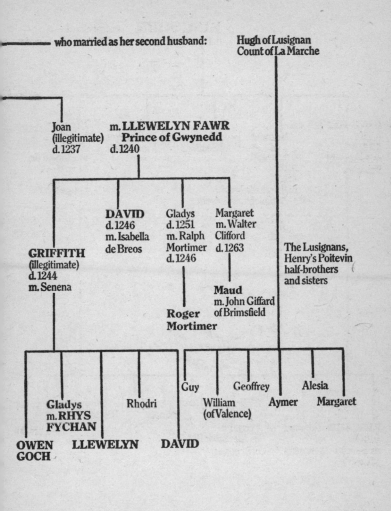

who married as her second husband: Hugh of Lusignan
Count of La Marche

Joan
(illegitimate)
d. 1237

m. LLEWELYN FAWR
Prince of Gwynedd
d. 1240

DAVID
d. 1246
m. Isabella
de Breos

Gladys
d. 1251
m. Ralph
Mortimer
d. 1246

Margaret
m. Walter
Clifford
d. 1263

GRIFFITH
(illegitimate)
d. 1244
m. Senena

The Lusignans,
Henry's Poitevin
half-brothers
and sisters

Maud
m. John Giffard
of Brimsfield

Roger
Mortimer

Gladys
m. RHYS
FYCHAN

Rhodri

Guy

William
(of Valence)

Geoffrey

Aymer

Alesia

Margaret

OWEN
GOCH

LLEWELYN

DAVID

The chronicle of the Lord Llewelyn, son of Griffith, son of Llewelyn, son of Iorwerth, lord of Gwynedd, the eagle of Snowdon, the shield of Eryri, first and only true Prince of Wales.

CHAPTER I

In the autumn of the year of Our Lord, twelve hundred and sixty-nine, King Henry of England, third of that name, brought to a triumphant completion his great new church of Westminster, the dream and passion of his life. For such was his devotion to the Confessor that the dearest wish of his heart had always been to create a worthy tomb for the precious relics of that great king and saint, and house it in a splendid church, as a jewel in a casket. And though his long reign – for this was his fifty-third regnal year since his nobles set him on the throne, a child of nine – had been troubled and torn constantly by wars and dissensions and feuds, by entanglements with popes and kings and princes, and though power had slid in and out of his hands, and the winds of other men's wills blown him hither and thither like thistle-down, for all these griefs and follies and misfortunes he had never relinquished that purpose and intent, but always returned to it as soon as he was master of his own actions.

As a child he had laid the foundation stone of the new work, when the monks in their ambitious zeal for their saint and their concern for the proper honouring of Our Lady grew dissatisfied with their old church and set out to rebuild, and in particular to add a great Lady Chapel at the eastern end behind the altar. Their plans outgrew their pockets, and devoured all the alms and grants within their reach, and when they despaired and owned their helplessness the king took the work upon himself as an act of piety. Certain follies of his own in the matter of

1

Sicily, certain unattainable ambitions, certain exasperations of his nobles and people tore him away from the work again and again, and counted almost fifty years away before he came at last to this happy consummation. But in this year of his blessed achievement I think he saw all that procession of life and death as but a painted scene of judgment upon a chapel wall, to be contemplated in peace for its colours when its perils were no more than half-remembered dreams.

And we in Wales, who had contended with him lifelong until the peace of Montgomery, then two years old, did not grudge him this victory, of all victories. Give him his due, in this passion at least he was not changeable, he who in all things else span with the wind and ebbed and flowed with the tide. He was happier building than fighting, and it showed in the quality of what he built.

It was in July, in the highest summer, when my lord Llewelyn's court was at Rhuddlan, that King Henry's messenger came, bearing a most cordial invitation to the prince of Wales to attend the festivities in October at Westminster, when the body of the Confessor was to be translated with great splendour and ceremony to the new tomb. It was an earnest of the easy relationship between these royal neighbours that the prince should be among the first to be bidden to the feast, and an even more marked sign of the times that the royal messenger should be that very Welsh clerk of the chancellery who had often served us, in the years of enmity, as our closest intelligencer to the English court. Cynan was not and never had been suspect, but before Montgomery he would never have been sent on the king's errands into Wales, his Welsh blood being reason enough for trusting him only close about the royal offices, and with the lowly work of copying, at that, whatever his ability. Now he came not as clerk and servant but as envoy in his own right, and with a groom to attend to his needs on the way. He did his formal office in hall with a beaming face but an earl's solemnity, but at meat at the high table afterwards he unbuttoned and was a boon companion, proving himself with a good clerkly voice when there was singing. This man I knew well from many meetings in old years upon Llewelyn's business, and to the prince himself Cynan's fine legal hand was familiar enough, but never before had they sat at one table together.

'I see,' said Llewelyn, smiling as he complimented him, 'that we made your fortune at Montgomery as well as our own. You may climb now in the king's favour with a good heart and a single mind.'

Cynan shook his head at that, and said there were no gains without losses, for he grew fat and easy now that his best occupation was gone. And so in truth he did, for he had still that white smoothness about him, but as if somewhat swollen, with the first signs of a paunch under his gown. He had been an old young man, and in time would be a young old man, changing without much change. His brow was by some inches higher, and time was setting about giving him the tonsure I had coveted in my boyhood and never attained.

'I was meant always to be a good doer,' he said, grinning a little wryly at setting himself among the stock we reared, 'but there's no thin living can wear away the flesh like the fret of danger, or keep the neck lissome like the eternal need to be looking over a man's shoulder. Now I rest easy, and turn my victuals into fair, fat meat. Your peace, my lord, may have made my head more secure on my shoulders, but it looks like turning my body into a bladder of lard.'

'God forbid,' said Llewelyn, laughing, 'that I should have to call out my guard again and break this land apart to keep you in hard condition. Are you so discontented with a quiet life? You talk like David. Where there's no mischief there's no sport! Though I think my brother's new little wife has broken him to harness, if her

3

spell holds, and of that we may all be glad.'

So lightly then he spoke of David, whom he had loved
best of his three brothers, and who had twice deserted
and betrayed him, and twice returned, half-grudging and
half-famished, into his too lavish grace.

'And do you carry,' he said, 'the like invitation to
David? I take it the Lord Edward would see to that.'
For King Henry's heir had grown up, until his thirteenth
year, in close companionship with David, then ward at
the English court, and that early alliance wrung them
both, and had cost us pains enough before our two
countries came to so arduous a peace.

'I do,' said Cynan, 'though what part the Lord Edward
needed to play is more than I know. The king is happy,
he wills less to no man. I think he calls every lord of his
acquaintance to share his own blessedness.'

'That I believe,' said Llewelyn, and smiled in some
wonder but little bewilderment at the image he had of
King Henry, who in happiness would scatter his own
substance of mind and body like largesse, and in appre-
hension or fright would strike out about him with feeble
but inexhaustible malice, like a child. In both he was
childlike. When he was wounded he would deal out
wounds to any who ventured near, when he was in bliss
he would spend himself like a fountain of love. But
always he must be the centre and spring from which ban
and blessing came. 'Tell me,' said Llewelyn, 'of how
things go with England.'

This order, tendered in open hall and before the entire
household of five hundred and more, Cynan understood
as it was intended, and regaled us freely with all the
current gossip and news of the court, but not yet with
any deeper observation drawn from beneath that surface.
The Lord Edward's preparations for his crusade, and the
king's for the great celebration in honour of his favourite
saint, said Cynan, between them had crowded every other
interest out of court. The list of those who had taken the

4

cross and intended to go with Edward to the Holy Land made a resounding catalogue of noble names, among them his brother Edmund, his cousin Henry of Almain, William of Valence, who was King Henry's half-brother, Gilbert de Clare, earl of Gloucester, John de Warenne, earl of Surrey, Roger Leyburn, and many more of the young men who frequented Edward's company.

'And the Lord Edward's wife intends,' said Cynan, 'to go to the east with him. She is as absorbed in this enterprise as he, and he thinks of nothing else.'

'So I have seen,' said Llewelyn, 'when he came to meet me in Montgomery in May, in the matter of the dispute in Glamorgan. Truly I believe he was bent on being fair, and we did get some business done, but while his feet walked the Severn water-meadows, I doubt his head was in Jerusalem.'

'Gloucester has taken the cross, no less than the rest,' said Cynan mildly. But he did not pursue that subject until the prince had withdrawn from hall into the high chamber, and had only a few of his closest with him, Tudor ap Ednyfed, the high steward of Wales – for his elder brother Goronwy, who had held that office before him, was a year dead at that time – the royal chaplain, and myself, his private clerk and servant. Then there was open talk of the dispute my lord had with Gilbert de Clare, earl of Gloucester, the only matter of large significance then troubling the good relations we had with England. Not, indeed, the only source of disputation, for when peace is made after ten years and more of border fighting and civil war, when lands have changed hands ten times over, and large honours been dismembered into a number of lesser holdings, with the best will in the world to word the agreement fairly and honestly, there must still be a hundred plots of land hotly disputed at law, and with reasonably good cases on both sides. The only remedy is in arbitration and give and take, in goodwill on both sides to do justice and keep

5

the peace. But land is land, and ambition is ambition, and all too often goodwill was in short supply when it came to sacrificing an acre or two of meadow or woodland.

The prince had every reason to be highly content with his gains in the treaty of Montgomery, for it had established him as lord of all Wales, and of all the homages of the lesser Welsh chiefs, recognised and honoured in his title and right. And he was bent on fulfilling his part of the agreement loyally, restraining his men from the border raiding to which they had been accustomed as of right all their lives, and paying punctiliously the instalments of the moneys due in fine for his recognition and alliance. If King Henry had such another prompt and cheerful payer, I never heard him named.

By the same token, he willed to abide by the prescribed arbitration in all cases where he held claim to land disputed by others. It was wearisome to wait out the delays, but he bore them with patience and good-humour. There was but this one matter that roused him to the edge of action.

In the south, in the land of Glamorgan, where the earl of Gloucester had a great castellany about Cardiff, he found himself now close neighbour to the prince, and fearing for his hitherto undisputed power, wished to extend northwards into the lands of Senghenydd, and create such another castle and administration there. The lord of Senghenydd was the last of a princely Welsh line, and had held as vassal of the earl, though only perforce, for his heart was with Wales and Llewelyn. And having his own suspicions of this, the earl had seized him and shipped him away to captivity in Ireland, at Kilkenny, and taken over Senghenydd as his own. When he began the building of a great castle at Caerphilly, to hold down the commote he had usurped, Llewelyn at once protested to the king, for this was plain breach of treaty. King Henry did his best to keep the peace between them, and to bring about some form of compromise that would satisfy both, but while the conferences and councils went on and on, so did the building of the earl's castle, and even the prince's patience was not made to last for ever.

Thus this matter stood when Cynan brought the king's invitation. And in the privacy of the high chamber he could offer some reassurance.

'The Lord Edward goes next month to confer with King Louis in France about the order of their sailing, the supplying of their ships, all the business of the crusade. In the summer of next year they intend to sail from Aigues Mortes. Gloucester is pledged, he *must* go. And when he goes, you have time to make your own dispositions, and to bring others, more accommodating, to reason. Two years and more! The king wills well to you, so does the Lord Edward. Oh, I grant you, the earl is already anxious to get out of his obligation, on the plea of his right to defend his border lands, but that goes down very ill with the Lord Edward, who is more than suspicious of the earl's good faith, and bent on forcing him to keep his pledge. It will be hard for him to stand out against his prince, especially when his own young brother is ardent for the crusade, and was among the first to swear. He cannot for shame let himself be displayed as recreant. It would take a brave man to outface Edward.'

'Or a foolhardy one,' said Llewelyn, 'and that he is.'

'So he may work his own undoing. But for my part I think he must resign himself to the crusade, and then you are rid of him.'

Then Llewelyn went on to ask him again of England, and how the days went there, and this time Cynan understood him in the deeper sense, and so answered him, with much thought.

'England,' he said, 'walks very gently and warily, like a sick man only a short while out of his bed, carefully watching every step before, and not looking behind. The wounds of civil war heal slowly, the worst wrongs to those who chose the losing side have been compounded by better sense, and the land is weary, and grateful for this new quietness. It came as something of a shock to them to be taxed, every free man on his belongings, to help to pay for this crusade, and they grumble as usual, but they'll pay, and take it as a mild penance or a thank-offering for peace in the land. The king is safe on his throne again, the succession secure.'

'And that better order that Earl Simon promised and died for?' said Llewelyn sombrely. 'And Earl Simon himself? All forgotten?'

'Nothing is forgotten,' said Cynan as darkly.

'And nothing changed!' said Llewelyn, with remembering bitterness.

Cynan shook his head. 'It is not so. Two things are changed, and for my life I cannot be sure whether for the better in the end, or the worse, or whether the one strikes out the other and leaves the land but a step from where it stood before. The crown came safe out of all that battering because the king was too soft to be crushed. Also the crown is a unity. But the baronage of England has been rent from head to foot, for it went two several ways and tore itself in half, and if it has not bled to death, it lies very sick. There was a balance there between king and baronage on which England depended for her power, and Earl Simon tried to restore it to true when it leaned perilously one way, and even to better the balance struck before. But God was not pleased to give him the victory, and now the scale dips heavily, for where is the force in the nobility to weigh against it? King Henry is old, and has learned a little sense, and moreover he is a weak man who finds it easier now to own his weakness. But when this overweighted power of monarchy is handed down to a powerful heir, then we shall discover the best and the worst of this changed order.'

Llewelyn watched him and said no word, for Cynan spoke as one equally bound to both England and Wales,

8

faithful in giving to us all the benefit of his wisdom and penetration, yet in his own fashion as true to England as Earl Simon de Montfort himself had been when he ripped her apart with the splendour of his vision and the passion of his virtue. King Henry's clerk knew what passed in the mind of his prince, and smiled at him his smooth and rueful smile.

'I take his pay,' he said, 'and while he wills well to Wales, so do I to him, and will not leave him. I, too, grow older. I am not sorry to sleep easy in my bed. But if ever he, or any other in his room, thinks to tear up this treaty and take to the old games, I shall remember my blood. I have not lost my old skills.'

'I will remember it,' said Llewelyn with a shadowed smile. 'Go on. You had more to say. What is this other thing you find changed that may restore the balance of the first?'

'It is that men's ideas need not die with them,' said Cynan, 'any more than scattered seed dies. In the stoniest of places they may root and grow. Even a man's enemies can learn from him. And if King Henry is too old, the Lord Edward is not, and has cold enough reason and shrewd enough judgment to take what he finds good, and make use of it, though he must take it from the hands of a man he has destroyed. Earl Simon will not be the first to turn his enemy into his heir. And England may be the better for it.'

I caught Llewelyn's eye then, and knew that he was recalling, as I was, the last speech ever I had with Earl Simon, on the high tower of the abbey church at Evesham, before the battle, as we watched the Lord Edward's army in a glitter of steel and wavering veil of dust draw in to our destruction, in confident purpose, without haste, forming their strict array on the march. 'I taught them that,' the earl said with critical approval. And after: 'If he can learn the discipline of battle, he can learn the discipline of statecraft, too. From his enemies, if need be.'

9

Those words Llewelyn had never heard but from my lips, I being then his envoy with the earl's army, but I knew he was hearing them now, as I was, in a voice not mine.

'Not England only,' said Llewelyn, with the face of his dead friend and ally still before his eyes, 'but I pray, Wales also.'

'There are signs,' said Cynan. 'Next to the cardinal-legate who made the peace it was Edward who did the most to curb the bloodiest of the victors, and save what could be saved for the disinherited. He leans to the sensible notion that men who pay the tallages and aids should have their own representatives to see they are fairly levied, and men who fight the battles and bear the weight of policy should have a small voice in forming it. And he is all for law. Yes, there are signs.'

'So nothing is utterly lost,' said Llewelyn.

'Nothing lost,' said Cynan, 'and nothing forgotten.'

He stayed with us the night, and Llewelyn wrote a cordial letter to King Henry, accepting his invitation to the feast. And when Cynan left us, it was to ride on across north Wales into Lleyn, to carry the like bidding to David, certainly to be accepted no less heartily. Llewelyn added a message of his own, with the hope that they might ride together in one royal party, to do Wales the greater honour and show a brotherly front. At that time, though David had been settled on his own agreed lands, approved by commission as his due, for over a year, they met but seldom except in formal council, for it needed time to restore without damage the old relationship between them. And that rather to accommodate David, the betrayer, than Llewelyn, the betrayed, who in the hour of his triumph at Montgomery had kissed and forgiven in honour of Wales and in the vastness of his own content. But it is not so easy to forgive the man you have twice deserted, when his largeness of mind only redoubles your deep discontent with yourself, and David

10

still went stiffly and formally with his brother and over-lord. His homage and fealty cost him dear because he had paid so little for them. I, who knew him better than most, yet never knew him well enough to know whether he would have welcomed the sting, had he been denied grace and countenance and humbled as he deserved, or flamed into open revolt and defiance. I think he himself did not know, for it was never put to the test. The only time he was shaken into complaining to me, it was that he was mislaid and received again with no more heart-burning than if he had been a strayed hound, both his defection and his return taken as events too light and trivial for passion or overmuch ceremony. That to Llewelyn he was worth neither a blessing nor a blow. Which was false, though fiercely he believed it. Llewelyn's passion was not as David's, a bitter fire consuming the heart within, but a glowing warmth that shone on the world without. But the one was as hot as the other.

Howbeit, David replied as civilly, and brought his party to join his brother's at Bala, in Penllyn, from which maenol the court set out in state, in good time to enjoy the fine autumn by the way, and reach Westminster a full week before Saint Edward's day.

I looked for their coming with both eagerness and pain, knowing they would come lavishly attended, and that among their retinue would be two closer to me than my own skin, one whom I longed for, one whom I dreaded, and that I could not have the one without the other.

They rode in on a September evening, before sunset. I was down by the lake, in the fields gleaned to a bleached white after the end of the harvest, and sun-gilded in the slanting light, when I heard first the horns sounding merrily in the distance, on the uplands to the north of the maenol, and then the moving murmur that is com-pounded of the easy thud and rustle of hooves in grass and gravel, and many voices in talk and laughter, the jingle of harness and the chimes of little bridle bells, and

11

the brief, cajoling calls of falconers after their hawks, a far-off music brought near even in its quietness by the stillness of the air. Then there was a high, pure peal of joyous laughter, a child's utterance in sheer delight of heart, and I knew the child unseen from afar, and turned back to the maenol to be beside my lord when he came out to the gate, as come he would, to welcome his guests. The bright procession wound down the bleached track through the deeper upland grass, and brought all its colours and sounds and voices down to the gate where we waited, half the maenol out to do them honour. David showed very splendid in black embroidered with silver, his head uncovered to the freshening breeze, the curving strands of blue-black hair tossed across his forehead, his eyes, that were blue as harebells, just clouding from their journeying innocence into the veiled withdrawal from which he gazed upon his brother. And he on a tall English horse, a red roan, Edward's gift, like the pretty white palfrey that nuzzled at his elbow, and the girl who rode it, astride like a boy, and booted in soft French leather.

David lighted down, and went before us all to bend the knee to Llewelyn, and kiss the hand that had reached to embrace him. I do not say he did it to offend, rather in stiff insistence on the hard identities of vassal and overlord, but there could have been no surer way of offending. Yet Llewelyn would not resent him, but let him have his way, and only offered him the kiss of kinship when he rose from his knee. They made each other the common offerings of enquiry and acknowledgement, the one in tolerant patience, the other in unsparing duty. Then David turned to his wife, and here we saw another creature, warm and eager, with the veil lifted from his gaze, and his long, arrogant, icy lips molten into a smile. She slipped her feet from the stirrups and reached down her arms to him, and he swung her easily aloft out of the saddle, and held her eye to eye with him and heart to heart a moment, before he set her on her feet and brought her by the hand to Llewelyn.

The kiss that David's stiff cheek had resisted was welcome to her, as was every gesture of friendliness and affection. Llewelyn had to stoop low to her, for she barely reached David's shoulder, and the prince was by the width of three fingers the taller of the two. And seeing her thus accept with impulsive pleasure what he had suffered like a blow or an insult, David, too, flushed and softened a little, though against his will and in his own despite.

She was then no more than twelve years old, and even for her years not tall, but sturdy and well-made. Nor was she beautiful, but for the bloom that all young creatures have. She had great brown eyes like a hind, innocent and wild, and curling hair of the same colour, and a soft, grave mouth given to rare but sudden and whole-hearted laughter. Loud and talkative enough when she was with David, she was quiet and shy in company, though not at all timid. And this was Elizabeth Ferrers, daughter of Robert Ferrers, earl of Derby, and wife to Prince David of Wales.

Child as she was, she was already once wedded and widowed. She was close kin to the king, her mother being his niece, Mary, daughter to the count of La Marche, Henry's eldest half-brother, a royal lady who had been married to Robert Ferrers when she was but seven years old, and her bridegroom only two years older. After the same dynastic custom they had married Elizabeth as a child to one William Marshal of Norfolk, who by his first wife already had sons old enough to be father to this tender creature. But her elderly husband followed the fortunes of Earl Simon, and died in that cause in the year of Evesham. Maid and widow, she had come into the king's wardship when her father, too, was dispossessed of all he had for his part in the civil wars, and since law had allowed her part of her dower lands from the Marshal inheritance, she had brought with her certain manors in

Norfolk when King Henry, at the Lord Edward's instance, bestowed her upon David in marriage. A match not to be missed, and David accepted it willingly, lands and lady and all, together with the Lord Edward's patronage and favour. Of all of which, I fancy, he thought he knew the relative values. Yet I saw for myself, now for the third time seeing those two together, a year married after the world's practical fashion, that Elizabeth had had something to teach him, and he had found himself learning without resentment. For every look they exchanged, every touch of their sleeves brushing, every intonation of their voices when they talked together, was eloquent beyond words.

I looked among the dismounting company within the courtyard for the face I most desired to see, knowing she would not be far from Elizabeth. For ever since David had brought his bride home, Cristin had been her closest confidante and attendant. David would have no other to care for the child, for in a world where he doubted most men and held most women gently enough but lightly, for Cristin he had and kept always a deep regard, and that alone was enough to incline his wife most warmly to her, even if they had not, from the first, been drawn to each other. And I was glad that Cristin should have a fair young creature close to her, to love and guard, she who had no child by her husband, and never would have child by her love. For we were cursed and blessed, she and I, in mutual loving blessed indeed, but cursed in that ours was a love forbidden and impossible of fruit, since she was the wife of my half-brother.

I found her among the first to follow into the maenol, Cristin, Llywarch's daughter, her black hair hidden under a white wimple, and a white mule stepping delicately under her. And as happened always with us at every new meeting, when I found her, her eyes were on me, and when mine held them they grew so large and crystal-clear in their purple-grey, the colour of irises, and so drew me into them like the seduction of deep water, that I died in them and was reborn into bliss, as a drowning man by the mercy of God and the grace of faith may sink through death into the peace of paradise.

She was within a month or two the same age as David, both being then thirty-three years old. We were long experienced in loving without greed or regret, she and I, and though we never spoke words of love, nor asked any fulfilment but the mutual knowledge we already possessed, neither did we avoid each other, nor any longer dissemble the truth that we had between us such trust and regard as few ever enjoy with man or woman. To what end? Godred knew very well how things stood with us, and knew that we knew, and by all means in his power, having glimpsed a passion of which he was incapable, had sought to drag it down to a level he could first understand, and then befoul. Who knows but it was Godred who kept us resolute in our purity?

So at this meeting, though I knew well that he was there among the company of knights and squires that followed David into the maenol, and needed no telling that he would be looking for me as hungrily as ever I looked for Cristin, I made no ado about going to her directly and with open gladness, and she gave me her hand, and said the same current words that I was saying to her, and let me help her down and take the bridle from her. Assignations we never made, but met when we met, and were glad. Surely we had, after our fashion, a compact with God to be endlessly grateful for what had been given us, and not to grasp at more. But we had never undertaken not to hope.

She had barely set foot on the ground, and her hand was still in mine, when he was there between us, clasping an arm of each in his long hands, and deliberately scoring against my wrist the silver ring he wore, the fellow to one I had once worn. His father and mine had long ago given the second ring to the girl he took for one night in the rushes of the hall at Nevin, and she, years after-wards, to her son, the fruit of that union. By that token I had known my half-brother when we met. He had not then known me, nor for some time after, nor had any word ever been said, even now, to make it clear that he knew me for his father's bastard, yet always, when most he willed to remind me how we three were bound to-gether, and how I might, if I willed, draw even closer, make myself his familiar and equal, and enjoy what now I only revered, always he contrived to twist that ring before my eyes, with its little severed hand holding a rose. But he had no power even to make us start, or loose too soon the clasp of our hands. With nothing to hide, why should we hide it?

'Well, Saint Samson?' said Godred, in that high, sweet voice of his, and linking his arm in mine. 'We are to go on pilgrimage together, it seems, to the Confessor's shrine. Three or four weeks of sweet companionship and easy living! I mean to enjoy you to the full, this time.' And with the other arm he encircled Cristin, and so drew us with him towards the hall, leaving the grooms to lead away the horses.

I am swart and plain, and he was lithe and fair and comely, with curling hair the colour of ripe white wheat, and round, gold-brown eyes. Yet she loved me, and not him!

'And Cristin shares my pleasure,' he said, closing his fingers possessively about her shoulder, 'though she is not so quick to utter it as I. We never forget, Samson, that it was you who restored us to each other, when we never thought to meet again. I speak for both – do I not, my love? This once join your voice with mine!'

She looked straight before her, and smiled. 'Samson knows my mind,' she said. 'There is no need to look back so far. He knows I forget nothing. But if you want me to say it, yes, I shall take pleasure in this journey together. Yes, I am happy.'

So he had his answer, but it was not the right answer, though he swallowed it with grace. For it was not what he wanted, it was outrage to him, that she should be happy, when he, though through his own curst nature, was surely among the unhappiest souls on earth.

During the days of our preparations it did happen now and then that I had speech with her alone, while he was busy with his own duties. It was not that at these times we spoke of our own affairs, but there were other things I had to ask of her that needed a degree of privacy, too. David was my breast-brother, my mother's nurseling, my own charge in his childhood, as now Cristin cared for the child he had taken in marriage, and I needed to know the best and the worst concerning him, for no matter how often he offended against Llewelyn and discarded me, yet I could not but love him.

'He is still sore,' said Cristin, 'and still denies with anger that his wounds are self-inflicted. He knows his own sins, but will neither repent them nor accept forgiveness for them. Edward embraced him when he deserted Llewelyn, and he despises Edward in his heart for embracing a traitor. Llewelyn in honour of his triumph tossed David's offences out of mind, and haled him back openly without penalty, never denying he deserved it, and David worships him for it because he could not have done as much himself, and hates him for it because so easy a forgiveness slights both the offence and the offender. They are two creatures made in moulds so different, and yet so linked, they cannot touch without hurt, nor be apart without loss. And yet he does love his brother! Sometimes I doubt he loves Llewelyn more than Llewelyn loves him. He could not so hate him if he did not.'

I asked, for God knows I had good reason to understand the power of personal happiness, what was to be hoped from this marriage Edward had made.

She was standing beside me in the twilight when this passed, having put her lady to bed, for that shy royal

17

creature awoke with the light and tired with the fall of darkness like all children. From the portal of Elizabeth's apartments we could see the silver of the lake like a spilled coin in moonlight. My sleeve was against my love's sleeve, and we were at peace, but for all these souls we loved, and for whom we desired the same peace.

Cristin said: 'She has tamed him. She does not know it – how could she? She is still half a child. There is no one so astonished as David. And how is that possible, since he knows his own beauty? None better! I think he never considered that a wife should look at him and find him beautiful. He took her as a chattel, a means to lands, and to the Lord Edward's continuing favour. I doubt he ever looked at her, until she had looked at him, and gone the way of most women who look at him. Half child she may be, but she is half woman, too. She looked at him, and she loved. Is it so strange? And you know him, he is gentle and playful with children, he awoke only when he found himself clasping a woman he had warmed into life, roused and ready for him.'

'He has bedded her, then?' I said.

'Surely! You have only to look at them. They have an understanding of the flesh.' It was true. There was no mistaking that radiance that shone out of them when they touched each other. She spoke of it with a calm face but a careful voice, regarding without envy but with secret grief what they had and we could never have. 'Her women told her, when they married her the first time, child as she was, what would be expected of her some day as a wife. She was prepared. And did you ever hear of a woman who complained of David's loving? He would have let her alone a year or two yet, I judge, if she had not stirred him. It charmed and moved him that she should love him and show her love.'

'And he,' I said, 'does he also love?'

'He is pleased and disarmed and startled, how can he choose but respond? It's a new delight and a great flat-

18

tery. Whether it will last, and keep its power, who knows and who can ever know with David? But yes, I think I would call it love. Whatever he does, he will never wilfully hurt her. But without willing it he might destroy her,' said Cristin with great gravity. 'Whoever loves David is in danger.'

And that was truth. And I was all the more glad that this proud, confiding and sensitive child should have Cristin watching over her. The time might come when she would need a friend, and nowhere could she have found another so brave and so loyal.

We rode for London at the end of September, a great party, not only to do credit to the royal house of Wales, but also to pay honour to King Henry, who by and large had played fair with us since the agreement, and who deserved his triumph. We crossed the Berwyns in brisk, bright weather, and had good hawking there. Llewelyn's falconer had in his charge not only the prince's own birds, but several he had been training as gifts for the king and the Lord Edward, and they made splendid proving flights along the way, and showed their mettle to such good effect that he was in high content with the fruit of his labour. We carried with us also venison for the feasts and for the king's larder.

At Oswestry we crossed into England, with no need of the letters of safe-conduct sent from the court, and that was pleasant indeed. So it should always be, yet men have free passage so seldom, and so briefly. But this autumn was blessed, even to the weather, and the ride into Shrewsbury, where we halted overnight at the abbey, was truly as serene as a pilgrimage, a dream of ease in those lush fields and softly rolling valleys. Yet on this road I had memories, too, for I had ridden it once in Llewelyn's service on the way to the parliament of Oxford, thus far the same road, and there was no evading the reminders of that journey, or the remembered face

19

of the man I had seen at the end of it, kneeling in grand, contained and private prayer at the shrine of St Frideswide. And Llewelyn, too, felt his presence, for I saw how he watched me, and willed not to be seen watching me, and hesitated whether to speak or be silent. Silent he was in the end, for of speech there was no need. He knew and I knew that the image of Earl Simon rode with us all the way.

After Shrewsbury we were on a way new to me, for we took the king's great highway called Watling Street, which they say the Romans made, and which drives by long, straight stretches headlong for London. One night we passed at the priory of Lichfield, and the next at Coventry, no great ride, for we had time and to spare. And when we were private after meat at Coventry, Llewelyn suddenly raised his head and turned to gaze to the south-west, and said, so low that I knew it was for none but himself and me: 'We are very close, are we not, to Kenilworth?'

I said that we were, that if he willed we could linger here a day, and he and I could ride there. If he so willed, alone. His face was fixed and bright, still as a royal head upon a gold coin, and even so coloured, a tissue of fine-drawn lines in gilt and umber. Those who thought him moderate and tempered and equable, a man well-set in the cautious craft of state, did not know him as I knew him. He and I were born in the same night, under the same stars, his mother was my mother's patron and mistress, there was no dividing us. And I knew him possessed and inspired, a soul like the flame of a candle on an altar, kindled and unquenchable in dedication to the cause of Wales. Yet in pursuit of that passion he had encountered one perhaps greater than himself, burning with a grander vision, and for a time those two flames had been one. If I forgot nothing, how could I conceive that he should forget?

'No,' said Llewelyn after long thought, and in a voice

so low I strained to hear. 'Not here! Kenilworth is not the place.'

In London we were very honourably lodged, the princes with their immediate households in King Henry's own palace of Westminster, some close officers, of whom I was one, in the guest-halls of the collegiate church of St Peter, the object of our pilgrimage, while the knights of the escort were sent on to that Tower of which I had so many old memories. Thus Cristin, being tirewoman to Elizabeth, remained in the royal island of Westminster close to me, while Godred was removed to the Tower, and both she and I could breathe freely and look each other in the eyes when we met with gladness and calm, untainted by the poison of his misery and malice, which neither of us knew how to cure. And by that blessedness, in part, I remember that great celebration of St Edward's day.

That is a wonder, that city of Westminster, in extent so small, in beauties so great, so teeming then with all the nobility of the land, for there was no earl nor baron nor cleric who did not wish to be present at the translation of the saint. In shape almost square, it is rimmed with water on every side, for on the east lies the Thames with all its ships and barges, while from the west flows in the little river Tyburn, to fill the long ditches that close in the royal enclave from north and south. And all this moated town is filled with the many and splendid buildings of palace and church, colleges and dortoirs and hospices and chapels, the gardens and orchards and cloisters of the monks, the stables and boat-houses and offices of the king, and everything needful to life, bakehouse and farm and fisheries, lodgings for good poor men, almshouses and mews and kitchens. I marvelled at the great press of guests this city could receive and accommodate, and yet at this time it was full to overflowing, and so glowing with ardour and excitement, so full of

21

voices and music, colour and movement, that the dullest heart could not but be stirred.

And there in the midst of this island city rises the long, lofty roof of the great church, visible from every part, from every part commanding and drawing the eye. The marvel within we were not to see until the great day of the translation and the first mass, but the marvel without was enough to hold us at gaze all the days we spent there in waiting. Such noble, springing tracery in stone, such grace of windows and portals, I had never seen. The monks, before their coffers ran dry, had themselves built the Lady Chapel they desired at the eastern end of the old church, and the form of this was fine, but time and the king's passion for his act of piety had outrun it far, and the body of the church which he had now completed, transepts and apse and choir, soared above incomparably tall and fair.

King Henry received Llewelyn and David in audience as soon as we came there, but I did not see him close until the day of the feast, only now and again running about his creation and vanishing again into his palace in transports of excited happiness, his master-mason and clerks and familiars hard on his heels like a swarm of bees. He was then sixty-two years old, and had lived through a long and war-torn reign that had destroyed many a stronger vessel, and though he had ridden out all the tempests he bore the signs upon him. Slender and graceful always, he was now very frail in appearance, his face worn and transparent, his fair, well-tended hair and beard blanched to an ivory-grey, and doubtless he was very weary, but the rapture of his achievement filled him with force and energy. If he had laboured on his kingdom with such devoted concentration of mind he would surely have been the best of kings. But at least, if his talents had not gone into statecraft, they had spent themselves on something lasting, lovely and worthy in the end, and I give him the credit due.

22

It had been the king's intention that he and his queen should wear their crowns of state upon the saint's feast, and that all things should be ordained in the same fashion as at a coronation, which meant that the customary writs had been sent out to all those who had special ceremonial rights and duties, and for some weeks they had been making great preparations for the occasion. But on the vigil of the feast King Henry made belated proclamation in Westminster Hall that he had had better thoughts in the matter, and deemed it presumptuous to assume the crown a second time, and especially felt it his part rather to be humble and joyful in his service to Saint Edward, than proud in his own estate. So the formal ceremonies were remitted, though all who cared to come to the festival might do so, and after the translation and the mass might remain to share in the banquet.

'That's but half the story,' said Llewelyn, when I attended him in the evening to make preparation for next day. 'It seems he's still beset with civil wars, though minor ones now. The citizens of London had laid out lavishly on plate and robes, since they owe service in the butlery on such state festivals, when the crowns are worn. But then the men of Winchester also laid claim to the butlery. It's a costly business, and no doubt either city would have resisted if it had been exacted from them as a duty, but neither was willing to relinquish it as an honour. There would have been quarrels, at the least, maybe a little blood-letting. He thought wiser to bow out of his crown gracefully and avoid the contention.'

It was too much, I said, to suppose that anything could ever go altogether smoothly and decorously with King Henry. Nothing he touched ever came finally to ruin, but always he walked creaking ice that cracked behind him, and came to land again safely by something a little short of a miracle.

'Ah, he'll ride this little storm,' said Llewelyn, 'at no more cost than the meat and wine he provides them. But

23

he has graver matters on his mind, too, when the light of his shrine is not too brilliant to let him see them. Gloucester has not come to the festival. And tomorrow being the great day, clearly he does not intend to come.'

From our view it was no bad thing that Gilbert de Clare should put himself in ill odour with both king and prince. All the more would they be disposed to listen, in the matter of the rape of Senghenydd and the building of Caerphilly, to the protagonist who did come at the king's invitation, and was prepared, as clearly Gilbert was not, to meet his opponent and consider sensible arbitration. By his intransigence and disobedience we could not fail to gain credence.

'He is mad,' said David, who was with us that evening, and throughout showed a front of unity with his brother, though during the past days he had been much in the Lord Edward's company. 'If he does not come he turns the king into an enemy for the sake of his favourite saint, let alone the matter of the crusade. And Edward is already bitterly angry with him for trying to slide out of his obligations. He took the oath of his own free will, like the rest, and Edward will hold him to it. Gloucester's party should provide one of the strongest companies. Edward is absolute that he cannot fulfil his undertakings to King Louis and to God properly if Gloucester breaks his oath. If he does not come in time for tomorrow, the king will send for him, and he had better pay heed. But my guess is, he'll come. At the last moment, with the worst grace, and insolently, but he'll come.'

But the morrow came, and the whole court and its guests rose with the dawn to make ready, but Gilbert de Clare did not come. Nor, in the end, was this the only vexation King Henry had to contend with on the supreme day of his life, for not only did the citizens of London stand so rigidly on their dignity as to withdraw after the great mass ended, and refuse the feast, while the men of Winchester crowed over them and stayed to eat and drink their fill, but there was also a grander and more bitter contention, which ended with London laid under an interdict for a time, though for all I could see it made little difference to life in the city, and no one fretted overmuch. The trouble arose out of an old rivalry between the two archbishops, for he of York had always insisted that he had the right to have his cross carried before him in the province of Canterbury as at home, and his brother of Canterbury had always resisted it. Now the archbishop of Canterbury at this time, the queen's uncle Boniface of Savoy, was very old, and too frail to be present at the great ceremony, and so his brother of York, Walter Giffard, had his way at the translation, and had his cross paraded before him, to the great offence of all his fellow-bishops, so that they made no move, when the time came, to join him in the procession round the new church, but sat implacably in the stalls of the monks, and let him cense the shrine alone. And old Boniface, when he heard of it, was so resentful that he placed London under interdict, and a month later he said his last mass in England at the coast, before sailing home to his native Savoy, where he died a year afterwards.

But as for the great concourse of worshippers that thronged into the church that day, I think these annoyances fell away from them unnoticed, as motes of dust vanish in a great brightness, or if they are seen at all, show like flying jewels. For truly that was a wonder. I think in this world there could be no building more glorious. The work the king had done – and rightly he can so claim, for though he had the finest masons and jewellers and metal-workers to labour for him, yet he himself had firm views on what he would have, and set it out in detail – comprised the eastern end of the nave, where his own royal chair was, the choir and the north and south transepts, the presbytery and the chapels and ambulatory of the apse, and beyond these to the east a short ambulatory leading to the Lady Chapel, which the monks had built some years before. And behind the high altar, encircled by the chapels, the new shrine of the saint was raised aloft.

Such was the extent of the work. But what can be said of the form, of the great soaring columns of marble that led our eyes upwards as we entered, so high we had to crane backwards to look up into the gilded ribs and bosses of the vault, of the carven shields, the diapered wall-spaces, the filigree windows, the traceries of screen and arcade, of the glorious colours of painted angels and sacred medallions, the grisaille glass studded with armorial shields. The sun shining through them filled all the vault with singing sparks of emerald and ruby and gold.

In this enclosure of splendour, to the chanting of the monks of St Peter and in the presence of all who could crowd anywhere within the walls, the relics of Saint Edward the Confessor were reverently taken in their casket from the old shrine, swathed with rich draperies, and carried on the shoulders of King Henry, his brother Richard of Cornwall, king of the Romans, the king's sons, the Lord Edward and Edmund of Lancaster, and as many more of the great nobles as could get a hand to the bier, to the new, raised shrine aloft behind the altar. Edward's great height so threw things out of balance that he was forced to let the coffin rest in his arm rather than on his shoulder, to accommodate his father, who was a head shorter. Where Edward went, who was not? Many fell short of him by head and shoulders, too.

Those who could not pretend to bearing any part of the blessed burden nevertheless reached a hand on one side or the other, at least to touch, and so walked slowly with the bearers, and among them went Llewelyn and David, one upon either side. Others came to touch but once as the coffin passed. So they carried Saint Edward up the stone stairway into his new chapel, a spacious place floored in red and green porphyry and Purbeck marble, with the great shrine of the same materials in the midst, studded everywhere with semi-precious stones and mosaic work, with a tiered feretory of solid gold at the top. And in this sumptuous tomb they laid him, and heard the first mass of the new church sung in his honour.

It so chanced that I had a place from which there was a clear view of the king's chair, and while mass was said I watched him, for he was so bright and pale that the light seemed almost to shine through him. His seat was raised, and the shrine of the saint was very lofty, and I think he could see, above the high altar, the golden crest of the feretory that marked the holy place. He never took his eyes from it, and for the first time I saw his face free of the single, strange blemish that had always spoiled his comeliness and kingliness, that drooping of one eyelid that cast shadows of doubt over his proffered honesty and gave warning of his twisting ability to deceive, a flaw he had handed on to his son. Edward sat close beside him, his seat lower, but his face on a level with his father's. I had them almost in full-face, the one oval superimposed upon the other, the old upon the young, until the light played tricks and seemed to make the young change places and blot out the old. Henry was grown so fragile and clear, Edward was so large and solid and full of blood and bone, his vigour and violence overwhelmed the king's small, pale flame, but could not extinguish it.

He was then thirty years old, this Lord Edward, a giant just coming to his prime, hardened and experienced in political contention and civil war, a man well-proportioned, long-limbed, moving with confidence and certainty in his body. He had large, heavy, handsome features, a great cliff of a brow, and his hair, which in childhood, as I remembered, had been flaxen, almost silver, was now so dark a brown as to be almost black, and his long, level brows appeared quite black. He affected rich but dark clothing, and little jewellery, having no need of adornment to draw eyes to him, his stature alone making him known wherever he walked. In repose, as I saw it then, his face was severe to grimness, attentive to the mass but not moved, as if his mind was on other business. His left eyelid drooped over the dark brown eye. I thought the flaw in him more marked than when I had seen him previously. Closed up in armour I had seen him last, dealing sharply-judged and unrelenting death at Evesham. But long before that, at Oxford, I had seen him close and spoken with him. He had the heavy lid then, but when he was moved or intent it hardly showed. When he followed Earl Simon and hung on his words it showed not at all. He was not moved now, or else the trick had grown on him unawares. I do believe he was devout, I believe his heart was set on his crusade in absolute and devoted duty, taking upon him both his father's oath and his own. But when I looked again at the king, I saw how far the father had out-stripped the son.

He had no such grand abilities, no such stature or prowess in arms, no force such as Edward had, and God knows he had many faults and weaknesses, and had led his own baronage, and us, and all who ever had to do with him, a devious and unkingly dance, as quick to turn and twist as any fox, being a timorous man who used what weapons he had. And yet to the end, and more than all at the end, there was a kind of innocence about him, as of a clean creature soiled by running in fright against obstacles that dirtied his robes but could not corrode his being. Often had I hated him and blamed him, and called him forsworn and devious, and so he had often been, and yet I watched his rapt and dedicated face there in St Peter's church on St Edward's day, and it was washed clean and pure like a child's, and yet deeply sorrowful and humble like a penitent's, and it seemed to me that in his supreme act of devotion he was confessing and repenting all the unworthinesses of his life, and from the heart paying for them as best he could, until

28

God should show him a better and surer way.

I looked at Llewelyn, who was not far away, and saw that he also was contemplating King Henry's face, though I think he had a narrower profile to study than I. His was a countenance I knew far better than my own, broad at the wide-set eyes, that were very straight of gaze and darker and deeper than Edward's, broad at the jutting bones of cheek and jaw, and these bold planes of bone all outlined by the spare curves of clipped golden-brown beard he wore. Not a face to confide too readily, but neither did it evade or conceal. I had seen it once as fixed and devoted as King Henry's was now, when he kept vigil with the sword he had sanctified to the service of a Wales which was then uncreated, as though he set himself to assemble from a scattering of shattered shards a single vessel of gold. And so he had done, and he was acknowledged prince of the nation he had made. It was another kind of achievement, but he knew and respected another man's apotheosis when it shone before his eyes.

So this one passionate devotion looked upon another as single and pure as itself, however different, and recognised and saluted it generously, smiling. And I remember thinking to myself that if God was of Llewelyn's mind, King Henry was assured of his absolution.

We stayed in Westminster for some days after the festival was over, and Llewelyn had two meetings with the king and the Lord Edward and their closest advisers, to discuss the vexed matter of Senghenydd, and put his own case as to which party was infringing the treaty there. Certain minor disputes concerning the borders were not difficult to resolve, with goodwill on both sides. But though King Henry, two days after the feast-day, had sent letters of safe-conduct to the earl of Gloucester, with the plain intimation that his presence was required as a matter of feudal duty, still Gilbert made no haste to obey. We could not wait his pleasure, but did make natural, though

I think fair, use of his absence to emphasise our own case. Then we left for home, taking a very cordial farewell. And this time we went not by the same way we had come, but by Oxford and Worcester, at Llewelyn's wish.

I had no clear idea then of what was in his mind, but when we drew nearer to Evesham, and he took his party for lodging not to that abbey, but to Richard of Cornwall's foundation of Hailes, I did guess at his reason, and when he announced that he meant to spend two nights in that hospitable place I was sure. Not as Llewelyn, prince of Wales, in royal progress of state, would he approach the place of the death and burial of Earl Simon, or make himself known to the monks who had buried his friend. But Evesham is but a little way from Hailes, and with a day in hand he might go there unrecognised and unexalted, like other men. I was ready when he sent for me to him, on the first evening, and shut himself up with me alone.

At the thought of an idle day David had frowned, restless for home once he was away from the court, and asked with his chill formality what he might as freely have declared as his intent, to ride on ahead, with the prince's leave, and be about his proper responsibilities in Lleyn. And I think Llewelyn was glad, for whatever had to do with Earl Simon's memory was tension and disquiet between them, recalling old discords not yet fully forgiven, even upon Llewelyn's side, much less on David's. So we were private, we might go where we would, as humbly as we would, and none to question us, even with his eyes.

'I have a consecration of my own to make,' Llewelyn said. 'Will you ride with me tomorrow, after David has taken his people off? They'll be away early; he's impatient for home now. Unhappy the man with two homes, born Welsh and bred English, and no fault of his own. He tears a string from his heart when he leaves the one, but once that's broken he cannot wait to get to the other, and bind it up again there. And he thinks I do not know!'

Unwilling to speak for or against David where we touched too near the grief he had helped to make, and the warfare in which he had taken the opposing side, I asked him where we rode. At that he smiled, but very gravely.

'You know as well as I, Samson. How could you or I pass so close, and not draw in to pay him honour? And I in particular, who have never yet seen that place. We will go to Evesham, you and I, and go as rustic and plain as any of the country people who frequent his grave. I want no honour, none of the respect given to princes, where he lies, until I have fulfilled both the oaths I made to his memory.'

I said I had somewhat of my own to vow to Earl Simon, and would go with him gladly. And Llewelyn thanked me as though I had done him great courtesy, which was his way.

When I left him, I met with Cristin in the hall of the hospice, coming from her lady's bed-chamber with a blue brocaded gown over her arm, to have some pulled threads of the embroidery stitched back into the pattern. She looked upon me with the radiant stillness that was better than any smile. Her night-black hair was loosed about her shoulders from its day-time braids. Silken and bright and heavy it was always, but absolute black, raven-black, with never a sheen of David's steely blue. It made her brow so white beneath that my eyes dazzled. Cristin went in the sun and the wind freely, and the sun would not burn nor the wind abrade her.

'She is asleep,' she said, seeing me eye Elizabeth's gown. 'She was tired out from the ride today. So much air and such a brisk breeze.'

'Asleep,' I said, 'until he wakes her?'

'He will not wake her,' said Cristin. 'He can be patient and tender to little things; it's with the great he has no

31

forbearance. They tell me,' she said, 'we are to leave you in the morning early.'

'It is true,' I said. 'David wants to get home. And my lord has other needs.'

'At Christmas,' she said, 'doubtless I shall see you.' For those brothers kept the feasts always in strict form, all the more because of the constraint between them, and the tie of kinship was sacred, so that at the Nativity or soon thereafter they must meet.

I said I trusted so, and wished her and her mistress a blessed journey home. And so we parted, as every meeting and every parting went with us, going from each other without a touch of hand or a turn to gaze. Of such small doubts and pleas we had no need. But with her image before my eyes I went out into the late October night, in the hush of the cloister, to breathe the chill and the darkness. Llewelyn, I knew, was gone to make his evening devotions in Richard of Cornwall's great church, for he was as devout as ever was King Henry, though the small, solitary holiness of the Celtic church, so spare and so sweet, haunted his mind and kept him safe from the worldly charm of such foundations as Hailes. God is somewhere within earshot of every altar, but nearer to our hermit-saints than to the lords of the English church. Yet a brave, demanding voice can reach him everywhere. So Llewelyn went alone to make his prayers for the morrow. And I left him to his vigil.

In the morning early David took his people forward for home, and Godred would embrace me fondly before Cristin's eyes, who might not do as much. He took delight in this brotherly close, and was adroit in so handling me, indifferent as I was, as to turn his ring inward upon his finger and leave the imprint of the hand and rose in the flesh of my arm, as though he stamped his ownership upon me with a brand, like a slave, a reminder of how I was tied to him by my bastardy, and she was his possession. But Cristin was not moved, or if she was he could get from her no sign of it. And then they were on their way out from the gates, and I was both delivered and bereft.

Then Llewelyn and I, in plain country brown like any village travellers, took two of the Welsh ponies and rode for Evesham, which lies to the north of Hailes, and about eight miles distant. A pleasant way enough we had, beside a little river, but the day was clouded over, and before we were halfway it began to rain, the soft, warm, wetting rain of the lowlands, and Llewelyn laughed, and said we should be well able to pass for poor, bedraggled pilgrims among the rest. For this tomb to which we were bound was become a place of great holiness and the resort of the common people in their need, as deeply revered as St Thomas's shrine at Canterbury by all the poor and unprivileged who had hoped so much from the living man. And even we knew, as far away as north Wales, that there had been miracles. The nobility of England, weary of discord and anxious to have their old errors put away out of mind, might accept the crown's verdict that Earl Simon had been rebel and felon, Edward might shun the abbey that held that abhorred body as a place unclean – though his avoidance might as well have been from shame as from hatred! – but to the common folk of England this was the resting-place of a saint, and they frequented it for their comfort, and made sad songs and joyful songs about it, publishing Earl Simon's miracles by word of mouth throughout the whole land.

We entered the town by the bridge over the Avon, that same bridge that Mortimer closed against him and brought him to his death. Busy and tranquil we found the place this October morning, and very fair and fat in its loop of river, the ground climbing towards the un-moated side, the north, where the walls of the abbey rose between us and the battlefield. At every step I drew nearer to that unhealed grief, with none of the duties and vexations and pinpricks of everyday to fend off from me the devastation of loss. For I had known Earl Simon, closely and well, all the last months of his life, and left him only when the head was hewn from his shoulders, and he lay dead beside his eldest son on the upland fields of Evesham. His advice and request that I should avail myself of my clerkhood and take refuge in the abbey with his attendant bishops I refused. But my little skill in arms could not weigh the balance in his favour, and what had I out of it but the grief and the grievance of seeing him die? Yes, something more I think I took away with me, a whole memory that did not turn back short of the last extreme, and so could live with the unforgettable talisman of his face, and need not turn its eyes away.

We were within sight of the great abbey gateway when Llewelyn said, in a voice that called me back from my own vindication to consider his thirst: 'Is this town much changed?' For he had never before seen it, except through my eyes.

I said no, not greatly. There were some new houses, as I remembered it, and peace had brought its own increase, and befriended a market surely always rich in goods, but now easy of access for buyer and seller even from far afield. But, no, not greatly changed. It was as I had known it. The abbey, also. A great and generous house, that had not turned its back upon its slaughtered saint.

'True,' he said, 'what need was there for change? They were hospitable to him living and dead.'

There were people enough going and coming about the courts of the abbey, and in and out of the great church. We lighted down from our ponies and left them in hand with a lay brother who came kindly to attend to any who needed him among the visiting folk. Damp from the soft rain, and dun amongst the homespun poor like veritable brothers, we went into the church. Neither he nor I knew where to look for the tomb we sought, but we followed those who went silently before, for all were bound to the same shrine. We who had come from the splendour of St Edward's translation stepped into another holiness, the antithesis perhaps, but not the contradiction, of the first. What can man do more than the best he knows? And if king and rebel – to give him that name he never earned – hold fast that vision, how are they opposed in the eyes of God?

It was in a dark but noble place, Earl Simon's tomb. Dark, for this was an old and massive church, not lofty like King Henry's building at Westminster, and the thick walls and narrow windows let in little light to the chapel where he lay. But the plain stone tomb was large and spare and grand, like his mind and spirit, a pure flame in an unrelenting austerity. There was a double step before it, each level worn into a deep hollow – dear God, in how short a time, and by how many humble feet! – and a place on the level surface of the gold-grey stone smoothed and polished into darkness, and also hollowed, somewhere in the region of that immense heart, but higher than by rights a heart should be, as the hewn stone was shorter than a middling-tall man should be, for there was no man living in England who did not know that the body within that tomb was headless. I know not who was the first who mounted the two steps and used his own judgment to know where to plant that first reverent kiss, but I bless him and envy him, and where his lips rested thousands upon thousands followed him and kissed, and after them, all in good time, Llewelyn and I.

When he had done so, Llewelyn kneeled upon the upper step, and I drew back from him to leave him private. There was a lamp burning at the head of the tomb, and on a narrow wooden prayer-stool there one of the monks kneeled. I suppose that there were two or three who shared this vigil among them, perhaps older brothers with infirmities to be nursed, for the one who kneeled there

35

when we came was shrivelled and bowed, and bulked no larger than a handful of fragile bones inside his habit. Men and women came and went as I waited, mounted beside the place where Llewelyn prayed, kissed the glossy, mouth-shaped hollow in the slab, and humbly withdrew to pray apart. But when Llewelyn arose from his knees and stepped back, so did the ancient monk who tended the lamp, and turned his head towards my lord, and then I saw his face, which was tiny and old, and worn to bone and spirit, and sweet and calm beyond measure, and his eyes, which were wide open and silver as the moon, whitened over with the veil of age and blindness. Some twenty years, I judge, he had not seen even the light of day, never a shade of difference between dawn and midnight. But he turned his face towards Llewelyn, who moved as silently as a cat, and he smiled with a strange, radiant smile, and came towards him with the careful, accurate gait of the blind who are certain of their ground. He came until he had only to stretch out his hand to touch Llewelyn's breast, and reached out delicately short of touching, and so stayed, his hand spread like a blessing and an entreaty.

'You are the man,' he said, in a voice as thin and small as a bird's chirping. 'My heart turned in me when you entered the chapel. I cannot be deceived. You are of his blood.'

'No,' said Llewelyn, wondering and moved. 'I am only one whom he touched in passing, like all the rest.'

'That cannot be true,' said the old man, shaking his grey tonsure, and drawing down his brows over the blind eyes as if to stare more intently into the face that fronted his own. He advanced his hand yet a little towards Llewelyn's breast, and laid it very lightly over the prince's heart. 'This – this declares you his. I know not of my own knowledge. I am told what is needful. I am told that I touch the son of my saint.'

'Father,' said Llewelyn, shaken, 'I do not lie to you.

36

There is no drop of the earl's blood in me. All his sons are dead or gone out of this land.'

'You have your knowledge,' said the blind monk, faintly smiling, 'and I have mine, and what is mystery and paradox to us is not so to God, who is the maker of truth as of all things. I tell you, I do but as I am instructed, and it is not possible that my knowledge should be deceitful. I say you are the son of my saint, and I bless you in his name, and in God's name.' With the hand that had warmed at Llewelyn's heart, dry and frail on its withered wrist like a dead flower on its stalk, he signed the air between them with a cross before the prince's forehead. 'May the prayers you have made here be answered, and the vows you have renewed come to perfect fruit.'

After a long silence Llewelyn said: 'Amen!' And so in my own mind I said, also, for I knew what pledge had been reaffirmed at Earl Simon's tomb. After I carried back to Wales the full story of the earl's death, Llewelyn made two vows in his memory, the first to extract from King Henry everything Earl Simon had granted him freely, recognition of his right and title to Wales and to the homages of all the Welsh princes. And that he had done. And the second vow was to bring to fruition the marriage he had asked and been granted gladly by the earl, and to make Simon's only daughter princess of Wales. That yet remained to do. Twice he had sent envoys to reopen the matter with the earl's widow, but the Countess Eleanor would not entertain his plea because of her promise to abstain from all moves that could vex her brother the king, or her nephew the Lord Edward. Withdrawn into France, and living retired at the convent of Montargis, she wanted nothing but to have peace, and dreaded the suspicion with which Edward might look upon any alliance between Earl Simon's friend and ally and Earl Simon's child. And very patiently and obstinately had Llewelyn waited for the passage of time to put that scruple and that fear out of mind, for who could believe, four years after Evesham, that any man or conspiracy of men could again revive a strong baronial party in England? Without Simon it was a dead cause. There was not a lord in the land who wanted the past even remembered. The present tired peace and slow and cautious healing was all they desired. But the countess held to her purpose and would not be moved. Neither would Llewelyn. He would have Eleanor de Montfort or he would have none.

'Amen!' he said again, very softly. 'Father, pray that prayer for me in this place now and again, and how can I fail?'

We went out hushed and thoughtful from the church, and the rain had ceased, and a watery sun peered feebly through the mist and cloud over the valley. In rapt silence we rode back half the distance we had to go, and only then did he say suddenly, in a voice low and diffident and hopeful: 'Samson, I have had a sign from heaven, have I not? A son, he called me!'

'So he did,' I said, 'and held by it. And blessed your intent in Earl Simon's name and in God's name. And surely such old, good men, drawing to their end after a holy life, cannot lie.'

'It must and shall come to pass,' he said, and he was speaking to the dead we had left behind us as surely as to me. 'A son to him I shall be, though not by blood. I shall be his son when I exchange the marriage vows with Eleanor, and take her home to Wales. God willing, his grandsons shall be princes.'

CHAPTER II

It was August of the following year before Edward got
his crusaders and their stores aboard his ships, and finally
set sail to meet King Louis in the east. He should have
joined him and sailed with him from Aigues Mortes, but
the dispute with Gloucester and other matters delayed
his departure, and he followed more than a month behind
the French king's fleet. They never did meet again in
this world. When Edward reached the crusader camp at
Carthage in November, King Louis was more than two
months dead. Not in battle, but of the terrible plague
that swept through his army in Tunis, killing in swathes,
and lopping off the head and the heart of that great
enterprise. The king died only a few days after Edward
sailed from Dover. Men remember him as a great and
good man, and so I think he tried to be, yet I cannot
think of him but with the memory of his judgment at
Amiens bitter in my mind, and often I think how much
of the anger and grief and violence of the world lies at
the door of good men, and how much injustice and
wrong they do in their certainty of good intent. Howbeit,
he is long dead, and no doubt there is judgment for kings
and popes as surely as for poor men, and a judgment
not of this world, but with unweighted scales.

As for Earl Gilbert of Gloucester, he fought off all
arguments and pleas, and evaded setting out with the
rest on this crusade, and Edward sailed without him, and
in great anger against him, but in the belief that he had
him securely bound to follow with his own force somewhat later. Gilbert, on the other hand, breathed more

freely once Edward was on the high seas, and had no intention of quitting his building of his new castle to go hunting Saracens or mamluks in the east. So Llewelyn's vexatious problem of how long to be tolerant and trust to arbitration to hold him, and when to lose patience and take action for want of law, remained acute during that summer. It was galling to be held up as Gilbert's excuse for not being able to quit his border honour, when we had done nothing to accost him, and he did much to affront us. On the other hand, Llewelyn did not wish to be, or even to seem to be, the first to resort to arms, whatever the provocation. So we still held back and waited.

It was barely two weeks after the Lord Edward had left England with his companions that we had an official visitor from King Henry, bearing royal letters, which in courtesy were delivered to Llewelyn in advance of the envoy's arrival, for he came well attended, and was of such importance that the court of Wales would naturally desire to have word of his coming, and be ready to do him honour. The king wrote recalling that by the terms of the peace between England and Wales the crown had retained one, and only one, Welsh homage, that of Meredith ap Rhys Gryg of Dryslwyn, at Meredith's urgent wish, but with the provision that should it ever please the king to cede that homage, also, to Llewelyn, the prince should pay for it the price of five thousand marks. His son Edward, said the king, had often pleaded with him to grant the said homage to Llewelyn, according to the prince's earnest wish, and at Edward's request his brother Edmund, to whom the homage had been given, was willing to cede it again in Llewelyn's favour. The king had therefore yielded to his son's entreaty, and was ready to grant Meredith's fealty to the prince of Wales, if Llewelyn would pay the promised five thousand marks at once, and to Edward, not to the crown, for the king wished the money to be a subsidy for the crusade. And because of the importance of the matter, King Henry was sending Robert Burnell, the Lord Edward's most trusted confidential clerk and adviser, to explain in person whatever needed to be explained further. So confident was he not only of acceptance, but of getting the money in full on demand, that he sent with Burnell the necessary charters for the exchange, his own grant of the homage, the Lord Edward's concurrence, and the Lord Edmund's willing cession of the fealty heretofore granted to him, all these to be handed over as soon as the money changed hands.

'So Edward has stood my friend,' said Llewelyn, elated and encouraged at this news. 'He would not have argued for me if he had still entertained any doubts of my good faith.' And I knew that he was seeing this move as one more sign that he might proceed with his design of pursuing the match with Eleanor de Montfort, without fear that her mother's doubts and reservations need be taken seriously. If Edward had no hesitation in trusting and working with the prince, the countess must realise that there was no longer any need for her to stand in the way of the marriage.

David, who happened to be in attendance by reason of council matters when the letter arrived, curled his lip at his brother's innocence. 'Edward has stood Edward's friend, as usual,' he said bluntly. 'He is to have the money for his crusading expenses, is he not? He – not Edmund, who surrenders Meredith ap Rhys Gryg to you. He got his twentieth from all free men, or he got at least part of it, and what's yet to come will go into his hands, too, but it's not nearly enough for his needs. He's over head and ears in debt now, when he's barely got his men out of England, and he'll be living on his creditors for years after he comes home. Edward's warm friendship for you is of recent growth, and serves a very useful purpose. Where else could he lay hands on five thousand marks on demand, and get a blessing with it? Oh, take what's offered, by all means, if you want the old bear,

41

and be glad of it – but not grateful! You are paying handsomely for your purchase.'

'I am paying what I undertook to pay, and getting what I have always wanted,' said Llewelyn, not at all moved by David's sour wisdom. 'If he has no cause for complaint, neither have I, each of us is getting what he wants, it's a fair exchange. But I do not believe this is only self-interest on Edward's part. It is not the first instance he has shown me of his goodwill. I would rather deal with him on the borders than with any other of the king's men. He has a better understanding, and longer patience.'

'So he has,' said David readily, but with the same dry tone and disdainful half-smile, 'and both in the service of his own interests, and no others. Take what he offers, if it suits you, but have the wit to realise that you owe him nothing, for it would not be offered if he was not getting full value for it after his own fashion.'

Said Llewelyn, amused and tolerant, but with some chill disapproval, too: 'You have had no cause to sharpen your tongue on him, to my recall. I thought you had great liking for him. There have been times when you have so indicated.'

David's dark and beautiful face did not change, but by the sudden light flush that stained his high cheek-bones I knew the mild sting had gone home. It was not so long since David had forsaken Llewelyn in time of war to join Edward, though God knows his motives may not have been near so simple as Llewelyn or any of us supposed. But he said only: 'So I have great liking for him. Too great for my good, perhaps. But not because I see him as big in the soul as in the body. He is a man, faulty like other men, and the more dangerous because born to so much power, and so largely gifted. I take him as he is. And you had better do the same, and enjoy what part of him you can.'

'You have had better opportunity to study him than

I,' Llewelyn owned generously, open-minded but un-convinced, 'but my experience is all I can use. Yours is yours, and there's no borrowing. And now there'll be no more studying him for a while; he's bound for the Holy Land, and for my part I wish him good use of my five thousand marks, for he shall have them, and I'll take back my old bear of Dryslwyn.'

'You were a fool else,' said David. 'I never said there was anything wrong with the bargain. But see it as a bargain, for so it is.'

So it was done, with no pretence or reluctance on either side, and the fealty and homage of Meredith ap Rhys Gryg, the old lord of Dryslwyn, the only Welsh prince then out of Llewelyn's jurisdiction, was restored to him.

The consultations that accompanied the transfer were brief and businesslike indeed, since the exchange suited all parties, except, perhaps, the over-persuaded and over-devoted Edmund of Lancaster. And what I chiefly re-member of them is the person of this same confidential clerk, Robert Burnell, already of formidable reputation, and to be ever greater thereafter. He arrived without great ceremony, attended well but not ostentatiously. I noted his seat and manner in the saddle before he alighted, for he rode like a merchant or a farmer, that is to say, as one who rides on his own errands, and not to be seen and admired by others, and therefore must ride well, sensibly and durably, to last out long days and hard ways, rather than to dazzle other men and wear out mounts. He had no affectations, but lighted down unaided, himself handed over his bridle to the groom, and eyed the way it was handled, even so, until he was content. So I saw, before ever I truly looked at the man and made note of his stature and visage, that here was one who had mind and eye and heart for every detail, and was not interested in the flowers of his office, however interested he might be – and he was, shrewdly! – in its fruits.

He was above the middle height, and straight as a fir

43

tree. His dark gowns were always of the finest cloth, never of the showiest cut. He was, I suppose, of much the same age as Llewelyn and myself, though I never enquired. If I am right, he was then around forty-one years of age, ten years older than his lord and friend, Edward. He had been in that prince's household since it was formed, when Edward was fifteen years old and being prepared for his marriage to the princess of Castille, and therefore fitted out with an appanage suitable to a married prince and heir to a throne. Burnell was from a small border family of no great importance until he graced it. His abilities were his appanage, and equipped him well enough to found a house and an honour, if he had not been a priest. As it was, there were great horizons open to him in another sphere.

'Old Boniface is dead,' David said to me, coming into my copying-room from the hall, that first evening, flushed and restless with wine, but not drunk. There was a core in him then, I dread of brotherly bitterness, that would not let him get drunk, his wits so raged against surrendering their edge. 'We lack an archbishop of Canterbury, and Edward has made his mind known. Did you not hear of it? Before he took his legions out of England he made a rush to Canterbury, to tell the monks what heavy responsibility they bear, having the election of the high priest in their hands. It was hearing of the old man's death in Savoy that sent him there, with a candidate ready chosen. He told them plainly he wanted Burnell. What could suit him better? Burnell is his man, heart and soul. That's why he's left here, ready and waiting, instead of sailing with the crusaders, as he intended. We shall see, we shall see, what the monks of Canterbury think of Edward's nominee.'

It seemed to me then that the chapter of Canterbury would hardly be likely to flout the wishes of the Lord Edward, but it had to be remembered also that he was now out of the country, and likely to be preoccupied with other high matters for some time to come, so that they had not to confront him face to face if they chose to ignore his orders. Nor was he yet king, at least not in name. In all else I must say his was the ruling will in England, and King Henry was content to have it so, finding his giant son a shield and comfort rather than a tyrant.

Whatever their reasoning, we heard later that the monks of Canterbury in solemn session had elected as candidate for the primacy their prior, a somewhat obscure person hardly known out of their own company, certainly with no great reputation for learning or doctrine. I have forgotten his name, and that in itself says most of what there is to be said about him. I do remember that the election caused anger at the king's court, and was received with cold disapproval in Rome. But the affair hung unresolved for two years after, and England was without an archbishop, because of a long and disputed interregnum in the papacy, and even when a new pope was chosen in the person of Cardinal Tedaldo Visconti, later to be known to Christendom by his chosen name of Gregory X, the new pope-elect was absent crusading in the east with the Lord Edward, and indeed had already become his close and loyal friend. When he returned to give his attention to his new duties, he examined the prior of Canterbury, and found him wanting in the qualities an archbishop should have, and chose instead the provincial of the Dominicans in England, Robert Kilwardby, a man of learning, purpose and character, who had never looked for the honour, and received it dutifully but with astonishment.

But in this summer of twelve hundred and seventy all this was still to do, and we saw Robert Burnell at work as man of affairs and trustee for Edward his lord. And I think that affairs of state were more his province than matters of faith and doctrine, and as archbishop he would have been wasted. He went straight to the heart of an errand, worded clearly, made decisions firmly and sensibly, was not to be diverted or provoked. By the time all was agreed, the royal charters delivered, and the fee of Meredith's homage paid in full, I found it no wonder that Edward should choose this man as one of the regent-administrators of his affairs and lands in his absence, and in the event of Richard of Cornwall's death, one of the guardians of his children.

He was of powerful build for his height, and moved like one in as firm mastery of his body as of his mind. His colouring was fair, with thick, short hair of a light brown, and eyes as light, flecked with green, and his smooth-shaven face was square and strong, every line sharply drawn. But all this force of decision and judgment he voiced in tones quiet, reasonable and brief. Llewelyn, as I saw, warmed to him, for good reason, being used to grappling with officials whose only intent was to avoid making any clear answer or bringing any doubtful matter to a conclusion. So it was no wonder that he took the opportunity of broaching with Burnell the issue of Seng-henydd, and his grievance over the castle building at Caerphilly.

'I know,' said Burnell, 'that both you and the earl of Gloucester have made out strong cases for your rival claims in those parts, both as to the commote itself, and the homage and fealty of its lord, who is now imprisoned in Ireland. You made representations to the king's Grace some time ago, to obtain his release.'

'I did,' said Llewelyn, 'for to my knowledge he has committed no treason against the earl, and it is no fault of his if two overlords both lay claim to him, and he prefers one of them. His Grace replied that it was open to me to bring action on his behalf in the king's courts against Gloucester, since the crown lawyers held that the lord of Senghenydd is of the Englishry. But I cannot bring such action without acknowledging the right of the court and the English dependence of Griffith, and this I do not acknowledge. The man is Welsh, and the land was his by hereditary right. I preferred the arbitration commission, old and good practice, drawn from both sides where disputed rights are concerned. But it moves not as such commissions used to do, but by legal delays and deferments which I find rather English than impartial. And meantime, Earl Gilbert continues to build. It is my contention that building should cease until we have agreement.'

Instead of bandying words to conceal art, Burnell spoke out freely. 'It is truth, you will find the nature of such joint commissions changed. I will not deny it. I do not say it was ever intended, but it is implicit in your lordship's present relationship with the crown. Think how great is that change. Never before has Wales stood in this same interdependence. You are nearer now than you ever were to the crown, and I tell you freely, English officials, by the very nature of your treaty, think of you as reliant upon the royal courts for the maintenance of justice wherever it touches both countries. Law *is* slow. I trust it may also be sure and just, but slow it is, and I well understand how that may gall. I cannot offer you hope of a reversal there. But as to the ban on building until the case is settled, I think there you have a strong argument, and it can be looked into. Can and shall, if I can procure it.'

'I have waited,' said Llewelyn, 'a great while, but to wait until the fortress is complete would be too much to ask of me. The earl claims he is in fear of Welsh incursion, and means only to make his own defence possible. But Senghenydd was never his, though he did impose homage on its lord, and it is not his own he is defending, it is what he had taken unjustly.'

'But you do not claim Senghenydd as yours?' said Burnell with his small, dry smile.

'Senghenydd belongs to Griffith, and should be restored to him, together with his freedom. Ultimately I claim

47

Griffith as my vassal, yes. By treaty I was given acknowledged title to the fealties of *all* the Welsh princes, saving
only this Meredith who is now also given to me. But
the issue of Griffith's allegiance and Welshness can wait
the slow processes of arbitration. What I claim now is
that building at Caerphilly should cease. De Clare should
not build, nor I destroy. But if he builds,' said Llewelyn
bluntly, 'then I shall destroy. I have let the work go too
far already.'

And Burnell smiled, and said that he valued the can-
dour of the exchange. He did not say, but it was implicit
in his manner, that he himself found Gilbert de Clare
a difficult, slippery and insubordinate man, and the Lord
Edward would not be gravely vexed to see him curbed.

'Yet I doubt,' said Llewelyn, after the envoy had
departed with his strong entourage and his treasure, 'if
that gives us free leave to do the curbing. Gilbert is
troublesome, but Gilbert is English, a marcher lord, one
of their own. It would be folly for us to rely too much on
new friendships, when they cross old ones.'

So he waited still for a while, measuring the days until
the point should come when for the maintenance of his
royal dignities he must act. And as I know, he was well
aware that miscalculation might be exceedingly dangerous, whether he moved too soon, and inflamed old
animosities, or too late, and encouraged insolent presumption of his weakness. And the danger of hesitation, of
threatening action and then not acting, or of acting by
derisory half-measures, was the most acute of all.

I believe that Burnell did urge the king to impose a
halt to Gloucester's building; he may even have succeeded
in getting Henry to make some gesture of prohibition,
but if so, it was ignored. And at the beginning of October
Llewelyn judged his moment to be upon him, and struck.

We went in force, led by the prince himself, for he
would not make this assertion of his rights through any
other hand, surrounded Gilbert's great earthwork, and

48

drove the English guards, builders and all, south in haste for their lives, though it was done with such method and deliberation that they recognised the impossibility of preventing us doing what we would, and withdrew without offering battle. Gloucester himself was not there, for parliament was then in session, and he was present in full cry, urging his right to build and the danger that threatened his lands, for once truly, though he did not know it. At the very hour, perhaps, when King Henry was writing urgently to Llewelyn that he had impressed upon Gloucester the necessity for keeping the peace, and that the prince should also observe the like restraint, we were setting fire to Gilbert's timber keep, tearing down his boundary walls, and levelling his earthworks. We destroyed everything, and then, to mark our own reading of restraint, withdrew from the entire commote, making no attempt to occupy it and hold it, as we could have done.

Of course there was great turmoil when the news reached the court, and Gloucester got something out of it in payment for his castle, for there was never any more said about his pledged duty to follow Edward to the Holy Land. Now he could settle vengefully in his marcher lands and purport to be the guardian of the realm as well as of his own claims. Llewelyn was loudly blamed for taking action, but that moved him not at all, and it seemed he had not gravely misjudged his hour, for king and council continued to urge the use of arbitration, and to support the meetings of the commission, though these still tended to talk endlessly and arrive nowhere, as before. However, we had a breathing space, and kept Senghenydd under careful watch, in case of further attempts to build. Gilbert was an incalculable creature, given to bouts of breath-taking audacity, sometimes deservedly successful, sometimes undeservedly, and sometimes disastrous, but also to long periods of unruly and incompetent muddling, arrogantly sure of his rightness

and tangling himself and everyone about him in quag-
mires beyond the capacity of other men. So one never
knew what to expect from him. I do not know whether he
had breathed in an emulous desire to outbuild King
Henry, from his belated and sullen visit to the abbey at
Westminster, but this year following found him at a high
pitch of excellence rare in him, choosing men ably,
appraising their plans modestly and sensibly, and giving
ability its head to design such a castle as barons dream of.
But until past the end of this year twelve hundred and
seventy we had no hint of what went forward, for the site
at Caerphilly remained desert.

Christmas we spent at Aber, after the old fashion, for
Llewelyn had still a strong attachment to that royal seat
by the northern sea. David and Elizabeth came for the
feast, in great content with each other. So wild, so tender,
so playful was David with this gay girl of his, I saw
again my breast-brother, the child who had been in my
care years ago, and had me by the heart still, for all I
could do. And I saw, I know not how, for her body was
not yet changed – perhaps in his constant care for her,
and the way he looked upon her mutely as upon a wonder
and a dread, but perhaps rather in her large and radiant
presence, that warmed the air about her even in the
frosts – I saw that Elizabeth was with child.

She was then barely fourteen years old, but more than
that in her true being, body, mind and spirit, having
loved so early, after being schooled earlier yet to the
needs of marriage, at a time when both marriage and
love were heathen and distant words to her. Whatever
doubts and dreads David had, Elizabeth had none. She
was all joy.

'He frets needlessly,' said Cristin, when I found myself
some moments alone with her in the night, under a cold
moon as we crossed from the buttery and kitchens to the
hall. 'She is ripe and ready, and without fear. But who
would have thought he would so wear out his heart for

her, and wrack himself to a shade with self-blame? What choice had he? She wooed him and won him, almost against his will, all against his conscience. If he seeks you out – he well may! – comfort him, and tell him not to be a fool. She has no need of any pity; she feels herself blessed.'

There was no word said, then or ever, of how her own years were running away in barren blossom from under her feet, of the great longing she had, and I shared, for the generation of the children of our own love, a happiness we could never have, and now saw shining so joyously in this strangely-matched pair. But at night in those feast-days, when Elizabeth with David led the dances, for all his vain wish to shelter and cosset her and force her to rest, then we felt to the full the ache of what we had never possessed, and surely never would in this world. As we valued and were grateful for those blessings we had, which were very great, so we saw clearly the magnitude of the last blessing we were denied. And Cristin's great eyes, iris-dark with longing, followed every movement as Elizabeth danced and sang and shone, and in the midst of her gaiety laid a hand so tenderly upon her girdle, where nothing yet swelled or quickened, caressing in rapture the very mystery of David's seed in her. Cristin watched like one famished, though her face was white and still and tranquil, and her hands folded in calm. Only to me did her eyes betray her, for even so I must have looked, envying David.

Yet my heart smote me suddenly, warning that there was one other who had good cause to know how to read the signs in her face and in mine. And I looked about me in haste and wariness, to find if Godred was there in the hall.

I found him among a group of the troopers of David's retinue, at one of the trestle tables drawn along the walls, easy and at leisure over their wine. He was standing, graceful and slender, with his shoulders braced against

51

one of the timber pillars, and his fair head leaned back against the smoky wood. The large, smooth lids drooped half over his full brown eyes, but I saw the bright gleam of interest and content and malice burning below his light lashes, and his lips were curved in a small, acid-sweet smile. He was staring steadily upon Cristin, but as I watched, as though my attention had drawn his, he turned his head and opened his eyes wide into mine, and his smile broadened into that comradely affection he used upon me, poisoned honey, yet God knows more deadly to him than to me.

I knew then that there was nothing he had not seen and appraised, no part of her longing or mine that he did not recognise, and was not willing to use against us. Slight and light he was, and found no fault with that and made no pretence about it, until he found he could neither tempt nor trick me into wallowing with him in the kennel, nor drag her down to the level of his own loving. He could not endure it that we had between us the one thing he had never valued or wanted, another manner of love, that could even live in abstinence.

Yet even then, when he had discovered jealousy by reason of the value another set on his wife, whom he himself never valued, he seldom resorted to her, or frequented her company, except as a means of tormenting me, or keeping David's goodwill. Other women he had in plenty, and his interest was small indeed in favours he owned by right. It was the one thing in him for which I was devoutly grateful, that his usage of her was civil but indifferent, and she could endure it without distress. It was myself he hated, and lived in the hope of destroying, and as one weapon blunted without effect he was for ever looking about him for another.

I dreaded he might have found one that night.

There was one other who had watched the happiness of David and Elizabeth with open pleasure and private pain,

and that was Llewelyn. He carried about his neck the
painted image of a girl twelve years old, only a year or
two younger than Elizabeth now. It was more than five
years since Earl Simon had betrothed her to the prince,
by this she was eighteen, and still out of his reach overseas, and the years of his prime were ebbing one by one
while he waited for her. And here he saw his youngest
brother in joyous wedlock with this eager child, and the
fruit of their love, the desired heir, already promised,
while he was barren and alone.

He watched them, smiling and tormented, and I saw
both the pleasure and the pain clear into resolution, for he
had received his third sign.

When I was alone with him in his own chamber, late in
the night after the hall was quiet and the household
asleep, he told me what I expected to hear, and I was the
first he told.

'It is time to put my fortune to the test again,' he said.
'I should be ungrateful if I neglected the clear signs
heaven has given me. When Edmund of Lancaster sails
with his force, to join the Lord Edward in Tunis, two of
the brothers from Aberconway have petitioned to sail
under his protection to France. They have missions to
Clairvaux and certain other houses there. They can as
easily be my envoys to Montargis. Surely by now the
countess must be reassured. I mean to renew my suit
for her daughter. You and I will prepare gifts and letters,
and trust in the word of the blind monk of Evesham.
He has promised me success, and I will not believe in
failure.'

I was glad for him, for the simple act of determining
upon action had warmed and liberated him, and while
we made our preparations it was eager anticipation he
felt, and the deprivation fell away from him. We drew up
letters very courtly and persuasive, recalling how Earl
Simon had exchanged vows with Llewelyn at Abbey
Dore, and we sent for the countess a mass-book very

delicately bound and illuminated in gold, and for her daughter a rose of enamel and gold-work, with the renewed pledge of Llewelyn's faithfulness to his bond, and desire and prayer for its fulfilment. The brothers of Aberconway were trustworthy and loyal, and so had been always to the royal house of Gwynedd, and above all they could be secret, for clearly he did not wish their errand to be known until he had his answer. It remained only for Edmund to fix a date for his departure, and though he was delayed a few weeks into the year by various vexatious matters and by King Henry's frail health, he got his levies away before the spring came. Then we drew breath and waited for news.

That was a quiet and prosperous spring for us in Wales, troubled only by the word that Gilbert de Clare was again busy building at Caerphilly as soon as the weather was favourable after the early frosts, and this time he had somehow gathered about him masons and planners of quality, and was bent on the erection of a fortress in stone. This at least had the merit, for us, of being a slower enterprise, so that we could afford to sit back and concentrate on formal protests to the court, invoking law and demanding a halt to this new infringement. Though Llewelyn kept tight hold of the borders of Senghenydd none the less, and got word very rapidly, wherever he happened to be, of what went on there.

For the rest, he steadily pursued his policies of settlement, of extending our cultivated fields wherever it was possible, of encouraging the growth of towns, and the founding of markets, and the use of minted money, all measures borrowed from England, truly, and necessarily so, since we had both to compete and co-operate with England. Those years since Montgomery were years of strong development towards a state, not feudal like England, yet learning from feudalism, and most beneficial to all his people. He had an eye, also, to the exact location of his castles, for the best control and protection of the whole land, and it had to be admitted that in the marches there were gaps not yet filled.

So my lord had enough and to spare to occupy his mind, and with the business of local justice he dealt always in person and with great care for detail. And as I remember, we were in session with a difficult family dispute involving the moving of boundaries and the abduction of a girl, in the prince's court at Carnarvon in the first days of April, when a messenger came in from Cynan in London, bringing both letters and a verbal report, he said of great importance. But he waited, none the less, until Llewelyn had the case before him judged and brought to agreement, if not wholly amicably, at least in such a shrewd knot that the parties could not break the accord without peril, and the girl restored to her parents undamaged. Then the prince withdrew, with none but myself in attendance, and in his own apartments the messenger came in to him.

He was a groom about the court, Welsh like Cynan who sent him to us, a lusty young man who made his living where he could, but kept one foot fast-rooted on our side of the border. So do all good Welshmen, for this soil is not as other soil, its stony austerity holds all its sons by the heart. Short and thick and dark was this young man, the very pattern of his kind, even to his tongue, which was not short nor thick nor dark, but long and sinuous and silver. But his matter was nothing for our comfort.

'My lord prince,' he said, standing before Llewelyn still dusty from his ride, 'I am the voice of princely events, and lack the art to tell them. My lord, it is no good news, pardon the bearer. Master Cynan's letter will bear out what I have to tell.'

'Speak out,' said Llewelyn. 'You are not the first to be burdened with an ungrateful errand; it shall not be your loss.'

'My lord,' said the groom, taking him at his word, 'on

55

the thirteenth day of March, at a city called Viterbo, in Italy, Guy de Montfort, Earl Simon's third son, fell upon the lord Henry of Almain, the Lord Edward's cousin, as he was hearing mass in the church of San Silvestro, slew him with the sword, and dragged the body out of the church to be mutilated in the square. Master Cynan said you should know of it, for your better advising.'

Cynan could not have known, when he sent that dire message, that Llewelyn's envoys were at Montargis, nor with how fell a sound the news of Guy's catastrophic vengeance came upon our ears. He sent the word to avoid what now was beyond avoiding. We had chosen the worst of times.

Llewelyn said, with a mute and mastered face: 'Tell me all you know. How did this meeting ever come to pass?'

'My lord, the new French king, Philip, was on his way home northwards through Italy with his crusaders, bearing back to France the bodies of his father, King Louis, dead of plague on the crusade, his young wife Isabella of Aragon, who died on the voyage home, his brother, the count of Nevers, and his brother-in-law Theobald of Champagne, the king of Navarre. All these high titles I learned from Master Cynan, who also writes them to you in the letters I brought. And with King Philip was also his brother, Charles of Anjou, whom the popes helped to the throne of Sicily some years past. This Guy de Montfort is now in his service, and his chief officer in Tuscany, so that he came to Viterbo to meet his liege lord. But when he heard that Henry of Almain was in that city with the French king's retinue, he was greatly disturbed, and came the next day to the church where he was, and killed and dragged him out, and so left him lying. My lord, this is all I know. Master Cynan has written more.'

With a mild voice and a shuttered face Llewelyn thanked him for his errand, and dismissed him to be fed and rested and remounted, with his reward in hand.

His reward for a blow to the heart. Cynan's letter was indeed fuller.

'God he knows, my lord,' he had written, 'what possessed the man to take his revenge thus, or, indeed, what possessed the Lord Edward to send his cousin with King Philip into Italy, where it was certain the vicar-general in Tuscany of Charles of Anjou must come to welcome his lord. There are those here who say that the Lord Edward sent his cousin, who was most dear to him, and once was a Montfort man, expressly to try to make peace with the Montfort brothers, and bring them to the king's grace, and it may be true. If so, he was sadly amiss in his judgment. Those two brothers, for Simon was in company with Guy when they entered the town, though he was not present at the church, did not know when they came to the meeting that Henry of Almain would be there in the royal retinue. This killing was not planned. They came, and then they heard of his presence. And Guy has sought him out and killed him. I know no more. It may be that you can read this riddle better than I.'

He had added a further writing a day or two later, when more was known:

'The Lord Edward, who has wintered in Sicily as the guest of King Charles, and proposes to sail for Acre very soon, has been informed of his cousin's death. There was talk of his being sent for to come home again, the main crusade being postponed by reason of King Louis' death, and King Henry being in poor health, but now his Grace is better, and it is certain the Lord Edward will hold to his oath and sail for Acre at once. The murderer has been deprived of lands and offices, but is at large, and having strong support from his wife's kin in Tuscany, and they very powerful, will find both refuge and sympathy there. It seems likely little will be done to avenge the crime until the Lord Edward's return, but he will not forget.'

'Indeed he will not,' said Llewelyn, laying the letters

by with a steady hand. 'He forgets few favours, but never an injury, and he greatly valued his cousin Henry. Well, it seems the madness of one hour can undo the work of years. Why? *Why* should he do so? What ailed him to throw away, if nothing else were at stake, all the sound work he has done for this new rule in Italy? All the laurels he has won? After six years!'

I remembered then how I had seen this same Guy lying in his blood on the field of Evesham, vainly trying to stretch out a hand towards his sire as he died. 'He saw father and brother killed before his eyes,' I said, 'their cause lost, their friends hounded and disinherited, the very dream in which he grew to manhood hacked to pieces. And he saw on the opposing part all those young men who had once followed and worshipped Earl Simon, and then deserted and brought him to ruin. To come face to face with one of them now, without warning, drove him to remember too much, and too bitterly.'

'But Henry was only one of many, and among the best of them, not the worst. Why single him out for vengeance?'

'He was there,' I said. 'And he was, I think, the most trusted of those who withdrew their allegiance, and the most missed. And close kin, nephew to the earl, cousin to Guy, and sometime dear to both. It is not so hard to understand the impulse to kill, but the act was an indulgence he should have been able to deny himself. Now he has destroyed himself, and set back the hope of reconciliation by years.'

'And with it my hopes,' said Llewelyn, 'or so I dread. We are back where we began. Edward will not forget or forgive this act. It touches neither Eleanor nor me, but will her mother dare to stand upon that view? I doubt it!' The countess was ageing and weary, and sickened with all matters of state and all involvement in the tangled affairs of England, for to say truth, her world had ended at Evesham, and without Earl Simon she was but a shell

58

filled with bitterness. 'Well,' he said grimly, 'until I have an answer I have neither lost nor won. It's still a matter of waiting. At waiting,' he said, ruefully smiling, 'I have had much practice, and am grown expert. A man should enjoy doing what he does well.'

I would not say there was much enjoyment for him in those six weeks we spent waiting for the return of the monks of Aberconway, but at least we were busy enough to help the time to pass, and we made good use of the opening summer. Gilbert de Clare was continuing his building in stone at Caerphilly, and all Llewelyn's formal protests, though they had produced great agitation among the royal officials, and many promises and reassurances, had not caused Gilbert's masons to lay by their tools. This was the season for building, and he was in haste to raise the walls as high as possible before the next winter's frosts called a halt. But between our preoccupation with these weighty matters we had a good spring for lambs, and favourable weather for sowing, also activities not to be despised.

Towards the end of May the brothers of Aberconway returned, having crossed the sea from France in the very ship which brought home under a mourning escort of knights the bones and heart of Henry of Almain, the heart to be enshrined in the king's church at Westminster, the bones to be buried in his father's abbey of Hailes. Since the news of the murder reached him, they said, Richard of Cornwall, king of the Romans, had turned his back upon the world, and was indifferent to the fate of his kingdom, and certainly to his own. It was barely a year before he followed his son out of this world, and was laid beside him in his own foundation. So those two sleep not ten miles from Evesham, where the king's felon and the people's saint takes his rest.

Brother Philip and Brother Iorwerth, the one old and reverend, the other young, both lettered and learned, were received by Llewelyn with all the more serenity and grace for the passion of anxiety he had to suppress, but they knew his mind, and delivered their embassage directly, and I think he was grateful.

'My lord,' said the elder, 'the letter we bring is but the formal acknowledgement of yours, and of your gifts, with the regard and respect of the Countess Eleanor. What further is necessary we were charged to deliver you by word of mouth. My lord, you will know by now that we came there to Montargis after the thing that happened at Viterbo, though we did not then know of it. The countess had already heard that news. She is deeply shocked by her son's senseless and terrible act, and more determined than ever that she cannot and will not countenance any move that will deepen the anger and suspicion that must follow. She pledged her word to do nothing that could touch or harm or disturb the realm of England, and she holds that the match you propose would be an infringement of her word. With the deepest regard for the lord prince's person, acts and motives, she will not attach her daughter to him or to any former ally of Earl Simon, for that would be to incur the displeasure and distrust of her brother the king, and in particular of the Lord Edward. She is adamant.'

Llewelyn said heavily: 'I had expected nothing better, since this death. From my heart I am sorry, but sorry, too, for the lady. Well, you did your errand faithfully. It is no fault of yours that you can bring me no comfort.'

Brother Philip hesitated but a moment before he said: 'My lord, after a fashion I believe I can. It was not possible for me to ask audience of the Lady Eleanor. But I have seen her, walking in the garden with her mother. And I have spoken with such of that household as I might. The lady is now eighteen years old.' He raised his creased old eyes that were experienced in reading men, and looked upon Llewelyn gently, and saw that the prince would not question him concerning Eleanor, and yet longed to know, and to have her spoken of. Deliberately

60

he said, measuring out words: 'She is of great beauty and great nobility. Those who serve her have serene faces and are quick to smile, and talk with her freely and eagerly. I have judged both men and women by this measure, and I know its worth. And this lady is still unaffianced, in a land where her name, her face and her fortune are all magnets.'

'There have been suitors?' Llewelyn asked, burning between his rapture at hearing her praised, and his dread of having her snatched away into a French marriage. His voice was low and level. Too low, too level. Brother Philip understood the use of the voice, and the constraints that can be imposed upon it.

'There have been many such, and of excellent repute.'

'And all rejected?' said Llewelyn. 'Like me?'

'Not like you, my lord, though all rejected. You the countess rejects, for reasons you understand. All others, though with the utmost gentleness, the Lady Eleanor has rejected. Her mother entertains all of good standing who come, but leaves it to the lady, and will not force her choice. And to this day, my lord, she refuses all.'

'She liked none of them?' said Llewelyn, carefully touching hope with aching delicacy, in case it should crumble away in his fingers.

'She gives no reason, my lord. But so consistent is she, it does appear that she may have a reason, to her sufficient. It may well be,' said Brother Philip, 'that she holds herself to have been betrothed by her father in childhood. It may even be that she clings to that bond with heart and will, and is resolved to await its fulfilment.'

CHAPTER III

Though Llewelyn took heart from what the brothers had told him, and held fast by his faith in his own resolution and the divination of the blind monk of Evesham, yet that year ever after seemed a dark and arduous one to us, and, for all the good summer season, brought little joy. It was not only the disaster of Viterbo, which was still spreading its echoes across the whole face of Europe as ripples wash outward from a stone cast into a still pool. It was also marked by a number of other deaths, closer to us, which in an unpractised unity such as Llewelyn had made of Wales, still unstable in its tensions between the old divisive ways and the new nationhood, made for changes and disruptions. Old princes passed, and left young, untried sons to step into their shoes. It was needful to keep a watchful eye and a ready hand upon every commote in the land.

The prince's old and faithful ally in Cardigan, Meredith ap Owen, was already a few years dead, leaving three sons to rule his lands between them. Now there left us also, in the summer of this year twelve hundred and seventy-one, two others who had played a large and turbulent part in Llewelyn's rise to greatness. On the twenty-seventh day of July died the old bear, Meredith ap Rhys Gryg of Dryslwyn, he whose homage had been sold to Llewelyn to help to pay Edward's crusading expenses. He was past seventy years, and had lived through many changes of fortune. He died at his castle on the Tywi, and was buried at the abbey of Whitland, and his son Rhys ruled after him. And less than a month later, at Dynevor, only a few miles distant, died Rhys Fychan, widower of Llewelyn's only sister, and dear to him, the nephew with whom old Meredith had fought and feuded lifelong, as though, for all they could not live in the same country at peace, they could not live without each other, either. Rhys they buried at Talley, beside his beloved wife, and his eldest son, Rhys Wyndod, then turned twenty-one, divided up his lands with his two younger brothers, Griffith and Llewelyn, the last named after his uncle, the prince. All three knew they could rely on the help and support of their kinsman, and of his namesake, the child of the family reconciliation, the prince was particularly fond.

But the death of their father was a shock and a grief to him, for Rhys Fychan was only three years his elder, and had been a loyal friend.

'I am reminded of my own end,' he said with a wry smile. 'I have lived forty-two years, and he was but three years before me. And how if the same hand should fall upon me in my noonday? It well might; it has on many younger. What can any man do but live as if he had a life before him? I know no other way.'

If he had spoken so before the high steward, Tudor would have taken it as a text for the sermon that was always on his mind, how the prince of Wales, more urgently than any his predecessor, having so much more to protect and to bequeath, owed it to himself and his people to marry and get sons to follow after him. For though Tudor knew of the old betrothal to Eleanor de Montfort, he held that marriage to be impossible, even undesirable, and his concern for Wales kept him rightly fretting for the succession. The prince turned a stonily deaf ear to all the advice the council persistently gave, but Tudor did not give up hope of persuading him at last.

Llewelyn read my face, too clearly, and laughed, though somewhat ruefully. 'I know! Rhys Fychan at least left three sturdy sons to take his place, and I stand to leave all at risk. But without faith there is no security, to look for it and loose my hold on what *is* secure would be a sin. I do and will believe that I shall make good all that I have sworn, and if I cannot, I will die still striving. God can provide, and also take away, if he will, what he has provided.'

This I remembered, and so did he, in consternation and sorrow, when later we heard of the saddest of all the deaths of that winnowing year. With father and mother very far off from him in the Holy Land, Edward's heir, John, a child of five years, sickened and died. No doubt he had the best nurses and guardians a child could have, but his mother had torn herself away from him to follow her lord, and a hard choice that must have been, and a hard deprivation for the child, and who knows if he did not die of it? A girl, the eldest, and a little brother were left, but the heir to the throne, after his father, had been taken, and men are quick to read signs and warnings into the bereavements of princes, ever since Pharaoh and his firstborn.

'God knows I am sorry for it,' said Llewelyn, grieving. 'Even in sons there is no security. The quiver can be emptied in less time than it took to fill it. I hold by my own way. What use is there in bargaining with fortune?' And he said, as if to himself: 'Poor Edward! He goes in the love and service of God, and God takes from him what he parted with, even for a while, only sadly and in duty bounden.'

I recall, looking back now at that time, that even as we spoke the Lord Edward's lady was again with child, the daughter Joan that was born in Acre on this pilgrimage. Before ever they reached England again she gave birth also, in Gascony, to another son, for she was fruitful, but her children died too often in infancy, or dwindled after a few years. It seemed that Edward, for all his giant stature and strength, could not breed true.

But there were two in Lleyn who could. In mid-August,

at the maenol of Neigwl where both Llewelyn and I were born in one night, Elizabeth gave birth to a daughter, strong, fine and perfect, bringing forth her young, it seemed, as placidly and neatly as any ewe in David's flocks.

'Never a day's sickness and never a complaint,' said Cristin to me after the christening, with the baby in a shawl in her arms, fast asleep with fists doubled under its round chin, and black silken hair short and lustrous like a cat's fell. 'She had danced all the evening, and he in a sweat over her, but not a sign of fear in her. And she went to bed and slept, so peacefully that so did he, and in the night, when she felt the throes beginning, she rose up very softly, not to wake him, and came herself to call me. I put her in my bed in the anteroom, where I slept to be near and ready, and not two hours later I put this creature in her arms, and she laughed for joy, but very softly still, because David was sleeping in the next room. By the time he felt the bustle going on all about him, and came out wild with uneasiness to see what had become of his wife, they were both sleeping, as snug and satisfied as cat and kitten.'

I asked if he had not been disappointed that she gave him a girl and not a son.

'Not a bit of it,' said Cristin, 'nor she, either. She thinks it the easiest thing in the world to bear children, and the finest, and promises him all the sons and all the daughters he can wish for. Besides, he sees his own stamp here, in this black colouring, and the blue eyes – she has his eyes – and that's a very powerful flattery. I thought he might take fatherhood lightly, truly I believe he thought so, too, until it happened to him, but we were far out. He has had a revelation – about himself, and Elizabeth and all the world – and it has shaken him to the heart.'

As for Elizabeth herself, there was no need to ask after her health, she bloomed like a rose, and would have no proxy-mothers between herself and her daughter, but shared the child only with Cristin. And this first girl they named Margaret. She was life's answer to a year over-burdened with deaths already known, and the fore-showings of deaths to come.

That autumn Llewelyn took serious thought how to proceed about the new castle at Caerphilly, for so far from halting his building there, Gloucester was pushing hard to raise the walls into a defensible state before the winter, so that the place could be securely held. If we were to move in arms at all, it had to be soon, and in force. Protests and arguments had produced nothing but counter-protests and counter-arguments, until we began to be certain that with the best of wills King Henry, in Edward's absence, was no longer able fully to control the earl's actions, while his council and nobles, who might have commanded formidable sanctions had they so wished, were some of them firmly on Gloucester's side, and privately anxious to help, rather than hinder, his consolidation of Senghenydd. Safe in Glamorgan, remote from the direct influence of Westminster, Earl Gilbert could do what he chose, in the certainty that his marcher neighbours approved, whether they dared say so openly or no.

So in the end, when October came in, and the building continued, the prince was forced to take action. There had been times when he would have struck upon lesser provocation and without any heart-burning, but now there was so much more to be lost, and so much more due in sober statesmanship to the nation he was creating, that he was deeply reluctant to take any step that might burn up into war, and disturb the loyal peace he desired to preserve with England. But once his mind was made up, he had lost none of his force and fire. He called out his host and took a great company south with him to besiege Caerphilly. Among the rest, David brought his muster gladly from Lleyn, restive for action and more intolerant of delays and irritations than his brother. It was the first time those two had been in arms together since David's defection to England, and that was eight years before. There were dangerous reminders there, but in the pressure of the moment they passed without harm.

I make no doubt we could have taken and destroyed Earl Gilbert's second castle, vastly as it was planned, as easily as we had done the first. But it was never put to the test. As soon as it was known that we had swept south and were encircling the half-built shell, King Henry in a great fright required equally rapid action from his council to bring about a truce before war could flare, and the council sent to Glamorgan the bishops of Coventry and Worcester, requesting a convention with Llewelyn. The prince was glad enough to accommodate them, though if need be he would have pushed his attack to a conclusion. On the second day of November they were brought into his camp and very courteously received. What they had to offer was sensible enough, and could well have been offered earlier if the will had been there. They were commissioned by the king to take Caerphilly into their care, and out of Earl Gilbert's hands. The site should be retained by the crown, and no further building should take place during the truce. But they required also that Llewelyn should withdraw his army from the commote, and be ready to conduct any further negotiations with his Grace's proctors at the ford of Montgomery.

'I am, and have always been, ready and willing to meet his Grace's proctors at any reasonable and fair place he may choose,' said Llewelyn, 'and if you give me the pledge that this site shall remain in crown custody, with that I am content.'

The bishops were careful to add in admonition, as no doubt they had been bidden to do, that King Henry had issued orders to the musters of the march and the border shires to stand ready to aid the earl if the prince of Wales should refuse to withdraw his forces.

'There is no need to tell me so,' said Llewelyn with a curling lip. 'If it is a threat, it does not affright me, and if a warning, it does not influence me. I will withdraw my army for a better reason, because I find the king's offer acceptable, and I take his word for its fulfilment.'

And he removed from Caerphilly at once, dispersed his southern levies, and took the men of Gwynedd home without so much as looking over his shoulder.

'You are trusting,' said David, dubious still.

'Even if I were not – and I do believe him sincere – there's no point in half-doing things,' said Llewelyn good-humouredly. 'It's either form and go, and no second thoughts, or else stay and fight. And if the king fears that would mean outright war, so do I fear it, and neither of us wants it. Whom could it benefit but Gloucester? If I gained a commote, I should have lost two years of solid work and the beginning, at least, of a secure peace. No, I'll keep what I have, and stake Caerphilly on King Henry's word.'

Thus that year ended in truce and the resumption of the wearisome legal arguments, but with nothing lost, and the castle in crown hands. And though the affair took an ill turn in the first weeks of the following year, and in effect Llewelyn lost the game, yet I am still sure that he did right to believe in the king's promise. Both Henry and his bishops acted in good faith, but the truth is that Gloucester was then possibly the most powerful man in the kingdom, and certainly the most lawless, and the old and ailing monarch had no means of mastering him, short of calling out the feudal host to make war on him, and if he had done anything so drastic it is certain they would not have obeyed. Marcher hangs with marcher, baron with baron, and Henry was not the man to overbear his troublesome vassals at the best of times, much less now in his old age.

Exactly how it befell we never did learn, but doubtless the force left to garrison the shell of Caerphilly during that winter was not strong, since Llewelyn had taken his army home, and the march was in any case alerted. However it was, Gloucester got possession of the place again, and manned it with such force that no one cared to try to wrest it from him. He may have raised an alarm of attack as his excuse to seize the castle, or he may have produced some devious point of law. However he contrived it, he was back in Caerphilly in January, and though the prince sent a formal protest to the king, and indeed got back from him, in February, a somewhat lame and apologetic letter attempting explanation and excuse, there was nothing more that could be done about it. David took fire and urged instant action, but Llewelyn would have none of it.

'To repeat what we did in November? To what end? You heard the bishops. Do you think that order has ever been rescinded? No, if I resorted to arms now it would mean the whole border aflame; it would mean war with England. The king could no more prevent it than he could prevent this move Gloucester has made. Caerphilly is not worth it, and I will not do it. I will not do it to Wales nor to England, and I will not do it to King Henry. His brother Richard is dying at Wallingford, and God knows how long after him Henry will be. My business is to conserve what I hold, and make the ground firmer under it. I choose to let Gloucester preen himself on his cleverness and keep his castle. But if he stir out of it to move against me he shall find out how little he has gained.'

And so this matter was left, in a manner satisfactory to none of us, but better than the ruin of war between two countries so recently brought to a peace still fragile. In these years Llewelyn had always a sure sense of how far he might go without wreck, and how much he should endure without outrage, and to this point I do not think

69

he had ever made a mistake. His eyes were always on his ultimate object, which was the firm establishment of the principality of Wales, founded upon rock, and linked by ties of friendship and respect with England. Bound as we were to that powerful and ambitious nation by a border half as long as our frontier with the sea, there was no possibility that we could live and rule ourselves in isolation from our neighbour. But equally, if we surrendered ourselves too lavishly to that alliance we were doomed to be swallowed up. This was both his peril and his opportunity, and between the two there was but a tiny step, to be crossed whenever his balance faltered. To this day I do not know, to my life's end I shall never be sure, when, or if ever, he failed of keeping that balance, or whether from the beginning of the world our doom was written, and with it his, however wise, gallant and devoted. When all is said, this is but the first of worlds, the last is yet to be; and what overturning of emperors and exalting of captives there shall be then, what abasement of victors, what laurels for the vanquished, all this is in the hand of God.

In April of that year of grace, twelve hundred and seventy-two, Richard of Cornwall died, that mild, moderate, sensible man who had tried his best to measure right and wrong and cast his vote with justice, who had had his ambitions and successes, and indulged his pride a little in his kingship over the Romans, that is, of some curious peoples in Germany, whom he visited from time to time, but whom we understood not at all, and he, perhaps, very little. He left but one son, Edmund, to follow him as earl of Cornwall, having lost his heir, Henry of Almain, at the hands of Guy de Montfort in that bloody act at Viterbo. He was, take him for all in all, a good, decent man. He was buried beside his son in his abbey of Hailes. After his death, King Henry saddened and dwindled, for he was a man fond and kind with his kin, and diminished by such departures. And his own sons were far away in the Holy Land, about God's business.

In the same month of April, for us in Wales, arose the business of my lord's next brother, Rhodri, who came between Llewelyn and David.

It was then the ninth year that Rhodri had been in the prince's castle of Dolwyddelan, imprisoned after his attempt to rescue Owen Goch, the eldest of the four brothers, who had been far longer in confinement because of his early attack upon Llewelyn in arms, at a time when they shared the rule in Gwynedd equally between them. Equality was not enough for Owen. He fought for all, and lost all; and at this late time I think there were not many among the ordinary people of this new land of Wales, so much greater than merely Gwynedd, and Llewelyn's unaided creation, who gave a thought to him any longer. But the scholars of the old school, and the ancient lawyers, and the bards, still raised their protests for him from time to time, for they could not get used to the notion of a Welsh state, but still thought of the old law as irrevocable truth and right, and of all Welsh lands as partible between all the sons of the royal house, though they knew as well as the rest of us that a return to the old way would soon tear the country into puny commotes and cantrefs ready to fall at a touch into marcher hands.

By this time I think their complaints were a matter of tradition and sentiment, and they would have been both astonished and confounded if Llewelyn had taken them at their word, and torn his work to pieces again to distribute among his brothers. Of the three of them only David had voluntarily accepted his lesser status as a vassal, and enjoyed his lands upon that ground, and for all his lapses since, had always returned to that stand, even in this last reconciliation that was still chilly and imperfect. Of the other two, Rhodri obstinately held to

71

his ancient rights, though he had never done anything to earn them. And Owen Goch, at the time of Rhodri's attempt on his behalf, had been offered his freedom and a fair establishment if he would accept the same vassal status David held, and had vehemently refused. To be honest, I do not think he had again been asked since that time. Llewelyn had been busy upon the affairs of Wales itself; it was easy to forget the angry, ageing, red-haired man glooming out over the lakes of Snowdon from the hilltop of Dolbadarn.

But now that we were no longer at war, with our eyes for ever fixed upon England, now that four years had passed with only the minor vexations inevitable in any legal settlement, Llewelyn began to consider once again all those other matters which had been shelved in favour of the greatest, especially as their right regulation could only add to the stability of Wales, and help to preserve our good relations with England.

'For there's no blinking the truth,' he said in private to me, 'it's not the best of recommendations to a prince that he has two of his own brothers in his prisons. Though God knows that was no novelty in Wales in the old days, if they did not kill one another outright, driven to murder by this same sacred law of the partible lands our romantics would like to revive.' He was not the first to abandon it, in fact, but had inherited the changed practice from his uncle and grandsire, though it was Llewelyn who came in for the odium from those who hated change. 'Now that I have time to breathe,' he said, 'I confess they are somewhat on my conscience.'

I said there was no need. 'Owen Goch had the half of Gwynedd, and was not content, but snatched at the whole. He deserved to fail, and to pay for it. And since then that first division is long outdated, for all the rest of Wales you have yourself drawn together, he has no rights in it. He had his chance to come to terms and get both lands and liberty at the price of his homage, and

72

he would not do it. What choice had you but to keep him safe where he could do Wales and you no harm?'

We were together in his own high chamber at Aber, late in the evening, as we often sat together, and he looked at me across the glow of the brazier and the dark red of his wine-cup, and laughed at me. 'All the justification in the world will not make my mind quite easy. You are becoming a lawyer like the English, Samson, and faith, so am I, for however much I may want a settlement, it will be on harder terms now than the simple act of homage. I'll take nothing less from Owen or Rhodri than a quitclaim of all their hereditary rights in Wales, engrossed on parchment, sealed and witnessed, something I can produce and they cannot deny. But for that I'd be willing to pay over not only liberty, but money, too, if need be, or land, provided they hold it of me, and not by any other right.'

'You made no such demand on David,' I reminded him.

'David offered his fealty. But I don't say,' agreed Llewelyn with deliberation, 'that I would not ask as much of him, were he now in the same situation. He is not. Whatever he may have done, he has never again raised the cry of his own birthright. And unless he gives me fresh cause, I will not ask anything of him, nor bring up again what has been done in the past. But surely there must be some inducement that could be offered at least to Rhodri, to get him off my hands and my mind. He's the weaker vessel, and the less able to keep his grudges white-hot for years. Let's at least try.'

Rhodri was then thirty-seven years old, and unmarried still, and I remarked, without much thought, that seeing how successful David's marriage bade fair to be, and how it seemed to work most potently upon his tempestuous nature, perhaps a wife could do as much to settle Rhodri. Llewelyn laughed, but then gave me a sharp and thoughtful glance, and said there might well be something in that. The restoration of the lands he had forfeited, upon terms, together with a proper match that would bring him lands elsewhere, might be temptation enough.

So we cast about quietly to find if there were suitable matches available, and made no move meantime, nor as yet did Llewelyn consult his council. There was a certain nobleman whose acquaintance he had made in Westminster, one John le Botillier, who had lands both in England and Ireland, and he had no sons, but only a daughter, Edmunda, who was therefore his heiress, and a very desirable match, and her father had let it be known that he wished to settle her in marriage. There was no haste in the matter, but upon enquiry it was plain that le Botillier was well disposed to the idea of an alliance with a prince of Wales and would be willing to consider any approaches made to him. The lady we had seen in London, at the festival, and she was now turned twenty, and handsome.

'We'll put it to Rhodri,' said Llewelyn, 'before taking it further. If he's compliant, it might do very well. Ride with me, Samson! I'll go myself, and at least deal honestly with him, not leave it to another.' And he said, when we were on our way to Dolwyddelan: 'My mother, before she died, told me to do justice to my brother. Do you remember? And I said I would do right to all my brothers. Easier to say than to do! Sometimes I wonder whether I know where right lies. When the rights of Wales come into collision with Rhodri's, or with Owen's, I see but one claim on me.'

I said, and it was true, that had they been other than they were, they, too, might have set the needs of Wales before their own. But by his tight smile I think he still doubted. Yet even in self-appraisal, and in his rare moods of self-blame and disgust with the shifts to which he was put in his quest, he never took his eyes from his grand aim, the establishment of a Wales solid and secure enough to survive its founder, and in pursuit of that aim he never repented anything he did, whatever its cost to him or another.

In the castle of Dolwyddelan Rhodri had a chamber high in the great keep, but he was allowed the run of the wards for exercise, under guard, and as prisons go, his was by no means of the worst. Sometimes he was even permitted to ride out in the hills, though safely escorted, for the castle stands high on a steep place, and the space within the walls is somewhat cramped. He had been visited, often by myself, once or twice in every year, and his wants and complaints, within reason, were attended to good-humouredly. Owen Goch at Dolbadarn was more closely kept, being a far more formidable person. Rhodri was querulous and critical, but not given to bold or decisive action. The marvel was that he ever brought himself to make that one rash raid, in the attempt to snatch Owen from his escort, though even that he did mainly for his own ends, needing an ally more robust than himself.

Llewelyn had him brought down from his tower apartment into the great chamber, where there was a good fire. Rhodri halted for an instant at the sight of his brother, and then came forward into the room with a wary and suspicious face, looking at us a little sidelong, which was a way he always had, from a child. Sometimes he even walked with a sidewise gait, as though too wary and secretive to approach people straight. He was not greatly changed after his long confinement, by reason of the air and exercise allowed to him. His reddish fair hair had no grey in it as yet, and he looked no older than his years.

'What, in person?' he said, curling his lip. 'I had not looked for such an honour!' He was not feeling as bold as his manner and words suggested, for I saw the rapid, nervous fluttering of his eyelashes, which were of a colour almost rosy. 'You've left me long enough un-

75

visited, there must be some important reason for this visit now.'

'There is,' said Llewelyn bluntly. 'A matter of business. I have a proposal to make to you, and we may as well sit down and be civil together while I make it.' And he sent for wine, and made Rhodri sit beside the fire, close to him.

'I look for no good,' said Rhodri sullenly, 'from any proposal of yours. You have never wished me well, or done me justice, why should I hope for better now? If you had any brotherly feeling for me you would have set me free long ago. What do you want with me more? You have done to me all that is needful, your princedom is safe enough, at my cost, and at Owen's. Go and enjoy it!'

It was David's complaint, though never voiced to Llewelyn, that the prince held him too lightly to care either for his love or his hate, which in his case was never true. But of Rhodri it was true enough. There was no way he could either anger or please my lord, never anything larger than irritation and weariness. So Llewelyn sat back among the fur rugs of the couch, and let his brother's petulant grievances flow over him and pass, like the humming of midges in the high summer. Neither smiling nor frowning, he waited for the feeble shower to spend itself. Then he said mildly:

'Hate me as well as you will, but listen to me, if you want your freedom and a life at large. For you can have it, but at a price. No, let me hear no exclamation, you know only too well there must be a price. We need not go into repetitions of what has been said often enough. Wales is one, and I made it one, and if it cost your life, and Owen's, and mine, I will keep it one. There is no change there; there never will be any change. But short of letting you or any break that unity apart, you wrong me, I do wish you well. I am here to prove it. Will you listen?'

76

Rhodri was so at loss, and so seeking within his own mind for perils that might still be threatening him, that it took some minutes to awe him into calm, and be sure of his attention. Then Llewelyn told him the entire bargain, bluntly and short, to leave no doubt.

'The father is favourably disposed. The lady is very comely, and a considerable heiress. And I will see that you are set up in a sum fitting to advance this marriage. The price is large. I own it. It is the only price that will buy you this opportunity. I want from you in return a quitclaim of all your hereditary rights in Gwynedd – for in the rest of Wales you have none, and never had any.'

Rhodri gulped, and gazed, and writhed, his breath taken by so unexpected a visitation. I saw how he leaned to the hope of freedom, recoiled from the surrender of his grievance and his claim, and yet could not but realise that the grievance had no hope of being recompensed, the claim no possibility of being acknowledged, whether he took this price or no. There was against him a mind far stronger and larger than his, and a cause not all, not chiefly, selfish, against which his own small struggles were vain. And he was being offered a very fine and comfortable position in the world, a wealthy wife, and his liberty. He leaned and clutched, and started back in dudgeon, and grasped again frantically before the hope escaped him. And Llewelyn let him sway back and forth in anguish as long as he would, without pressing.

'In return for the quitclaim,' he said, 'I will pay you the sum of one thousand marks to acquire this marriage, but the quitclaim I must have.'

'And if I refuse?' said Rhodri, quivering. But to me, at least, it was already clear that he would not refuse.

'Then you remain here as my prisoner, and you have quitclaimed to me all that I require of you, but without any repayment. Let us say,' said Llewelyn, in the gentlest and most reasonable of voices, 'that I stand to gain what I need, whatever your answer may be, but if your answer is yes, and if you make it good, then you also stand to gain a wife, an estate, and a figure in the land. It is not an even choice,' he said, with some distaste, 'but at least it is fairly stated. And you know, for all your grudges, that what I swear to, that I perform.'

And Rhodri did know it, as all men knew it who dealt with Llewelyn, for after he had wrestled with his venom a while, and we had kept silence and borne with him, he said in a strangled voice, and wringing his hands together in rage and relief equally mixed: 'Very well, I agree! I will give you the quittance you want.'

The agreement was drawn up and sealed at Carnarvon on the twelfth day of April, with the approval of the council, though since it was a personal bargain, accepted upon both sides, they had no call to sanction or prohibit. Nevertheless, their blessing, given with great relief at the solution of one long-standing problem and reproach, was worth much, and their witness to the deed far more.

Rhodri was brought down from Dolwyddelan to Carnarvon still under guard, for Llewelyn would not quite loose him out of hold until he had his quitclaim safely sealed. But it was not difficult to see the lavish company that attended him as escort rather than guard on a prisoner, and from the day of his acceptance he had been allowed the services of his own household and clerks, so that there should be nothing underhand about the bargain. By the time they rode into Carnarvon Rhodri was no longer a pressed partner in the deal, having conned over all its advantages to himself at leisure, with no envied and resented brother by to poison the picture for him, and the prospect of an Irish heiress, with a goodly estate in trust for her, and a pretty face to match, had begun to seem far more desirable than a tenuous claim that grew every year more impossible of realisation. So it was no sullen and reluctant prince who brought his retinue into Carnarvon to seal the bond, but a cheerful

78

giver who went about with a small, sidewise, sleek smile, as though he had reached the conclusion that he was not doing at all badly out of the exchange, but had better not reveal as yet that he was aware of it.

In a great conference of council and clergy Rhodri and his clerks delivered the prepared deed, by which he quitclaimed, for himself and his heirs after him, to the prince and the heirs of his body, all his rights and claims by heredity in the lands and possessions of north Wales, and elsewhere throughout the whole principality – though naturally this need not preclude the grant of lands to him to be held of the prince by homage – in consideration of the payment of one thousand marks sterling with which to acquire the marriage of Edmunda, daughter of John le Botillier. The deed also made solemn promise that he would not disturb, or procure others to disturb, the peace of the prince's realm, against his present willing surrender and quitclaim. And to this document he added his seal, together with the seals of the bishops of Bangor and St Asaph, and the abbots of Aberconway, Basingwerk and Enlli, with leave to add also the seals of the arch-deacons of the two northern sees. A great number of witnesses, headed by Tudor the high steward of Wales, and including Llewelyn's own law clerks, subscribed to the agreement. Rhodri was at the same moment fast bound, and utterly free. From the time the deed was concluded he was at liberty, and a first payment of fifty marks was made to him at once, to pay his expenses in opening negotiations with le Botillier. Which he set about eagerly, with every prospect in his favour.

And indeed he was not so bad a match for the lady, and not an ill-looking fellow, though vague and colourless beside either Llewelyn's glowing brown or David's raven blackness and brilliance. And in the first exchanges everything went well with his suit, and the father, certainly, was in favour of the marriage, and exactly what befell to break off the arrangement we were never told, for by then the matter had naturally passed completely into Rhodri's hands, and whatever it was, it caused him great chagrin and anger, and he was in no mind to share it. By such grains of gossip as leaked out, it seems that though le Botillier was in favour of accepting Rhodri, his daughter had other ideas, having both a lover and a mind of her own, and contrived to place herself in a situation so delicately compromised that her parents found it wise to let her have her way, and betrothed her to the young man in question. Whether this is true or not, certainly she was married, shortly afterwards, to one Thomas de Muleton.

Now perhaps Rhodri could have borne this rebuff somewhat better if his marriage plans had not been made so publicly and before so great and solemn a concourse, but as it was, the collapse of his hopes could not but be noised abroad just as publicly, and he took it very hard, for though marriage plans are made and unmade in business-like fashion all the year round with no heart-burning on either side, yet to be the favoured suitor with the parents and to be rejected and outwitted by the girl is less common, and very shaming. From the moment he got the news of the final break Rhodri shut himself up from sight, fearful of covert smiles and castle jokes such as follow the unfortunate, and brooded in the blackest of moods. And within a week he vanished from among us, took his portable treasure and rode away in the night, and the next word we had was that he had entered Chester and confided himself to the justiciar there.

Llewelyn made mild enquiry, not anxious to interfere with his brother's plans, if Rhodri intended to shake off the dust of Wales, only wanting precise news; and I think he would have been willing then to pay a further instalment of the money due, but Rhodri had already ridden south, presumably to London to ask hospitality and service at court, so as we had no further word the prince shrugged, and let him go.

'With goodwill,' he said, sighing, 'if he intends to settle in England, for I am rid of him, and he may do very well there, where he has no claims and no grievances, and no ambitions beyond his reach.'

None the less, it had an unpleasant flavour for us that a prince who found his life soured in Wales should naturally make for King Henry's court, as if fleeing for refuge to the enemy, whereas we had been at peace and in very reasonable friendship for five years.

'It seems we have not yet succeeded in changing men's minds,' said Llewelyn soberly. 'He could have gone openly for me, why should I hinder him?'

'Why, indeed?' said David to me, after hearing this. 'He has what he wanted from him, signed and sealed, with a dozen or so reverend churchmen as sureties, and half the nobility of Wales as witnesses. There's nothing any lawyer, English or Welsh, can do to break that bond, and nothing left to fear from Rhodri. Now he has not even to pay him or feed him. Why hinder his going, indeed!'

He had come to me, as he used to do years before, in my copying-room, where I was busy with some documents concerning cases to be heard in the prince's local court. We were sitting by candle-light, for I had worked so late that even in August the light was gone, but for a violet afterglow over the sea. Elizabeth was not with him on this visit, and without her he was restless and out of humour. The black mood could not endure in her presence, at least not thus early in the charm of their marriage, but now it sat upon his shoulders for want of her, and perhaps in some measure for shadowy regrets and remembrances concerning Rhodri.

'Both you and King Henry,' I said, 'have good cause to know and admit that the prince pays what he pledges. *You* have no call to speak slightingly of his usage, whatever Rhodri may claim. Take care your own debts are paid as punctiliously as his.'

I meant debts not in money, and he so understood me, for he smiled at me darkly across the table, his elbows spread among my parchments and his chin in his cupped hands. His finger-tips pressed deep hollows into his lean cheeks below the rounded and polished cases of bone out of which his eyes shone so wildly pale, clear and bright.

'Ah, now you preach like my true priestly breast-brother,' he said. 'I have heard the note before, I should miss it if ever you gave me up for lost, and cast me out of your prayers. Oh, yes, I have debts still undischarged, have I not, Samson? Twice forgiven, twice restored. I have a great load of amends to make, and gratitude to show, and service to render yet before I shall be clear of my indebtedness. Do you know of a slower and a deadlier poison,' he said, pressing his fingers deeper, so that his long lips were drawn up in an angry smile, 'than having to swallow favour undeserved? Never to be able to find gratitude enough to buy it off, and never to be able to spit it out in rank ingratitude? I'd liefer be treated as an equal and slung into Dolbadarn for twenty years with Owen!'

Knowing him, I said without excitement: 'That is a lie. And you know it.'

He drew exasperated breath, and gnawed his lips for a moment, eyeing me glitteringly from under his long black lashes, and then he laughed.

'Yes, that is a lie! I might wish to prefer such dire payment, but in truth I like my freedom, and my comfort, and my own will, and I suppose if my deserts threatened me again I should again use my wits to cling fast to all those good things, and slip sideways from under the lash. Sweet Samson, I shall come to you no more for confession and absolution. You know me too well. I get no flattery.'

'No penance, either,' I said.

'True, that should bring me still,' he owned, 'seeing what I've just admitted. I wonder if I could ever take to

82

hating *you*, Samson, for letting me off too lightly?'

'As you hate him?' I said, and watched him flinch and frown blackly, and clench his even white teeth hard upon his knuckle, but never for all these writhings take his eyes from mine. Such he was, he could look you in the face as clearly and challengingly as an angel, both while he lied to you and while he told you blazing truth. If he could not come to terms with a man, or a cause, or a world, still he would not turn his face away. Once he told me outright that he was afraid of death, but he never averted his eyes, not even from that enemy.

'You deceive yourself,' I said, 'you do not hate him.'

'Do I not?' said David mildly, still gazing like one interested and willing to learn.

'Think, sometimes, that you have what he lacks and envies you, married happiness, and a child...'

'Children!' said David, and let his lips soften into quite another smile, thinking of Elizabeth. 'She is again with child. But no one knows it yet but you, Samson. She says it will a boy this time. She says it as if God had told her. Yes, I have what he may well envy, have I not?' And then he did lower his eyes, but to look within, at this mystery he hoarded within himself, as if he watched the seed burgeon. And more than that, a mystery beyond that mystery. The slow, deepening curl of his lips was triumphant. He enjoyed, he delighted in, his victory over Llewelyn; he prayed it to continue. It was a large and crushing revenge for every real and imagined injury.

'You teach me,' said David, softly and sweetly, 'where gratitude is truly due.' And he rose, the candles quivering faintly in the wind of his movements, and stretched at large, and smiled down at me. 'I will remember it in my prayers,' he said, and turned to the door. 'I'll leave you to your labours now. Good-night!'

In the doorway, the soft blue light from the summer sky flowing down all the outlines of his dark figure like moonlit water, he turned and looked back. 'To think,' he said, wondering, 'that he had always this weapon of the quit-claim, if he had cared to use it! They say every man has his price. I wonder what he would have had to offer Owen? Or me, for that matter?'

'He has never asked you,' I said, stung, 'he never will ask you, for such a quitclaim.'

'As well!' said David, soft and muted in the doorway. 'I would not give it to him if he did.'

In October of that year Pope Gregory X, that Cardinal Tedaldo Visconti who was recalled from the crusade to take up his office, and there in the east had become close and faithful friend to the Lord Edward, examined and rejected the prior of Canterbury as candidate for the primacy of England, looked warily but briefly at Edward's choice, Robert Burnell, that formidable cleric of affairs, and passed carefully over him to choose Robert Kilwardby, the Dominican. So the national province had an archbishop again after two years, a man of scholarship, piety and intellect.

And one month later, in his palace of Westminster, King Henry died as he had lived, among the turbulent outcries of a populace preoccupied with a minor quarrel over the mayor of London. His death was hastened, as many believed, because of his hurried pilgrimage to calm another local disorder in Norwich, which otherwise flickered out without great damage. All his life he was haunted and hunted by such annoyances, yet he had reigned for fifty-six years, and survived everything life and England could do against him. He lived to see his dearest dream take shape in this world, in his church at Westminster, and few men have that joy. And he died, for all the turmoils he had provoked and suffered, better regarded than in his youth, and the mourning for him was not feigned nor formal, though muted by the natural erosions of time, for he was old, and had had his span fairly.

Since the deaths and burials even of kings give but very

brief warning, Henry was in his tomb before ever we heard of his departure. The official word from the regents and the royal council did not reach us until the twenty-sixth day of November, being sent out along with the formal letters in the new king's name to all his sheriffs and officers in the land. But we had fuller information three days before that, for Cynan sent his lively Welsh groom to bring us the news, his master's letter supplementing his own account.

'His Grace was buried,' Cynan wrote, 'in his abbey church four days after his death, and they have laid him, according to his wish, in the tomb from which the relics of Saint Edward were translated three years ago. By one means or another he will make his way into heaven. The Lord Edward being absent, the council and his own proctors have taken charge, and for four days England had no king, though there was never any question of his peaceful succession or his welcome. After the funeral mass, before the tomb was closed, all the bishops and barons and others present went up to the high altar, and took the oath of fealty to King Edward. A new seal has been made for him, and King Henry's seal was broken by the archbishop of York after the oath had been sworn by all. The first to swear was Gloucester, who was sent for to the king on the day he died, and has pledged himself to forgo all old grudges against Edward, and guard the kingdom for him until he comes, and all the signs are that he means it and will do his best. They have written to Edward to let him know of his father's death, and urged him to return quickly. By this time his term in the east is over, and he must be on his way back, but as far as is known it was his intention to winter with Charles of Anjou in Sicily, as he did on his journey east. Now he may change his plans, but equally he may not, for he made good certain of his arrangements before sailing, and has absolute trust in his proctors to act now as his regents.'

These proctors were the archbishop of York, Robert Burnell, and my lord's cousin, Roger Mortimer, his troublesome and aggressive kinsman, neighbour and enemy in the middle march. Those two had an old rivalry that was also, after its fashion, a friendship. So we knew with whom we should have to deal in any disputes or agreements that might arise.

'So the old man is gone,' said Llewelyn, pondering his own regret with some surprise. 'I have fought him most of my life, and never thought I might grieve for his death. But we had grown used to each other, and there was a certain security in that. Now we begin afresh. And not with Edward, not yet.'

The old man was gone, and the new man not yet come, and there could be no homage rendered until he did arrive in person in his kingdom. The oath of fealty, that the baronage had taken at the high altar after the burial, could indeed be sworn in the king's absence, but the meeting of hands was impossible, and it was somewhat unusual, though not unknown, for the two acts to be separated after this fashion. So we expected only to continue our dealings with England as before, until Edward's arrival, and were prepared to be as accommodating with his regents as we had tried to be with his father.

At this time Llewelyn still had a number of matters at issue with England, and had listed his complaints after the normal fashion, and we were in process of arranging a meeting of the commission at the ford of Montgomery, the usual place of parley. When, therefore, he received a letter from the regents, he expected that it should be appointing a date for this arbitration. It was indeed a summons to the ford of Montgomery for an official meeting, but not of such a neighbourly kind as we had looked for. The regents sent a writ to order him to attend in person at the ford on the twentieth day of January of the coming year, to take the oath of fealty to King Edward in absence, in the persons of those who would be sent to represent the crown.

This writ came to us in December, and bore the date of the twenty-ninth of November, and there was about this indecent haste an ominous note of incivility which both stung and amused Llewelyn. King Henry had been dead just two weeks when they called the prince, with less ceremony than would have been used to an earl. Surely they were pressed with business then, a great burden of legal adjustments necessary after the passing of one king and the succession of another, and they sent out all their official writs and documents in great haste, and made little distinction between persons. And yet this pricked and clung like a burr, even in my skin, and I am sure in Llewelyn's. But he also was a busy man, and wasted little indignation on the summons.

'The dogs bark as loudly as they can when they are barking for a lion,' he said good-humouredly. 'Where's the haste, when I cannot do homage until Edward is here to close his hands on mine? Why should I swear my fealty to the king's shadow? I'll wait for Edward.' And he went on with the business of his commote court, which was then occupying him, and for all I could see, forgot the whole matter.

Now this is of importance, for some have thought that even at this time he had it in mind to avoid repeating to the son the homage he had rendered to the father, seeing this change in the monarchy as his opportunity to hold fast what he had gained and achieve a completely independent status for Wales, in alliance, certainly, but an alliance equal on both sides, without hint of vassalage of any kind. But this is false, and even the suggestion has arisen only of late. He had no such move in mind. He said as he meant, for in all border disputes he had relied more upon Edward than upon any other, and had very solid trust in him. But for some of his officials he felt no such kindness, and to affront them, I confess, was not unpleasant to him. They had caused him trouble enough.

87

But to avoid his homage, no, he never entertained such a thought. By treaty he had pledged himself not only to King Henry but to his heirs, and as he had pledged, so he kept. But he did not think it of any importance to make a ceremony of vowing fealty while homage was impossible.

He was more displeased, I believe, shortly after, when he received a curt reminder that there was one sum of the indemnity to England in arrears, and another instalment due at the Christmas feast. Which was true enough, though he had already despatched the arrears about the time of the king's death, and it was receipted later, and reminders in advance had never been customary or necessary, for there was no man in the treasury who did not know that the prince of Wales was not only the promptest payer the crown had, but in fact the only prompt payer. The monarchy was eternally in debt, Llewelyn almost never, and never for long.

'This is insolent,' he said, tossing the letter aside to me. 'When they appoint me a day to put right the wrongs done to me in the borders, as I have asked and asked, then I'll pay them the next money due, and not before. And the earlier Edward comes home, the better pleased shall I be. I thought Burnell, at least, had a finer understanding.'

I said that I read in the tone of this demand, rather, the loud and arrogant voice of his cousin Mortimer. And at that he laughed, and said I might well be right, for Roger was a bull who made head-down for his adversary. And back he went to his work, and let the crude demand lie. I know on what terms we had dealt with England, and I say, and say again, that in this attitude he was justified, and I, who loved and lived for him, never thought then that there was any need to advise or persuade him to any other tone. Those who say the change was in him, they lie. He changed only when all changed. And had he remained constant when all changed, what would it have availed him? Nothing!

At the Christmas festival at Aber, according to custom, David came visiting, to preserve the proper form, but without his Elizabeth, for she was near her time, and therefore, to my grief, without Cristin, who was never parted from her, and to my ease, with our Godred, either, for he resisted being parted from Cristin. This I put down, though not quite easily, to a desire to look like a good husband, for of real and loving care for his wife he had none, but a man must keep his status and his face. It was a snowy Christmas, as I recall, white across the salt flats and crusted with frost along the edge of the sea. The mountains hid in sparkling mist well into the new year, and we in the maenol under the cleft of the hills had a snug, smoky Christmas, no way troubled, unless it was by David's fretting for his beloved girl. We told him again and again she had the best of care, which he acknowledged, and that she had borne her first daughter in joy, within three hours, and laughing, which also he owned and vaunted. Even so, he grudged every moment away from her.

Consequently he did not stay long with us after the new year began, but was in haste to get back to Lleyn, though he knew that Cristin would have had a messenger on the road hot-foot to him if there had been any need for his return. But he waited for a meeting of the council which was held in the first week of January, being still insistent upon his duty, even when his mind was elsewhere and he contributed little. He did, however, prick up his ears and look very thoughtful when he heard of the arbitrary letter from the regents, though Llewelyn mentioned the matter but currently in passing, with reference to the need to hold something in reserve to force amends for border infringements. For there is no doubt that these had increased since King Henry's death, not in any drastic fashion, but by local raids, and some interference with merchants and the passage of goods. I do not think this was in any sense official policy, or that the regents countenanced it or knew much about it. It was rather that with one king dead and another not yet come, those who lived a lawless life by choice in the marches, remote from the seat of power, and in the tenancy or service of almost equally lawless lords, felt themselves freed from any strong surveillance, and indulged their normal sport to the full. By the time law could get to them, they were again dispersed and about their innocent business. This was the case generally in the march, but in the centre and the south, especially where we were neighbour to the vast and powerful honours of Gilbert de Clare of Gloucester and Humphrey de Bohun of Hereford, it was not merely the lesser people who plundered as opportunists, but there were also some planned and methodical incursions by the lords themselves into land manifestly Welsh. The regents were able and hard-working men, but carried a great load, and were held by the sheer weight of their documentary business to London, where the needful offices were. The prospect of their coming in person to examine and suppress the raiding in the borders did not terrify the marchers at all. They might deal out verbal penalties from Westminster, but distance was blessed, and they were not Edward. So the borderers made hay while the good weather lasted, and the only means we had of preventing was in arms, and that we were anxious to limit to what was clearly fair defence, short of actual retaliation.

'I have never been long in default with the money I am pledged to pay,' Llewelyn said, 'and I do not blink the fact that it is due by treaty. If I withhold it or delay it, it can be said that I am failing to fulfil my terms, and that goes against my grain. But it is truth that these pinpricks along the border have become dagger-wounds, and to my mind the terms of the treaty are already being broken from their side. I have lodged my complaints so often that I grow weary. The only direct weapon I have to my hand is this money. Perhaps I have been too prompt up to now. They write me into their accounts a month ahead of time, and have spent half what they get from me before they get it. It may cause them to read my letters more carefully and keep their own bond more exactly if I hold back what is now due. Let them perform their part, and I'll perform mine.'

Tudor approved, though cautiously. Some of the council were prepared to go further, having border troubles in their own commotes, and all shrugged aside the summons to the ford as of little importance, which was certainly Llewelyn's own opinion. He preferred direct dealings with Edward always, and had found them by far the best way of getting grievances attended to and wrongs righted.

'When the king comes home,' he said confidently, 'we shall have no more trouble and misunderstanding, even if there's no lasting cure for a contentious border as long as men are men. I rely on Edward's goodwill and good sense. It is these officials who offend.'

So with general approval we held back the payment due that Christmas, though it was his habit to have the amount ready and waiting, so far as that was possible, whenever it fell due. And with that the council dispersed. But David, frowning and thoughtful, sought out Llewelyn before he gathered his people and rode for home.

'Take care,' he said seriously, 'how you deal with these regents. Never take them too lightly; they are not light men.'

'Did you disapprove?' said Llewelyn, surprised. 'Why did you not say so?'

'No, it's well enough to stand upon the treaty, and insist they do their part. But don't take it too far, if you'd be wise. These officials *are* Edward. Make no mistake. Edward will not uphold you or any against them; they represent his name and right – however they

91

conduct themselves. They may do in his absence things he would rather they had not done, but if they are done in his name they will be law and binding, and he will maintain them, and oppose all those who challenge them. Even you!'

All this he said earnestly but coolly, as he performed all his vassal duties, not as a brother warning his brother of unwisdom. And I, who was watching his face and guessing at the mind behind it, judged from the distant spark in his eyes that more than half of him was already away with Elizabeth, and in a vision he held in his arms the son she had promised him, the first of a line, the founder of a dynasty. For all the controlled austerity of his face, there was triumph in his eyes. It was the first time I had ever seen him look upon Llewelyn with something near to pity. Punctiliously he warned him of possible danger. Once I had said to my lord that as often as David's right hand struck at his brother, his left would reach to parry the blow.

I went down with him to the stables, and walked beside him as far as the gate when he rode, swathed in furs against the cold. I asked him to give my greetings and service to Elizabeth, and to Cristin, and when he said he would, his voice was quick and warm, and he laid a hand upon my shoulder. There was little he did not know concerning Cristin and me, though I think Godred remained to him a bright, shallow mystery.

'I would you had my happiness!' he said, and meant it.

'Do you wish as much to him?' I said.

David shook his shoulders impatiently. 'It is his own choice to be barren and alone. It is not yours.'

'He will not always be so,' I said, and prayed that my heart might be as certain of it as my voice sounded.

'You think not?' said David.

'Surely not! God forbid I should look forward hopefully to any death, but the Countess Eleanor cannot live for ever, even if she continues adamant all her life, and nothing else stands in the way. After all this time, who can raise any objection?'

'The Countess Eleanor is no more than a dozen years or so older than he is,' said David, and his voice was slow, considering and cool. 'No man can tell when his time will come. He may yet go before her. And here is this heritage without an heir, and he values it so little! A kingdom, and he will not give it a prince!'

It was the same text to which Tudor spoke frequently and at length, though less often to Llewelyn these days, knowing it would be vain. But Tudor said these things with anxiety and exasperation and sorrow. In David's voice was none of these; it kept its soft, speculative level and the calm of its music unshaken by any indignation. A very beautiful voice he had, but as I knew from my own long alliance with him, it could fret and scald and slash with passion enough when he so pleased.

'While I,' he said, so softly and drily that he seemed to be speaking to himself rather than to me, though I knew it was meant for my ears, and meant to disquiet a little, 'I have heirs – perhaps a prince by now! – but no kingdom. Thus is this world arranged at cross-purposes, Samson. Have you never wished to move the pieces into a better pattern? Or do you still believe God knows best, and should not have his elbow jogged?'

'Go home,' I said, 'and take your mischief with you, and forbear from plaguing your wife as you delight in plaguing me.'

And at that he laughed aloud, and stooped low from the saddle to embrace me about the shoulders, and rode out of the gate with a plunge of his heel and a swirl of his cloak, keeping the rimy edges of grass along the coast road to avoid the glassy ice. And after him his retinue, well-mounted, rich and bright with colours, equipped and harnessed most princely, a king's retinue.

CHAPTER IV

A small judgment awaited David and Elizabeth that January for their too much pride and delight in their fruitfulness, for the expected son was a second daughter, as fine and dark and bold as the first, but not so beautiful, taking after her mother rather than her sire but for the black hair. She came as sweetly and readily as the other, for this lady was gifted for bearing as few women are, and all her children lived and flourished, and she, meantime, remained so young and vigorous that after some years of tending her girls she appeared rather as their elder sister than their mother.

This girl they named Gladys, after David's only sister, many years dead in her bloom. And I think that the check to their exultation was but mild and brief, for they both loved their children, and took great pleasure in enjoying them. Moreover, Elizabeth had proved her gift of giving birth, and he his generosity in engendering, and as for the sons, it was but a matter of time. So the little one was never made to feel she must pay for her error in not being a boy, but was cherished and worshipped from her birth. And as love is a rare virtue, and surely prized in heaven, so I count the family blessedness of those two perilous and hapless creatures as their justification and their crown. By this time David so loved, as she deserved and exulted in his love. He was a creature hard to trap, but she had him in the snare of her own immeasurable worship. He never swerved from her, never again looked at any other woman, he who had ensnared all the beauties of England and Wales before Edward cast this innocent child-widow in his path, brown as a mouse, mild as rain, plain as a little sister.

'Is he happy?' asked Llewelyn, in some doubt, when we got word of the child's birth. 'He wanted, he expected, a boy.' Of his voice I knew even those tones that were lost in the quietness of his speech. He suffered what David never knew, all his bowels cramped with longing, for he was all a man, and obstinately celibate for his love. A passing strange thing is love, outside the regulation of the flesh, entering into the spirit. I have seen his face so translated by desire, he passed beyond David's recognition.

'He is happy,' I said. 'You need not fret for David.' But for Llewelyn my heart turned and curdled in me, remembering David's grievance and David's vaunt, crying aloud that he had a prince without a kingdom, or would have soon, while Llewelyn had a kingdom without an heir. With all the goodwill in the world on Llewelyn's part, and, for all his stiff-necked insistence on his vassal status, a great deal of obdurate and hurtful love left on David's, yet this division of their personal fortunes was no way helpful to the restoration of the old trust and affection between them.

In the early spring of that year twelve hundred and seventy-three we had news from Cynan at court that disquieted Llewelyn more than he would confess. King Edward on his slow way home from the Holy Land had sent his wife into Spain, both to visit her brother the king of Castille, and also to conduct certain minor matters of business on his behalf in those parts, while he went into Italy, to Orvieto, to renew his friendship with Pope Gregory the crusader. The queen was then carrying another child, and had with her her baby daughter Joan, born at Acre. Doubtless she was glad to rest awhile in her native country, before she went on into Gascony to meet Edward there. He had written to his council that he would make haste to get home, but kings never have quiet from affairs, and there were some restive lordlings in Gascony who were still prepared to outface even Edward, so that his presence was needed there. In the end he delayed a whole year.

But as at this time of which Cynan wrote, he was with Pope Gregory at Orvieto. And there he learned that Guy de Montfort, the murderer of Henry of Almain, was still at large, sheltered and safe in the territories of the people of Siena, having his father-in-law, the Red Count of Pitigliano, as a most powerful ally. Edward in great fury demanded aid from the Sienese to hunt down the assassin, and though they refused him, they did so in fear and trembling, and Siena and Florence and other cities of Tuscany begged the king not to resort to war. So, doubtless, did his friend the pope, and Edward could not well go against him, but he did use every possible legal threat to induce Guy to submit himself to the church's condemnation and penance. His unremitting hatred and rage appalled all who witnessed them, not that Guy had not earned it, but that its intensity and deadliness were more and less than human, giant like his body, but not subject to any curbs or temperings of time, or resignation, or magnanimity, as human rages should be.

'In the end,' wrote Cynan, 'he has failed to get his enemy into his hands, but has done the best he could to destroy him, inducing the pope to issue against him the most frightful bull of excommunication possible. He is left no human rights, he can hold no lands, own no property, take shelter nowhere without imperilling those who shelter him. With that the king has had to be content, and has now left Orvieto on his way to the pass of Mont Cenis. But from all I hear, feeling in Italy is not near so unfavourable to Guy, and as soon as the king's back is turned there will be ambassadors enough willing to try to bring the man to submission and absolution. More ominous is the revelation of King Edward's mind towards those who incur his displeasure.'

'As well,' said Llewelyn wryly, reading this dolorous account of the turbulent fortunes of Earl Simon's third son, 'that I am making no move at this time, and can make none, in the face of the countess's absolute rejection. At waiting, I believe, I am the most accomplished of princes, certainly the most experienced. I can wait yet a year or two. Even King Edward's animosity must wear itself out sooner or later. At least I can take good care of Wales, while I wait for the day when I can lay it at Eleanor's feet.'

At this time he was concerned to repair certain gaps in the main border defences, which he wished to ensure by means of a string of castles, as the English did. From the north, by Chester, he had Mold, and Whittington in Salop, and safe support at Dinas Bran, but in the middle march, over against Montgomery, his position was less well established, and for some time he had been planning to place a new castle, a strong building in stone, somewhere in that region, and preferably in conjunction with a town and a market. He chose the crest of a great ridge overhanging the valley of the upper Severn, just where the lesser river Mule flows into it, in the cantref of Cydewain, perhaps four miles from the ford where our conventions met, and five from the royal castle of Montgomery. From the summit of that hill, where the rock breaks through the turf, there is a glorious view over all that grand valley, for many miles to the south, and less widely to the north, while across the river valley the folded hills rise again, hiding Montgomery, but revealing all the river crossings between. It seemed a most defensible site, and the river junction below a very profitable place for a township, access being both good from all directions, and controllable from the castle. As soon as the weather was favourable for the moving and cutting of stone and laying of foundations, building began, with a great army of workmen and masons.

This place the people of Cydewain called Dolforwyn,

the 'Angels' Meadow', and the township Llewelyn founded beneath it, where the rivers joined, we called Abermule.

About the twenty-fourth day of June, when the building was forward and in good heart, and Llewelyn in the summer weather, after some weeks encamped below the hill to supervise the work, had withdrawn with his entourage to Dinorben, he was astonished to receive a visitor in the person of the reverend prior of Wenlock, which is a Cluniac abbey in Salop, not too far distant from those parts of the border, bearing a letter from King Edward's regents, issued through the royal chancellery. The prince received the reverend father with all courtesy, and such soldierly hospitality as we could offer him in a summer camp, and contained his curiosity about the message until we were out of the presence of the messenger. For the prior was old and gentle and very benign, and knew no more than we did what he carried, being charged only to deliver it, and to bring back the prince's answer.

'I have a premonition,' said Llewelyn, hesitating to break the seal, 'that these lieutenants of the king use the most innocent and well-willing to carry their worst crudities. It is one way of disarming offence.' But he would not give it to me to open and read to him, being, I rejoice to remember partly at my instruction, fluent in Latin as in Welsh, and almost as good in English, if his French, like mine, was something wanting. He read slowly, burning visibly into pure, silent anger, his burnished summer brown flushing into copper-red, but all in stillness. When he looked up at me, the skin of his face was drawn tight over starting bones, his eyes, which were normally peaceable in their deep, rich peat-brown, had red flames tall and bright in their depths.

'This is not to be borne,' he said, smouldering but quiet, torn between indignation and disdain. 'They have run mad with the glory of being deputies to greatness. Do you know what they dare to write to me, Samson? They straitly forbid me to continue with my plans to build

98

a castle at Dolforwyn, or to found a market town at Abermule, to the hurt of his Grace's crown rights and neighbouring markets. They forbid me! In my own Welsh lands! What market rights has England on this side of Severn to be infringed? None! And what right has one sovereignty to forbid another to build or found within its own territories? None! I am not even appropriating a site from a vassal of my own. I am the one person who has the right to build there without asking leave of any man living.'

And this was true, for Griffith ap Gwenwynwyn of Powys, the greatest of his vassals and the last to come to his fealty, held only a part of Cydewain. Nevertheless, I fancied then that Griffith was not best pleased by the founding of the castle, having an eye to his own trade rights and privileges at his castle and town of Pool, though that was a matter of eight miles distant from Abermule, and it could hardly be said that the prince was encroaching, trade with England in those parts being brisk, and the border not as turbulent as further south. But Griffith was jealous of his power, and grudging of his homage even when he came to it finally of his own free will and for his own ends.

'This outdoes their order to rush to swear my oath of fealty to a couple of abbots, almost before Henry was in his tomb,' said Llewelyn, and suddenly laughed, though angrily, remembering how little sleep he had lost over that. For having chosen, and stated his choice firmly, to wait for Edward in person, I think he had quite forgotten the matter of the summons to the ford of Montgomery, assuming that his decision would be accepted, and the matter dropped until the king came home. Whereas, as we afterwards learned, on the January day appointed in the original order, the abbots of Dore and Haughmond, escorted by a company from Montgomery, duly attended at the ford of the river, and waited until well into the afternoon for Llewelyn to come to the meeting. And since that was a bitter winter month, and the ford a bleak enough place in such weather, no doubt they had hard things to say in private about the prince's contumacy. Nevertheless, the regents must have shrugged off their too zealous attempt and recognised Llewelyn's right to prefer a direct meeting, for from that day nothing more was ever heard of persuading him to the oath until the king's arrival.

'But this shall not pass so simply,' he said warmly. 'Insolence and presumption towards me I can repulse without aid, but when they presume grossly against the laws that unite and separate England and Wales, they injure more than me, and do no service to their own lord, and he shall know it.'

'Will you send an answer by the prior?' I asked, thinking he might prefer rather to send a formal protest to Westminster by Welsh clerks at law, or even by one of Tudor's sons, who often did such errands for him where ceremony was advisable.

'As well by the prior as by any,' said Llewelyn, 'since he will respect the seal, and be witness to whom it was superscribed if others show less respect.' And he asked: 'Where, according to Cynan's last despatch, is the king arrived now?'

Then I caught his drift, and approved, and so did Tudor when he heard, and those few of the council who were then with us. For according to Cynan, who was well informed about all the news from Edward's wandering court, they were now on their way to Paris, after delaying a while among the queen-mother's relatives in Savoy, and by the end of July they should be guests of King Philip in the French capital. Moreover, the king intended to take to himself a great part of the business of England, now that he was so close to home as France, and a steady stream of messengers, envoys, clerks, clerics and barons was already crossing and recrossing the Channel on his affairs.

'Good!' said Llewelyn. 'Then they will have no excuse for detaining in their own hands any letter expressly addressed to the king.' And he dictated to me the following letter:

'We have received the letter written in your Grace's name, and dated at Westminster on the twentieth day of June, forbidding us to build a castle on our own land near Abermule, or to found there a town and establish a market. We are certain that the said letter was not sent with your Grace's knowledge, and that if you were present in your kingdom, as we would you were, no such mandate would ever have been issued from your royal chancery. For your Grace knows well that the rights of our principality are entirely separate from the rights of your realm, notwithstanding that we hold our principality under your Grace's royal power. You have heard, and to some degree have seen for yourself that we and our ancestors have always had power within our boundaries to build castles and fortresses, and to set up markets, without prohibition by any man, or any announcement of such work in advance. We pray your Grace not to give ear to the malicious suggestions of those people whose desire it is to exasperate your mind against us. Dated at Dinorben, on the feast of St Benedict, the eleventh day of July.'

Thus with clarity, force and dignity did he reply to the unjustified and illegal demand made upon him, and with absolute confidence exempted Edward from any part in the insult. And in this I think he was right. Even now I think so. And the letter was sealed and clearly superscribed to the king in person, and the prior's attention called to this when he undertook to carry it, as I am sure he did faithfully. But it had to pass through other hands than his before ever it could be delivered to the one man for whom it was intended.

'And the building,' said Llewelyn shortly, 'goes on.' And so it did, in the face of the garrison of Montgomery, so that its progress could hardly have been overlooked.

Now in the matter of this letter, which plainly is of great importance, I must set down here that we never heard word more of it, nor, indeed, of any objections to the founding of Abermule, or any attempts to prevent the raising of the castle on the hill above. I do not know what happened to the letter. It may be that it was duly sent on to King Edward, that he entirely agreed with what Llewelyn had written, and instructed his regents to cease interfering with the prince's actions. I say it *may* be so. But in that case I should have expected the king to write personally to Llewelyn in acknowledgement and reassurance, for he was punctilious in correspondence and courtesy in the normality of business. And no such reply ever came. Or it may be, and for my part this is what I believe, that the regents, in spite of the personal nature of the letter, arrogantly considered it within their mandate to open and use it freely, and retain it in their own hands instead of forwarding it to the king. Its content may well have persuaded them that they had better not attempt to press a demand which could be so firmly resisted at law, let alone in practice, and therefore they took no further action, and perhaps were very glad to let the attempt go by default. In either case, the effect upon the building of Dolforwyn was the same, but the effect upon the future relations of Wales and England was by no means the same, for if the letter remained in the chancery records, then Edward can never have been made aware of his lieutenants' overbearing and illegal demand or Llewelyn's justified resentment of it, and he cannot have seen and known what absolute faith Llewelyn had in the king's goodwill and intent to do right, and how little in his officers. If, therefore, that letter was detained and suppressed in Westminster, then I say that whoever took that act upon him took also a heavy burden of guilt upon his soul.

Nor had he any excuse, for by the end of July a great

number of the nobility were flocking to France, some to greet Edward, clear some point with him, and return, some to accompany him and work with him in his duchy of Gascony, whither he departed late in August to rejoin his queen. There were messengers enough and to spare, sailing weekly from Dover. Even though affairs kept him in Gascony so long, from this time the reins of government were in Edward's hands, though the regents still held great power at home, and I could not but remember David's warning that Edward would support his officers against all men as though they partook of his sovereignty.

However, there was still a year to run before Edward came home. This delay was not at first expected, for in August, about the time the king left Paris for Gascony, Llewelyn received a letter from the justiciar of Chester, Reginald de Grey, informing him that the king had fixed on the octave of Easter of the next year for his coronation, and cordially inviting the prince to be present. It is true that in the same letter he reminded Llewelyn of the amount of the indemnity still owing, and requested payment, but that hard touch of business was softened by a more friendly request that Wales would supply venison for the king's larder on the occasion, as Llewelyn had sometimes done before when a feast was toward.

The prince replied as warmly, acknowledging the invitation, guaranteeing to provide the venison by the date required, and diplomatically evading the question of the money, since he had only David and one or two other of his counsellors with him at that time, but promising a proper answer to the regents at Michaelmas. For as he had complaints to those officers still unredressed, he chose to conduct any correspondence about the money also with them, pointedly making the two issues one. A course which had not yet produced for us much in the way of amends or compensation, and for them nothing in sterling, but he persevered, and hoped for Edward's coming.

Later, because of the many matters occupying the king in Gascony, this date was changed to the nineteenth of August, by which time many things had also changed.

As I remember, it must have been after the building of Dolforwyn began that Griffith ap Gwenwynwyn's eldest son, Owen, began to frequent David with open admiration, and to spend much time in his company. This Owen was a man about twenty-seven years old, a good-looking young fellow enough, not over-tall, and not burly like his father, but rather taking after his English mother, Hawise Lestrange, who was the daughter of a former sheriff of Salop. Slender and well-proportioned like her, and of rather fair colouring, Owen had followed his father's example, no doubt due to her influence, and adopted the English manner of dress, harness and all besides, being to all appearances a marcher lordling rather than a Welsh prince. Indeed, the English called these men of Powys by the name of de la Pole, after their castle of Pool, and often in the past, before he came to the prince's peace, Griffith had taken part with the English of Shrewsbury against Wales. But at this time they had been ten years in fealty to Llewelyn, by no means to their loss, for in the treaty of Montgomery they, too, had gained and kept some lands won with the prince's aid.

Griffith ap Gwenwynwyn was the greatest vassal the prince had, and he valued him accordingly, and also respected his hardihood in battle and his forceful qualities in peace. The community of Wales would have been maimed without Powys. But their relationship had been always a matter of shrewd business, not a close friendship, such as the prince had had with his brother-in-law Rhys Fychan, or Meredith ap Owen of Cardigan, both now dead. To come down to stony truth, they did not love each other. Griffith grudged the prince's ascendancy, even while he subscribed to it for his own gain, for he was a proud and envious man, whose narrowed eyes measured every vantage, and his tongue complained of every slight, real or imagined. Llewelyn disdained such jealous and calculating minds – Griffith would have said he could afford to, being supreme – but made what accommodation his warm nature could manage, to make the alliance work harmoniously. And so it had, whatever the difficulties and reserves, for ten years.

'I'm glad Griffith's boy has fallen under David's spell,' said Llewelyn once when we rode from Dolforwyn, late that autumn. 'I have been prepared for some coldness in that quarter, knowing our friend's temper, though God knows Pool is far enough away to hold its own in trade, and my castle is no threat to him. But if his heir is cultivating my brother, the sire can hardly be nursing too great a grudge. That one has his family well in hand. All but his wife!' he added honestly, and laughed, for that lady, elegant and fragile as she appeared, was known all along the march for her iron will and quiet but steely tongue, and the thin white hand she extended for kissing was rumoured to have a firm and regal grip on her husband and all her children.

Dolforwyn was then rising against the sky in a great rectangular enclosure of walls and wards, without corner turrets, for the height of the ridge was such that it commanded a view all around, and a well-manned curtain wall would be its main defence. The keep was first planned upon a square base, but in the building the masons changed to a round tower, for what reasons I now forget, but the shell rose sheer and strong, almost ready to be filled with household and garrison. It was a noble, solitary, sunlit place, the river like a silver serpent below.

'By next year, say Easter, we'll have a garrison and a castellan within,' said Llewelyn, 'and take good care that Griffith and his lady shall be among the first guests, and very honourably received. Whatever I can to reassure him, that I'll do.'

In such a mood, contented but cautious, did we approach that Christmas season. And as was the custom still, we repaired to Aber for the keeping of that feast.

David came from Lleyn with all his household, and a retinue of knights and troopers somewhat larger than usual. He was in great finery and very wild spirits, and constantly Elizabeth watched and worshipped him, herself seeming the quieter for his exhilaration, as though he dazzled her into stillness. There was nothing to be observed about her body yet to make me wonder, she was slim as a willow, but that quality of brightness about her caused me to look for enlightenment to Cristin, who was close at her side with the year-old Gladys in her arms. Cristin understood the look, and smiled her slow and radiant smile. When it was possible to have speech together she told me it was as I supposed.

'She is again with child. But not a word yet. There's hardly a soul knows but David, and now we two. She wants a son for him, she will have a son. She so prays, heaven can hardly deny her. But she dreads some stroke of fate if she lets it be known too soon.'

'And David?' I asked, watching the arched security of her arm under the child, and the easy way her body leaned to balance the weight, and all the natural accomplishment of motherhood that came by grace to one deprived of all hope of bearing children. I marvelled that she, so deeply aware of loss, should yet be so little saddened, for she had genuine joy in these daughters not her own.

'This time David is sure. This time it will not fail. He is as you see him, exalted as high as the mountains. But he has his moments of doubt, too, and then there's no going near him. I never knew him so lofty when up, and so black and brittle when down. And he has six months or more to wait in this perilous state yet! You would think his fate was in the balance this very December.'

During that Christmas festival we saw far more of his

106

ups than his downs, the stimulus of company, music, wine
and feasting naturally turning him towards the light. He
drank more than was usual with him, he danced, and
sang, and rode, and hunted while the weather was bright,
and was never still for a moment but when he slept.
Sometimes, indeed, his gaiety seemed too feverish and
too strung, designed to fill his days to the exclusion of
all thought. And what I noted most was that never once
that December did he seek me out, as often in the old
days he used to, in the late evening when he tired of the
music and smoke and ceremony in the hall. He spoke
me blithely in passing, among other people, but never
did I encounter him alone. For my part, I would have
done so gladly. For his, as I came to understand, he
wanted no close companionship with me, for I knew
him too well.

Llewelyn beheld his brother's elation with pleasure,
seeing him drop at last the formal deference he had for
so long preserved in his dealings with his prince. 'If he
is coming out of his sulks with me at last,' he said to me
privately, 'so much the better for us both. It has been
hard to know how to have him without offending, he
is thornier than a holly-bush.'

So when David proposed, if he might, to stay on
through January with all his people, and prolong this
family party, Llowelyn was glad, and said so heartily,
forgetting the extreme caution of his recent handling to
throw an arm about David's shoulders and hug him
boisterously.

'You could do nothing to please me so much. Stay as
long as you will, and most welcome. You bring life into
the court with you.'

So he said, and in the circle of his arm David stood
stiff and still, like a man of ice, for his face had blanched
into a blue, burning whiteness, and his eyes, as I have
seen them do at other times, had closed their shutters
against the world and were staring within, in fascination

107

and grief and horror, as though he saw every evil thought or act of his life graven into his own mirrored face. So he was for an instant only, and then his ice melted, and the dark, smiling grace came back to his countenance, that was turned, large-eyed, upon Llewelyn. Something brief and graceful he said, and escaped out of the embrace, and Llewelyn let him go without another thought. And all that light-hearted company stayed, all through January and into February, though now I cannot think that one heart among them was very light.

At the new year it was fine and cold, but towards the end of January the sun removed, heavy cloud came down and swallowed the mountains, mist closed in and devoured the sea. Aber was an island in blank greyness, and the sky drooped ever lower and heavier upon us. Then the snows began, great, drifting snows that blocked all roads. Deprived of riding, the court settled down equably to pass the time at home in the maenol, and sit out this bad weather. Stores were ample; we had no need to worry. Only David, restless and uneasy, prowled the wards like a caged beast, and eyed the sky a hundred times a day for a break that did not come.

I say, only David, yet there was a manner of echo from his disquiet that ran also through the men of his retinue, and had them edging along the walls from stable to hall, and hall to armoury, as though waiting for something of which they were half afraid.

'Would not you tread warily,' said Godred, grinning and holding me affectionately by the elbow, as we watched David lunge through the outer ward, 'if you were groom or page of his? But there's nothing ails him that a quick thaw won't cure. He hates to be cramped.' All which was true, and there was no need to say it to me, nor could I imagine what there was in his words to keep him quietly giggling to himself, though he was given to such secret communings meant to be heard but not understood, and in the course of them he laughed a great deal. 'Hates to be cramped in his acts or in his ambitions,' sighed Godred, 'and if you shut him in he'll break out. A nice, quick thaw, say in the next week or so, would suit him royally.'

But the thaw, when it came, suited no man, for at the month's end the snow turned to torrential rain, that went on day and night, with gales that ripped the mists away and drove the black clouds headlong across our sky, but never tore a chink between us and the sun. The little river that ambles down to the salt flats through Aber became a rushing flood, all the lower meadows stood under shivering water, and all the streams burst their banks throughout the whole of north Wales. From the hills the snow dislodged in half-melted floes, swelling the floods. There had never been such a season. Cramped we were indeed, for there was no sense in stirring out of the gates. And David's fever burned clear white like the hottest of flames, but the fiercer he burned, the more silent he became.

All that second day of February he walked apart when he could, and his eyes looked within, as though he had shut himself into an even narrower prison than the maenol of Aber. That was the day that the clouds first thinned and broke, and the rain ceased, when first we saw the mountains again, and the shore, and even the distant silver line of the island of saints across the sands of Lavan. So far from releasing David into his former buoyancy, this change turned him mute, distant and still, with an air of listening to something, or for something, that we could not hear. He watched the sky, and looked out over the subsiding waters as the brook sank slowly towards its proper bed, and his face was as still and inexpressive as stone. In the evening, when the meal was over, and the hall smoky and red with torches, Elizabeth missed him from her side, and when he did not return in a little while, sent me to find him. She was anxious about him by then, for though he showed to her a face more like his own, and for her could smile and speak reassurance, yet she knew there was something amiss with him, and feared he was ill.

In the wards the snow was melting raggedly, drawing crooked white edges under every wall. There was someone standing just within the shadow of the great doorway, and as I drew close I saw that it was Cristin. She laid a hand upon my arm, and that was a rare thing, for us to touch each other.

'He is in the chapel,' she said, knowing my errand without need of telling. 'He has been there alone all this while.'

'She has missed him,' I said, 'and is uneasy. He will not want that.'

'No,' she said, 'not at any cost.' And she took her hand slowly from my arm, and I crossed the wet, dark ward and went in to him.

He was not kneeling, but standing close to the altar, and the only light within being the altar lamp, its red glow shone upward into his face, and I saw it for a moment fixed and drawn in fire, like the mask of a man in hell. Or like the face of a man wrestling with terrible and blasphemous prayers. But when he heard me enter, and swung round to face me, then the half-lit face I saw was quite calm and resolute, and the blue eyes mildly veiled.

'Samson?' he said. 'Is it you?' I was in darkness, but he knew. 'Always my careful shepherd! Am I not free to take my thirst to the spring like any other man?' His voice was light and mocking, but a tone higher than I knew it.

Being in no mind to try to take from him what he was plainly unwilling to share, I told him flatly that I was sent by his lady to find him, for she was afraid he sickened. And at that he uttered something neither sigh nor laugh.

'So I do sicken,' he said. 'I sicken God, man and myself, but it is not a sickness of the body that makes me loath-'

110

some.' And the next moment he said lightly: 'Say a prayer for a fine night, before you follow me in, for if the roads are passable I'll be on my way to my own tomorrow.' And he went past me with a large, easy step, and made his way back to the hall and his wife, and kept his countenance and his tranquillity the rest of the evening.

But in the night I could not rest, I hardly know why. It was not simply the recollection of words and actions so strange and yet so small, it was rather something in the air after that long isolation of the floods and the rains, a fearful stillness that hung on the night now that the endless streaming, whispering, rippling noises of the waters were hushed. When the whole maenol was asleep, the silence was as tall and wide as the night, and charged with uneasiness. I lay listening for any sound to make the void again populated, and how many imaginary footsteps I heard I do not know, but one I heard that was not imaginary. It passed by my tower chamber towards the stair, and halted for a brief moment outside Llewelyn's own sleeping apartment, which was close, for I had always a corner very near him, and if ever he needed anything in the night, it was me he called to him. When those quiet feet paused, I rose up silently from my brychan and girded my gown about me, for who would thus stand motionless in the dark outside my lord's door? But in a moment the footsteps resumed, slipping away until they ceased, the stairway swallowing them up.

I needed no light to find my way anywhere I pleased about Aber, and it seemed that this restless one after midnight needed none, either. He knew this place as I knew it. I let myself out and went to open Llewelyn's door, very softly. In the darkness within his long, peaceful breathing measured the depth and tranquillity of his sleep. Whoever had ill dreams in Aber that night, the prince had none. I closed the door again upon his rest, and eased the latch silently into place, and for a while

111

I stood guard outside his room, waiting and listening. But there was no more movement, and after a time I went back to my bed, and there lay waiting in vague disquiet without understandable cause, until I fell asleep.

It was but a shallow and wary sleep, for what awoke me next was the first faint change in the darkness, hardly a lightening, rather a softening in the texture of the night. Dawn was still more than an hour away, but for early February it was a clear night and with stars, and by our northern reckoning rather warm, a heavy, moist air. I had lain no more than ten minutes drowsing and wondering, when of a sudden my door was opened and someone came in. There was almost no sound in her coming, all in a moment she was there, barefoot in her nightgown with a shawl round her shoulders, and over the shawl the spilled marvel of her black, silken hair, stirring round her like living darkness, and curtained within that marvel her pale, bright face, with huge eyes limpid and iris-coloured like the first promise of morning that came in with her, and its first freshness that breathed in her breath. Thus for the first time came Cristin to my bed, and departed again as virgin as she came. For what had Godred's occasional marital demands to do with her virginity?

I started up naked in the skins of the brychan, and could not arise before her because of that nakedness. And for want of better words – for of such there are none – I said her name: 'Cristin!'

In a whisper she said: 'David is gone! He never went in to her. His pillow is unpressed. Samson, I dread for her. She was asleep too soon to wait for him. She does not yet know. But if she awakes and misses him, God knows what may befall her. There is nothing else can cause his son to burst her womb untimely, but if she fears for David she may miscarry. Samson, find him!'

I clutched the furs about me, and watched the vision that was my Cristin, a light that dazzled my eyes, though

112

but half-seen in darkness. I said: 'Go back and stay with her, and tell her, if she wakes, that all's well, he rose for sheer wakefulness, and I am with him. She knows he has his moods, she may believe it. And I'll find him.'

She said, in that clear thread of a voice, under her breath and barely audible, as she herself was a phantom faintly shining in the absence of light: 'God bless you, my dear love!' Not a word more. And she was gone as she had come, and I was alone.

I rose up hastily and did on my clothes, and went out, down the stair and through the silent passages and rooms, through the hall where all the sleepers stirred and snored. Everywhere I passed like a shadow, stretching my ears after any sound or movement to betray another wakeful presence, but there was none. Nor did I believe he would be anywhere there among other men. The place for which I made with the most confidence was the chapel, where once already to my knowledge he had taken some struggle or distress of his own, only to be called away without an answer. But he was not there, either. And the first pre-dawn light was beginning to soften the black of the east into dove-grey, and I dreaded that Elizabeth would awake and come forth herself to search for him, before I could make good what I had promised her, that I should be with him.

There was no possibility that he would be in any of the guest lodgings in the wards, only those public places remained, the stables and mews and store-houses, and what should he want with them? The watch on the main gate was awake and aware, and had had an undisturbed night, and seen no one stirring.

It was almost by chance I found him, as I stood in the inner ward, turning about to look if anything moved anywhere around me, or any shape broke the merloned line of the wall. And he was there, he or someone, a tall blackness swathed in a cloak, motionless against the sky above the postern gate. He neither saw nor heard me.

113

His back was turned, for he gazed steadily out over the wall to the south-east.

I mounted the wooden staircase to the guard-walk, in the corner close to where he stood, and went to him without any great care to conceal my approach, but without any deliberate utterance, either, for it was so strange to see him standing like a carven man, black and still and cold in the February dawn. I knew by the infinitely faint bracing of his shoulders the moment when he knew he was no longer alone, and by the want of any larger movement that he knew very well who it was who came. His face was tight and pinched with the cold, as if he had stood out the night there, but it was quite still and calm, a dead calm, as if something had ended, something the passing of which was not yet recognisable as either to be mourned or welcomed. His eyes never shifted their gaze from the hills, but it was a drained, exhausted gaze, no longer urgent. He said not a word, but when I touched him he turned and went with me, and at the head of the stairway he withdrew out of my hand, and went before me down into the ward. And there was Elizabeth coming out from the tower door in a flutter of blue, dressed and cloaked and anxious, with Cristin at her shoulder.

There was light enough then to recognise us by manner and gait and stature across the ward, and we came as a relief to them, walking towards them as we did in the most commonplace way in the world. They could not see the frozen blankness of his face. Elizabeth cried out his name, at once glad and reproachful, and flew to take him by the shoulders, and suddenly he heaved himself out of his torpor with a shudder and a moan, and recoiled from her, evading the innocent embrace.

'Don't touch me!' he said in a soft, wild cry. 'You'll soil your hands!'

The look of astonished hurt and disbelief on her face, in that first moment of doubt and uncertainty she had ever suffered from him, struck him clean out of the trance that had held him bound, and he realised what he had done. He flung up both hands and shut his palms hard on his cheeks, and shook out of him, like gouts of blood: 'A bad dream – I have had a bad dream!' And before she had time to question or to weep, he leaned and caught her up passionately and tenderly into his arms. 'Lisbet, it's over now! It's gone! All's well now – all's very well!'

The fright went out of her face readily. She laid her arms about his neck and caressed him, lamenting with the serenity of past and mistaken pain: 'Where have you been? Why did you go away from me?'

He carried her away into the tower, back to the bed-chamber he had deserted, and certain am I they lay and loved like starving creatures until they fell asleep in each other's arms.

We two were left in the ward, between the dwindling banks of snow under the walls, looking after them with still faces. Until Cristin said: 'I do not know what it is we have seen. But I know it is well that only you and I have seen it. And I hope that you and I have seen the last of it here. I think I should not like the echoes, if there were to be echoes.' And she gave me her hand, as we went slowly back together into the hall, for the chill that was upon us needed some unlooked-for grace to warm it out of our bones.

And when David and Elizabeth appeared again among us, he was himself, alert, calm and rational, only perhaps a little quieter and more chastened than usual, like a convalescent out of danger and grateful for it. There was no more listening and prowling, no extremes of elation and depression, rather two or three days of harmony and reason. And as soon as the roads were reported pass-able, he took leave of Llewelyn, and his whole party left for home.

So for some time we believed, Cristin and I, that we had

115

indeed seen the last of that night's alarm. Nevertheless, there were to be echoes. And she was right. When they came we did not like them.

CHAPTER V

On the sixth day of that same February the king's regents sent one William de Plumpton to Chester, to take delivery, or so they hoped or professed to hope, of the instalment of money under treaty which had not yet been paid, and which Llewelyn was withholding as a means of enforcing settlement of grievances. It was hardly a reasonable expectation that the envoy should get anything to take back with him, in any case, seeing the floods were still out wherever there was river or stream flowing, and the marshes round Rhuddlan remained a lake, so that it would have been almost impossible to reach Chester by the day of his visit. I do not say Llewelyn would have complied even had the season been favourable, but at that time it was pointless even to try.

By the end of February, when the court was at Criccieth, travel was normal again, and the regents sent to complain of non-delivery of the money. Llewelyn replied, as he did consistently in these exchanges, to the king personally, though whether his letters ever left England is doubtful. He wrote freely acknowledging that he was bound to pay the amount due, and informing King Edward that the sum was ready and waiting to be paid to the king's attorneys, provided the king fulfilled faithfully what was equally due from him under the treaty. In particular he asked that the earls of Gloucester and Hereford, and after them the marchers in general, should be ordered to surrender those lands they had illegally occupied and were as illegally detaining. Whereupon payment should be made immediately.

Whether this letter ever went overseas or no, it did bring a measure of response, for the king, or the regents in his name, ordered a commission to be sent in May to Montgomery, to arbitrate on the mutual charges of breaches of the peace, and to try to bring about a treaty with the earl of Hereford. I see in this the hand of the king himself, or else of Burnell, the most reasonable of the regents and the closest to his master's mind, whose chief difficulty in border matters was to curb the impetuosity of his colleague Roger Mortimer. Marchers make very poor arbitrators on marcher affairs, as judges do of their own cases.

We were again at Aber, towards the middle of March, when a messenger came riding in from Llewelyn's master-mason at Dolforwyn, which was almost ready to be garrisoned, though much work remained to be done as soon as the new building season made conditions possible. A small guard had camped in some discomfort through the winter, and it was Llewelyn's intention to visit the castle and give his mind to the siting of the new town as soon as he could. The message he received hastened that day, though not as we would have wished.

'My lord,' said the envoy, a trooper of the guard, 'I am bidden to tell you of suspected treason. At the end of January the prior of Strata Marcella sent to us to say that one of the brothers, on an errand into Pool, had seen unusual activity about the castle, and great numbers of armed men, it seemed to him in preparation for some foray, for he saw how they were busy about the stables and armoury, furbishing weapons and fletching arrows, and both the Lord Griffith and his son Owen – Owen especially – directing all, as if for some great move. He promised to send word again if this company set out with intent, but we had no further word from him until he sent to say that they must have left secretly, by night, for certainly they were gone from the castle, which was about its business as always, and no more men within

118

than usual. My lord, you recall those days of heavy rain and great floods. The prior set watch, and the brother appointed saw a strong company come riding home into Pool, also by night, and in sad order, half-drowned and without any booty or prizes. We judge the floods turned them back. But we do not know from where, for the prior's watch was on the castle gates, and the castle is the end of all roads at that place.'

'I know it,' said Llewelyn, braced and intent. 'It is all but in the river. It must have been no more than an island and a causeway then. True, they could have come from any point. And we do not know when they set forth?'

'No, my lord, only when they crept home again like drowned rats. And that was the night of the third of February. We have the prior's word.'

'His word I take,' said Llewelyn truly, for there was not a single Cistercian house in north Wales that was not his loyal ally. 'But your captain and the master of my works have their own opinion, I think. Speak out what they have to say.'

'My lord,' said the man warmly, 'I speak out my own thoughts as well as theirs. Ever since you began the building of Dolforwyn, we have had word again and again how Griffith ap Gwenwynwyn resented your presence there. It was the common gossip of Pool that he feared for his market, and also kept close touch with Sprenghose in Montgomery, and made good certain the king's men there feared the same prejudice to their gains. I do not say the English have any part in what he planned. I do say he is ready to lean on them if he brings down judgment on his own head by his own actions, and has sought to prepare their minds to come to his support. We think Griffith planned to attack your castle of Dolforwyn by stealth, perhaps intending to blame the English, since they have shown concern about the foundation, and meant to accomplish this raid now, before

119

you have a full garrison there to defend it. We think he meant to destroy what you have built, and your guard that holds it for you, but the winter barred his way. My lord, the upper Severn has been out of its banks more than three weeks, high over the water-meadows and into the rock of the hillside. Close as we lie, I believe they had no means of reaching us.' And he said, watching the prince's face: 'I do not think the lord prince is any way surprised.'

'No,' said Llewelyn, 'no way surprised.' He did not love this house of de la Pole, and was not loved by them, and only advantage had ever drawn or held Griffith to him, and only advantage would hold him now, and yet Powys could hardly be spared. He sat back in his chair, and thought, and there was no pleasure in it. For the sake of Wales he would not cut off Powys, not for his own life, if he might retain it by any decent means. But for the sake of Wales, just as surely, he could not let any treason pass unpublished and unpunished. He shut his eyes for some minutes, to look beyond the hour.

When he opened them again, he was resolved. 'I will deal,' he said. 'I am grateful beyond words to your master, to the prior and his brethren, and to you for your honest embassage. Now I will deal accordingly.'

It was late in March when Llewelyn set forth with his high steward and his immediate court to inspect and approve the work done at Dolforwyn, and there we kept the Easter of that year. It had been his intention to do so in any case, and his going there in state provoked no suspicion and gave no forewarning, nor did it occasion any surprise that while he was in the neighbourhood he should send for his greatest vassal to attend him, and bring his eldest son Owen with him. They came with disarming smiles, attentive and dutiful, the father a big, powerfully-made, greying man with strong features and a keen sense of his own dignity and state, the son almost

120

as tall but lightly made and graceful. Both of them, I thought, were a little too effusive in their compliments, and their eyes a little too wary, but the relations between the princes, however profitable to both, had never been personally warm.

In the hall of Dolforwyn, still largely a shell, half-furnished for living, and before Tudor and most of the members of his council, his clerks and personal household, Llewelyn stood up before those two, and himself told them that they were under suspicion of deceit and disloyalty, against their sworn fealty to him and to Wales.

They started back from him open-mouthed, in utter dismay, I am sure not feigned, for they had thought their abortive moves had passed unknown, and been devoutly thankful for it. They cried out their innocence of any such offences, and their unswerving loyalty to the lord prince and their own fealty.

'At least, my lord,' cried Griffith, 'let us know our accusers. Whoever they may be, let them meet us face to face, and make their charges here, where we can refute them.'

'There shall be proper opportunity at law for you to refute the charges,' said Llewelyn, 'and for this time, if you seek an accuser, I accuse you. The council are here to see that justice is done to you, according to Welsh law.' And this he said with emphasis, knowing that Griffith had a way of preferring English law if he could get it, and also that the causes at issue between England and Wales, formerly always judged by an arbitration commission, had of late slipped nearer and nearer to becoming suits in the royal courts, which was by no means what he understood by the terms of the treaty, and posed perilous pitfalls for Wales in just such cases. He did not intend that Griffith should be allowed to inveigle this cause into a king's court.

'I do not know who can have poisoned your mind against us,' protested Griffith vehemently, 'but I swear
121

there is no truth in what they have told you. And if I am to be able to defend myself, at least I must know of what I am accused. Can I prove every moment of my loyalty, and my son's loyalty? Let me know what acts are alleged against me, at what times and places, that I may be able to bring evidence to the contrary. And time – I must be allowed time to bring my witnesses.'

'You shall have time enough,' said Llewelyn. 'We intend to set up here today a bench of judges to hear and examine both your evidence and mine, and take whatever witness they please in this neighbourhood. You shall have a day assigned, and a place, to answer. And the charge I think you should know, as you have said. It is known that at the end of the month of January you gathered in your castle of Pool a large company of armed men, with horses and supplies, and that they rode out secretly by night upon some as yet unproved errand, I say treasonous. Thanks to God who sent the floods, they never achieved whatever their purpose was. They were seen re-entering Pool, also in darkness, on the night of the third of February. And you, my lord Owen, were seen to be their leader.'

'It is false!' cried Owen, paler than his shirt, and his voice cracking. 'Whoever says so, lies!'

'When you come to hear the sworn evidence,' said Llewelyn drily, 'I think you will wish to take back that word.'

The young man drew in his horns at that, doubtless wondering desperately with whom he might be confronted, and how much the observer could know. But still they argued sturdily, why should they do so, what cause had they ever given to be thought disloyal, and what advantage could there possibly be to them in raiding and pillaging in the depths of the winter, if that was what was suspected? Against what manor or maenol or settlement, to be worth so secret an enterprise?

'Against this very castle and settlement, which you

122

never liked,' said Llewelyn, 'and which you have spoken against more than once. It does not deprive your own market, nor infringe your rights, I am building on my own lands, but as I have heard, you would not have been sorry to see this place razed – all the more, perhaps, if it could be put down to some lawless action by the Englishry, who have also been casting ominous eyes at it for the sake of Montgomery. In the end *you* may tell *me* where you rode. I would advise it. If this matter is cleared fully, there shall still be access to my peace.'

After he had said this I saw those two, father and son, exchange one rapid and stealthy glance, and look away again, and I wondered if Llewelyn with his customary bluntness had not given away more of his case than was altogether wise, though I knew why he did it. It was his wish to show them at once that their best policy was to make a clean breast of the affair and accept whatever penalty was imposed, with the implicit assurance that it would not be extreme. He did not want out-and-out hostility, for fear Wales should be maimed of one of its vital provinces. Nor, indeed, was his ever a mind for extremes, which produce counter-extremes in the recoil. What he had now suggested seemed rather to calm than to alarm them. They continued to protest total innocence, and absolute confidence, but they accepted a day some ten days ahead, the seventeenth of April, for the hearing, and the place was fixed at Llewelyn's manor of Bach-yr-Anneleu in Cydewain, which was handy for both parties.

'Very well,' said Llewelyn, 'name your arbitrators.' And he himself for his part chose Tudor, with one of his brothers, and Anian ap Caradoc, who was one of his chief law clerks. Griffith named one of his own officers of Powys, and his justiciar, and one other whose name I have forgotten. It is a long time since I saw those documents. Then they chose and agreed on the prior of Pool, as a just man bound to neither side, to fill the seventh place. And those two withdrew from Dolforwyn to set about preparing their defence. They went wary, anxious and wincing, but not desperate, and I think their heads were together even on the ride home.

The seven judges in the meantime were at liberty to examine and take statements around Pool and Dolforwyn, but I think Griffith had taken good care to get out of the castle any of those men who knew what had been planned, and little fresh information was gleaned, except the curious fact that the company of armed men, clearly a war-band, had left Pool castle not merely one night before their re-entry, but four. The poacher who had been out in the woods that night was none too anxious to tell what he had seen, but did so honestly, and the justices turned a blind eye to what else he had been about. It was a puzzling detail. In such weather, what could Owen have been doing with his men for those four days? Apart from that we got rumours and little more.

On the seventeenth of April the judges sat at Llewelyn's manor, and Griffith ap Gwenwynwyn and his son came before them. But it fell out somewhat differently from what we had expected, for as soon as the court was convened Griffith and Owen asked leave to speak, and said outright that they pleaded guilty to the offence with which they were accused, that they had indeed plotted treason against the lord prince, in despite of the fealty they owed him. They desired to confess their fault and throw themselves upon the prince's mercy.

Llewelyn did question a little concerning those four full days lost.

'My lord,' said Owen, who had led the unlucky expedition, 'when we found the valley road impassable, rather than abandon the enterprise we tried to make a circle through the hills and come at Dolforwyn from the north side, and though we made a part of the journey, we crossed between the brooks that drain into the Bechan, and then we could go no further, nor get back with safety, and it took us two days to make our sorry way home to

Pool. My lord, now in more blessed condition I thank God there was no harm but to us who invoked it.' He was a smooth young man, and bent on salving his threatened prospects if he could by any means do it.

'Well,' said Llewelyn, 'I have done. You are confided to your judges.'

Then those seven justices conferred, and with no voice dissenting – bear in mind always that Griffith's own justiciar was one of the seven – they accepted that plea of guilty, and gave their verdict that in view of the absolute confession of treason, the two accused were placed, as to their bodies, lands and possessions, at the disposal of the lord prince, to do with them and all things theirs whatsoever he would. Thus everything Griffith owned passed into Llewelyn's hands, to give back or retain, as he pleased. And what he pleased he had already considered, weighed and measured, to balance enforcement with remission, and penalty with clemency. He was as pale and grave as his traitors when he made his mind known. And they – I say it, who saw them then, and know what plaintive play they made thereafter with their wrongs – they were immeasurably happy with the outcome, having expected worse, even with their careful precautions.

'The most of your lands and possessions,' said Llewelyn, 'I am moved to grant back to you. There are certain exceptions,' He named them, all territories which had traditionally been in dispute between Gwynedd and Powys. They lopped Powys perhaps of one-quarter of its ground. 'You may make your petition for the remainder,' he said, 'upon conditions.' And those conditions also he set out in full. Griffith and Owen had every opportunity to protest against them, had they so wished. They were main glad not to make any such protest. I think they were astonished and gratified at the modesty of their loss.

Nevertheless, I own it was not easy for Griffith to swallow the indignity, when he was forced to go on his

125

sixty-year-old knees before the prince, and ask humbly for the restoration of the remainder of his lands, for him and his heirs, pruned of those small parts beyond the Dovey, in Cyfeiliog, and of thirteen vils near the river Lugg, and most of Arwystli. To the conditions attached he assented, not gladly, but that was not to be expected, and I do not think they were unjust or excessive. First, Owen was taken into Llewelyn's keeping as hostage for his and his father's loyalty. Then also twenty-five of the chieftains of the lands regranted to Griffith were to give their fealty instead to the prince, and swear a solemn oath to be faithful to the prince as against Griffith if he again offended. And last, all the parties had to agree that if Griffith or his heirs again attempted treason against Llewelyn, then the prince should have the right to take possession again of all the lands in the traitor's hold, and keep and enjoy them for ever. The compact was not complete until Griffith, with what grace he could, authorised this seizure in the event of his own default.

On the following day he and his son executed a deed likewise rendering all their possessions forfeit to the prince if Owen should attempt to escape from Llewelyn's custody, and be lawfully convicted of such an attempt. His parole was thought hardly a strong enough guarantee, and since it was far less trouble, and more agreeable for him, if he could be out of close ward and merely an enforced guest at court, a sanction of such severity might hold him as effectively as bars.

We remained in Cydewain until the time came for the May meeting at the ford, where Edward's commissioners duly came, and some of the mutual complaints were dealt with by sensible give and take, though others proved more intractable, and there was little but parchment progress with the envoys of the Earl of Hereford. But something of interest we learned there, for it came out that Rhodri, who had shaken off the dust of Wales in chagrin after his marriage plans foundered, was now in

126

London, in the service of the queen-mother, and moreover, had found a more complacent bride, and one just as profitable, for he was married to a lady who was an heiress in Gloucestershire.

'Who would have thought it?' said Llewelyn, relieved and amused, as well as heartily glad for him. 'Without benefit of my thousand marks, all but fifty, he has done as well for himself, after all. That's one load off my mind. Beatrice, she is called, it seems, and they say a pleasant lady. Who knows, he may have run at the right time for his own fortunes.'

There had never been any further mention of that debt owed to Rhodri, and there was little point in pursuing him with it, even had we known until then where to find him. And shortly thereafter he went abroad to France in the queen-mother's retinue. Llewelyn shrugged aside the commitment for the time being, since there had been no claim laid upon it. But for his brother, though the least to be remarked of all his brothers, he was pleased and assuaged. The old law of lands partible equally between brethren, though he stood out against it all his days for the sake of Wales, Wales as a people, a tongue and a nation, hung heavy upon his heart. Such a curse it can be, to be one of four brothers, in a land that keeps such customs. How much easier was Edward's lot, by all men acknowledged as the sole heir to monarchy, and even the lot of his brother, accustomed to accept and illuminate his lesser but glorious place, having its own rights and not encroaching upon the greater.

'I have even heard,' said Llewelyn, 'that this lady is with child. Rhodri is from good stock. Who knows but my grandsire may repeat himself out of Rhodri's loins as well as any other? There may be greatness yet from what I fear I reckoned too small. Let's, at all costs, wish him well!'

So we went home cheered rather than burdened, satisfied that the evil of Griffith ap Gwenwynwyn was curbed and frustrated, and that what ill effects remained from that collision could be softened and soothed away by our usage of Owen, while he remained with us. I know that Llewelyn had in mind a fairly early release, and reassuring patronage in the meantime. The young man went with us dutifully, nervous, attentive, almost obsequious in his determination to wipe out the past, and Llewelyn took care to pay him some civil attention in return, though they had little in common. Such relationships are not easy upon either side.

On our way back into Gwynedd we halted overnight at Corwen, in the vale of Edeyrnion. Some of the solid men of those parts came to the prince with various pleas and petitions, and among them was a miller, a stout man and enterprising, who had his mill a few miles up the river from that place, and since there were often people wishing to cross the Dee by his boat and save themselves a league or two on foot, he came to ask licence to provide a ferry and man it at that spot. It was a reasonable request, and quickly granted, and I went to write him the needful licence and get it sealed, and afterwards walked up with him some way along the riverside, to take the evening air, for it was a fine night after a stormy day.

It so happened that the river was running fairly high, and is always rough water there. I remarked that he would need a sturdy ferryman if his service was to operate on any but summer days, and he allowed that there were times when he would not ask any man to risk his life on that crossing, though most of the year he knew it himself well enough to master it, and he could find men at least as good to do the work for him. I said, eyeing the broken water, which was storm-brown, that I would not care to tackle it myself even now, in late May. And he laughed, and said this was nothing, this would not hinder him.

'You should have seen it in those winter floods we had. Man and beast, we were up in the roof of the mill, though we stand high, and we had to wade to get out. I mind one night when it was at its worst, there came a company riding downstream and wanting to cross. What they were doing out in such numbers God knows, forty of them if there was one! But they came shouting, was there not a ford a little higher, for they must get over. And I laughed in their faces, asking after a ford, when a man had to ford his own fields, let alone a torrent like the Dee. Then they would have me take them across in my boat, but I would not have attempted one trip, let alone the four or five I should have had to make. And with horses? Not for the world! I think they would have taken the boat by force, they were so urgent, but that they were afraid to handle it themselves when it came to it. They were even mad enough to think of trying to swim the beasts across. But not mad enough to do it!' he said, and laughed.

All this I heard at first but currently, as of mild interest between two companions passing the time, but before he was halfway through his story I was sharply intent, and hearing echoes in every word, for could there have been two such parties out in such weather, and on such urgent business that only God could turn them back with his storms? I asked of him: 'What night was this? Can you recall?'

'That I can,' said the miller confidently, 'for the next day was the first break in the clouds, and by evening the rain stopped, though it was ten days before the Dee was back in its bed. It was the first night of February.'

Two days out from their muster at Pool, and two days before their draggled return. It was too apt to be untrue. The company that Owen had led out of the castle stealthily by night had ridden, not up the Severn or through the hills to the raiding of Dolforwyn, but hard towards the north-east, only to be turned back by the Dee in flood. And if that was true, then upon some blacker business than Dolforwyn, or why should they compound so willingly with that story and throw themselves gratefully on Llewelyn's mercy? If they had not had worse to fear by letting the case be pursued further, they would have fought it out in the court and denied everything but some local brawl not threatening their fealty.

'But I tell you this,' said the miller with certainty, 'though they rode on downstream to try elsewhere, I'm sure they never got across Dee that night, nor that sennight, either.'

No, thought I, they never did. And I asked him, with no too great show of interest: 'What could they have wanted so desperately on the way north, in such weather? Was there anything to be noted about them out of the ordinary?'

'Out of the ordinary enough, come to think of it,' said the miller, 'when we have such order as the prince has made in the land. They were armed, every man, with bows or steel.'

After I had left the miller I took that singular story back to Llewelyn, and repeated it for his ear alone.

'Have up young Owen,' said Llewelyn at once, 'and let's see what he has to say to this. But first ask Tudor to come to me. No one else.'

I took my time about finding and bidding in Owen ap Griffith, that the prince and Tudor might have time for consultation. For beyond question the boy would deny, and cling fast to his own story, but more depended on the manner of his denial. He went in with me very quiet and wary, but in his situation so he well might, and we did not hold that against him as proving or disproving anything. He saluted the prince very respectfully, and sat but gingerly and stiffly when he was bidden, eyeing Llewelyn with apprehensive eyes.

'Tell me again,' said Llewelyn amiably, 'for I wish to be informed in every detail, all the course of that wild ride you made in the floods to try to reach Dolforwyn. We had but the outline before. Now fill in the colours.'

130

'I fear,' said Owen, licking his lips, 'the lord prince wishes only to remind me of an iniquity I already regret, and would wish out of mind. But I have deserved it.' Which was no bad beginning, considering all things, and as I have said, there was more of his secret and guileful mother in him than his overbearing father. And he drew breath and described, with increasing confidence, in the end almost with relish, every mile of the way, which brooks they had crossed, where they camped miserably overnight, where they found themselves perilously bogged between rivers in flooded heath, never too stable even in better weather. A good story it was, all the more as he cannot then have expected to have to produce it, and must have been improvising.

'That is comprehensive enough,' said Llewelyn at the end, 'and leaves not an hour unaccounted for of all those you wasted in this quest. So the miller from upstream here is wrong, is he, if he says you were ranging with this same band along the Dee on the first night of February, seeking a crossing, when by rights you say you should have been somewhere in the peat-bogs north-west of Dolforwyn? If he says that *you*, leading this migrant company, tried every means to get him to ferry you over? Mistaken, do you think? Or lying? Or dreaming, perhaps?'

Owen turned a yellowish white like old parchment, and shrank where he sat, but he kept his countenance better than I would have thought was in him. Twice he swallowed hard – we watched every move – and tried to find a voice to answer, but I think he was giving himself a little time, all he dared, for thought. They came in the night, they were many, cloaked. Could the miller know any man of them again? It was Owen's only weapon, and he clung to it.

In a dry and laboured whisper he said : 'My lord, I will not claim any man lies, when I do not even know him. I must answer only what I do know, that I was not there,
131

nor any men of mine. I have told you where my men were that night. To my shame! Is not that enough?'

'Shall I send to the mill,' asked Tudor, 'and have the miller come in person to testify?' And Llewelyn said: 'It would be well,' and still watched Owen. But the young man had played it off in the only possible way, desperate wager though it was, and had no option now but to sit out whatever came, and still steadily deny.

'Then there were two companies of men out in arms for no good purpose,' said Llewelyn, 'in two separate parts of my realm, were there? Some forty in number in each? And both at the same most fortuitous time? It is asking a lot to ask me to believe it.'

'My lord, how can I answer for other men? I have told you the truth, and I am paying the price asked of me. What more can I do?'

So he said, and clung to it through all questioning, even when Tudor and Llewelyn from both sides pressed him hard and fast, and with whatever traps they could devise. Later, the next day, the miller was brought, and Owen was confronted with him, but so straitly that the man was told not to show recognition or nonrecognition or say a word in the young man's presence, the more to agonise him with doubt of the outcome, that if he feared enough he might prefer to confess and be done with it. But he feared confession more, knowing what he had to confess, than continued obduracy.

'My lord,' he said, sweating, 'let me know if this fellow claims he saw me that night and knows me again. For if he says so, then indeed he lies, though he may have seen armed men, and may say so in all good faith.'

'He does not claim to know you again,' said the prince honestly. 'In the dark, among so many, it would be a very long chance. And your livery and any marks of your household I'm sure were well hidden. No, *he* is not the liar. But I bid you now, think well what you are about, for it's you I hold, and on you it depends how I hold you.

132

I want the truth of this strange business, and however you deny, I tell you to your face I believe it was you and yours trying to cross the Dee that night. You had much better cleanse your breast now, for in the end I shall find out all.'

From the green pallor of Owen's face I fancy he was even then equally sure of it, but he could not do other than persist in his denial, and so he did, against all pressures. Thus he came into a stricter keeping, and from a guest became a prisoner. But nothing could we get out of him. Nor now could we let it rest, for doubt of what lay behind it. All through June and into July Llewelyn had his clerks and agents questioning about the Dee and also in Cydewain, for north of the Dee we never heard word more of this armed band, thus confirming that they never got across the river. But in Pool by this time everything was so dissembled and dispersed that there was nothing to be learned there. And it was not until well into July that the prince received at Rhuddlan a letter from Cynan, brought by that same Welsh groom of his.

'The bearer,' wrote Cynan, 'has recently been in the king's castle of Montgomery with me, on some minor business, and having better access to the gossip of the stables than I, learned somewhat more of the matter of your troubles with the lord of Powys. I do not take gossip for proof, but it is worth noting. You may not know, but the garrison at Montgomery are very well aware, that one very close to you paid a visit to the castle of Pool in November of last year, and was a guest there more than a week, and that without any ceremony, but rather softly and with few attendants, which is not his habit, and without his wife, which is even more strange. There are some in the neighbourhood who whisper that he may not be quite innocent of taint in the treason to which Griffith and his son have confessed. If I trespass, hold me excused. The precedents you know better than I. I speak of your brother, the Lord David.'

Llewelyn sat long, after he had read this, withdrawn into himself, before he roused himself with a great effort to question the groom, who said out freely what he had heard, and knew the difference, too, between common castle gossip and the grain of hard but ambivalent truth within it. Then with thanks and a reward, and in his normal calm manner, the prince dismissed him.

'Dear God!' said Llewelyn then, to himself rather than to Tudor and me. 'It must not be true.' But he did not say that it could not be. And I, for my part, was so stunned that at first I could not bring my mind to connect and examine as it should have done, and make sense of what I knew but he did not, those night hours in February when David deserted his bedchamber and his wife to stand out the cold of the night on the wall like a sentinel, while the distant mischief he might well have had a share in brewing either succeeded or failed. As soon as I remembered his face, in the chapel as on the guard-walk, I knew that he had known. Something, if not all. But what he could have had to gain, by some furtive raid on Dolforwyn or any other of the prince's garrisons, was mystery to me. The torment was, that in his love there was so much hate, jealousy and resentment that he was capable, in the last anguish, of acts unfathomably sense-less, so long as they were sufficiently hurtful.

So little was I enlightened at that point, that my dismay and my understanding stopped there, when I had so much more knowledge, had I been able to arrange the pieces in their true pattern. If, indeed, to this day I know the true pattern. Perhaps only God knows it, and just as well. In his hands justice is assured, and mercy possible.

'Griffith's son has been paying court to him a year and more,' said Llewelyn, vainly fending off what he knew he must do. 'Why should he not pay a visit to Pool, since he

134

was welcome there? There's nothing in that.'

'Softly, and almost unattended?' said Tudor. 'Without his wife and children?'

'It is not like him, no. But what is like him? He changes like the sky. I will not believe he has taken part in anything aimed against me.'

'Would it be the first time?' said Tudor harshly.

I said, and it was labour to say it: 'I have somewhat to tell you that perhaps should have been told earlier. But I thought it was over and done, and no grief to any man. Hold me excused, for I did not deliberately keep it from you, but only let it lie as something finished, something I had no cause to remember. I have cause now!'

Llewelyn turned his head and looked at me curiously, all troubled and saddened as he was, and a little smiled, seeing me as lost and daunted as he was himself. 'Tell me now,' he said.

I told him everything I recalled about that night, even to what David had cried out to Elizabeth when she ran to clasp him, how she should not, for she might soil her hands. And I remind him how, after that night, David had been gentle and calm and almost humble, like a man grateful for deliverance out of danger. 'For so it always was with him,' I said, 'that as often as his right hand struck a blow at you, his left hand would reach to parry it.'

'It was God parried it this time,' said Llewelyn grimly, 'with snows and rains.'

I said: 'David prayed.'

'For better weather to prosper his design?' said Llewelyn.

'So he bade me pray,' I said. 'But what his own prayer was at the chapel in Aber before I came, only God knows, and David.'

'I have not judged him,' said Llewelyn heavily. 'Not yet. I shall not be his judge.' And he laid aside Cynan's letter with a steady hand, and said to Tudor: 'Call a council, and let them deal. I am the complainant, they must advise me what to do.'

And so in due course they did, with one voice ordering that David should be summoned to appear before a court at Rhuddlan on a date in the middle of July, to answer to a charge of implication in treason. As I remember, he sent back word, as it were with raised brows and a disdainful smile, that in view of the tone of the summons, which was to him incomprehensible, he must refuse to appear except under safe-conduct. Llewelyn without comment issued the required letters. But his face, when he thought himself unobserved, was so full of grief that it was hard to bear.

And just at this most unhappy time came the news that Edward was again in Paris on his way home, and that his coronation had been fixed for the nineteenth day of August. All England was waiting for its king, and we hung upon David's word from Lleyn, David's word which was always and endlessly fatal for us, as if he had been created to destroy what his brother built, whether he would or no. For if he was fatal to us, how much more fatal was he to himself.

'In the name of God,' said Llewelyn, wrung, 'how can I go to Westminster for this crowning? What, and leave this dangerous riddle still unsolved behind me? Unless I can get to the bottom of it and resolve all, I will not go to England. I'll send and excuse myself from attending, and by all means send venison for Edward's feast, but I'll not leave Wales in such a tangle of treachery and secrets. He will have to hold me excused for the sake of my own realm, and there's none should understand that better.'

As he had said, so he did. For indeed there was great danger to Wales in the eruption of such a case at law between the prince and his own brother, worse than the more understandable clash with the lord of Powys, and it was vital that Llewelyn should be seen and known to be present in his principality, and in full control of its destinies. The stability of Wales was too new and fragile to withstand any shocks. Moreover, David accepted the letters of safe-conduct, and condescended to set out to face the council at Rhuddlan in the middle of July. At that time Edward was on his way from Paris to Montreuil, and thence, after concluding a sound trading pact with the countess of Flanders, he soon embarked for Dover.

Now I know that afterwards there were many men willing to swear that even at this time the prince had resolved, in his own mind, not to attend King Edward's coronation, and to reserve his fealty and homage if by any means he could, having turned against the king on the suspicion that he had some part in, or at least approved, the border infringements that constantly plagued us, and even the affair of Griffith ap Gwenwynwyn. But I know that this is not true, that his mind towards Edward was as it had always been, and he had not then even considered the possibility of enmity or ill design on Edward's part. I know, for I wrote the letter at his command, that was sent to Reginald de Grey in Chester as late as the twenty-sixth of March of that year, pointing out that he had not yet been informed of the king's intended date of arrival in his kingdom, or the new arrangements for his coronation, and asking to know as soon as possible. And this letter was sent from Aber just before we set out for Dolforwyn, which was *after* the first news reached us of the treachery of Griffith ap Gwenwynwyn. It never entered his head, until much later, to suspect Edward of anything, or to seek to evade the fealty and homage due to him. He would have attended the coronation in due state, and certainly in friendship, if it had not been for this far more grave matter of David's implication, and the dangers it threatened to the unity of Wales.

Thus David came with a small retinue of knights to Rhuddlan in the latter days of July, when Edward was already preparing to embark for England. Elizabeth he

137

left at home in Lleyn, not only because of the grave nature of this visit, but for good reason enough, which he told court and council with proud and ceremonious intent upon entering the hall. He looked as always immaculate and graceful, stepping clean through all the foulness he engendered at his worst, and spurning those impulsive human virtues he showed at his best. Alone he came before the assembled council in hall, leaving his train outside and wearing no weapon, and he stood well back from us all, to be single and beautiful as he well knew how, and said in a clear voice:

'My lord prince and brother, you must excuse me some small delay in obeying your summons. Family affairs kept me. If you can forget for a moment the cause for which I am called here, and be glad with me, I pray of you that goodness and grace. In the morning of the day before yesterday my lady bore me a son.'

Thus very becomingly he announced his news, but his face was not as his voice, but arrogant and bright, his eyes blindingly blue with triumph, and upon Llewelyn he suddenly smiled, and his smile was sweet, cruel and vindictive, as he avenged himself in advance for whatever could be said of him or done to him. But it was his mistake, for though he never looked at me, it was then he struck all the pieces of that puzzle together in my mind, and I remembered his voice saying, in wilful mischief then not wholly serious, but now, perhaps, gone beyond mischief: 'A kingdom, and he will not give it a prince! While I have heirs – perhaps a prince by now – but no kingdom!' And truly now he had his prince, while Llewelyn was still barren and alone.

If his intent was to pierce to the heart, as I think, then it fell blunted. For Llewelyn was large of mind and generous, and could not, for all his own longing, grudge blessing to another, even his suspect brother. Indeed, in another way David's shaft did him good service, for it disarmed the prince's judicial sternness to such purpose

138

that I think he began almost to doubt what his own ears had heard, even to feel a little ashamed of suspecting his brother. He gave him joy openly and warmly, and enquired after Elizabeth. And even David, I believe, was shaken into some small burning of shame at being so rewarded for his venom, for he flushed as he made answer:

'My lady is well, and the child well, I thank you. He is whole and strong and perfect, and we have called him Owen.'

Judge how difficult it was, after such an exchange, to bring the affair back into the shape of an impeachment. But Tudor was not and never had been dazzled by David, and reminded the assembly drily that it would be well to proceed to business.

'You say well,' said David as roundly. 'I am here to listen to certain charges against me, as I understand, and to answer them as best I can, or to be appointed a day later to answer them. It is fitting that my own affairs should be left out of it. I am at the prince's and the council's disposal.' But always he kept in his eyes that blue, exulting, affronting brightness, and still he smiled upon Llewelyn.

Then Tudor spoke out what he knew, and what we suspected, and told him strongly: 'You stand impeached of conspiracy and treason. If you can show that these facts mean something other than they seem to mean, and that you are clear of all offence against the prince and his realm, we are ready to hear your answer.'

'My answer,' said David, aloof and cool, even scornful, 'is to deny that ever I entertained, since those my offences that are all too well known, any wrong intent against the prince, or committed any traitorous act, or joined in any dark conspiracy against his power or his possessions. I say that I am guiltless of what you allege against me. That part of your story that is true I accept, that is, that I did visit Owen ap Griffith at Pool, at the time you mention. Why should I not? I went there for no ill purpose, but because I was invited. If there was any plotting done in that place, I knew nothing of it and saw and heard nothing of it, and if there was any action taken, as you say and as Owen now says, by the men of Pool against your head, my lord, then it comes as news to me as to you, for I had no part in it. I deny all your charges. And since I hear them now for the first time, I ask leave to examine them at more leisure before I refute them all, as be sure I shall.'

'It is within your power,' said Llewelyn, 'to refute them now, or at least to make fuller answer than a mere denial. That every man accused can make, guilty or innocent. Will you not satisfy us now, and set suspicion at rest?'

'These are serious charges,' said David, 'and to me particularly serious, since I am your brother, and owe you closer allegiance than any.' So proudly, and with such lofty injury he said it, I swear Llewelyn for an instant felt himself the one accused. 'This I promise you, you shall be satisfied, with a full and final answer, but that requires other witness and other proofs than mine, and I need the help of my own clerks to muster evidence. Either accept my word, and discharge me now from all blame, or appoint a day for me to come to trial, and give me fair time to make ready my defence.'

'So be it,' said Llewelyn heavily, for he had hoped to be rid of that load without a further delay. 'It is your right.' And the council conferred, and at the prince's urging set the date for the hearing later than otherwise they would have wished, in October, at Llanfor in Penllyn. And David, on his word to appear there, was dismissed, and left Rhuddlan without waiting to exchange a word in private with his brother, that being the only smart he had left to administer, like a blow in parting.

After he was gone I was torn two ways, whether or no to speak out to Llewelyn what was in my mind. But I could not deny him what might well be strength to his case, and I knew I could trust him not to let it prejudice David's. For the whole torment of this matter was that even in our suspicions we could well be wrong. The men of Pool had confessed their treachery, but David denied all, and for all the weight of circumstance, his visit to Pool, his strange behaviour at Aber in February, there might be no more in his guilt than the harbouring of a partial knowledge, even a suspicion, which he did not reveal. Of so much, in my heart, I knew him guilty, but his guilt might go no further than that.

In the end I told the prince all, all those things David had said concerning his children, and in particular the son of whose coming he was so sure, and who was now newly arrived in this world.

'I dread,' I said, 'that since becoming father to children he has found his lands growing too cramped for him, and for his ambitions for them, and has turned yet again to his old complaint, that all Welsh land is partible, and he has never received his due. For himself he accepted his lesser estate, but for them? It is his aim to leave a dynasty well endowed, and to send his son out into the world like a prince.'

'That I can understand,' said Llewelyn wearily, 'though even so I could not countenance or condone it. Wales is not truly mine, or only mine as everything I am or have belongs to Wales, all but the soul. What is not mine I cannot give away, even if I would. Yet I do understand his impatience with me, who live alone and sleep cold, and nurse, as he says, a kingdom without an heir. And I had thought he had wit enough to see, and knew me well enough to be sure, that I am *not* without an heir, though I have none yet of my body. If I die unwed, David *is* my heir, and his son after him.' But in a moment he said sharply: 'No! He *was* my heir! If he proves guilty now, does he think I will let Wales go to one who turned traitor to Wales?'

So David had had everything to lose, and nothing to
141

gain, and that was always his fate, to spend all his energy and wit to waste, and only in moments unguarded, and very lightly valued, to give out those small acts and impulses of warmth that endeared him to so many men. I do remember how once he broke to me the news of my mother's death, with such skilful sweetness, and a touch so gentle, and tears in his own eyes, for she had been his nurse. But not even his affection was a safe gift, though precious, and worth the risk.

'But the mystery remains,' I said, 'for what would it profit his purpose to muster an armed band from Powys, and seek to enlarge his lands by force? No, it will not do. He would do better asking you for more, and he could have made a good case, with his first son in his arms. And you would have listened. He should have known it!'

'I am as lost as you,' said Llewelyn. 'This matter is very dark, and I will use all the men I have to seek out and find some light upon it. I pray David will show sense and speak out whatever he knows, but I cannot rely upon it. Our own hunt must continue.'

And so it did, both in Powys and along the Dee, and to some extent in David's own Lleyn, for if he had plotted, then some of his own people must be in the plot. Nor was this the only anxiety we had then, for word had come from Maelienydd that Roger Mortimer was building a fine new castle at Cefnllys, a stone fortress, whereas the treaty gave him leave only to repair the old one and put it in good order. A wooden enclosure and keep is a sensible means of defence on a border, but a stone castle with ditches and fortifications is a base from which to move outward, and we knew enough of my lord's cousin Mortimer to know that he would not scruple to use that base illegally if he saw the opportunity, and would hang on tooth and nail and with all the resources of law to what he got without benefit of law. Only a day after David had left us, in the castle of Mold, which he had set out to inspect, Llewelyn wrote a letter of protest to

King Edward about the building, with a sting in it for Mortimer above the open reproach, for he was one of King Edward's regents, and should have been foremost in maintaining his law and treaty obligations. But Roger was always a headlong creature, and would not brook restraint.

A miserable August we had of it, while the summer weather invited to joy, and the harvest began in very good heart. For with the whole burdened business of a principality there was now overladen this distress and suspicion between brothers. And still Owen ap Griffith in my lord's prison clutched at his wellknown story and would not part from it, though fright ate at his innards, and sturdily he swore that there had never been collusion between him and David, but he felt simple admiration and worship for David, and his only act had been against Dolforwyn, for dread and envy of its influence on the market and township of Pool.

And while we in Gwynedd agonised, and sifted, and probed after the truth of a complex matter, King Edward of England landed at Dover on the second day of August with his queen, and his daughter Joan of Acre, and the baby son Alfonso, born in Gascony, two foreign fruits brought back from the crusade. After the voyage, though undertaken in the best time of year, doubtless they were all glad to break their journey and rest as guests of Earl Gilbert of Clare at Tonbridge, and the Earl Warenne at Reigate, before they made their state entry into a London cleaned and festively arrayed for their reception, on the eighteenth of the month. At Westminster all the space within the island enclosure was filled with bright pavilions, and all the halls painted and furbished for the occasion. And on the day following, being a Sunday, Edward and his queen were crowned in the abbey, and for fifteen days thereafter all London feasted and made merry. But without the prince of Wales.

And to record a small act of restitution or revenge,

according as you view it, from the ceremony in the abbey the archbishop of York was firmly shut out by his superior of Canterbury, because he insisted on his right to have his cross carried before him. So his former victory at the translation of Saint Edward was fully requited at the coronation of King Edward.

As for Llewelyn's absence, there was never any sign that the king took it amiss, or failed to accept his excuses. Whatever men may have said afterwards in late wisdom, there was no ill-feeling then begun, no slight intended, and none suspected.

The time for David's appearance at Llanfor drew near, and Llewelyn removed the court to Bala, and there waited for the day of the hearing in depression and agitation of mind, but resolute to have out the truth and deal full justice. For the sake of his own pride and position he could do no less, but even more for the sake of Wales.

On the day appointed the council sat, and the bench of judges were prepared, and everyone waited for the accused to appear. But all that day passed, and the dark came down, and until full midnight we waited, that it might not be said we made him defaulter before his due day was ended. For there are delays and accidents on the road, and a man may be forgiven a lamed horse or a detour to ford a stream. But midnight passed, and David did not come. And then we knew he would not come.

Llewelyn had sat out the death of the day grave and silent and with a motionless face, like a stone man in his chair. When it was dead past question, he turned his head towards Tudor, and said:

'Take a guard of twenty men, and fetch him. Bring him in chains.'

CHAPTER VI

―――――――

That I was sent with that party was an afterthought on his part, and a concession. Not only had I almost a confessor's privilege with David, however he used me in despite of it, but also I was the person who knew the truth concerning that night at Aber, and I, better than any other, might relate to those events whatever David might do or say now at bay. We had great need of all the evidence we could glean. So when Tudor rode with his armed guard, I went with them into Lleyn, to the taking of David.

I think Tudor already had it in mind that we should not find him. I know I had. Once before I had ridden to Neigwl to recall David to his duty, and found him flown, and that with less reason than now. So we asked at Criccieth if anything had been seen of him, but the answer was, nothing. Certainly he had not ridden through that town or halted at that castle. The castellan said that to the best of his knowledge David's court was at Nevin, and thither we went, but Tudor detached two men to ride northwards of our course, for if he had indeed run, and not by way of Criccieth, he must have gone by the pass of Bryn Derwin, where once in his turbulent youth he had stirred up Owen Goch to make war on Llewelyn for the whole of Gwynedd, and been unhorsed and made prisoner. The first of his three betrayals, forgiven in a year. I was sure in my heart then that this third would never be forgiven.

We came down to the outer sea at Nevin in the blue autumn afternoon, the sun faintly overcast, the sky and

145

the sea melting one into the other without division. Above the outer fence of the maenol there was smoke drifting languidly, but thin and rare, as from only one or two low fires. And there was a guard at the gate, but only two men, and they lethargic and dispirited, and at sight of us approaching in some fear and more resignation. About the yards a few maids moved, in the stables there were only two or three work horses, but the stock grazed in the outer meadows, cattle and sheep. The castellan, a man of the local tref, came out from the hall and stood before us, blank-faced but erect, for he had his orders from his lord, and he was still in his lord's service until another took possession.

'In the prince's name,' said Tudor, sure now what to expect, 'where is the Lord David?'

'He is not here,' said the castellan. 'He bade me say to the prince, or to the prince's messenger, that they are welcome to what remains in Nevin and in Lleyn, since he cannot take it with him where he is gone.'

'He is a defaulter and recreant,' said Tudor, 'and we need no permission of his to take possession of all his lands and goods. He has failed of his day and of his sworn word. You had better look to your duty to the prince now, for you are without any other master.'

'I know it,' said the man, with a wooden face. 'Now I have done his last behest, and I am free of him. Ask me what you need to know.'

'Where is he gone? When, and by what road? Is there still time to overtake him?'

'I doubt it,' said the castellan. 'He left, with the most of his armed men and his family and attendants, in the night, four days ago.' That was a well-judged time, not so soon as to be still under close watch, since if he went about his business confidently and calmly to within four days of his hearing it might seem to all men that he was sure of the outcome, and in no fear of facing it. And not so late that he could not, by night, get his party across

146

Wales either to Chester or Shrewsbury before he was hunted. 'The road he took he did not confide to me, there were none in the secret but his guard, not even the lady. But I know they set off by Bryn Derwin, and it's my belief they'll make for Shrewsbury by Cymer, and pass well south of Bala.'

'They'll have circled round us the night before we sat waiting for him,' said Tudor, 'and gained two miles for every mile we rode westward. Still, we'll make the attempt.' And he sent two riders with fresh horses and orders to get remounts by the way, on the fastest route eastward, to enquire at all halts and alert all garrisons, and two more back to Llewelyn to carry word and get his orders.

'And now,' said Tudor grimly, 'let's see what he has taken, besides a wife hardly recovered yet after his son's birth, and that same son, and two small girls. With that burden we may take him yet.'

I knew already who else was gone, I knew it by the strings of my heart stretched out to breaking. God knows how he had accounted to Elizabeth for that night flight, though she would have followed him wherever he led. But I am sure he never let any word of it out to Cristin until they mounted and rode, for though she was in his service, or in his wife's service, she would not have let him go without a fight, for his own sake no less than for Llewelyn's. But when she was faced with the decision, and no time for argument or prevention, she would go with Elizabeth and the children. What else could she do? Unwilling, unhappy, loyal, knowing to what risk and sorrow he was dragging his defenceless lady, Cristin could not desert her. She was gone, and I might never see her again. Gone with Godred, for certainly Godred knew all, while I was left here without even the sweet anguish of seeing her face, and knowing that she loved me.

We went through the maenol, the castellan attending. David had taken his gold, his jewellery, all his portable treasure, and by the emptiness of the stables, some

147

thirty knights and troopers, no doubt carefully chosen, together with his wife and children, with Cristin and perhaps one other maidservant to care for them. Nevin was an empty shell, deserted by its lord.

As soon as Tudor's messenger reached him, Llewelyn sent out riders to all his garrisons along the border, and they scoured the Welsh side of the march, but in vain. David was already through the net and gone to earth in England, and for some weeks we heard of him no more. And still we did not know what lay behind all this coil of conspiracy and treachery, and had no way now of probing to the final truth.

'Yes, one way, perhaps,' said Llewelyn. 'We know him guilty now, and do not know of what, and I cannot leave it there. Let's see what someone else can make of this flight, someone who does know what the crime was, and is still in my hands to dread paying in full for it. Let Owen ap Griffith in his prison know that David is fled. And if he so receives the news as to think we know more than we do, so much the better, he'll sweat the more.'

So it was done. And sweat he did, being left now to bear the whole burden of the prince's revenge, and the more it delayed, the more did he fear it. All in all, I think he did well to sit out the rest of that month without blabbing, for as he was left to carry all, so he had the option of speaking out without contradiction, and piling the whole crime, or the lion's share of it, upon David.

I remember that November of Edward's first regnal year as a fatal month, the time when an opportunity for accord and understanding was not so much neglected or missed, as snatched away wantonly by chance, never to be repeated. It may well be that the fortunes of Wales turned about purely because of this mishap, and if that is true, then no man was to blame for it, and all the wisdom on earth could not have prevented it.

This is what befell: As soon as his coronation was

well over, and he had looked about him and secured control of all those matters outstanding in Westminster – and I repeat, with no sign of dissatisfaction or reproach at Llewelyn's absence from his crowning – King Edward turned to an accommodation with Wales, such as his father had achieved before him, and with every expectation of a peaceful continuance. He sent to the prince, early in November, to ask him to send envoys to meet him at Northampton, to make arrangements for receiving Llewelyn's fealty and homage in person, as the prince had desired, at a place and time agreeable to both. And Llewelyn gladly sent his proctors as requested, for it was no advantage to him to have this matter hanging unresolved, any more than to Edward. The messengers came back satisfied with their reception, and reported that they had agreed to the date the king had suggested, which was the twenty-fifth day of this same month, and the place, which was Shrewsbury. It was a sensible and proper arrangement, and Llewelyn had no fault to find with it.

But in the days immediately following the return of the envoys, came also the hoped-for message from Owen ap Griffith's custodian. Terror for himself had overcome Owen's obstinate silence. He begged that he might have audience of the bishop of Bangor, or some other reverend man, and cleanse his bosom by confession.

'Now we may learn the truth at last,' said Llewelyn, relieved, and as glad as it was well possible to be, with David so heavy on his heart. 'Whatever it may be, I shall be grateful to have it out in the open. I had best not make him face me on the occasion. We'll hale him out to Bangor, and confront him with bishop, dean, chapter and all, if it will make his tongue wag more freely. But, Samson, be present for me. I would have you stay unseen, and take down what he has to say.'

Relations between Llewelyn and the bishop of Bangor at this time were most cordial, and so they were with all the abbots of all the Cistercian houses of Wales. In St

149

Asaph, in Anion II, he had a most difficult and contentious prelate, so jealous for the privileges of his see that he resented others having any rights at all, and was endlessly embroiled in lawsuits of all kinds. Anion had even complained of the prince to king and pope as hostile to the church, by which he meant hostile to Anion, or at least a match for Anion, and all the Cistercian priors of Wales had combined to send an indignant letter of rebuttal to the pope against this slur on a most just and devout prince. But Einion of Bangor was loyal, humane and reasonable, and with deep concern accepted the task of taking confession from Owen ap Griffith. In the chapter-house of his cathedral this meeting took place, in the middle of November, and I, who recorded it, remember it still, word for word as it unfolded.

They brought in Owen from his prison, greyish-pale from close confinement, and fretted and thin with his long companionship with fear. He had not been ill-used or starved, and his modish cotte and chausses were still elegant, and his light brown hair and short beard well-trimmed, and yet he looked both wretched and neglected, so eaten up with fear was he. He looked from face to face round the circle of reverend men, with uneasy eyes, all in one rapid glance, and came and kneeled at the bishop's feet, and kissed Einion's hand with obsequious fervour.

'There is something you wish to say to us,' said the bishop, 'for the relief of your soul. You may speak out without fear. Confession will be health to you.'

It was rather for the best advantage of his body, to my mind, that Owen had made up his mind to speak, sure that everything was bound to come out, and thinking it wiser it should come from him, and he get whatever remittance was possible out of it. He joined his hands in entreaty, and cast down his eyes nervously, and made his confession on his knees. I had thought he might even then be exercising some devious discretion as to what he

150

told and what he omitted, and rearranging truth to his own best showing, but no, it was a straightforward tale he told, now that his mind was made up. If he revealed all, then nothing more could emerge to damn him.

'My lord, to my shame I have not only offended against the prince's grace, but in fear I have lied to cover my worse guilt. I desire to make full confession now, in the hope of your lordship's intercession and the lord prince's mercy. But I am in your hands and in his, to dispose of as he pleases. I acknowledge it, and whatever he does with me, I make no complaint. I have deserved his anger. But I would have this burden of secrecy and sin off my heart at all costs.'

Not all, perhaps, but it was worth a bold cast to try to salvage something out of the wreck. The bishop bade him speak, and promised to do for him, body and soul, what could be done.

'Do you make this statement of your own free will, or has any threatened or forced you, or put the words into your mouth?'

'My lord, no one has prompted me, I speak of my own free will, being sound in mind, and knowing what I do. I am come now to a better condition, I would make such restitution as I can.'

'Then speak,' said the bishop, 'and put away doubts and fears.' Which in Owen's situation was easier to say than to do, but he judged the fear upon that side to threaten him less than elsewhere, and plunged into his story.

'My lord, you know already that the lord prince got wind, early in the year, of my father's disaffection and mine, and how we had put into the field a war party with evil intent against him, and how he believed that we had attempted the destruction of his castle of Dolforwyn, out of jealousy and despite because of our rights and privileges close by at Pool. And when he impeached us of this offence, seeing that it was useless to deny, we confessed our guilt, and let it be thought that the rivalry

151

of Dolforwyn was all the matter of contention, and that we had indeed intended its razing, and nothing more. My lord, we lied. The enterprise was larger, and the sin, too. And it touches also, most deeply, the Lord David, who is now fled into England. I was set to win him into our plan, and so I did. In everything we did, he was a willing partner.'

'And who,' asked the bishop, 'so set you on to seduce him? Was it your father?'

For the first time the young man faltered even in his desire to have this ordeal finished. 'No,' he said, very low, and writhed, and in a moment got out, even lower: 'My mother!'

'Then your father took no part? Did he know of your plotting?'

'He did know. He did take part. But not the leading part. Do not ask me further to accuse her! I was guilty, let that be enough.' And indeed he had said enough already to be understood by any who had ever known that slender, steely lady of Pool, Hawise Lestrange the marcher's daughter. Into whatever plan she conceived, she could drive both husband and son, and that without ever raising her voice.

'Go on,' said the bishop.

'My part was to win over David, and I did it. He has often shown discontent with his lands, and he is bold and able. He entered into a bond with us to enlarge both his estate and ours. He promised his eldest daughter to me in marriage, and he promised my father, and me after him, both Kerry and Cydewain to be added to Powys, in return for the armed aid we pledged him to accomplish what he most desired. I was to lead a strong company in secret to the lord prince's maenol at Aber, and that we sought to do, but the floods turned us back at the Dee and prevented our evil.'

'You say it was to Aber you were bound?' said the bishop, still astray and in great amazement. 'In the name of God, with what intent? What could you hope to do there, in the very heart of the lord prince's power?'

'What God in his wisdom prevented,' said Owen, and knotted his hands in dread of his own words, and wrung out frantic tears. 'We conspired to murder the prince in his bedchamber, and make the Lord David prince of Wales in his place.'

In the blank hush that came upon us all I heard not even a breath, and then the long, faint sigh of every man present, so soft that it might have been the sound of the sudden, bleak November sunlight creeping across the flagged floor. The bishop sat chilled to stone. My pen had stabbed deep into the parchment and splayed its point, blotting the leaf. God knows what we had expected to hear, but it was not this, never quite this. Bishop Einion drew back a little from being touched by Owen's shaking hands, and himself shook with anger and disbelief.

'Wretch, do you know what you say? Are you lying still for some purpose of your own? If this was what you intended, the Lord David surely cannot have known it was meant to go so far.'

'I do know!' said Owen, shaking and weeping. 'As God sees me, I am telling the truth. The proofs are written and sealed, my mother keeps all the agreements we made in a coffer at Pool, you may send for them. David's seal is there. He did know! He knew all! On the second night of February we were appointed to reach Aber in the darkness, and he was to let us in.'

Then there was no more mystery for me in all the curious detail of that night in Aber, David's face in the red glow of the altar lamp in the chapel, tormented and ravaged between exultation and loathing, David's restless prowling as he watched the weather, his words, his frozen vigil above the postern gate, that was barred but not guarded. Llewelyn was never as careful of his personal safety as he should have been, and who knew it better than David? Who could better lead a party of armed raiders to the prince's bedchamber in the dark, and in silence? But God had prevented, and saved him from the act. No one could save him from the intent. And perhaps only God, not even David, knew the content of those desperate prayers of his that night, whether they were for clearing skies and hardy fellow-conspirators and a princely heritage for his son, or that God would tear the skies open and send down the torrents of judgment to make an impassable moat about Aber. For as often as David's right hand launched a blow at Llewelyn – David who never repented his evil against any other – his left hand would reach to parry it.

'He gave me to know,' said Owen, bleeding words freely now that the worst was said, 'that if he had no son of his body, by marriage with his first daughter I should be his heir.'

David must have laughed at that, knowing already what they did not know, that his Elizabeth was again with child, and certain in his own mind that this time she could not fail of providing him a son. And so she had, and the grand inheritance David had earned for him was a shameful exile in England, bereft of all lands and honours. So far had he overreached himself.

'He was to let us in by the landward gate, and lead us to the lord prince's room. And when Llewelyn was dead, then David's men and mine would take possession of the maenol and name him prince in his brother's place. And to this we all swore, and set our seals, if you doubt my word. But the floods turned us back, and the day passed without that terrible sin.'

'I thank God!' said Bishop Einion.

'And we thought it was over! That we had done no more than sinned in intent, and wasted our labour and time, as we deserved, that we were safe, and it had all passed without effect and without detection. But time and vengeance have pursued us ever since, thus slowly and surely, without any haste.'

'God's time is endless, and his patience without limit,' said the bishop. 'Never think that he has forgotten, or failed to see.' And he said heavily: 'Have you done? Or is there yet more to tell?'

'I have done,' said the poor wretch, grovelling.

'I cannot yet give you absolution, there is more required of you than confession. Do you empower me freely to say to the lord prince all that you have said to me?'

'Oh, my lord, with all my heart I entreat you to, and to lift this burden from me. I want to make what amend I can.'

'I will speak for you,' said the bishop, 'but with a heavy heart. Yet if you mean that truly, there is grace to be had.' And he sent for those guards who had brought the prisoner, and committed him again to their charge, to be returned to his prison. And I wrote to the end all that I had to write, and took it with me to await the prince's bidding, after the bishop should have spoken with him. But all that while that I waited – for it was no short telling – I could not cease from seeing David's face, after the night was passed and he had lain lost in his wife's arms until late in the morning, a face so weary and so at peace, as though after his own confession. I remembered its wondering humility and gratitude, washed clean of all greed and desire, even if that state of chastened bliss lasted not long That was when he had thought, like Owen but with how much more intensity, that it was over, that his mischief had been prevented and his better prayers heard, that he was delivered from evil. While at every step the shadow of his act, which was itself now only a shadow, trod hard on his heels and waited its due time to lay a hand upon his shoulder.

'Once I have heard it,' said Llewelyn when I went in to him, 'now let me hear it again as you took it down from his own lips.' And I read to him, he sitting perfectly quiet and alert and calm, all that deposition of Owen ap Griffith,

155

how the prince's death was to be brought about by the connivance of his own best-loved brother, and that brother exalted to his vacant sovereignty over the principality he alone had made, single-handed, out of chaos. By the time it was done the last daylight was dying, for the days were short then, and I got up to go and trim the candles, but he put out a hand with a sharp, pained gesture to halt me, and: 'Let be!' he said. 'There is light enough left for me to see where I am going.' So I sat down with him again, and waited.

'Once,' he said, musing, 'he rode at me headlong on the field of Bryn Derwin, mad-set to kill or be killed, but that was in open combat, face to face. I had not thought he hated me enough to conspire with so small a creature to spit me to my bed while I slept. Explain him to me, Samson, if you can, for I am lost.'

But I said never a word, for there never was any creature living under the sun could truly explain David, least of all David. He knew himself, and even his lies were never disguises from his own self-knowledge, but knowledge is not understanding.

'Though it is but a step,' Llewelyn said out of the gathering dark, 'from seeing Wales as his inheritance after me, since I am celibate, to growing impatient at the waiting. He is not the first to want to hasten the succession. The same impatience has been the death of more than one Welsh father, since time was. Strange that I never saw it as having any influence between him and me. And now, Samson, tell me, how often am I to turn the other cheek?'

'No more!' I said. 'Now you must think only of yourself. He has made himself the enemy, it is none of your doing.'

'No,' said Llewelyn, 'there's more at stake. Bear with me an hour or so, Samson, while I think for Wales.'

In all that he said and did then, it was for Wales he was thinking, and for that cause he was able to suppress his
156

own desolation and grief and anger, and forgo his own revenge.

'I am walking a ridge between two abysms,' he said after he had been some time silent. 'The two most powerful men in Wales, after me, have made common cause against me, and what I do now against them every princeling in Wales will be watching, and what I do must be seen to be justice, that they may accept it and take warning, but it must not be seen to be tyranny or cruelty, or others will be antagonised. I stand to lose allegiance whether I am too harsh or too merciful. If they conclude they may lightly break my peace, and not be crushed, some will do it, as they did it lightly in the past when Wales was not one, but many. If they think the measures I take too extreme, they will fall away out of indignation. If only I had had this land twenty years longer, even ten years, without interruption! It would have withstood all forces bent on breaking it apart. But this is a perilous time. We are not yet what some day we may be, God willing. We are not a state, not even a people. We are a loose bonding of little lands and tribes and families, of men who see no further forward, as yet, than tomorrow, and for a small, snatched advantage today will throw even tomorrow away. There is no man but Llewelyn can hold Wales together. If,' he said, very sombrely, but with resolution rather than misgiving, 'if Llewelyn can.'

I waited and was still, for he needed no word from me. For a while he, too, was silent, and then he resumed: 'I may not take revenges like other men. I may only bring offences to justice. Did you ever consider, Samson, what a cruel deprivation that may be, that afflicts kings and princes, not to be permitted to hate and resent, and feel outrage like other men?'

I said, only too truly, that it was not a deprivation from which all kings suffered. In the darkness he laughed, but somewhat hollowly.

'But by their own deed, duly sealed,' I said, 'all Griffith

157

ap Gwenwynwyn's lands are forfeit to you.'

'No,' said Llewelyn. 'Only if they offended again, and that I cannot charge, for this, however magnified now, is the past offence. So much justification I have for being patient and lenient. Not for their sakes, God knows, though I would rather have them as allies than enemies, but for the sake of Wales. Owen I hold, and will hold. He is safe enough. David I have lost for the time being, and he must wait. But Griffith is there in Pool, and thinks this whole matter over and finished, for his part in it, for he knows nothing yet of his son's confession. I do not want Griffith dispossessed, I do not want him prisoner, I want him bound to me, with all Powys – for Powys I cannot spare. I want him shaken and chastened, but not broken or humiliated further, so that he shall be glad to hold fast to me and keep his own. And if I can bring him to a manner of reconciliation and renewed fealty, I will do it. I must preserve the wholeness of Wales as best I may, and at whose cost I may, liefer my own than break this land apart.'

'News travels fast, even when few seem to know it,' I said. 'Griffith knows of David's flight before now. He may draw the same conclusion from it as his son drew. There is need of haste.'

'There is,' said Llewelyn sombrely, 'but of care, too. And I have not forgotten that there are only a few days left before I must set out for Shrewsbury, to meet King Edward. I am bound to him by treaty, and I agreed to the twenty-fifth day of this month, and go I must, though I would rather far that I had this matter of Griffith and Powys safely behind me, and could come to my first formal meeting with Edward as master of all Wales past question, with no dissentient. My fealty and homage would be paid on so much sounder a stand, and I could press my demands over the borders with so much stronger a voice. But there is no time. Until I come back from Shrewsbury, the less that gets out about Owen's tale, the

158

better. We'll not alarm Griffith too soon if we can avoid it. And it may be that the next move will come better from a prince already safely installed in fealty and alliance with the new king of England, and invested with his overlord's authority in the marches as well as his own.'

'And David?' I asked.

'There is nothing I can do about David at this time,' said Llewelyn heavily out of the mourne darkness. 'Neither embrace him nor kill him. As well! I might be tempted to kill rather than to embrace. When next I meet with David we may finish, one way or the other, what was begun at Bryn Derwin.'

On the twenty-second day of November, therefore, the prince, with a large escort and in noble state, set forth on the journey to Shrewsbury to meet with King Edward there, and to swear the oath of fealty and perform the act of homage to the sovereign in person, as he had always intended and considered himself bound to do, for though he maintained his position that the treaty had been frequently infringed, he did not hold those infringements as being grave enough to cancel his duty under it. As he was pledged, so he meant to do.

Had those two met at Shrewsbury that day, my story and my prince's story and my country's story might have been altogether different, blessedly different. And this is the lost moment for which, I see, no man can be blamed, but only some malevolent chance as wanton as lightning-stroke. For at Shrewsbury we were met, on what should have been the eve of that encounter, by a messenger bearing a letter from the king, written at Cliff, which was a hunting-lodge he had in Northamptonshire, on the very day Llewelyn set out from home. Edward had got so far, when he was taken ill with the sudden and violent bursting of an abscess, and was so much weakened that he could not continue his journey. He wrote regretting that illness prevented him from keeping his engagement, for he could not ride, but said that he would try to arrange another mutually agreeable date and place as soon as his health permitted. He did not fail to add a reminder that there were arrears of the money due under treaty still outstanding, and requested that they be paid, for even on a sick-bed Edward was a man of business. But having stated his reasons for withholding those sums many times, and also his willingness and ability to pay them as soon as he got satisfaction on his part, Llewelyn did not then pay much attention to that part of the letter. For since his first priority was thus frustrated, he was able to turn his mind and attention, with relief, to the second.

'We go home, then,' he said at once, roused and fierce, 'and set about the business of Griffith ap Gwenwynwyn.'

He wrote in reply to Edward's letter, also regretting that the meeting was prevented, and by such an unwelcome cause, and wishing his Grace a speedy recovery. And then we turned our backs on Shrewsbury and rode hard for home.

Our best hope, unrecognised, we left lying broken behind us.

Of those five nobles and clerks that Llewelyn chose to go as his ambassadors to Pool, led by Cynfric ap Ednyfed, Tudor's brother, I was one. Always he relied upon me to render an account faithful to the last detail, and I think found in me a mind tuned like his own, so that what I distrusted he took care to examine carefully, and where I found matter for sympathy he was at least willing to examine and withhold judgment. Whatever his reason, I was among those chosen. We had our orders, strict and precise, for his will was to win back Griffith and Powys with a whole heart, and he was prepared to go far to ensure success. Our task was to present ourselves formally at Pool as representatives of the prince of Wales, and to inform Griffith honestly of the content of his son's confession, without prejudice to his reply. For we were to invite him, and by all possible means persuade him, to return with us of his own accord to the prince, not as a prisoner but honourably as our companion, to make his answer to what his son Owen alleged, either to clear himself freely of the charges therein made, or, if he pleaded guilty to them, as the occasion was already past and had accomplished no evil, to confess to them and throw himself upon the prince's mercy, which he was assured should not be denied.

This, I swear, is what Llewelyn charged us with when he sent us forth. Do you know of another prince, so threatened and so abused, who would send his envoys with such large terms to his enemy?

On the last day of November, in a cloudy and melancholy afternoon light, we five rode into the town of Pool, and down to the river meadows where the castle was raised. We bore no arms, and went unattended, in token of the openness and honesty of our intent, and at the castle gates asked audience of Griffith in the name of the prince of Wales, his overlord, on matters of state. Peaceable as our aspect was, it aroused a great deal of fluttering within, until Griffith sent word in haste to admit us at once, and himself came hurrying out in his furred gown to meet us on the steps of his great hall. His heavy-featured face wore a fixed and somewhat ungainly smile, with little true welcome in it, but a great effort at appearing welcoming. He bore himself as though nothing had happened since April, when he had confessed to disloyalty and resigned himself to the loss of some part of his lands and the enforced absence of his eldest son. Having cleared that account in full, his manner seemed to say, there can be nothing in this visit now to trouble my conscience, and nothing to fear. But his eyes looked sidelong and were not quite easy. Whether any word had reached him of Owen's confession or no, certainly he knew of David's flight.

Our part was to be grave, detached and impartial, for it

161

was possible, if hardly probable, that Griffith had not been admitted to the fullest extent of his lady's and his son's design. Princes can be dispossessed and their lands usurped without going so far as murder. But I grant you it was not likely he should be innocent, and our errand was to make it clear to him, even so, that he need not dread extremes if he returned willingly to his fealty. When he brought us into his high chamber and dismissed all other attendance, Cynfric as spokesman delivered our embassage.

'You know, my lord, as all this land knows, that the Lord David has fled to England, instead of standing his trial on suspicion of plotting against the sovereignty of the lord prince. The prince sends you word by us that since that flight your son Owen has voluntarily made a full confession of conspiracy to treason and murder. He charges that you are also implicated, on these heads.' He recited them, with date, place and time. Griffith sat stiff and erect in his chair, his countenance motionless, only his eyes flickering now and then from face to face round the circle of us. 'The prince urges you,' said Cynfric, 'to return with us to his court, and to make your answer to his face concerning these charges, either to clear yourself and satisfy him, if you are innocent, or to repledge your fealty and ask for and obtain his clemency by confession if you are guilty. The event is past, and for what was then known of it you have already made reparation. If you will accept the prince's grace and return to your troth you need not fear that mercy will not be forthcoming.'

Griffith asked, in natural anxiety, after his son.

'Your son is in close hold,' said Cynfric, 'but safe and well. No harm has come to him, no harm will come. His offence is purged. If the same honest peace can be made with you, the matter is over.'

Griffith sat for a while in glum thought, and then roused himself to play host worthily in his own castle, shaking off the heaviness of uncertainty.

'You must give me time to speak with my wife,' he said, 'and consider what I do. Stay overnight, and give me the privilege of feasting the prince's ambassadors, and after dinner I will give you my answer.'

And that we did, accepting it as a good sign, for surely he was visibly resigning himself to the inevitable agreement, having so much to lose by enmity and so much to keep and conserve by humility and good sense. He presented us to his lady, who kept a calm, unsmiling face, ceremonious but not gracious, and sat among us at the high table as stately as a queen, and jewelled. Hawise Lestrange was as tall as her lord, but slim as a willow, with long, elegant hands and long, elegant face. Without the slightest friendliness she took excellent care of our entertainment that night, and very lavish it was. In particular we were pressed to drink our fill, but in Griffith's house, and on our errand, we did not care to deplete his stores more than we need. He had not yet given us an answer, or we might have been more disposed to carouse with him. But after dinner he excused himself and left us to take counsel with his wife, and came again with a calmed and resolved face.

'I thank you for your errand. It shall not be vain. Tomorrow I promise I will ride with you to where the lord prince is, and I will satisfy him of my troth.'

Well content, we went at length to the chambers prepared for us, two small tower rooms upon different floors reached by a stone stairway in the wall, Cynfric and I in the upper room, our three colleagues below. From this sleeping-place all the noise and bustle of the hall was so distant as not to be heard. I marvelled how soon the whole castle fell silent, and since we had ridden much of the day, and sat content and well-fed in smoky hall all the evening, I fell asleep and slept deeply.

Too deeply! Even when the sounds of nocturnal activity did draw near, they failed to rouse me. Not until the

163

sudden weight of hands bearing down out of darkness pinned me to the brychan, and a great palm gripped my mouth, did I start out of sleep, and try to spring up in alarm, but by then it was too late to do more than struggle fruitlessly under the heavy body that held me down. I heard the threshing of Cynfric on the other side of the room, and someone cursed him horribly, and then two bodies fell crashing to the stone floor, and all the time there was a muted grunting as of a man gagged with cloth, or a smothering sleeve. How many there were of them it was hard to tell, but enough, six at least to deal with the two of us. Griffith took no chances. They had brought no lights into the room with them, they knew where to find us without benefit of torches.

It took them some time to subdue Cynfric, and they were not gentle, for he had awakened more readily than I, and done some small damage to one or two of them, even with no weapon but his hands. But they had us both pinioned at last, and muted, and hobbled our feet, too, before they dragged us out to the stairway. There were two or three others waiting there with torches, men of Griffith's guard, and all of them as blown and exercised as those who had fallen upon us. The door of the room below was standing open. We had little doubt that our companions had been overpowered first, and that we were being hauled away to join them in captivity. And I remember thinking even then that Griffith was mad to toss away so viciously his own best hope, one he was lucky to be offered.

Pool castle was strange to me, I knew only the hall and those tower chambers, and we were dragged down so many staircases and along so many stony passages that I was lost. But I knew we were down beneath the level of the hall, and it needed very little guessing to expect some lightless prison below ground, without window, where too curious visitors could be tossed for security, and have no notion what went on in their absence; or why they were so disposed of. Killing I did not look for. He had little to gain that I could see even by throwing us into his dungeon, but nothing at all by killing us. Nor, in fact, did our captors do us any great hurt, however unpleasant the hole into which they finally thrust us.

A narrow door opened on a steep flight of steps, down which we were rolled hastily when they had unbound us, and we fell among other bodies in darkness. Hands reached to prop and steady us, and voices hailed us by name, challenging and anxious, for they had feared worse for us. We in our turn, ridding ourselves of the cloth that gagged us, told over all their names. We were five sorry ambassadors, and five very angry prisoners, but prisoners we were, and there was nothing to be done about it, against a garrison of hundreds, and without even a dagger among us.

'The more fools we,' said I, smarting, 'to put any trust in any promise or oath of Griffith ap Gwenwynwyn. We should have known he had some lying trick up his sleeve.'

'If we are fools,' Cynfric said, groping for a wall for his back in the stony darkness, and stretching out his legs resignedly before him, 'Griffith is a worse fool. He has tricked himself out of Powys now. He could have kept all he had at the price of renewing his oath and leaving his son a while longer as hostage for him. Now he has beggared himself and abandoned his son. Grace will not be so easily come by after this.'

Seven days we spent in that stinking hole, but at least after the first day they gave us some light, and regularly they fed us, even if they did thrust our meat in to us like feeding hounds. The dungeon folded into three cells opening one from another, which at least, when we could dimly see, gave us a measure of decency. There was but the one way out, and as often as they opened the door at the stairhead they set it bristling with long lances to fend us off. But to say truth, we saw no profit in compelling them to complete Griffith's work by killing us, whether in desperation or by accident, when we were as certain of Llewelyn's eventual coming as we were of dawn, though neither could we see. And after we had once tried questioning the guards who brought us food, and found them charged not to answer, and afraid to ignore that charge, we ceased from questioning, and sat down doggedly to wait. The misuse of ambassadors was something Llewelyn would not endure, that we knew. And as he had shown great patience, so he could show equally great vehemence and vigour at need.

We counted the days by the meals they brought us, and by our count it was the seventh day of December when the narrow door above us opened without three or four lance-heads immediately bristling through it like the spines of a hedgehog, and opened wide to the wall instead of gingerly by a hand's-breadth, and further, remained open. The guards we had begun to know did no more than peer in and then draw back respectfully out of the light. A head we knew far better leaned in and narrowed its eyes into our stinking darkness.

'Cynfric?' said Tudor's voice dubiously. 'Are you all safe below there? Come forth and be seen!'

'Here!' said Cynfric, mounting towards his brother as the first of our line. 'What kept you so long? We feared we might have to keep Christmas without you.'

They embraced, for all the stench we brought up with us. There were other known faces crowding in behind Tudor, first reaching to touch us and be sure we were whole and well, then laughing at us, for we must have been a forlorn sight, unshaven, unwashed, draggle-tailed and cold. They brought us triumphantly into the inner ward of the castle, where Llewelyn was posting his men, not for the garrisoning of Pool, but for its destruction. They were already bundling faggots to his orders, laying logs and brushwood under the walls, and marshalling the garrison and the fragments of the household to be despatched into the world for refuge.

For no good reason, except that I was just emerged from darkness, I looked up into the December sky, chill and distant with frost, and very still, and against that pallid grey I saw at the top of the tower Griffith's war-banners fluttering limply down to wither over the merlons of the wall. He had not stayed to lend his own defiance to that barren gesture, I knew it then. Once we were underground, and the castellan and his men ordered to stand to for siege, Griffith had taken his leave in haste, and there was but one way he could have gone. As often as I hear of the power and prowess of this lord of Powys, I remember how he ordered up the flag of war, bade his seneschal stand fast and defy the world, and then took to his heels into England with all his family, and all he could carry of his wealth. I have the measure of Griffith, having known him. Whatever the dominant, Griffith would find a means of ingratiating himself with it. Whatever the climate, Griffith would grasp a place in the sun. Even if he mistook the hour and missed his hold, Griffith would find a means, and quickly, to amend his standing. Whoever died, for personal passion or for a cause larger than personality, Griffith would survive.

Llewelyn came leaping down from the guard-walk on the wall, in leather hauberk and booted to the thighs, to reassure himself that we were all sound and whole. He was alight like a flame, very bright and steady-burning in the December gloom, but it was an angry brightness, and until he had spent it in action he would have no inner peace. Too much patience and forbearance had eaten him from within, and now his indignation at least had room to range.

'I delayed too long,' he said, smouldering, 'and bore too much, and at your cost. I thank God you have come to no harm. When ambassadors are so used, there's an end of tolerance. I should have struck the moment the

167

word reached me. I marvel I did not. I'm grown so used to holding back, I delayed yet again, and sent the abbot and prior of Cymer to hunt out Griffith in his new lair and offer him a last chance to return to his fealty and renew the unity of Wales, with the promise of mercy still. I began to dread,' he said, and shivered, 'that I had lost the power to strike hard. Now I feel like a man restored.'

'Regret nothing,' said Tudor firmly. 'You did right to make even that last bid for his allegiance, if only to let the world see where the right is, and how far you have gone to reconcile him. Now, if he has eyes, King Edward must know these are obdurate traitors who have gone to earth in his borders. Time and time again they have been offered the chance of return, and still refused.'

'Well,' said Llewelyn, heaving up his shoulders largely, 'whether I did well or ill, it's done. Now we have other things to do. Since Griffith refuses to restore the unity of Wales, I will, without leave or aid from him. Now everything he has is doubly forfeit, for this offence is worse than the other.'

We asked if they had had fighting, for in our prison no sound from without reached us.

'Very little, and half-hearted at that,' said Llewelyn. 'Griffith's castellan had no great appetite for the defence, small blame to him, when his lord had none! He surrendered at the first assault. The place was well manned and provisioned, too, and the outer buildings cleared and burned for action – that's part of our work done for us. Take your ease, for we'll bide the night here before we send the castle after its barns.'

So all we who had come out of the dark went to cleanse ourselves and find or borrow fresh clothing, to stretch our cramped limbs and take exercise, or rest in better comfort bones bruised and stiff from stone. And that seemed to us a delectable day, not only because we were alive and free, but because the sovereignty of Wales was also at large, justifiably and manifestly, and the happier for it.

For action can be happiness, whether it turn out in the end to be ill-judged or well, after long and frustrating abstinence.

That night after we had eaten in hall the prince held a field council, having with him more than half of his own council of Gwynedd, though not of the other lands of Wales. And there he told us what was in his mind to do, which was to proceed through all the lands and tenements of Powys, if possible peacefully, if necessary with the sword, to take over all manors and strongholds of those lands, and set his own officers over them, annexing Powys to his own inheritance. Legally he had every justification in the deed executed by Griffith and Owen at Bach-yr-Anneleu in April, by which they ceded everything to him if they again offended against their troth. Morally he had every right even without that deed, since Griffith had himself needlessly abandoned both his oath and his lands, piling fraud on fraud and felony upon felony. And during that month of December it pleased me to see Llewelyn forget, in the flush and purposeful haste of conquest, the bitter inward sadness and desolation of David's treachery. I knew that ease could not outlast action, but at least it renewed him for a while.

The following day we packed and marched, having first seen Griffith's garrison out of the castle, to be distributed among certain of the maenols under the control of officers of our own. And the castle of Pool, once empty, we fired behind us, and left a party in the town to complete the destruction after the fire died and cooled.

We went like an east wind through Llanerch Hudol and Caerinion and Griffith's remaining portion of Cyfeiliog, proclaiming the prince's lordship everywhere, installing his officers, planting his garrisons wherever they were needed. There was little resistance, no more than a scuffle here and there, and no bloodshed. Yet so deep is the sense of hereditary possession in Wales that this procedure, however justified and however sound in law,

169

seemed to the bishops shockingly drastic, and they wrote to the prince in mid-December urging moderation. Though plainly, since the lord of Powys had deserted his lands and refused the generous offer of freedom to return to them, his forfeiture was a matter of practical management as well as of law, for someone had to administer Powys. Griffith had swept away into exile with him his wife, his second son Lewis and his younger children, and an estate without a head can very rapidly rot into disorder. We had annexed the whole of Powys by then, making a circle northward through the cantrefs of Mochnant and Mechain, and withdrawing gradually into Gwynedd, leaving the land firmly settled.

At Rhydcastell, which is a grange of Aberconway, we drew breath on the twentieth day of December, and Llewelyn chose to pass the Christmas festival there. From that place he replied to the bishops, pointing out that their appeal for an accommodation and peace between the parties had much better be addressed to Griffith and David, who had both resisted the prince's efforts to achieve just such a consummation, and obdurately refused to return to their sworn fealty. It was not he who had prevented a reconciliation, nor he who first caused the breach by plotting murder.

In the stillness after action he was suddenly at loss, brought face to face again with the reality of betrayal, which he had done nothing to deserve. He was always hard put to it to comprehend the curious, secret, complex jealousies and hatreds and motives of those whose natures were not open like his own. Where he saw reason to complain, he complained at once and forthrightly, where he had a grievance he blazed it out of him, and then it was done. Also he listened to the complaints of others, not always with understanding, but always willingly. I never can discover in my own mind how he and David came from the same seed and the same womb, or how they came to love so much, and claw each other so deep.

Rhydcastell was a pleasant enough manor, sheltered and close to the rich, wooded valleys of Conway and its tributaries, but I cannot say the Christmas we spent there was a happy one. It had a certain sense of achievement to celebrate, not without satisfaction, but quite without joy. There were too many reminders of the disaster which had begun, unrecognised, a year ago, and of the false serenity we had felt then, and the brightness of Elizabeth and her children making the court at Aber gay. Now they were somewhere in England, in an exile that could please no one, and dependent on patronage for their maintenance. Such an inheritance had David laid up for his new-born son by snatching at the future too soon.

But until the beginning of the new year we had no certain knowledge of where they were. Then on the second day of January came a friar of Llanfaes, who had been on pilgrimage to other Franciscan houses, and halted some days at Westminster, and he brought a letter from Cynan.

'They are in Shrewsbury,' said Llewelyn, when he had read. 'David and Griffith both, with all their households. And their heads are together as before, and their men are still in arms. So says Cynan. More, he says it is known that they have sworn a new oath of mutual support – against whom, we hardly need ask. Once they had burned their boats, there was little left for them to do but turn on me and make me pay for all – that I understand. But listen what Cynan has to say further! This is the meat of the matter! This is what caused him to write, for the rest I could have learned by other means very shortly. "The king has issued a mandate, *not made patent*, to the sheriff of Salop, instructing him to allow the fugitive Griffith ap Gwenwynwyn, with all his household, to dwell in peace in the town of Shrewsbury until he should receive any contrary order. And your brother, the Lord

171

David, who is in Griffith's company there, has certainly written to the king appealing for aid and maintenance for himself and his family. The families of these two lords are large, and include, as you know, many well-armed men. They may not be the easiest of neighbours to your borders." '

So blunt and open a warning, sent from the court by one of Edward's own chancery clerks, I had not expected, even though the bearer was also a good Welshman. It seemed to me that Cynan was not far from the moment of choice, and it was clear, when that breakage came, what his choice would be.

'I take the point,' said Llewelyn grimly, 'and I will secure my borders in the middle march, and be ready. From David, from Griffith, I look for nothing but growing hatred and despite now. Since they have refused return, and there's never any standing still, they have no way left to go but deeper into their own venom. But that Edward should give them protection and countenance! You see what Cynan says – "*not made patent*"! With good reason, for by that sign he must know he does vilely to harbour traitors. I would not have believed he could bear to signify approval to treason.'

'Don't judge too hastily,' said Tudor. 'Do we know what gilded story the king has been told? Would David go to him with the truth? No, he'll have made it a very different tale, with himself the wronged and persecuted brother driven out of his lands into exile. You know him, how fatally plausible he is. The king is his only hope of advancement now, he'll play on him with every device and charm he has.'

And so I said, too, and his charms and devices were many and seductive, and from childhood he had kept some hold and claim on Edward. And yet I was not satisfied, for all the story of that conspiracy to kill, unearthed by painful stages over a year of searching, was by then notorious through the whole of Wales, and

172

could not have failed to penetrate into England and reach the court, since they had their agents everywhere, just as we had. It was hard to believe that Edward did not know where the truth lay. But it could still be believed that he withheld judgment until he had heard all sides of the matter, and the order to let the felons live openly in Shrewsbury might be only a temporary measure. So I said, and Llewelyn heard me with a dark and doubting face.

'There is more in it than that. Fugitives is the word Cynan uses, surely of intent. It was Edward's word to the sheriff. He might well keep his mandate close! The treaty made at Montgomery forbids either England or Wales to receive and harbour the fugitives of the other. He knows he is breaking treaty. He cannot choose but know. Never tell me there's a line of any document concerning his rights that Edward does not know by heart.'

One of his law clerks present, who had been an envoy at the drawing up of that treaty, looked a little uneasy at this, and frowned like a man searching his memory, and said that as to the wording, the lord prince was slightly in error, for the word 'fugitive' did not occur in the king's responsibilities towards Wales, though it did in Llewelyn's undertakings towards England.

'The phrase, as I recall, is that King Henry promised, for himself and his heirs, "inimicum vel adversarium principis vel heredum suorum non manutenebunt contra principem vel iuvabunt." '

'Is that not to vary without differing?' said Llewelyn impatiently. 'Are not David and Griffith my enemies and adversaries, and is not Edward now maintaining and aiding them against me? If the word "fugitivum" had been added, what difference would it have made?'

To him there was indeed no difference, because he did not play with words like cards in a game, but held fast to conceptions of duty, undertaking and honour. What use was it to tell him, even if we had then grasped the rules

173

of the game, that Edward could claim the exiles he entertained had not yet, from his land, attempted any move against the prince, to come within the terms of the treaty? Or that Edward's lawyers would have a thousand arguments, even if the exiles did continue their treasons from without, to prove the treaty was not infringed, and Edward not obliged to take any restraining action?

'He knows,' said Llewelyn quite positively, to himself rather than to us. 'He knows what he is doing! He is doing it of intent. I have not provoked him, I have not evaded my obligations under treaty, there is no personal matter at issue between us. *He* has made the first move towards enmity. Take note of it!'

And so I did, in great trouble of mind, yet not quite recognising what I saw. For this was the moment when Llewelyn's belief in Edward's good faith was first, and fatally, shaken. Thereafter there was no return to the old, easy, honourable enmity, played out fairly and with honest men's regard and respect for an honest opponent. Never, until they came to blows. The battle-ground was the only ground where they could meet.

At night, when Llewelyn called me to him to play the crwth before he slept, he said, softly but abruptly after long silence: 'I have not yet pledged him fealty or done him homage. It is the only weapon I have, if he takes arms of his own choosing against me.' And he looked up at me and smiled, seeing my uneasiness. 'No, I have no hope of withholding my homage for ever. I owned it due, and I shall pay it. But, oh, Samson, if I could with honour, how gladly I would! To have Wales entirely separate, entirely free, a state equal with England!' And he closed his eyes upon the vision, for he was very weary. But in a moment he opened them again, and said wryly, quoting an old Welsh proverb: 'Truth is better than law! But how shall we prove it, against the tide, if Edward maintains that law is better than truth?'

CHAPTER VII

There is no man can say that Llewelyn acted rashly or in haste during that spring season after Griffith's flight, or took his own way without consulting his council. He was more than usually careful to sound out the opinions of the elders, and to weigh the consequences of what he did before taking action. He made no complaint to the king, and no sign of knowing where his enemies were lodged, much less of being aware that they stayed there with the king's sanction and approval, and virtually under his protection, until they themselves took action and showed all too plainly that they were based on Shrewsbury, and moreover were freely allowed to make armed sallies from that town, against the terms of the treaty. This forbearance on his part was primarily to protect Cynan, or any other royal servant of Welsh birth, who might come under suspicion of sending us secret information, but also to demonstrate to the whole world that the offence came first from Griffith's men, and Edward could no longer plead that they were not conducting themselves as 'enemies and adversaries of the prince, contrary to treaty.'

The first raid into Cydewain came late in February, a rapid strike from Shrewsbury into the lands south of Pool, and a quick retreat, driving off several head of cattle and burning barns full of grain. One villager was killed in that fight, and a number of families left homeless. Llewelyn, when he heard of it, sent for one of the chief men of that part, and took a detailed statement from him, as an eye-witness, that no one might be able to challenge his story. Then he wrote formally to Edward, setting forth the truth of the matter, whence the onslaught was launched, what booty had been taken, and by whose men, naming names, and making it clear that no intelligent man could fail to note how the king's officers, though they had not taken any part themselves, certainly had done nothing to prevent or restrain the attack, as undoubtedly they could have done. Nothing on such a scale was begun from Shrewsbury but the bailiffs of the town and the sheriff of the shire knew about it. But they had not banned the raid, nor taken any steps to punish the offenders since.

Soon afterwards there were two more such raids, briefer but also hurtful, into the commotes of Deuddwr and Ystrad Marchell. The Welsh there defended themselves stoutly, but could not pursue the retreating enemy into England. Each time Llewelyn wrote again, always fully, and in March King Edward finally sent a reply, in very correct but distant form, saying he had received the prince's letters complaining of various trespasses along his borders, partly following the reception of the prince's enemies into the march, partly from other causes, but not having with him those advisers he would wish to consult in the matter, he thought it better to leave dealing until his proposed Easter parliament in London, when all his counsellors would be present. And he asked that Llewelyn would send to that parliament legal envoys fully instructed in the matters at issue, and promised to do whatever was right according to treaty.

It was a very civil letter, and promised fairly enough, but there were things about it that troubled me, as though I saw again between the lines the heavy droop of the eyelid over the wide brown eye, hiding half the king's thoughts. Why, for instance, did he lump together these specific complaints concerning the traitors and rebels with the ordinary infringements to which we had grown almost accustomed along the border? They belonged in a category very different, and Llewelyn had most markedly
176

distinguished between them. And where was the need of consulting all his parliament and council, nobles and clerics, some three months after he himself, consulting no one, had issued orders that the fugitives should be free to live as they pleased in Shrewsbury? The time to take counsel would have been before he opened his arms to traitors.

'He is playing the delaying game with me,' said Llewelyn, and the suspicions he nursed against the king grew larger and blacker. Nevertheless, he did send envoys, expert in law and fully briefed concerning the facts, to the king's Easter parliament, and of talk there was plenty, but still all of promises without action. King Edward wrote, early in May, that he had heard the complaints of the envoys, and had instructed the sheriff of Salop to fix a day for meeting according to custom, to discuss such complaints from both sides, and to make mutual amends for any injuries done. The present ambassadors, he claimed, were not fully empowered, and therefore no judgment could be arrived at in Westminster concerning the trespasses alleged to have been committed against the prince by the king's magnates.

This, after Llewelyn had named them! '*His* magnates!' he said angrily. 'The two greatest are *my* magnates, and my traitors, and he dares lay claim to them? What is he about? Is he so preoccupied with other business that he has not realised how great is this offence and this danger? Or is he welcoming it after his own fashion, and looking for profit from it, all in good time?'

Nor was he the first of us to begin to suspect as much, for Tudor had already voiced to me a similar dread. Moreover, before long the king's attitude hardened, and he no longer empowered de Knovill, the sheriff of Salop, to meet with our envoys and make amends in the old way, but ordered him to make none, nor accept any from us, until Llewelyn should have regularised his position by performing his homage to Edward, though up to that time

177

no further arrangements had been made, nor any further demand, for that formality, and it was Edward's own illness that had prevented it before. We did not know of this prohibition until later, but we saw for ourselves that no meeting ever took place, and no redress was made. Moreover, the depredations of Griffith and David from Shrewsbury grew bolder, and were carried out by such formidable numbers that we suspected – it may be wrongly – that their own forces were augmented by some of the king's men, perhaps not officially ordered, but willingly serving as auxiliaries, and sure that de Knovill would turn a blind eye.

Llewelyn complained once again, in terms stronger and more direct than before.

'Write to King Edward,' he said, 'that since my envoys returned from parliament there have been no less than six further raids made on my territories by the men of Griffith ap Gwenwynwyn, who are maintained and protected in the county of Salop, and their crimes publicly defended there. Of the booty they took on these six raids, from all the border commotes of my realm in this region, part has been sold openly in the markets of Shrewsbury and Montgomery, which can hardly be done without the knowledge of the authorities responsible for those towns. Four horses belonging to me have been taken from the groom travelling with them, and my man publicly beheaded. The peace can hardly be maintained if such felonies are permitted. Though the king's own men are not directly to blame, yet their maintaining and protecting of the criminals is as great a peril to peace as if they themselves had committed the offences. I therefore pray your Grace to do justice, and order your sheriff to arrest the felons, whose names, should they be still unknown to your Grace, I can and will supply. I expect justice and fair amends from you, and the prevention of such disorders in the future, and I beg for an answer to this letter by the bearer.'

This was sent on the twenty-second of May, from Aberyddon, and could hardly have been more explicit.

'But not wholly true, I doubt,' said Llewelyn bitterly, 'for I tell you, I am no longer sure that I expect from Edward any measure of justice or any amends.'

This was also the mood of most of us who had followed this exchange of letters. Looking back now, I am not sure how far we were just in our turn to Edward, who had all the complex business of state upon his mind, of which this affair of the Welsh traitors may have seemed to him only a minor part. Yet I am not satisfied with this, because of small, perilous points, like his insistence on treating David and Griffith and the complaints against them in just the same way as he treated Llewelyn's legal wrangles with de Bohun over disputed lands farther south, as though all these men were his own barons. This he knew was not the case, and his continued refusal to differentiate cannot have been anything but deliberate. At this time the only grievance he can possibly have had against the prince was the withholding of the money due under treaty, and again and again Llewelyn had stressed that it was ready and waiting to be paid if the king would also perform what was due from him under treaty, that is, to curb and compensate for the border infringements of which we had cause to complain. But Edward was a proud and domineering man, and a single grievance was enough, even if he had not chosen, in that month of June, to provide himself with a second and greater.

On the twenty-fourth day of the month he issued a summons to the prince of Wales to present himself at Chester on the twenty-second of August, to take the oath of fealty and perform his homage as a vassal. True, he offered letters of safe-conduct for the journey into the town, but it was not yet forgotten, in Wales or in England, what the worth of Edward's word had been to Henry de Montfort at Gloucester, and to many another whom he chose to consider as rebels and obdurate, or his parole

179

and solemn oath when he was hostage to Earl Simon, and turned recreant without a qualm.

The messenger who brought the summons was a young clerk we did not know, and therefore Llewelyn merely thanked him for his errand and offered him entertainment overnight, making no show of what he felt concerning the matter of the message. But the young man smiled, and said: 'I am entrusted also with another piece of news, I will not say all welcome, since it concerns a death, but perhaps not all unwelcome. And I am bidden to mention to you the name of Master Cynan, who taught me the message. For I am his sister's son, and I owe my place at court to him.'

'Then you are doubly welcome,' said Llewelyn heartily, 'and I look forward to hearing all your uncle's news over dinner. Speak out his message now, whatever it may be.'

'My uncle bids me tell you,' said the boy, 'that the king has received word, only a week ago, of the death of his aunt, the Countess Eleanor de Montfort, at the convent of Montargis, where she has lived since she left England. Her daughter, the Lady Eleanor, is now in the guardianship of her brother Amaury, still unwed, still unaffianced. To the best of my uncle's belief, it is she herself who has resisted all offers made for her. If you are still of the same mind, my lord, your way lies open.'

Late in the evening I looked for him and could not find him, though he had presided at the high table as always, with a calm face and a commanding eye, and been gracious to the young man, Cynan's nephew, who had brought him two such momentous and perilous messages. Not a word had he yet said to us of either, gone beyond indecision, beyond exultation or despair, forgetful of the king in the sudden sense he had of being near to Eleanor, as though the miles of air between had shrunk, so that he could all but stretch out his hand and touch her cheek. I should have known from old experience where to find him, and there he was, when I thought on the certainty at last, alone in his chapel before the small altar light, not on his knees but standing erect, his eyes upon the little silver glimmer that flowed reflected down the cross, and in his cupped hands before him the painted and enamelled medallion that Earl Simon had given to him long ago, the image of a child's grave and marvellous face in profile, with the heavy braid of dark-gold hair coiled upon her shoulder. Twelve years old she was when that portrait was made, hardly older when her father betrothed her to the prince, and now she was a woman grown, twenty-two years old, and I had not seen her for those ten years, and except in this image, Llewelyn had never seen her.

'God forgive me,' he said, very low, for he knew who came in to him without looking round, 'God forgive me that I can be glad, when she has lost a mother she surely loved. But if she has waited, as I have – oh, Samson, if she has indeed waited for me with a single heart, as I for her – then even she may be glad at the heart of her sorrow. And when I see her face to face, and take her hand, it shall be my life's work to make her glad, and fend off from her every sorrow and every doubt. At Evesham I was promised I should be his son. The blind man blessed me, in Earl Simon's name and in God's name, and wished me fulfilment. It cannot fail!'

I wondered then if there had ever been times when he had doubted of winning her, for he was human like other men, and could not be always constant in faith. But it is all one, for I believe, whatever the exaltations and despairs of his spirit, he had never contemplated giving up the fight, and to die still pursuing an ideal is not defeat, but victory. Now it was so near that his extended hands touched the hem of her garment.

'I must not take her consent for granted,' he said, 'nor her brother's approval, either. She has never seen me, I am only a name to her, remembered for the sake of her father. But now at least I may send and offer for her in

181

good faith, and she may say yes or no to me, and at no other person's leave but hers will I take her. There is a wine-ship of St Malo lying in Caergybi now, and ready to leave. My envoy and notaries shall sail with her, and with good weather they may be in France within the week. This Montargis is south of Paris, is it not?'

'Twenty leagues or so,' I said, 'perhaps twenty-five.'

'And Montfort l'Amaury, from which her family came?'

'Closer still, very close to the city.'

I had never been over the sea, but often, in the days when I was Llewelyn's envoy in Earl Simon's retinue, I had talked with his son Henry, and sometimes with the earl himself, about the lands in France which they had left to put down deep and powerful roots in England. As for Eleanor, I think she had never seen France until her mother took her away after Earl Simon's death at Evesham. She was born in Kenilworth, the youngest of her line, and the only daughter after five sons, three of them now dead, one just absolved from excommunication but still rightless and landless, one, the last, a scholar of Padua and a papal chaplain. To his care she was now committed, and with his goodwill, in no way bound by promises made to Edward, as her mother's had been, she could be married.

'In a month,' said Llewelyn, his eyes steady and bright upon the flicker of silver light on the altar, 'I may get her answer. I would to God I could go myself, if she consents, and bring her home, but I dare not turn my back here. It is her dower, and her son's inheritance, I am nursing now, and I must hold it safe for them. But, Samson, if she consents – you knew her, she will not have forgotten! – I would have you go as my proxy, and speak the words for me at our first wedding.'

Not until the wine-ship had sailed, and with it Cynfric and the prince's best notaries, with his proposals and gifts, did Llewelyn turn his attention to King Edward's summons to Chester. But when he did, it was clear that a part of his mind had been busy with it in secret. For things had changed greatly since he set forth to meet the king at Shrewsbury on the same errand, and illness prevented. He had then had no complaints or grievances against the king, and no suspicions of his motives and intentions. Now he had all these, and to a grave degree.

'Since we have some weeks of grace,' he said, 'this shall be done in proper form, and not I, but the council of the princes of all Wales, shall make the decision.' And he called such a council to assemble in the next month. All the magnates of his realm received his writs, and all attended.

Llewelyn read out to the assembly the king's summons, and laid it on the table before them.

'Less than a year ago,' he said, 'I received such a summons to Shrewsbury, and set out to obey it and keep that appointment. But then it was at a place and date agreed between us, and I had nothing to argue against it. I will not keep secret from you that I would gladly see Wales free of all obligation to any other monarch, if I might do so upon terms of peace with our neighbours, and without breaking faith. But that I cannot do, as yet. I made a treaty with King Henry, and I am bound by it still, and do not wish to repudiate the bond. Provided the king, as the other party to the agreement, keeps its terms and performs his own obligations, I have promised him homage and fealty and I shall pay it. But a treaty requires the keeping of faith by both sides. As to my own part, I have not until this time, as I see it, defaulted in any point. I have held back the recent moneys due under treaty, but I have said repeatedly that it is ready to be paid as soon as reparation is made for violations of my borders and acts of aggression against my men. Until a year ago I would have said, also, that King Edward has kept to terms, and respects the treaty. Now I am less certain. Hear my reasons, and tell me honestly if I am making much of little, and finding malice where none is.

183

'As to the infringements of our borders, they began before the king returned to England, and in part I know they are to be expected, and cannot be charged against him. Nor dare I claim my own men are invariably guiltless. But see how these troubles have increased during this year since he came home, when I expected them to be strongly taken in hand. I have written letter after letter, detailing every violence, every offence; he cannot say he is not informed. There has been offered no remedy.

'Again, and still closer to the mark, those traitors who conspired against my life fled at once, when charged, to England, and that in David's case when he had every opportunity to defend himself in court, and in Griffith's case even after his son's confession, and after clemency had been twice offered to him if he would come to my peace. They were sure of their welcome, or why make such a choice? Do all princes welcome their neighbours' traitors with open arms? Princes of goodwill, with no evil intent? Even if they shelter and maintain and tolerate them, do they leave them at large on the borders of the land they have offended, and allow them to raid across those borders at will? I think not. Yet this is what King Edward has done. He cannot say he was not told the full truth about their conspiracy, he cannot say he has not been told of their depredations from Shrewsbury. Still there has been no remedy, and no change.

'I have been long in looking beyond this point, but I am come to it now. In all that Edward now does, and all that he deliberately refrains from doing, I see the gradual erosion of the treaty of Montgomery. I am driven to believe that he means, when he has weakened it enough, to repudiate it, and be free to conduct the old enmity against Wales, in the hope of conquest, and that he will use my brother, and Griffith ap Gwenwynwyn, and any other such powerful tools as may fall into his hands, to that end.

'Now consider, and tell me, in the light of all this, how am I to reply to this summons to Chester?'

They hesitated long, pondering, all watching him with doubt and anxiety, his young nephews of Dynevor most earnestly. The elders among them, I think, had reached the same suspicion long before Llewelyn opened his mind to it. But it was Tudor who took up the argument, and very gravely.

'I have gone this road,' said he, 'a stage further even than the lord prince. This murder was planned for February of last year, while King Edward was still away from his kingdom – true enough. But how far away? In Gascony, and then on the road to Montreuil and Calais. For a good year before he came home there were couriers running back and forth to him across the sea, and half the business of England was in his hands, and half the court of England overseas in his company. Was it so hard for those who planned our lord's death to send their messages back and forth among the rest? How if the assassins were sure of their welcome in England because it was promised in advance?'

I was watching Llewelyn's face when this was said to him, and I knew then past doubt that such a thought had never so far entered his mind, being so alien to his own nature, which he was all too apt to attribute as candidly to his enemies. I knew, too, that now, at Tudor's instance, the notion struck deep as a sword-thrust, and would not be easily dislodged, however he contended against belief.

He sat roused and startled. 'Are you saying,' he asked with care, 'that the king may have been a party to the plot to kill me?'

'I am saying more. I am saying that the king may have instigated it,' said Tudor stoutly.

'I cannot believe it,' said Llewelyn. 'He may be willing to go far in his lust for conquest, but he could not stoop so low as to suborn murder. It is impossible!'

'How so, my lord? Only in the sense that this king regularly performs the impossible. It was impossible a noble prince should pledge his good faith time and time again in Earl Simon's war, and time and time again break it, but he did it. It was impossible he should give his parole, with the most solemn oaths, and callously discard it, but he did that also. Consider the circumstances! Has he not all his life been close to your brother? Has not David once before deserted Wales for England, and served Edward, even in arms, to the best of his power? Who was it wrote into the treaty the provisions for David, that he should be re-established in at least the equal of what he had before? Did Edward scruple to make use of a traitor then? To reward a traitor? You know he did not! Strange, indeed, if such an attempt on the lord prince's life were timed so carefully to herald the king's home-coming without implicating him, and he unaware of it, who had the most to gain. Stranger still, when it failed, that those who did the work should fly so directly into his arms, unless he owed them protection for their services. It would suit King Edward very well to have David installed in your place. David is his creature. You belong to yourself and to Wales.'

'You make too strong a case,' said Llewelyn, very pale, 'though I won't deny a certain logic. It may not be as you say, but only that circumstances give it colour.'

'True,' said Tudor, 'that it *may* not be as I have said, but not true that I make too strong a case. I make the case we must make, and must consider fully, before we can know what it is wise to do now. For the end of it is, that it very well *may* be as I have said. And that is more than enough. Has he behaved all this year as if intending justice, or has he nursed the murderers, given them aid and protection, allowed them to run riot over his borders with impunity, against your rights and your lands? You know the answer better than any!'

Then Madoc ap Griffith of Maelor spoke up. So many of the older princes had passed from the world in those last few years that Llewelyn's council showed as a circle of young men, with only a few of Tudor's generation to add experience to their ardour, and Madoc, who was the eldest of four brothers, ranked almost as an elder of Wales among these glowing boys. He was shrewd, reasonable and provident, a good man in council.

'There is one further point to be made,' he said. 'The king summons the lord prince into Chester to do his homage, and while Chester is a border town, it is also a royal garrison town, and to enter it is one thing, to leave it may be quite another. I have in mind the precedent of the lord prince's father, who accepted a king's word and went into the Tower as his guest, but never left that place again alive.'

'The king has offered safe-conduct,' said Llewelyn fairly.

'So he may, and he may even be honest in offering it. At the best, let us say he is. Even so, he puts no restraints upon your traitors and would-be assassins in Shrewsbury. We know he allows the Lord David access to his own court and person, what reason have we to suppose the king will curb his freedom if he attend him to Chester? A murderer can just as well strike in Chester as in Aber, once he is sure of the king's indulgence. And that's to put the best construction upon it. At the worst, if the king set them on once, or sanctioned what they suggested, so he can set them on again, and still, in public, wash his own hands.'

'Madoc is right,' said Tudor. 'It is not safe for the prince to go into any royal town where his enemies may move about at will, and in arms. It should not be asked of him. It was always the custom to meet in the open at the border, either at the ford of Montgomery or some similar spot, as the dukes of Normandy used to meet the kings of France on the Epte. If the king is sincere in wishing to continue the treaty and keep its terms, he should be willing to ensure that homage may be performed in a safe place. It is my view that the lord prince should take that stand, give his reasons, and decline to go into Chester.'

Then several of the others present also spoke, some doubting if the king could be planning expansion by

187

murder, but all wary of allowing Llewelyn to go into an English city, where, if treachery was indeed contemplated, he would have no means of extricating himself. Llewelyn sat and listened to all, himself adding nothing more, and it was clear to me that he was greatly shocked by what had been suggested, but almost as much by his own slowness to recognise the full extent of his danger as by the danger itself. Had not David, even, in his devious way, constantly warned him against putting any trust in Edward, or taking his intelligent self-interest for goodwill?

'Give me your counsel, then, man by man,' he said when they had all done, 'am I to go to Chester or no.' And one by one they spoke out, from the eldest to the youngest, and every man said no. By the measure of the threat to the treaty, our one safeguard against England's greed, by the measure of the distrust all felt towards Edward, not one was in favour of compliance with the royal summons. It came to the youngest present, Llewelyn's nephew and namesake, not yet eighteen. The boy flushed red with passion as he said: 'No, do not go! For the sake of Wales, do not put yourself at risk.'

'I am at risk whether I go or refuse to go,' said Llewelyn, and smiled at the young man, who was dark and bright and beautiful, like his mother before him. 'I am at risk every day of my life, waking or sleeping. So are we all. It is a good thing to remember it, sometimes. But Wales I will risk as little as I may, God and you guiding me. I shall do as you have advised. I will write and set down yet once more those injuries I feel should be amended before I swear fealty, and the reasons why I will not come to Chester. I will make reasonable request for a safer place, and declare my own intent to keep honourably to terms if Edward will do the same.'

'It might also be well,' said Madoc, pondering, 'to prepare such a statement as may be offered to another authority, if the king is not minded to be accommodating.'

'I had thought of it,' said Llewelyn. 'Pope Gregory is

a wise and just man, and easy of approach, as I have heard. I'll give my mind to it. If we are to look for friends in need, we'll go to the highest.'

Thus armed with the approval of all his magnates, the prince answered Edward's summons as he had said, courteously but decidedly, declaring his willingness to assume all the duties implied or stated in the treaty, provided Edward would do the same, and in particular charging him to end his illegal support for those who unquestionably had been and still were acting against the prince. This was the chief stumbling-block, being by far the most serious breach of treaty. If that was set right, and a safe and proper place agreed for their meeting, Llewelyn would take the oath and do homage as was due.

Edward, so we heard, was very angry when he received this letter. In the first place, whatever some men may have said, wise long after the event, concerning the previous considerable delay in regularising Llewelyn's position as vassal of the English king, there never had been any prior refusal or even avoidance, for only once before had the prince been summoned to the meeting, and then he had set out without any resistance or reluctance to keep the engagement, and only Edward's illness had prevented the matter from being completed. Consequently this firm and reasoned refusal now came as a shock to the king, who could never bear to be denied. Whatever his own motives, he had certainly expected unquestioning compliance on Llewelyn's part. Then also, he had made the journey to Chester, certainly not only for the prince's sake, but publishing the fact that the homage was to take place there, and an offence against Edward's dignity and face was mortal. He could be generous to those who threw themselves at his feet in total submission – if that may be called generosity, for rather was it that when they so satisfied his desire to dominate he ceased to care about them – but firm and steady resistance drove him to ever-mounting ferocity. He at once issued another summons, ignoring everything Llewelyn had written to him concerning the place and the terms, to come to him at Westminster, three weeks after Michaelmas. Chester had been declined, he flung Westminster itself, the very centre of his power, in the prince's face.

'I have taken my stand,' said Llewelyn grimly, laying this new summons aside, 'and I shall not depart from it. I cannot go back. If his aim is to convince me he has designs on my life, he makes progress. From Westminster to the Tower is not so far, as my father discovered, but from the Tower to Westminster is a lifetime's journey. This I'll answer, but not until answer is due. Let him wait until the day he himself has appointed, and he shall have all the answer he deserves, and as civilly as before. But he is mad if he thinks I will come to Westminster at his bidding.' And he turned again, quite calmly, to the composition of his manifesto to Pope Gregory, who was Edward's friend and fellow-crusader, and yet was honest enough to be trusted by those who held Edward to be their enemy. We were well advanced with it by then, and it was a lengthy document, first outlining again, as a reminder, the main terms of the treaty of Montgomery, negotiated and blessed by a papal legate, which should by law and right govern the relations between Wales and England, then detailing the main counts on which England was now breaking those terms.

By then we knew that the crown was paying money to keep David and his household. The entire plot against the prince's life we set down for Pope Gregory to read, with all the raids mounted since that time from Shrewsbury, and winked at, or worse, by de Knovill, the king's sheriff, at the king's orders. And lastly we complained of the king's persistent citing of the prince to places unsafe for him, where his felons and traitors were free to move about him at will.

So grave a document was drawn up with the counsel

and participation of all the chief law officers and elders of the prince's realm. Whoever says he acted of his own might, and arbitrarily, he lies. Whatever was wisest and most earnest in Wales took part in this appeal to the chief arbiter of Christendom. When it was drawn, we were as men drained and fulfilled, who could do no more, having done their best.

On the day that we had it ready, Cynfric and the notaries came back from Montfort l'Amaury with letters and messages from Amaury de Montfort and his sister, the Lady Eleanor.

So strange a day it was, hot and long and dusty with harvest, the sky a pallid blue clear as crystal, and never a cloud in all its bowl. And we were newly come to the full understanding of danger, and had accepted it and made our dispositions because there was no alternative, and yet that day was so full of the bright solemnity of joy that there was no room in it for any other passion or repining. From the moment Cynfric rose from his knee before Llewelyn, and showed him a beaming face, and held him out letters, there was no looking back.

'These,' said Cynfric, 'from Amaury de Montfort, on behalf of his sister and his house. And this from the Lady Eleanor, who speaks for herself, to the same effect, and to your comfort and worship.'

So he conveyed at once the purport of what was afterwards read and re-read many times for its savour, as slowly and lovingly as the finest wine satisfies a great thirst.

To the match, so long delayed but never abandoned, her kinsmen consented, in the terms of the settlement there was no dispute nor demur. But what best pleased Llewelyn was her own letter, written with her own hand. I know, for to me he showed it that night, in the summer twilight, after we had heard mass.

'For you knew her,' he said, 'and you will know the very voice in which she speaks these words to me, and I think it must resemble his voice, as surely her mind resembles his mind.'

She had written to him, at once with noble formality and so blazing and direct an intimacy that it was as if she walked towards us in the fields with outstretched hands:

'To the most noble and puissant Llewelyn, prince of Wales, greeting and reverence. My dear lord, though I have never seen you but through other eyes, yet I have known you from my childhood, and what my father did not live to tell me concerning his pledging of my hand to you, my mother did tell me, though only in regret when she also told me why that marriage was impossible. You know how and why she felt herself bound. But having been promised the impossible, I have chosen not to lower my eyes to anything less. The pledge made at my father's will I have kept at my own. That we may join our hands very soon, and see each other face to face, and that God may keep you safe and glorious until that day comes, is the prayer of your affianced wife, Eleanor de Montfort.'

I said: 'Yes, this is Eleanor. The very note of her voice, and the large, straight look of her eyes. She is his daughter, no question.'

'Now we have a double errand overseas,' he said, glowing. 'The envoys to the pope shall sail with you, they for Rome, you for Montargis, and with as little ceremony as possible and as little delay, for it may well turn the scale for us if we get our case into the pope's hands first. Edward will not be far behind, once he gets wind of it. Tudor has the ship in hand – there's a merchantman with a Winchelsea master loading timber and wool from the Aberconway granges, and he goes next to Calais for cloth of Flanders. Go to her, Samson, stand in my place with her and speak the vows for me, and come back in her household when she comes home to Wales. There is no man but you I want for my proxy.'

It needed no saying that I would do for him whatever

he asked of me, and to do this I was glad from the heart, and yet it was a time when I was loth to leave him. Only when it came to such a separation did I truly see how the clouds had gathered over him black and heavy, and all in the course of a year, when he had done nothing to dare the thunder. To this day I do not know what to believe concerning the possibility that Edward procured or encouraged the conspiracy against Llewelyn's life. I do not know whether he actually was guilty, nor do I know whether I believe in his guilt. I do know, from what came later, that he was quite capable of it, but as at that time I doubt if he had considered such a course or recognised what use he could make of it. Rather the assassins first fell into his hands with their armed men, as apt tools for provocation without committing himself, and then he saw what use could be made of them, and once launched, how far the matter could be taken. If that be true, then David was guilty not only of Llewelyn's wrongs and dangers, but also of the temptation and corruption of Edward.

'I wish I left you in more settled case,' I said, 'with this business of homage and fealty safely over.'

'Or put clean out of the reckoning,' he said, and laughed. 'If I could refuse it outright without myself breaking treaty, I would do it. But if he comes to terms and does his part, it is due and I must pay it. Should I hope for him to continue immovable, and give me my bid for freedom?' And he shrugged off the tempting dream, for he did not believe it would go to that length, and knew the dangers if it did. 'God gives with one hand and takes with the other,' he said. 'If my secure peace is the price to be paid for Eleanor, I'll pay it without grudging.'

Of that journey, the first and last ever I made out of these islands, my telling must be brief. The ship from the Cinque Ports took us up off Carnarvon from one of Llewelyn's own coastal boats, the abbot of Cymer, his chaplain, and the notary Philip ap Ivor, the prince's envoys to the papal court in Rome, and I, alone, sailing to join the household of Eleanor de Montfort at Montargis. It was then September, but a very pleasant autumn, blue-skied and breezy, excellent for sea-going, though I am not gifted in that kind, and even a brisk wind and some feathering of the waves were enough to make me queasy. The master of the ship was a great, thick-set man shaped like one of his own wine-casks, and of the independent and masterful mind of all the Cinque Ports men. He owned his ship, and it was to him the same as owning a kingdom. Even Edward, after the civil wars, in which the south-coast sailors had favoured Earl Simon's cause, had found it expedient to make peace with them on generous terms, and turn their minds to the future and the promise of good trading conditions and royal patronage, rather than trying to take revenge for their siding against him. He was not always so reasonable with those who wielded no sort of power to make his revenges cost him dear.

This master, who had been one of the last to abandon the piratical harrying of the royal ships at the end of those wars, and had held out until it was clear not only that he could do no further good, but also that he had his chance of coming to the king's peace without penalty, talked freely of those days and his own exploits, and spoke the name of Earl Simon boldly and simply as one revered and remembered, as saint and legend. Also he knew many ballads and songs about the earl and his heroic deeds, and his miracles, and could sing them very well, and when he found that I was interested he repeated them over to me that I might take them down and learn them. That was enough to seal him my friend, and he put himself out, the weather down the coast being easy and brisk, to show me something of the governance of a ship, the use of the steering oar, and how the great sail might be manipulated to suit the wind. But I did not tell him that I had known that great man who was his idol, nor that I was bound to the dwelling of the earl's only daughter, to speak the marriage words with her in my prince's name.

He was a good man, stout and fearless, and both able and daring in his use of his ship. I would we had had him on the return journey, it might have turned out very differently. What he could not run from he might very well have rammed.

All down the coast of Wales we had favourable winds and clear skies, and I saw the long, beautiful shore of my land as I had never yet seen it. But after the passage of the headlands of Dyfed the winds grew stronger and the sea rougher across the open water, and round the toe of England the crests of the waves were white and high. I was grown used to it by then, and could walk the deck securely even as we leaned and creaked in the swell, and I began to take pleasure in the voyage for its own sake, which had been to me, until then, only a mild hardship between me and the fulfilment of my errand. I marvelled no longer at our master's sense that his own element, which he rode and ruled and endured more than half the time he spent living, was the true and manifest reality and freedom, and the land was a kind of prison full of limits and bars, where he felt himself cramped and diminished. Once in the mid-sea there was no man was his master, neither king nor pope, though he respected both as he required to be respected.

It was a long journey across the south parts of England, so drawn-out that I learned somewhat of the ground of English power, which habits mainly in this southern land. Here are those parts fronting France, which is a very great country and in peace and alliance with England, hence the power is redoubled as long as this amity continues. We of Wales habit but a part of the western fringes, and have no such access to the wider world of Christendom. Popes and kings listen to us as best they can, but we are a voice from very far away, and out of a strange land. England lies between us and all those ears that otherwise might hear our complaint.

In sudden cloud and mild rain we came to our master's home port of Winchelsea, and put ashore part of our cargo, all the timber and half, perhaps, of the wool. Then we made across to Calais, in the last week of September, and there disembarked, the abbot and his colleagues to take the long road to Rome, I with them as far as Paris, for under the abbot's holy shadow travel was safer and more respected by the sheriffs. And at Paris we separated.

I had but a short way to ride from the capital city, to the castle of Montfort l'Amaury, from which place Earl Simon's family took their being and their name, and where Eleanor's cousins of the French branch made their principal home. For a party from that place was to ride with me to Montargis. I had very gay company, therefore, for the rest of the journey, those twenty or so leagues to the convent founded by Earl Simon's sister Amicia. Round this family foundation there lay rich estates and a fair town, and all the guest apartments of the convent, and the houses of grace to which the Countess Eleanor had retired with her household after Evesham, were full of the relatives and knights and friars attendant on Eleanor, her daughter. She was niece and cousin to kings, and provided already with the household of a princess.

We came there in the late afternoon, in time to show me those fair fields about the convent in the slanting light before sunset, all golden. It was then past the middle of October, but still serene and mild. Amaury de Montfort came to me in my lodging to conduct me to his sister.

He was then about twenty-seven or twenty-eight years old, cleric, scholar and wit, a papal chaplain and a man to be reckoned with in Christendom. I had not seen him since he was fifteen, in the old days at Kenilworth, and I doubt if I should have known him again, for he had grown somewhat away from the family build and the family face, hair and complexion darkening with time, his countenance lengthened and narrowed instead of keeping the massive, bony grandeur of the earl's imperial head. His

196

cheeks were olive and lean, his eyes very dark and deep-set, and intensely brilliant. They say he had a sharp and biting tongue that made him many enemies, but that I had no occasion to experience, for to me he was open and gracious after the manner of all his house.

He had not known, until my coming, who would be sent from Wales to be Llewelyn's proxy, and but for my name I am sure he would not have known me, as there was no reason he should after so long. But the name Samson touched some old memory. He looked at me with fixed attention, and then unlocked his thin dark brows and said: 'Yes, now I remember you! You were the prince's man with my father, at Kenilworth before Lewes.'

'I was,' I said, 'but there was no reason why I should stay in your mind for so many years on that account.'

'But on another account, perhaps,' he said. 'My brother Guy, when he escaped from England and the king's prison after Evesham, told us the whole story of that battle. You were bidden to leave my father's battle-line and go with the bishops, and you refused to leave him.'

'So did others,' I said. 'Earl Simon was not an easy man to leave, once drawn to him.'

'Some did not find it hard,' said Amaury, suddenly grim, and I knew he was thinking of all those young men who had made the earl their idol for a while, but fallen away when the road grew steep and dark. And in particular of Henry of Almain, the best of them and the most bitterly resented. Amaury had never reconciled himself to the loss of his family's English possessions or his own clerical prebends in England, and continued from France and Italy to wage legal war against all who now held them. I might even have considered him far more likely than Guy to have committed that murder at Viterbo, had it not been known and proved that he was in Padua at the time, and had not spoken with his brothers for some time previously.

I asked after Guy, as we walked together through the

197

courts of the convent and into the cloister garden from which Eleanor's apartments opened. For Pope Gregory had ordered his incarceration in one of the fortresses in papal territory, after his submission, and all we knew since then was that he had been absolved from excommunication, but not from any of the other bans imposed upon him.

'He is still a prisoner in Lecco,' said Amaury. 'It is not the most rigorous of custodies, it might well be possible to slip out of it, and our cousin John would be willing to set him up in some sort of command if he could, but it's impossible anywhere in papal lands. And all this is due to Edward!' It needed no great penetration to see that there was no love lost between these two cousins, however well-disposed the cousins of Montfort l'Amaury might be. We had reached the green enclosure outside Eleanor's rooms then, and suddenly Amaury looked up straightly at me, and said seriously:

'You realise how ill Edward may take this marriage?'

I was surprised, and said what seemed to me obvious, that no one in his right wits could possibly attribute any share in Guy's guilt to his innocent young sister, who had never taken any part in the dissensions of the past.

Amaury smiled again, but darkly. 'How well do you know Edward?' he said, but not as one requiring or expecting an answer. And I thought no more of it then, for we had stepped into the cool stone doorway, and entered a long, low-ceilinged room, lit by two candelabra branching from the walls. At the far end of the room, where long windows still let in the sunset light, three women were sitting in tapestried chairs about a table, two of them stitching at the same piece of sewing, a blue, brocaded gown spread across the board to let them take each a sleeve. The third, who sat with her back to the sunset, with her book lifted before her to receive the light, was reading to them in a full, clear, childlike voice, low-pitched and moving. I did not know the poem she was

198

reading, but it was a love-poem. When she heard our steps on the stone she laid by her book, and rose and came round the table to meet us, and so stepped from the sunset light that made an aureole about her, as round a virgin on an altar, to the light of the candles that fell full upon her face and breast, and caused the hieratic image to flower suddenly into a woman sculptured in dark gold and ivory.

At twelve years old she had been tall for her age. At twenty-two she was only a little above the middle height, but so erect and slender that she seemed taller than she was, and the coil of braided hair above her great ivory brow, still honestly wide and plaintively rounded like a child's, caused her to move with a marvellous, upright grace, as if she balanced a heavy crown on her head. She wore a gown of a colour hardly darker than parchment, but its silken texture and the candle-light turned it to the same muted gold as her hair. And she gazed at me, between long lashes almost black, with those wide-open, wide-set, translucent, green-golden eyes I remembered, so huge and clear that only honesty and goodness dared look straight into them, for fear of their mirroring magic.

I looked at her, and I saw again the young, ardent, grave face of her best brother, Henry, dead with his father at Evesham, and the noble, austere head of Earl Simon himself, as first I saw it in the church at Oxford, with great eyelids closed, and deliberate lips silently forming the measured words of his prayers. She was all the nobility of her house in one flower, and all the beauty. Those English chroniclers who afterwards wrote of her in superlatives, as most beautiful and most elegant, did not lie.

She stood with the soft candle-light flowing down the folds of her gold and reflecting from her whiteness, with a half-smile on that mouth of hers, that folded together firmly and purely as the leaves of a rose, and gazed upon me for a moment with the sweet, courteous grace she

199

showed to all strangers. But as I stepped before her into the same charged space of light, and she saw me clearly, her eyes burned brighter gold, and her lips parted in joy.

'Master Samson!' she said, and held out her hands to me.

I clasped and kissed them, moved beyond measure that she should remember and recognise me after so long. Behind me Amaury said drily: 'I see you need no office of mine here, you are old friends.' And he went away quietly and left us together. The two ladies went on serenely with their sewing. And I sat down with Eleanor de Montfort, and talked of Llewelyn. And it was as it had been at Kenilworth, when she was a child, and questioned me of Wales, and of the prince I served, and learned of me that he was a man to be loved, since I so plainly loved him.

On the eve of the marriage, in the cloister garden by the fountain, she said to me: 'You were the voice that first sang him for me, in such clear tones that I could not but be drawn. And you were the brush that first drew and painted him before my eyes, in such radiant colours that my child's heart fixed and elected him. And then my brother Henry also talked of him much, with affection and admiration. I never saw my father again, after he had finally met with Llewelyn, but when my mother told me that he had accepted the prince's proffer for me, it was as though a choice I had made in my own heart was confirmed and vindicated and approved, as well by heaven as by my father. For to me he had always been as the pillar of a church, quite upright and incorruptible, and his will, which had never been other than gentle and loving to me, was heaven's will. What use was it, then, for her to tell me in the same breath that what had been promised could never be? I understood her reasons, but I knew she was wrong, that it could be and would be, and all I had to do was wait.'

'And if he had been less captured, and less constant?' I said. For marriages are made and unmade for many noble children, with old bridegrooms who die, with distant bridegrooms who are cut off by war or by changes of alliance, with opportunist bridegrooms who happen on a better match before the first can be completed. Few such arrangements, however sworn, would have survived the years and the disputes that had threatened theirs.

'That was not how you had shown him to me,' she said serenely, and smiled. 'It was he who asked for me, at a time when others might well have been thinking better of the idea, had they toyed with it, for it was the last summer, and Edward was already loose, and the shadows gathering, and all those who looked first to their own security were drawing off and changing sides. If he pledged himself to me then, and was as I had seen him through your eyes, then he would not lightly turn from what he had sworn.'

We were sitting together on the stone rim of the fountain, before the evening came down, and she put out her hands and cupped them in the sparkling fall of the water, letting it fill her palms and spill over in silver. She gazed into the quivering pool as into a crystal, with a face grave, assured and tranquil.

'But even if he had changed,' she said, without sorrow or blame or wonder, 'that could be no reason for me to change. A woman should have her own truth and troth, as well as a man. If I could not marry according to my father's will and my own, then there is room enough for me at Montargis, within the rule as without.'

'And did you never have any doubts of the ending?' I asked.

'No,' said Eleanor, and smiled, opening her fingers and letting the mirror of silver dissolve through them into the stone bowl below. 'None. Never.'

The next day, in the church of Montargis, in the

presence of a great company of her kinsmen and knights, she was married in absence, and made her vows to Llewelyn, prince of Wales. And mine was the hand that clasped her hand, and the voice that spoke the proxy words for my lord, after so long of waiting.

Before that celebrant company, with those vows in my ears, and that woman beside me, a woman like a lamp of alabaster shedding radiance, I caught my breath once on the words given me to say, and Eleanor's beauty pierced me through suddenly like a sword of flame, and for that one moment it was no golden girl of twenty-two years hand-in-hand with me, but a slender woman approaching forty, raven-haired and iris-eyed, and it was to Cristin, no less than to Eleanor, that I spoke the sacred vows of love, not knowing then if I should ever see her again, but knowing that I must never hope for more than the bliss and pain of beholding her face and standing ready to serve her, even if time turned back and restored her to Wales and me.

So sudden and so keen was that visitation that I turned my head to look her in the eyes, those deep eyes that changed colour with the light from clear grey to royal purple. There never was a time that we two met, and I looked for her among many, but when I found her her eyes were already fixed and unwavering upon me, drawing me down into her being. But here I came to myself, beholding a different vision, the face beside me younger and lovelier, and not turned to me, but gazing straight before her towards the altar. A pure face in profile, clear as a queen on a coin, one large, confiding eye open wide to confront whatever came, a folded, dreaming mouth, Eleanor as Llewelyn had viewed her for ten long years of waiting, in the medallion her father had given him, looking with a grave, high confidence into her future, towards a bridegroom and an estate fitting her nobility. She, too, had waited, she who had never swerved from her certainty, and admitted no doubts. None! Never!

She had me by the hand, and her clasp was warm and vital and sure. And I, too, believed. I was ashamed to disbelieve, having her silent faith like a pillar of flame beside me. So I completed with all my heart the words that justified her, and renewed and registered my own vows in heaven.

CHAPTER VIII

There was a week or more of preparation and packing after the marriage, for it is no light matter to get such a large household moving, with all the treasure and plate and clothing belonging to its members, and such a number of officers and servants in attendance, not to mention several horses belonging to some of Eleanor's knights, who had favoured and valuable beasts and would not leave them behind. There was also some discussion about the best way to proceed, for the distance to St Malo from Montargis was much the same as to Calais, but to embark at St Malo would shorten the sea route by several days. Amaury pointed out that to go by St Malo it would be necessary to enter Brittany, and the duke of Brittany was close ally of England, and his son married to King Edward's sister Beatrice. He did not expect any interference with our passage, but had pricking thumbs about the advisability of letting any word of his sister's marriage reach Edward until we were all safely in Wales, and the whole matter an accomplished fact. But as against any risk from that quarter, we could save a number of days on the journey, and be in Wales the sooner. In the end it was agreed to send an agent ahead to charter two ships at St Malo, while the slow cortège followed at leisure and halted at Avranches until all was ready. And that we did.

Winter travel is no light undertaking, and that promised to be a hard and capricious winter, but Eleanor's party rode in very good spirits, and everything then seemed hopeful and bright. We were delayed at Avranches for most of November and into December, first by the need to find two good ships, and then by very contrary winds which kept us from embarking for some while longer. But before Christmas everything was ready, and the prospect of keeping the festival at sea did not in any way discourage Eleanor. All the lading was done before her own party rode from Avranches, and on the eve of Christmas Eve we put to sea.

Eleanor would have me stay in the leading ship with her immediate household and officers, her brother, her two ladies, and some of her knights, the remainder with most of the friars and the minor officers and the horses being in the second ship. These ships of France were built somewhat higher out of the water than the Winchelsea ship in which I had made the passage over, and I thought were less manoeuvrable to the winds, and less speedy and stable, but they had more comfort for the ladies, the stern-castle having a very neat and solid cabin built within it, and the fore-castle the like, though smaller. We had good winds to take us out from the Channel westwards, the seas were not rough, indeed the master complained rather of lack of wind than of too much, and altogether, even in cramped quarters, Christmas passed in simple but devout good cheer. For Eleanor was happy, and her happiness made a glow all about her that exorcised all fears and doubts. There was never any lady so ready and careful as she – but it was not care, for it came to her by nature – to see to the comfort and content of all those who served her, and the more joy she had, the more did she wish to see every soul about her joyful.

In those days, while we were making well out to sea to clear the toe of England, she would be always out in the weather, cold though it might be, with a cloak wrapped about her and a scarf over her hair, narrowing those eyes that never else were narrowed, to peer as far ahead as vision could carry her, towards Llewelyn and Wales. She walked unconcerned along the planking when the ship swayed, and balanced on the fore-castle like a willow, yielding and recovering, leaning her long fingers on whatever sailorly arm offered, and smiling towards her lord.

'What is that land?' she said, pointing where a low blue line, heaving just clear of the long level of the waves, and barely darker and more stable than their flow, showed ahead of us. 'Is that England? Cornwall, it would be here?'

The master said no, not England, but the first glimpse of the nearest of the Isles of Scilly. 'We'll round them, and keep well clear. You may not so much as see England, but only your granite cliffs of Dyfed, and the coast of Wales.'

'Soon, soon, I pray!' she said. But he said it might be several days yet, for the winds grew slack and capricious, and he could but do what was possible. And then she said, with that immense sweetness she had, that she was in his hands, and so rested, and would not for the world press either him or God, but was grateful to both.

Such she was, this princess of Wales. And of such there are few. But shortly we learned even more of her, and she, it may be, of herself. For we grow by conflict, and whatever challenges us calls forth what is within, and often we have guests dwelling with us we did not know until fate knocked at their door.

It must have been about the turn of the year, though my memory here is at fault and I cannot pin down the exact day, while we were circling round those blue-green islands in the ocean, leaving England well away on our right hand and out of sight, that the look-out called down from his chilly nest above the mast to warn of two sail bearing south towards us, one upon either hand. It was no way strange that they should be here, in this stretch of sea, since the islands were furnished from Cornwall, but the separate courses of these two seemed to him to be curiously matched, as though they trimmed sail to keep abreast but apart. They looked like ordinary merchantmen, and he gave warning of them only for the steersman's

206

information, lest he should be surprised by the apparition of one or the other on his flank.

The steersman shouted back to him, and as the two shapes emerged a little larger and clearer out of the faint sea-mist, he shifted his course by a point to pass between and give them both a wide berth. It seemed to us, watching them grow from mere bobbing gulls to looming barques, lower-built than our ship but larger and faster, that they closed in slightly towards us as they came. And from the nearest of the islands, as I looked astern towards our sister ship, I saw a long, dark shape suddenly surge out from the hazy blue of the shore, like a sped arrow, one of those low, snake-like rowed boats such as the Norse raiders or stray pirates from Scotland and the northern islands used. The look-out noted it at the same moment, and sang out its discovery.

'I do not like this,' said Amaury, watching the three, and noting how they ringed us. 'Surely the sea-ways are cleared of piracy since the peace?'

'Never cleared,' grunted the master, brooding, 'but in more than four years I've met with none. This looks too planned to be honest.'

'Can we run between them and get clear? If they have to come about to chase us we may gain time enough to outrun them.'

'We can try,' said the master, and try he did, with a rigged sail and a relay of rowers, but those two ships coming to meet us had gauged their own powers and ours, and had time and seaway enough to close in before we could slip between them. By this time, when we were forced to ease to avoid ramming or being rammed, or closing within their reach, we could see the men moving on board both of them, assured and intent, too plainly giving all their attention to us. They seemed well crewed, but showed no arms, and thus far no disposition to attack. Their tonnage, though, appeared to be considerably greater than ours, and very well tended and maintained, no beggarly keels such as prey on the lonelier sea-routes for a murderous living.

There was a big fellow in a frieze cloak on the forecastle of the ship closing slowly in on us from the left. I caught the gleam of mail when the wind ripped back the folds of the frieze, and saw that he wore sword and dagger. Eleanor's knights were all out on the deck with us, quiet and watchful, and more than one was already buckling on his own harness. Eleanor stood in the doorway of her cabin, her two ladies peering anxiously over her shoulders. She said not a word so far, she simply listened to what those said who knew the seas better than she, and watched the approach of those two unknown barques with measuring eyes, waiting for enlightenment.

A long, echoing hail came to us across the water. The cloaked man cupped his hands into a trumpet about his mouth and bellowed down the wind: 'Heave to! I have a message to you!'

'Send it from there!' roared the master back to him in French for his English, and still we crept forward. They risked damage to themselves if they tried to lay alongside us too suddenly, without crippling us first, and now we were fully abreast of the pair, in between them, and even drawing past by inches. Amaury saw it, and hissed at the captain: 'Now, break for it and row, we may clear them yet!'

The captain bellowed an order, the rowers heaved mightily, the ship leaped under us, and indeed we might have got clear away, if we had not been so absorbed in the two large ships as to forget the long-boat from the islands. It had circled our sister ship, which was slower than we, and lain off at a small distance, watching and listening. It seemed harmless to us, formidably though it was manned, for it was so low that boarding us from that serpent-shape would have been impossible. But that was not its purpose. As our rowers bent into their oars, so, with a sudden shout, did theirs. The boat sheered forward through the water like a dart, overhauling us at speed. Its raised, iron-shod prow sliced through our steering-oar, severing it with a violent shock and flinging the steersman across the deck to lie stunned under the gunwale, then plunged on, hardly checked, to tear all the oars on our steerboard side to flinders. The ship was brought up shuddering, and heeled about round its crippled side, splinters of wood flying. In the island boat, as it sailed past us and drew clear in a flurry of spume, the crew shipped their oars and stooped their heads low for protection, letting their razor-sharp prow do the work of destruction for them.

We were flung about the deck like leaves in a gale, and clung by whatever came to hand until our helpless ship partially righted herself in the water. By that time the larger of the two pirates had closed in on our other flank, until with a creaking and tearing of timbers she ground our remaining oars to pulp, and dragged groaningly alongside us. Then suddenly great numbers of men came surging up from where they had lain hidden, all along her side, dragged us close with grapples, and came swarming over the gunwale, with weapons naked in their hands, twice, thrice the number we had on board.

The tall man in the cloak, red-bearded and armoured, advanced upon us at their head. We closed in a half-circle about the women, and drew in our turn.

'Put up,' said the stranger, halting ready, 'and come to no harm, or fight, if you see fit, and take the consequences. You would be ill-advised.'

It hardly needed saying. We were a handful, and he had a small army. Nevertheless, Amaury in his rage, and perhaps seeing before the rest of us what lay behind this interception, launched himself forward and lunged at the man with all his might, but the other merely stepped back from him, not accepting single combat, and three or four of his henchmen closed as one on Amaury and bore him down by sheer weight, wrenching the sword out of his hand and clubbing him to the deck with the hilt of it. He lay stunned, with a trickle of blood flowing from his scalp, and then all his fellows leaned hand to hilt and would have flung themselves upon a like fate, if Eleanor had not caught two of them, the nearest, by the sleeve, and cried sharply: 'No!'

It drew all eyes to her. Until then she had been clinging unnoticed in the doorway of the cabin, shaken by the heaving and shuddering of the ship, and in deep shadow behind our ranks. But at her voice everyone fell still, and when she stepped forward we opened a passage for her, though watchfully, and keeping close on either side.

'No,' she said, 'no more of that! I want no killing, and no violence.' And she went to her brother, and so did the two Franciscans of her company, and raised him gently, dazed and bleeding. 'Take him and tend him,' she begged them. 'I must speak with this man.' There was no fear in her voice or her face. I think I never saw her afraid for herself. And the friars helped Amaury away to a pallet in the fore-castle, and she remained, facing her captor squarely, slender and straight and gallant, without pride or pretence. He looked at her beauty, and was struck dumb for a moment.

'If you have business here,' she said calmly and courteously, 'your business is with me. All here are my people, I take responsibility for them. What is it you want with us?' And she added, in the same serene tone: 'You do not look like a pirate, and I had not thought that pirates would be so well-found as you seem to be, or need so many men to crush so few. We are two unarmed ships on a lawful journey. Of rights you have none. Of demands clearly you have. Let me hear them.'

'I am armed,' said the bearded man, 'with authority enough, and have a commission to perform, and I intend to perform it. There is no intent to offer either offence or violence to you, madam, nor to any who serve you if they obey my orders.'

'Whose orders?' said Eleanor. 'Let me know your name and title. Are you a knight?'

'Madam, I am. But my name and rank are very little to the purpose. The orders I give, I have also been given.'

She smiled a little, not unkindly, as if she did not wonder that he preferred to keep his name out of the affair, but she did not press him. 'Given,' she said, 'by whom?'

'By the king's Grace, Edward of England.'

'Ah,' said Eleanor, unsurprised, 'I had begun to understand as much. I have never heard that my cousin had a trading interest in piracy, so I imagine his interest is in my person rather than in any ransom I could pay.'

Her opponent could have been in little doubt then with whom he spoke, but there were two other women standing there in the background, wide-eyed and pale, and he wished to be certain. 'You are,' he questioned, 'the Lady Eleanor de Montfort?'

'No,' said Eleanor, looking up at him within hand's-touch, with those wide, gold-flecked eyes that showed him the mirror image of his own diminution before her. 'I am Eleanor de Montfort, princess of Wales.'

He was struck out of words, for this was not within his orders, but he could not disbelieve her, confronted with those eyes. 'And what does the king of England require of the princess of Wales,' she asked patiently, 'that has to be extracted by these extravagant means?'

'These ships,' he said, recovering himself in some suppressed fury, 'and all in them are taken into custody at the king's orders. You and your ladies shall not be molested, but the men of your household will be kept under guard until the king's pleasure is known.'

She frowned over that, and said carefully, no longer baiting him but bargaining seriously: 'These ships are under charter to me, but their masters and crews have no responsibility in this matter. All Master Derenne has done is to hire to me his ships, his men and his skills, and the

211

king has no right or need to exact any penalty for that, whatever he means to do with me and mine. Have I your word that as soon as we are on land I shall be allowed the use of my own treasury to pay what I owe, and that ships and crew will be permitted at once to return to France? It would be unjust to detain them.'

'I cannot give you such a guarantee,' he said, uneasy, 'it is not within my competence. It does not rest with me.'

'Be so good, then, as to make known to the king that I make that request for them. That at least, I suppose, you can do?'

'I can and will,' he said.

'And may I keep my friars with me? They will attempt nothing to trouble you.' She did not ask for her brother, for she knew by then that whoever was allowed to go unbound, he would not be. There was a heavy load upon her, and she had to think for all her people. The friars were allowed her. 'Where are you taking us?' she asked.

'Into Bristol, madam.'

'Very well,' said Eleanor, and turned to leave him, as though that ended her need to endure his presence. But she looked back to add, thinking of the shattered oars and the broken steer-board: 'They have good repair yards in Bristol, I understand. I hope the king will bear the cost of putting Master Derenne's ships in order.' And she went away without a glance behind, to where the friars were cleansing and binding up Amaury's broken head.

They put an armed crew aboard either of our ships, and rigged a makeshift steering-oar to get us into port. Our sister ship was not damaged, having been boarded without bloodshed in the consternation when we were crippled. All of us men aboard they disarmed, and transferred us to their own vessels, though Amaury bitterly complained of being forced to leave his sister in the hands of such fellows, and with only her servants and friars to guard her. I doubt if he truly feared any affront to her, for she was the king's cousin and the king's captive, and Edward would have required account of any injury done to her, however he himself injured her. It was rather a way of being insulting to our captors, since Amaury could do them no other harm, and a means of ridding his heart of some of the venom and frustration he suffered. For indeed our happy expedition had turned into disaster, and we had no way of getting word to anyone who might help us, Llewelyn least of all.

In the larger of the Bristol ships they let us take exercise on deck under close guard at times, and that was the only glimpse we had, for the rest of that voyage, of Eleanor, the distant flutter of a scarf or the gold of her hair unbraided to the wind, on the stern-castle of Master Derenne's ship in line before us. She, I think, complained not at all. It would have altered nothing, as Amaury's ferocity altered nothing, and she was more concerned with ways of dealing that might, perhaps, lighten the burden for some of us, and better our sorry circumstances. She thought much, and was wary of both resentment and despair, neither of which could be profitable. Before we reached Bristol she had made slaves of most of those seamen who had been sent to capture her, and friends of more than one, though the knight who had planned the capture and been in charge of it she avoided and treated with cold civility.

Concerning this man I have since learned something, though not much, and after we were landed in Bristol I never saw him again. It is possible that Edward, though willing to hire and pay for such dubious services, did not particularly desire to be reminded of them afterwards. The man's name was Thomas Archdeacon, and Cynan later kept close watch on the rolls, and discovered that in May of the year then beginning, twelve hundred and seventy-six, the sheriff of Cornwall was empowered to pay to a man of that name the sum of twenty pounds, to cover his expenses in carrying out some unspecified mission on the king's behalf off that coast. There cannot be much doubt what that commission was. I would not say he was very well paid for his trouble.

The year was already in its first weeks when they put us ashore at Bristol, and we were hurried away into close confinement in Bristol castle, to await the king's orders as to our disposal. There, as I learned later but guessed even then, Eleanor exercised her reasoning, her firmness and her masterly good sense to support the power of her beauty, and so worked upon the governor of the castle that we were well used, as far as leniency could be taken without risking our escape, for none of us had given any parole, and it would have been worth the castellan's office if he had let us get away from him. She also procured the release of the ships, and saw to it that their expenses were paid at her cost. Truly she was Earl Simon's daughter, feeling and generous to the least, as to the greatest, who served her, perhaps more punctilious to the least because of their greater need. Nor would she owe a penny, nor rest until the last owing was paid.

At the end of January we knew, from the activity about us, that King Edward had made clear his pleasure concerning us. Eleanor with her personal household was to be conducted to honourable captivity – such is the phrase of those who lose all honour by enforcing it – at Windsor. Her brother and her knights were bound for imprisonment in Corfe castle until it should please Edward to release them. Helpless to protect Amaury and her fellows, Eleanor turned her mind to enlarging her permitted household to contain as many of us as she could. She fought for the friars, with good hope, since the orders command a degree of reverence, and most men prefer not even to seem to be oppressing the church. And she fought also for me, insisting that I was her clerk, and she could not be adequately looked after without me. Edward might still have known me at sight, and left me to rot. But the governor of Bristol did not know me, and my Latin and French being adequate

214

to convince him, he accepted her plea and added me to her company.

The day I was restored, which was the eve of our departure under strong guard for Windsor, she talked with me very gravely and intently. It seemed to me that she had lived a year's experience in one month, and grown taller, more serene and of greater authority, all the lines of her glorious face drawn finer and clearer as though challenge made her doubly alive.

'Samson,' she said, 'help me to understand, for I must know what is expected of me in order to be able to confound it, and what is believed of me if I am to refute it. Why has my cousin done this cruel and indefensible thing to me? He knows he has no right, law has no part in it. What does he hope to gain by imprisoning me? Or to prevent?'

I told her then what Amaury believed to be true, and what he had hinted to me when I came to Montargis. 'You realise how ill Edward may take this marriage?' In our crowded cells in Bristol he had elaborated on that theme with bitter venom.

'Your betrothal to Llewelyn was made by Earl Simon when those two were allies with the barons of the Provisions against the king's power. It was a very potent alliance, though it failed in the end for other reasons. Amaury believes Edward sees the accomplishment of the marriage now as a deliberate step towards reviving a baronial party, again allied to Wales, against the crown. That he sees you as the focal point of a dangerous rebellion aimed at his sovereignty and his life.'

She thought that over for some minutes in silence, and then shook her head with decision. 'I do not believe any sane man could entertain such a fear. It is ten years since the party of the barons was broken. What signs of life has it shown since? After the first disordered years of revenge, everything has been at peace, and everyone has been glad of it. If you raised the cry of de Montfort now, not one

215

magnate would rally to it. Not one! If I know it so clearly, Edward would have to be a little mad not to know it. He has nothing to fear from that quarter.'

'Amaury would say,' I told her, 'that on that subject Edward *is* a little mad. Especially since the death of Henry of Almain.'

'Yes,' she owned sadly, 'for that indeed he may hate us, but it surely gives him no cause to fear us. I could believe that he might strike against me for his revenge, if I was the nearest de Montfort. But out of genuine fear of some conspiracy against him...? Amaury believes this,' she said, considering. 'Do *you* believe it?'

'No. Edward is as shrewd a judge of possibilities as most men, he knows he is as firmly seated on his throne as any man who ever occupied that seat. He knows the old baronial cause is dead, he cannot be genuinely afraid of its revival. But he may very well use that as his pretext for what he wants to do.'

'And that is?'

'To break Llewelyn,' I said. 'To force him to concede everything, to swear fealty and do homage without guarantee of any recompense, any reaffirmation of the treaty, any correction of the present abuses. He has tried already with threats and demands, but he lacked a weapon terrible enough. Now he believes he has one.'

'So I am to be the means of bringing my husband to his knees in total submission, am I?' said Eleanor, opening her gold-flecked eyes wide. 'My cousin may even expect me to add my own pleas to his open threat. Does he know how long we have waited already, without being broken by worse threats than his? A year or two in Edward's prison I can bear. I could not bear it if Llewelyn so mistook me as to think I valued my freedom above his honour and dignity. If we had some means of getting word to him!'

I said that with patience and care, so we might have, once we were in Windsor, for the court must come there now and again, and even in the king's retinue there were quiet Welshmen like Cynan and his nephew, who had not forgotten their origins.

'If only I could send you back to him,' she said, 'I would, but I dread there'll be no chance of that. We shall be well guarded. I must deal as best I can. I could be angry, but anger is waste of time and passion, when it changes nothing.' And by some steely magic of her own she did abjure anger, she who was Earl Simon's daughter, and had inherited his scornful intolerance of the devious and unjust. She steered her solitary course with resolution and method, winning over one by one those persons who came into close contact with her, and who, from castellan down to turnkeys, had surely expected very different usage from her. As at Bristol, so at Windsor, when they brought us there, Eleanor conducted herself as would a state guest, gracious and gentle to all, with never complaint or mention of her wrongs, as though they fell beneath her notice. Nor was this course one merely of policy, for as she said, these simple people who brought her food, tended her fire and guarded the enclosed courtyard where her apartments were, were none of them blameworthy, but forced into this confinement as she was, and they deserved of her, and received always, the great sweetness of address and courteous consideration which were natural to her. It was not long before they began to love her.

Within the suite of rooms in that closed yard, the princess's household moved about freely, for it was a corner walled in every way, with but one gate in and out, and that strongly guarded. Escape was as good as impossible, unless someone among the guard should turn traitor, and there was no hope of that. There was a little patch of grass, wintry and bleached in that January weather, and a shrubbery and garden. Some care had been taken to ensure her comparative comfort while keeping a very fast hold of her. The comfort she acknowledged with grace, the precautions for her safe-keeping she never seemed to see. When she asked for a lute, they brought it, and also at her request, a rebec for me, since I had told her I could play the crwth, which is not so different. If she wanted books, they brought those, also. For freedom she did not ask, or appear to notice her deprivation. There was only one person to whom she would prefer that request.

She had her own chapel there, and was provided a chaplain, though she preferred the company and service of her own Franciscans. There she lived a confined and tedious life with her two ladies, and waited for Edward to acknowledge by his appearance in person the deed he had countenanced, and to demonstrate by his approach that he was not ashamed of it. I know that she wanted him to come, that even in such circumstances – in particular in such circumstances! – it was a discourtesy that he did not visit and face her after what he had done.

'He *must* come,' she said, reassuring herself when she doubted, 'he is too proud to shun the ordeal for ever and leave me to his underlings. He will get no ease until he has faced me. Neither shall I. I want to make plain to him, to his face, what I took care to tell his jackal the moment he seized me, that I am already a wife. Whatever Edward can alter, and spoil, and frustrate by keeping me caged here, he cannot undo my marriage.'

But it was two months and more before the court came to Windsor. We had no news all that time, we lived in a bubble cut off from the world, like all prisoners, and for us, seeing in what situation I had left Llewelyn in the autumn of the previous year, it was an anxious matter to have this sinister silence veiling all. Unknown to us, his envoys were still at the papal court, but Edward's ambassadors had followed them there hot-foot with a long *ex parte* account of the worsening relations between England and Wales, including the statement that the summons to Chester had been at Llewelyn's request and to suit Llewelyn's convenience, which I knew to be untrue, for it came quite unexpectedly, without consultation, and Edward had already broken off in advance all his pretences at making amends in the borders. Pope Gregory took the Welsh complaints seriously, and did intervene with Edward, advising further arbitration and deprecating any hasty action. But that was a year of misfortune in Rome, and in the first few months the pope fell ill, and died, and the resulting interregnum left Wales without a protector at the highest court in Christendom.

We were likewise ignorant that the king had again cited Llewelyn to go to Winchester to do his homage, late in January, at that very time when Master Derenne's crippled ship was limping into Bristol. Again the prince had replied that it was not customary to demand that he should go into England, that it was not safe for him, and that his council would not permit it. He had not then heard of the fate that had befallen Eleanor.

Edward's response was to summon the prince again at once, to appear three weeks after Easter, at Westminster, for which season and place a parliament had been called. Llewelyn as steadily repeated his conditions, and his refusal until they were met. But this time he did know of the gross offence offered to Eleanor, and wrote denouncing it, and demanding that she should be released and sent safely to him. If Edward had counted on forcing his submission by this means, he had judged very badly. It was impossible, after that monstrous illegality, for the prince to give way by one inch, or have any dealings with the author of such a crime but upon arrogantly equal terms of armed enmity, or finally with the sword in the field.

But none of this did we then know. And when, in mid-March, the bustle of great preparations and the coming and going of many officers about the castle of Windsor made itself heard even in our fastness, we stretched our ears and gathered what we could from the servants who attended Eleanor, and guessed that King

219

Edward was bringing his queen and his court to spend Easter there before parliament sat at Westminster.

'Now,' said Eleanor, 'he cannot slight me further by leaving me unvisited, as though he had had no part in bringing me here. He *must* come!'

Never until then had I known her to let her hunger and grief sound in her voice, and even then it was for no more than a moment, and she was almost ashamed of it, and flushed as she shook the weakness away from her. But I knew that her sorrow and longing were very great, as great as the acknowledgement she allowed them was small, and the crisis of meeting Edward face to face and maintaining her position was to her the first great step towards her ultimate victory, in which she never ceased to have faith.

From beyond our walls we heard bustle and haste, fanfares and music and commotion all that day, and in the evening the merry-making in the royal halls sent its echoes to us in waves on the wind, but no one came visiting to our island.

Not until the third evening did he come. She was pale with waiting then, and wanted to fill up the moments that brought no arrivals with whatever came to hand, for fear of their echoing emptiness. We were making music, she and I, and the girls with their sweet, light voices, playing and singing a French tune they knew well, I following by ear on the rebec, when the door of her parlour opened, and the doorway was filled with a man's giant shape. There had been so little noise, and we, perhaps, were making so much, that for some minutes we did not mark his entry, but went on with the song, and though that was honest, and not designed, yet it fitted very neatly with Eleanor's needs. Her head was bent with love over the lute, and her hands on the neck and strings were fleet, devoted and beautiful, when doubtless she should have been instantly at the king's feet with her mouth full of entreaties. By the time one of the girls observed him, and fell mute, we were close to the end of the refrain, and we three who were left finished it neatly, and looked up at one another, smiling, before we understood that we were observed, and by whom.

That was an ample enough room, though small as palaces go, and its doorway just large enough to let in giants. His thick brown hair scarred the stone of the arch above him, and his great shoulders filled the opening from side to side. That night he was all sombre brown and heavy gold, with a thin gold coronal in his curls because it was a festival, and he presiding in state. In these years of his maturity his features were large, heavy, smooth and handsome, with a monumental stillness when he was not in anger. Of grace he had none, but he had a grand, practised command over every part of his vast body that caused him to move majestically, and passed for grace. His drooping eyelid was very clear then, and shocking in its furtive meanness. I understand that I do him injustice, but I do so in the truth of what I saw. So did nature do but dubiously by him, marking him with this flaw. And perhaps she knew her business!

I never was so aware of the grand, wide honesty of Eleanor's eyes as when she laid aside her lute, that evening, and rose to meet him. Never so aware, and never so proud and glad. She barely came up to his breast, and she over-matched him with those great, golden eyes that mirrored to him, without any design of hers, his inescapable imperfection, where she was perfect.

God knows what he had expected, but whatever the expectation, she would always come as an astonishment. She made him the deep reverence due, as did we all, but he had eyes for nobody but Eleanor.

'I am glad,' she said, 'your Grace has the charity to visit your prisoners, since it is at your pleasure we are here. Your Grace's invitation to England would have been more appreciated if it had been rather more formally phrased.'

'Madam,' said the king, in some constraint, as well he

221

might be, considering the sting of her words and the sweetness of her voice, 'I much regret the necessity for putting you to this inconvenience.'

'So do I,' said Eleanor, 'and I have no possibility of amending it, but your Grace has that option, if you care to use it. It would be a much simpler matter to unlock the doors and lend me an escort and horses, than to commission Bristol pirates to seize me in mid-ocean. And I think it would be more likely to win you whatever it may be you want of me and mine.' Her voice was both brisk and serene. I would even say there was a faint, rueful smile in it.

'I did not come,' said the king, goodhumouredly enough, 'to ask your advice on policy, madam. I am sorry that you should be the victim in a matter in which you have been no more than the innocent tool, but I need you here as hostage for others less harmless than you, and here, I regret, you must reconcile yourself to staying until I can safely release you. I came, rather, to see for myself that you are in good health and spirits, and have everything you need for your comfort and maintenance.'

'I have not,' she said with emphasis.

'You have only to ask,' he said, and bethought him in time, and added with the surprising echo of her wry smile: '– within reason!'

'Mine is a request eminently reasonable,' said Eleanor, 'in a new-made wife. Nothing can ensure my comfort until you restore me to my husband. No!' she said in a sharp cry, seeing him open his lips to refuse her out of hand. 'Do not so simply dismiss what I am saying! This once let us talk like sensible cousins at odds about a matter which is subject to reason, and try to find where we can meet, and how we can dispose of those misunderstandings that divide us. You *are* my cousin. You used to call me so. You would not deny that I have never done you any wrong, nor wished you any. Whatever you may have against my house, do not make me the scapegoat, nor,

222

above all, read into my marriage any sinister designs that have no existence but in your thoughts. Sit down with me, cousin, and pay me the compliment of listening to me, for it is my life you are playing policy with now, and you have no right to use me as a chessman, no right to make or unmake my marriage, no right to tell me whom I shall love. You have might, and that is all. It would be better to use it sparingly, and let reason have its say, too. Then, if you withstand me, having heard my arguments, you need never hear them again, for I will never again ask of you what I am asking most gravely now.'

'I have nothing against you,' he said, reluctant but dazzled. 'I have said so. But I will not countenance this marriage until the prince of Wales has regularised his position, and done homage as my vassal.'

'You are not asked to countenance it,' she said calmly. 'God has already done that. You realise, do you not, that I *am* his wife?'

'The marriage is not yet consummated,' he said bluntly, 'and can be annulled. Indeed, cousin, you might even thank me some day for giving you the opportunity to think again. With your person, and your lineage ...'

She smiled then into his face, with a spark of real amusement. 'So might many a good Christian count or baron have whispered into the ear of *your* Eleanor, through all those five years or more she lived with you virgin as a child. Would you have liked that any better than I like your suggestion now? No, believe me, this marriage will never be undone by anything short of death. I promise you that. Come, now that you are here, give me twenty minutes of your time, drink wine with me, and listen. Then, if you are not moved, I am done.'

He gave in to her then, though with a guarded face and wary eyes. And certainly he did listen, and certainly he watched her steadily, and with both eyes wide open, too, which meant that he was shaken out of his common granite assurance, though there was no telling what the result

223

would be. And she, making her one great bid, the first and the last, to bring Edward to terms which should make a common future possible, used her marvellously pure and honest face and her lovely voice to charm and convince him, and wore out the very fibres of her heart in the effort. Even then I was curiously aware, without understanding fully, that she was fighting as much for Edward as for herself and Llewelyn. And, oh, if she could have triumphed then, she could have changed the world.

She told him exactly what her marriage meant, what it was and what it was not, how she had clung to her betrothed as a matter of faith pledged, how constantly Llewelyn, too, had sought to renew and complete the contract, not suddenly now, as a gesture of defiance against England or an attempt to revive a rebel faction, but year after year throughout, before ever Edward came to the throne, when Welsh relations with King Henry were at their best and most cordial, and it would have been lunatic folly to attempt or desire disruption. She showed him, beyond all rational doubt, that it was a match made out of mutual love and desire, and contained within it no dark designs to trouble the peace of any man, but concerned only two people in the world, and further, that to attribute to it such unworthy aspects was mortal insult to those two people, besmirching what was to them sacred, and multiplying for the future all the possibilities of misunderstanding and illwill. She told him what damage he had already done by his act of piracy and abduction. And then she showed him how by releasing her he could more than make amends, for she, of all people who might attempt it, was best equipped to undo the present wrong without revenges, and more, to interpret him to Llewelyn as now she was interpreting Llewelyn to him, with every hope of convincing each of the other's integrity, and bringing about a better-grounded future.

She had the eloquence of angels, and their immense, compelling gravity. I saw her father looking through her face. But she was talking to a monarch, not a man.

When she had done, and it could not have been better done, she was so drained that her face was whiter than snowdrops. He sat gazing at her still, and he said: 'That you are saying what you believe, that I grant. I never held you to blame for the use others might make of you. But I cannot accept your truth as justifying those behind you. You have lived a cloistered life, you know nothing of this rough world, or what men are capable of. I will say of Llewelyn that he could not have a better advocate. But I'll keep the weapon I have. I am sorry that you should be the sufferer. I will do what can be done to make your stay less irksome. If there is anything that can give you pleasure, ask for it.' He was rising as he said it.

'I have asked,' she said, 'and you have refused. I shall not ask again. There is nothing else you can offer me to compensate.'

He looked about the room as he crossed it, marking the lights, the furnishings, to see if anything was missing. 'You could have the freedom of Windsor,' he said unexpectedly, 'if you would give me your parole.'

Out of her languor and weariness she smiled. 'You are paying me half a compliment. Did you realise that?' It was true. When in his life before, or perhaps after, did Edward ever offer to accept a woman's parole? Or so much as realise that she might possess honour, as surely as a man? 'But only half,' she said, 'or you would know what my answer is. No, I will give you no parole. If I can escape you, I shall. But be easy, I shall use no murder, nor piracy, nor violence as the means.'

He did not wince at that. He was never ashamed of anything he did. But he did pause at the door to look at her again, with a kind of grudging wonder. 'Very well!' he said. 'Then I regret you must stay in close ward. A pity! You could have made your own lot so much easier.'

'Well, if you dare not let me out,' said Eleanor, 'you may let others in. I can be visited, if you trust your

225

castellan to use discretion. It would pass the time for me, and we may as well put on some show of civility. I do not intend to make my visitors listen to my grievances, your queen and her ladies need not fear, if they are so kind as to come and see me.'

'You shall not be neglected,' he said, 'while we are here.'

'And something else I can and will beg of you,' she said, 'and that is mercy for my people. Their only crime has been to follow me. If you will not release my knights, at least ease their captivity. And my brother....'

He cut in upon her there with a darkened face. 'Ask nothing for your brother! Keep to your own distaff, and leave the men of your house to me.' And he turned and went out from her without another word.

She sat for a long time tired and sunk deep in thought after he was gone. 'Strange!' she said. 'He *does* believe it! He is still afraid of us. He still hates us. He can credit the impossible, provided it discredits a Montfort. I fear I have done my lord a very ill favour by linking him in marriage with a woman of the house of Ganelon.'

Nevertheless, after that day she was visited, for the queen herself set the pattern, and it was certain that the queen did nothing without the king's leave and approval, more likely at his orders. Eleanor took the opportunities she was given, and set herself to win the good opinion of all those ladies who came to see her, and presently, having the management of her own household within her constricted quarters, herself began to invite and to entertain, to cast a cloak of normality about her unhappy position. Having her nature, it was hard indeed not to be liked. Before the Easter parliament was over, at which Llewelyn certainly sent by his envoys the same adamant reply, the same terms for his homage, and the same indignant demand for his wife's release, Eleanor had won over most of the women who frequented the queen's society, and made the queen herself a half-unwilling friend.

'If he cannot love us,' she said, 'at least let's see if I can make it harder for him to hate us.'

She kept her word, and never, to any of her visitors, said one word of complaint, or anything that could embarrass those who were free while she was captive. And Edward could not choose but know how gallantly and gently she bore herself, and with what arduous patience. But while I was there he did not come again.

Late in April, after the day Edward had appointed for Llewelyn's homage at Westminster was come and gone, as vainly as its predecessors, we had two other visitors, however, even less expected than Edward. There was a spell of mild, fair weather about that time, and as the little courtyard and garden were well sheltered but admitted the southern sun, we had carried out benches for the women to the grassy patch, and they were sitting there with the sweet spring light upon their embroidery, while Eleanor tried out softly upon the lute a tune she was making to a French love-song. Her two ladies bore captivity more lightly than she, living much as they would have lived anywhere. But she had lost flesh in her waiting, for all her gallantry, and the sweet, vivid face was closer every day to that glorious mask of bone and intellect I had first seen solitary among many, in prayer at St Frideswide's tomb in Oxford. Nor was her ordeal yet near its end.

The single gateway that admitted to our court clashed open while she was fingering out, with a private frown, a difficult vocal line, and marking its notation on a leaf beside her. She did not immediately notice, but I did, and looked round. Eleanor's chamberlain, old in the service of her mother, came trotting across to her from the portal, and stooped to her ear. She looked up, turning her head towards the gate, and she was smiling, and a little surprised. She laid the lute aside, and got up to meet her visitors. Under the stone archway David walked, stooping his head where the roof leaned low, and holding Elizabeth by the hand.

I never was more confounded, even knowing him as I knew him, which was to know that no man on earth could ever know him and be secure of what he knew. He had envied his brother, grown impatient with waiting for the succession, let himself be seduced into a dream of murder – I say a dream, for I do not know if ever he truly contemplated the reality – fled his brother's judgment, and from the shelter of Edward's shadow done his worst and bitterest to stamp out of existence any remnants of their feeling as brothers, avenging himself on David no less than on Llewelyn. And now he came visiting to his brother's wife, wronged and captive as she was, bringing his own most innocent, loving and bewildered child-wife as unwitting advocate for him in the approach. He came with a white, taut face, deep-eyed, solemn and brittle, most delicately groomed and dressed, David inviolate in his beauty, so clean after all his flounderings in and out of the mire, and so vividly coloured, the blue-black hair curving in blown sickles round his cheeks, and the raven lashes curling back widely from his harebell-blue eyes. He was near forty, and still he kept his wild, vulnerable face of a clever boy, and not one of his scars showed in him. Never, life-long.

And Elizabeth, herself immaculate in valiant innocence, went bravely with him wherever he led her, and never knew she was his armour against all threats, and namely the threats from his own nature and his own memories. While he clasped her hand, he could believe in himself as she believed in him, whether she understood or no. The sweet brown mouse with the shrill, child's laughter was grown into a woman now, a little thicker in the body, a little rounder in the face, mother of four children, still giving birth as neatly and smugly as a cat, and every bit as ready and protective of all her brood, including her spouse.

I never asked and cannot claim to know why he came, whether in pure curiosity to see what manner of woman

228

his brother had chosen, or to preserve a position of his own in balance between the courts of England and Wales, or whether in truth he felt compunction towards this girl who had never wronged him, and had no part in the tangled fury he felt towards Llewelyn, and desired at least to touch hands with her and exchange some human words, even if he could not avow his guilt and ask her forgiveness. I did not linger to hear, though I think it was a very formal and restrained visit, in which Elizabeth played the chief part. But what did flash into my mind at the first sight of them approaching was the use that I might make of them, and I stooped in haste to Eleanor's ear, and said to her:

'If she speaks of her children – and she will – ask her to come again and bring them to see you!'

Then I went away out of earshot, out of sight of them, for fear David should call too much attention to me, since so far I had escaped Edward's recognition, and passed simply for Eleanor's Welsh clerk. If Elizabeth came again with her children, in all likelihood so must Cristin come as their nurse, and so I should not only gain a spring of cool water for my eternal thirst, but with God's help get some word of what went on outside the walls, and send a message to Cynan.

I kept out of sight until they were gone, and then went to Eleanor, who sat looking after them very thoughtfully. 'So that is David,' she said slowly. 'Now was it at his wish they came here, or did she compel him to it out of the simple kindness of her heart? She was happy when I asked if I might see her children. She likes to give pleasure. And she will bring them. Now what is it you hope for from that?' And when I told her I hoped for a chance to send word out to be carried to Llewelyn in Wales, she quivered as a high-bred hound quivers, waiting for its release. 'Oh, if I could but tell him that I stand with him, that I have no regrets, that I ask nothing of him but to maintain his truth and his right, as I will mine here. Yes, it would be

229

worth anything. Better yet if I could send you safely back to him, you who know my mind better than any.'

I said I should be loth to leave her, but most vehemently she urged that he had the greater need of me, for hers here was but the passive part, and all she had to do was to refuse to be moved, while he had to sustain his country and his cause, even to the edge of war if need be. For to give way once to Edward was to be condemned to give way eternally. And she made me promise that if ever the chance offered, I would take it, as in duty bound to rejoin my lord.

After two days Elizabeth came again. The good weather still held, and Eleanor with her ladies was again in the garden, which began to seem very cramped and poor in that blossoming spring. The guard at our gate opened for Elizabeth without question. Clearly David was well installed in his old place at Edward's side, and Edward's bounty was paying for David's household. But he did not appear with his wife this time. She came in flushed and proud and glowing, with her two little girls dancing beside her, one clinging by either hand. The elder was then approaching five years old, the second turned three, and both as active and bright as butterflies. And behind this trio came in my Cristin, in a loose grey gown, bearing in her arms David's son and heir, Owen, then within two months of his second birthday. There was a third daughter left behind at home with the younger nurse, for she was only five months old, born in Shrewsbury.

Our eyes met the moment Cristin came in. It was always so. But I was aghast at what I saw, in spite of the radiance of her look, that told me there was no change within, for without she was so direly changed. She carried the little boy as lightly on her arm as once I had seen her carry a new lamb down from the hills of Bala, but her step was heavier and slower, and her face was fallen hollow and white, her eyes sunk deep within her head and the eyelids faintly puffy and soft, her lips also a little swollen. I could not move nor speak for dread that she was fallen gravely ill, and she so cut off from me and from all who knew her best, all but this child-woman Elizabeth, who lived only for her children, and did not seem to see the change in their nurse.

Eleanor and Elizabeth sat down together in the sun, and the two ladies-in-waiting came in haste to enjoy the novelty of the children, and began an animated game with them on the grass. Elizabeth held out her arms for her son, and Cristin gave him to her. With a flash of her eyes Eleanor signalled to me that I had my freedom and opportunity, for she could very well hold this little group together and happy.

Cristin drew back from them gently, and turned and walked with me, away beyond the shrubs and bushes, into the cool of the ante-room. I watched her poor, fallen face and ached for her. Even when we sat down together, we who for years had so seldom been alone with our love, for a while I could not speak. Then I got out in dread:

'What is it with you? Are you ill?'

'No,' she said, and smiled, and even her smile was pain. 'No, not ill. Listen, Samson, for we may not have long. I am charged with a message to you. You have friends here, others besides me. They have a plan to bring you safely away out of this place, and home to Wales. If you will go? Will you go? We dare not attempt more. Her they will never let out of these walls, nor out of their sight. You they may.'

I told her then what had been in my own mind, to get word to Cynan that might be sent on to Llewelyn, in reassurance at least that his wife was heart and soul with him in his stand, and desired him to make no concessions for her. But I knew, even without Eleanor's urging, that if the chance offered to get back to him I must take it, all the more as the clouds gathered more ominously.

'One will come to the governor, while the court is still here in Windsor,' said Cristin, 'with the request to borrow

231

you, as being fluent in Welsh and versed in Welsh law, to copy some documents for David. Oh, never fear, David's seal will be available, and David is so close to Edward, no one will question it. There will be horses waiting for you at a safe place.'

'And leave some poor soul to answer for stealing or copying David's seal?' I said, doubtful. 'Or bring David himself into suspicion?'

'No need,' she said. 'Your guide is coming with you. He also is Welsh, and if there is to be fighting, he wills to be home and fighting beside his own people. No one else will come into suspicion.'

'No one but you,' I said. 'You could suffer for me. Who else could have brought me this message?'

'No,' she said, shaking her head. 'You need not fear for me. I am strongly protected, no one will point at me. I wish to God I could ride with you, Samson, as once we rode together to Llewelyn, but I can no more go and leave her now than I could when he brought us to the border, all in innocence, and only then let me see where we were bound. Now we go armed, David and I, enemies bound by a truce. But whatever evil he may have done, he will not let any harm come to me. I am the cross that dangles before his conscience, I am the voice saying: Repent! He cannot do without me, he would be lost.'

Her voice was soft and wild, and her low laughter very bitter. I asked her: 'Was it he who warned Edward, and had him send pirates to seize our ships at sea? Is that also to his account?'

'No,' she said, 'that was not David. That word came from Brittany, while you waited for the good winds. Hard to keep secret the passage of such a party, and Edward has his spies everywhere. Do not put down to David more than his due, his load is heavy enough. He can see no end now but destruction for himself or Llewelyn, he feels himself far past forgiveness. Now he wants to bring on the ruin he foresees, to pull down the house over himself or wipe

232

his brother out of the world and try to forget him. Since there's no going back, he is frantic to complete what he has begun. If I left him, there would be no one who knows the truth, no face that has only to appear before him to remind him of the judgment. David needs me even more than she does. It would be hard for me to leave him.'

I said again, for her voice was so low and grievous, and her face so burning with white despair: 'Cristin, something has happened to you! You are ill!'

'No,' she said, 'I am quite well. Will you go, Samson? Promise, for my sake! I want you free, and far away from here.'

I promised, for she clung so to my hand, and her hollow eyes devoured my face with such longing. 'Yes, I will go. Whatever you wish I will do, but don't ask me to go from you gladly. And you so changed, so pale and strange! If it is not sickness, it is worse. For God's sake, do not keep it from me! Something terrible has befallen you....'

She heaved a great, shuddering sigh, and clasped her hands under her breasts. 'Yes, something has befallen me indeed. I did not want to own it, I did not want you to know, but it is written in my face, and you'll get no rest now for thinking and dreading. He has found a way at last of avenging himself on you and on me. So simple it was, and yet he never thought of it before! He, who fell into bed beside me and snored the night away dreaming of all his other women, suddenly he grasped what would most surely destroy me, and strike you to the heart. Since we came to England he has never let me alone, night after night after night with his hate and glee and pride in his cleverness.'

She stood up abruptly beside me, and spread her arms wide, to show how her girdle was tied high under her bosom, and her body gently swollen under the grey woollen gown.

'Do you not see what God and Godred between them have done to me? I am four months gone with child!'

233

CHAPTER IX

In this desolate situation I was forced to leave Windsor –
my lord threatened, my lady captive, my love pregnant
with Godred's monstrous progeny, a dagger, not a child,
begotten in hate and despite. Ever since he married her,
for policy and establishment like most marriages, he had
slighted and misprized her, now he persecuted her with his
attentions only to poison and kill both her and me. She
said to me before she left me, with a calm more terrible
than her desperation: 'I will never bear any child but
yours!' But I knew, and so did she, that she could not harm
the life within her, however she shrank from it in horror.
She would bear it and she would care for it, and Godred
would gloat as he watched her wither, and the incubus
devour her, and savour the thought of me eaten alive in
Wales by the same disease. Above all, what cruelty to the
child, to create it out of hatred and cherish it out of malice,
making it a death before ever it lived, when she could so
deeply have loved a child engendered in kindness. And
even worse if he came, in his own way, to love and value
it for the damage it had done on his behalf.

So judge in what anguish I went to my duty.

I told no one. I was tempted for a while to entrust
Eleanor with that whole story, and pray her to stand friend
to Cristin if by any means she might, for her heart was
great enough to find room for the miseries of others, even
when it might well have been full of her own. But I did
not do it. There was no possibility of confiding Cristin's
secrets, her darkness and her need, to any other soul, so

passionately were they hers. So I was compelled to let her carry that burden alone.

Duly they came for me, early in one of the first evenings of May, a young servant in David's livery, bearing a written request with David's seal, begging leave to borrow the services of the Welsh clerk, for some intricate copying that required knowledge of both Welsh and English law, since he had only his immediate household with him on this visit, and had left his own law-men in Shrewsbury. Clearly David's demand, thus proffered, was almost as good as Edward's order, it being assumed without question that he had Edward's sanction and approval for everything he did. And a clerk is no great matter, and hardly likely to risk breaking loose on his own when he can sit comfortably enough, even in a virtual prison, under the protection of his lady's name. So nobody made any bones about asking Eleanor's leave, which she graciously gave, and for the first time since entering Windsor, I passed that iron gate that sealed off the princess's prison.

The last look I had from her, shining and private like a blessing, went with me down through the town beside my guide, and across the river to the house where David was lodged.

There was nothing difficult in our escape, because no one was hunting us. We simply rode out of Windsor towards the north-west, briskly and confidently as though we were on approved business, and were never questioned until we reached Wales, though we pressed hard at first, and rode well into the night, lodging having been prepared for us at a grange near Oxford. There we slept out the rest of the dark hours, and went on with fresh mounts in the dawn.

'We can be easy enough,' said my companion contentedly. 'No one will have missed you, not yet. The castellan will think you are detained overnight on David's business, and I take it your lady will make no mistakes, know nothing and say nothing?'

235

I said he might rely on that. He was from Lleyn, and had been homesick, he said, ever since he had been fool enough to cross the English border in David's train, and was main glad now to be going home, where he belonged. If there was to be fighting, as everyone seemed to expect, it was not for Edward of England he wanted to fight.

I asked after Cynan, and whether he had made proper preparation to defend his own innocence if suspicion should fall his way. But my companion did not even know the name, and was surprised at the question. Then who, I asked, were his fellows in my rescue, and who had arranged access, in any case, to David's seal, since that could hardly be Cynan's work.

He looked at me along his shoulder, and considered how much to tell me. 'His orders were that you were not to know, but I thought you must have guessed it. The Lord David's seal will have been mislaid somewhere about his household, where anyone -- meaning your servant here! -- might have got hold of it, and in due time it will be found again, no doubt very convincingly. He wants none of his people implicated, you need not fear. I am the scapegoat, once I'm safe in Wales, and I shall have no objection to that! But as to how it was planned – why, the simplest way possible. Who do you think affixed David's seal to the request for you, if not David?'

It was not the surprise it might have been, once I accepted it. It fitted still with that image I had of him, for ever torn, so that in England, when he had cast in his lot there, half at least of his heart fought for Wales, and in Wales a hundred ties of almost equal potency drew him back towards England, and never, never could he be content anywhere, and never could he be faithful, because faith to one land was treason to the other.

'Then all this is his work? The relay of horses, the night's lodging, all?' I thought of Cristin, who had wanted me away from her, very far away where I could not see her anguish or be a tormented witness of the birth she dreaded, and I could believe that David had had her, too, in mind. For there were some for whom he had always a kindness, and to them, after his fashion, he was faithful.

'All his,' said the young man. 'Playing one hand against the other for plain wantonness, or wishing himself back where he can never go again – who knows? But if that was it, he'd grudge it to us – and it was he offered me the chance, and only smiled on the wrong side of his face when I jumped at it. He's snug enough there at the king's elbow, and has picked the stronger side, on the face of it. But it's my belief he'd change with you and me if he could.'

God knows he may have been right. Certain it is that David had deliberately extracted me from Edward's grip and restored me to Llewelyn, to the old land and the old loyalty, into which he was certain he himself could never enter again.

Llewelyn was at Rhydcastell when we came there after that journey, late in May. We were barely dismounting and leading our jaded horses into the stable-yard, when someone must have run to him with the news, where he was newly in himself from riding, and stripped to shirt and chausses, for it was an early summer, and hot there between the hills. He came out in haste, his bared breast russet-brown, and the small lines of thought and frowning graven into his brow in ivory against the sunburned gold, which the bleached brown of his clipped beard did no more than outline in a single shade darker. The marks of the summer were on him, but the marks of the winter, too. Not all Edward's harassment, not all the border malice of the marchers, operating with their master's tacit approval, could have honed down the lines of that bold, bright face to this fine-drawn carving, or put the first traces of grey in his hair, either side the brow. He was fretted for Eleanor, as she for him. Those two had never yet seen each other in the flesh, and they were pared away to spirit and longing for love.

He cried: 'Samson!' in a shout of joy, and came to embrace me, and of his gladness I was so glad as to be shaken almost to tears. 'I thought I had sent you to your death,' he said. 'You are whole and free, thank God, you at least! Come in with me and tell me all you have to tell, let me know the best and the worst, for I am starved. No man of mine could get any true word or any comfort in Westminster. I have begged in vain, and thundered in vain, they would tell us nothing but that he has her, and all her company. You, too, Samson! And now you are here! If I can accept a first miracle, so I can believe in a second!'

I told him in a breath what seemed to matter most. 'She is well, and unshaken, and sends her true mind by me. I am here with her blessing and at her wish.'

He laid his arm about my shoulders, and turned suddenly in revulsion from going within, and haled me away instead into the fields, to a high, grassy knoll that looked down upon the valley, and there we lay in the rich green grass together, in the scent of the little spicy pink flowers of pimpernel and centaury, and the sweet air of freedom. And I was grateful to him for this blessing, that we had no walls about us, no listeners, no echoes. Under that sky it was possible to believe in the victory of truth, and the reunion of divided lovers.

There I told him all that melancholy and angry history, from first to last, dredging up for him out of my memory every look and every word of Eleanor's, and indeed not one was ever forgotten. And it was like the sudden bliss of steady and gentle rain upon a great drought, slaking the thirsty soil, setting the sap flowing in new life, filling the world with a young, green sweetness in which all the flowers of hope burst into bud. He lay with his chin in his hands, and listened, sometimes asking a quick question, perhaps only to imagine again her voice repeating its calm and queenly defiance.

'Whatever he may hold against me,' he said, not angrily but heavily, 'whatever suspicions he may have of me, it was vile to make her the victim, and viler to try to use her as a weapon. And I tell you, Samson, when first I got word of it, I was in two minds, and if I had been a free man I should have massed all my power in one great thrust, hopeless or not, as much to destroy him as to deliver her. But I am not free to be senselessly brave and throw my life and all away. I hold Wales in my hands, this land I have half-made into a nation, and cannot abandon now. It is hers as well as mine, but most of all it is the hope of the future, of my sons by her, and of other men's sons, every soul who speaks the Welsh tongue has rights in it. I have not had long enough!' he said, drumming his fist tormentedly against the thick grass. 'It is not made, but only making! If I had had ten years more, if King Henry had lived ten years longer, this danger need never have been. But I have not had long enough! Not long enough to wipe out all those centuries of disruption.'

'You could not have delivered her,' I said, 'you could only have fallen helpless into Edward's hands, which is what he wants, for if you fall, Wales falls.'

'I know it!' said Llewelyn. 'It would have been folly to abandon the way of law for the way of war. My envoys are still at the papal court, waiting for a new appointment now Gregory is dead. God rest him, he did his best for us. I have sent further letters. The new pontiff will know from the first of Edward's crime. I had complaints enough before, now this becomes my chief and first complaint, and manifestly just. No, it would have been mad to rush to arms, I should have destroyed my own case, for I take my stand on the treaty, which he wants broken and discarded. If he could goad me into being the one to shatter it, he would have won. But, oh, it was hard not to fight for her!'

I said: 'She is of your mind. You cannot yield now, not by a single point. The terms you stand on are just, and you have offered homage according to treaty and custom.'

'I have done more,' said Llewelyn, half enraged with himself even for that. 'I have offered to take the oath of fealty to his envoys, if he will send them to me, to satisfy him until we can agree on a safe place to meet for homage. He has refused. He stands absolutely on my total submission, and my consent to attend wherever he summons me. I stand absolutely on seeing the treaty honoured and reaffirmed, its breaches repaired, and my wife sent to join me, before I will take the oath or lay my hands in his. It is deadlock. This one concession I offered, to break it, and he refuses. I shall make no more. I shall not offer that again.'

'She above all,' I said, 'understands the necessity for standing fast against him. "I could not bear it," she said to me, "if Llewelyn so mistook me as to think I valued my freedom above his honour and dignity. I ask nothing of him," she said, "but to maintain his truth and his right." If you once give back an inch, he will press you back again and again, toe to toe, and give you nothing in return.'

'I confess,' said Llewelyn, brooding, 'I still do not understand him. He was not always so with me. Why this stony enmity now?'

'It is the first touch of resistance,' I said, 'that turns Edward mad. What does not move at his thrust, even if it mattered nothing to him when first he laid hand on it, becomes to him the total enemy, and he cannot rest until he has hurled it out of his path and ground it to powder under his feet.'

'He should sooner have practised on Snowdon,' said Llewelyn grimly, 'than on Eleanor and me.'

Afterwards I told him, when what most mattered was done, what I had until then withheld, and he pointedly

240

had not asked, who it was who had won me out of Windsor.

'So I supposed,' said Llewelyn drily. 'He had always a kindness for you, in spite of all the times he used you ill. It is the one thing that still does him honour. As for me, I have been through this to-and-fro of his once too often. David is dead to me.'

But concerning Cristin I did not tell him anything, not because I grudged him the half of my load as I would have given him the half of my joy, but for a simpler reason that confounded me more. For when I opened my lips to speak of her, my throat closed, and I had no voice. So I accepted the judgment of God, and held my peace.

In the months that followed Llewelyn manned his borders, fended off the offences that grew with every week, and steadily sent complaints, with details, times, witnesses, in every case that came to his notice. To Rome he sent again to remind the new pope, whose election we awaited with hope and anxiety, of the utterly illegal detention of Eleanor, and all the other, lesser wrongs which defaced the treaty relationship between the two countries. And at the beginning of July we heard, with great joy, which of the candidate cardinals had been elected. He had taken the name of Adrian, as he had been the cardinal of St Adrian, but we knew him by another name.

'They have chosen Ottobuono,' cried Llewelyn, understandably elated, 'Ottobuono Fieschi. The very man who made this treaty, and took pride in it. He was our friend then, and laboured honestly for us. Praise God, we have a friend there who knows every article of the document he himself fashioned. He will not let it be repudiated.'

We rejoiced indeed, with what seemed to us good reason, knowing this to be a man of incorruptible goodwill, and knowing that he understood as well as we did the importance of the treaty he had worked out at the end of the barons' war. We rejoiced too soon. He was all we believed him, but he was also old and frail. That was a year of deaths. Before August was out, when he had been pope but one month, Adrian the Fifth died.

Wales was again left friendless. There came in a Spanish pope, with a great reputation for learning, and having a progressive and forceful mind, or so we heard, but one that knew nothing of us, and had never set foot in these islands, much less played any part in bringing them to an arduous and equitable peace. I do believe Pope John listened, and did his best to hold a balance, but it was Edward who first got his ear, and Edward, crusader, vassal of France, king of England, duke of Gascony, was universally known, and carried weight in every court of Europe and the east. It would have needed a voice more peremptory than the thunder of God to shout him down.

I do not see what Llewelyn could have done in that year that he did not do, to make known the true state of the case. In April, while I was still captive in Windsor, the dean and chapter of Bangor had written to the archbishop of Canterbury, repeating the full facts of the conspiracy of David and Griffith against the prince's life, as Owen had confessed them, so that Archbishop Robert should not be able to plead ignorance of the crime and criminals that Edward was harbouring, and the seriousness of the breach of treaty that that protection constituted. In June Llewelyn himself also wrote to the primate, who had urged him to keep the peace in the march, pointing out how frequent were the disturbances of that peace caused by English attacks, now so constant and apparently so organised as to amount to a state of war. In July, again, he sent a complaint that his men, going on their lawful business to the fairs and markets of Montgomery and Leominster, had been robbed of their goods, and some hundred or more imprisoned, and one at least killed, and that the marchers made no secret of their intent to continue such seizures, in defiance of the treaty.

'Even if we cannot get justice now,' he said, 'at least we'll make sure the truth is on record, for other and less prejudiced minds to judge. For I'm sure Edward never writes one word of cherishing my traitors and assassins, or seizing my wife, but only and always that he has summoned me to do homage and I have refused him. And not even that is true.'

Long afterwards Cynan told me of the letter Edward wrote to Pope John in September of that crisis year, when I am certain he had already not merely made up his mind to resort to war, but actually set the machines of war secretly in motion, before ever he got his desired condemnation of Llewelyn from his parliament. What Llewelyn had guessed at was accurate enough. There was not one word of any offences on the king's side. David and Griffith might not have existed. He wrote only of the homage refused, and then charged all the border clashes to the prince's account. You would not have known from those despatches, said Cynan, that there was in the world, much less in Edward's prison at Windsor, a lady who was princess of Wales by right.

Llewelyn made one more reasoned attempt to forestall fate, but reason had little say left in this dissension, except the cold reason of Edward's resolution on conquest. The prince again sent envoys to the Michaelmas parliament, bearing letters offering fealty and homage on the terms due by treaty, and not otherwise. What Edward claimed he most wanted, Edward was offered, upon terms which did no violence to justice or to his rights, as he was doing violence to the rights of others. But this was not absolute submission, and that was the only answer he would consider.

He took the last step, and took it deliberately and coldly. He called a full council of his chief prelates and magnates, and demanded and obtained from them the unanimous judgment that the prince's petition should not

243

be heard, but that the king should go against him as a rebel and a disturber of the peace. The marches were to be put into a state of immediate defence – defence, being, of course, Edward's word – and the feudal host was summoned to muster on the day of St John the Baptist of the following summer, at Worcester.

These formal orders, being promulgated during that parliament, were common knowledge, and our envoys brought the news back with them. What lay behind we had to estimate for ourselves, for certainly Edward would not sit still through the winter.

'This is no threat of war to come when the host gathers,' said Llewelyn. 'It is war now, and I fear we shall soon learn it. If he times his muster thus for midsummer, half a year away, he means to have a good part of his work done for him before ever he takes on that expense. This will be every marcher lord for himself, with a free hand to raise what forces he can and take what land he can. And we with a long and uneasy border, laced with the lands of small chiefs who may well fear to be squeezed between two rocks, and rush to take cover behind the greater. We have seen it so often before!'

In council and in camp, travelling the length of his land before the worst of the winter set in, he was resolute, cheerful and practical, improving wherever possible on the dispositions he had already made. But I know, who was always beside him, how his heart was eaten with foreboding and grief over those two springs of his life, Eleanor and Wales.

'We'll still keep plying him with approaches,' he said grimly, 'as long as it's safe for bishop or clerk to travel into England, and as long as he'll issue safe-conducts. He shall not be able to say it was I who broke off all contact. I have never sought to avoid my obligations to him, but only when he performs his part will I perform mine. That I'll keep repeating as long as I can get an envoy within earshot of him. Whether he'll listen is another matter. I

244

think his ears have been stopped all this year, if truth were told.'

I thought so, too, but if continued diplomatic missions could postpone action even for a few weeks more, we should have our ally, winter, on the doorstep, and frost and snow might hold back what Edward certainly would not curb willingly. And all the council agreed with the prince's consistent messages, patiently repeating that this war was not to the purpose, that right should be done on both sides, and could not be one-sided. But Llewelyn had long ceased to believe in any success from reasoning.

'If I am to pay now,' he said to me once, as we looked out from the walls of Dolforwyn across the Severn towards Montgomery, 'for what I failed to do for Earl Simon, God grant I may not be asked to pay it through his daughter!'

As for me, at this time I was torn so many ways that there was no rest for me night or day, for not only was I racked with all the cares that oppressed my lord, and troubled deep by the recollection of what Eleanor's distress must be, on his behalf rather than her own, but also I could not get out of my mind, waking or sleeping, the thought that the tale of Cristin's months was come to an end, and somewhere far from me, perhaps in Chester, where we heard David had taken his men to join the garrison, the time of her labour was come upon her, and she already turned forty years old, and bearing her first child, in peril of her life and of her peace, in hatred and despite, in fear and loathing, poisoning what should have been a youthful joy. And she was mine, heart and soul mine, and I would have died for her, and I could do nothing to help her.

We kept Christmas but poorly and on the move that year, for the most part at Dolforwyn and in the marches of Salop, where Llewelyn thought well to draw in from certain outlying lands to shorten his line, rather than lose men to the forces from Montgomery and Oswestry, which were already skirmishing along the river valley. Before we left that castle we received a rider who had made his way through the English patrols and swum the river with his horse to get to us, and came weary, draggled and muddy into Dolforwyn, but vigorous and grinning still. And that was the young clerk Morgan, Cynan's nephew.

'You must forgive me, my lord,' he said, when we had fed him and given him dry clothes, and brought him to Llewelyn, 'that I bring no letters. What I bring you I carry in my head this time, and it's my head I risked to bring it. My good uncle has taught me a long list of what the king has in hand for Wales. Will you hear it?'

And he delivered it word for word as he had learned it. How Edward had set up three commands along the march, the first at Chester, where the earl of Warwick was commander, with David as his lieutenant, the second here opposing us in the middle march, under Roger Mortimer, and the third in the south, where Pain de Chaworth commanded from Carmarthen. The king's own standing corps of knights and troopers was divided between the central and southern commands, and the commission of all three commanders was to collect supplies, recruit foot-soldiers wherever they offered, and above all, to receive local Welsh princes to the king's peace, offering them protection in the future for their defection, should England and Wales again come to terms. And protection meant that once they had pledged their fealty to Edward, out of natural fear, that fealty should be retained in any agreement afterwards.

'They are issuing proclamations inviting all the small men along the march to get out of the line of battle,' said Morgan very earnestly, 'and some are wavering, and may well fall. This is the king's first weapon, he will use it to the full, and even spend to make it effective. When the lion roars, even well-bred hounds, of good gallantry, take to the bushes.'

'Small blame to them,' said Llewelyn ruefully, 'when they have no better training yet. I have seen it coming, friend, I know what I face.'

'And further, my lord, my uncle bids me tell you that the king has sent overseas for war-horses, he is buying more than a hundred in France. He has sent to Gascony for crossbowmen, and approached the king of France to allow the shipping of men and horses from Wissant to England. In December he sent out writs for the feudal levy, for the first day of July, at Worcester. As to the bowmen from Gascony, this is but the beginning. He will get more. And he is furbishing all the ships of the Cinque Ports fleet for sea service.'

He drew breath, after so much talking of matters learned by heart, a ruddy, well-made young man, bringing with a good heart news that might be bad or good to us, according as we made use of it. 'I am finished, my lord, I know no more.'

'We're bound to you for your trouble,' said Llewelyn, smiling at him, 'and something troubled because we are bound. You did very well by us in getting here. But how can we ensure that you get back as safely?'

'Never fret for that, my lord,' said Morgan cheerfully. 'I am not going back. My uncle does not expect me. I am a Welshman, and I can use sword or lance, as you please to employ me. I have come to add one more, for what he's worth, to the forces of Wales.'

With a full heart the prince made it clear to him that his worth was as great as his welcome was warm, and prayed that Cynan, who remained behind to bear the possible vengeance for his nephew's defection, had made provision for his own safety.

'It was he who bade me go freely,' said Morgan, 'and he can very well take care of himself, he is not answerable for my follies, and has my leave to disown me as hard as he will. He said he might yet be of service where he is,

247

now that he has made his choice, and of messengers God will provide at need.'

Such crumbs of honest comfort and gladness we had, and not a few. But those who thus came to join us at the risk of their lives were the poor and landless, who had nothing but their lives to lose. With those minor chieftains, especially those who inherited but little by reason of having many brothers, it was another story, and we knew from the beginning that it must be so. The smaller their patrimony, the less possible was it for them to raise men enough to defend it by force, and Wales was but a word still, there was hardly one among them who was prepared to let go of a commote in the borders in order to help his neighbours inland to preserve the heart of a country.

Before the year ended, Mortimer had raised so great a force at the king's pay at Montgomery, and had so many added companies from Lestrange and Clifford and Corbet, all with lands there to enlarge, that we were pressed back in a number of skirmishes from the borders of Salop, and soon they were encroaching into Powys. Griffith ap Gwenwynwyn had naturally remained sitting hungrily there on the fringes of his own lost lands when David went to join the earl of Warwick at Chester, and was more eager even than the king's own men to recruit and mass supplies, and push the advance into southern Powys, to get back his own, however justly forfeit. And before the first month of that year twelve hundred and seventy-seven was over, the earl of Lincoln had brought a strong force to join Mortimer's command, and they were rolling us back far into Powys, and setting up Griffith again in his lordship of Pool, though as a vassal holding from the king, a mere baron of England.

Wherever Llewelyn himself fought, the fortunes of the conflict were stayed, at least for a time, the magic of his presence was such, but he could not be everywhere, and when his back was turned the faint-hearted began to count their chances after the old manner.

'It begins,' said Llewelyn grimly, when we heard of the first defector in Maelor, and he left the middle march as well held and supplied as he might, and went north to try to secure other waverers in the parts near Chester. He also sent his last embassage to Edward, who still graciously gave safe-conduct, to preserve his own appearance of patience, though with no intention of listening, to present once again his offers of terms to avert out-and-out war. The only response was Archbishop Kilwardby's commission to his brother of York, certainly at Edward's direct order, to pronounce sentence of excommunication against the prince, and this was done. It meant little in practical terms to us in Wales, but it did express Edward's final and absolute refusal to listen to any terms but abject surrender, or consider himself longer to have any human obligations to the rival he desired to overthrow.

As for the progress of this war that was not yet officially a war, the king's strategy during the period of preparation was clear. He reserved his use of the feudal host for the final blow, and spent the months between in such a campaign of recruitment and reinforcement as had never been used against us before. His officers built up, chiefly at Chester, but also at Montgomery and Carmarthen, great reserves of food, arms and horses, and provisions of all kinds, and also took on large numbers of men at royal pay both as workmen and soldiers. Thus while no war had begun, from three bases, widely spaced, three considerable armies were gnawing away, as opportunity offered, great pieces of Welsh land, and either turning them over to marcher barons to be held and garrisoned, or fortifying them for the crown. At the same time crown officers were busy proclaiming, as Morgan had foretold, Edward's willingness to receive Welsh chiefs to his peace upon favourable terms.

Now this may seem to be invitation only to cowards and traitors, but indeed it is not necessarily so, and

Llewelyn never quite condemned those who succumbed. Consider the position of such a one as Madoc of Bromfield, one of four brothers, whose lands south of Chester jutted perilously into English territory, being surrounded more or less on three sides, and situated between two very strong English bases. Such a promontory of Welsh ground he could not defend against the crown forces alone, nor could the support of his overlord long maintain it. He had a choice between fighting for it until he was driven back out of it or killed in the fighting, abandoning it and withdrawing with all his forces to join Llewelyn and make a stand further west, or else accepting the king's offer and transferring his allegiance in order to keep his lands. He need not thereupon promise also to fight on Edward's side – though some did – it was enough if he ceased to fight against him. And to make his choice in this dire situation such a young man had only the guidance of a long past of holding and preserving a man's own small principality, a tradition barely changed as yet by Llewelyn's proffered vision of a Welsh nation. It was no great wonder that so many, in the most dangerous and exposed positions, gave way and made their peace. What was wonder was that so many stood out, and refused the bait.

Thus in the month of January both Madoc and his brother of the region south of Dee sued to Chester that they might retain and enjoy their lands unmolested if they came to the king's peace, and David and the earl of Warwick received them into fealty.

Further south, in Brecknock, the earl of Hereford, who had for so long been preferring claims to certain lands held, and acknowledged as being held, by Llewelyn, raised a large force on his own account, and turned the war to his own advantage by possessing himself of those lands before he began at leisure to make his preparations to join the king's muster. It was because of the strong pressure just to his north, from Mortimer and the earl of Lincoln, that he was able to manage this with so little effort, for we were fully occupied on the Severn. And still further south, along the Towy, the royal forces from Carmarthen under Pain de Chaworth began a great drive up the river. And here they were assured in advance of one willing ally. Rhys, the son of Meredith ap Rhys Gryg, Llewelyn's sometime ally and later unrelenting enemy and unwilling vassal, held the castle of Dryslwyn and the lands about that part of the river, and he had been very quiet and careful up to this time, islanded as he was among the sons of Rhys Fychan, the prince's nephews, who were fiercely loyal. But when Pain drew near with a considerable force, Rhys ap Meredith very pliantly bargained for terms, was promised he should hold his lands as before once the war was over, if he would but swear fealty to the king and allow them to be used as a royal base while fighting lasted, and closed very happily with that offer. He was, I think, of all those many who deserted Wales, the only one who deserted gladly, having inherited his surly old father's quarrel.

With Dryslwyn secured, the command in the south could take its time about subduing the other princes along the Towy. Llewelyn had no opportunity to go to their aid, for he was fully occupied in the north, making fast his line against the threat from Chester.

We had left the castle of Dolforwyn well garrisoned and provisioned, and its position was strongly defensible, but one thing we could not ensure for them. By fatal chance that was an early spring almost without rain or snow, a circumstance that not only negated many of our defences by marsh and river, but also dried up the well at Dolforwyn. Llewelyn said bitterly that the error was his, that he should have made better trial of the water supply before he placed a castle there, but the season was unusually dry, and once the combined forces of Mortimer and Lincoln had moved up the Severn valley to the siege, the castle could not long hold out, nor could we come to their relief. Early in April the garrison surrendered. So brief a history this castle had, and so tragic, full of contention, deceit, warfare and loss.

At no time during this winter and spring did the royal forces strike any direct blow at Gwynedd itself, the heartland of Llewelyn's power. No, their efforts were all directed at gnawing away the edges of his outlying lands, and lopping away from him one by one the lesser princes who supported him, thus denying him, when the time came, both men and bases outside his own hereditary principality. But in other and more devious ways they struck close to home. In May an indignant page-boy, who had overheard talk not meant for his ears, came rushing to Tudor with what he had gleaned. Rhys ap Griffith ap Ednyfed, who was a nephew of the high steward and a trusted bailiff of the prince, had sent a petition to the king from Llewelyn's very court, seeking the royal peace for himself and his brother, and what the boy had overheard was their agreement on flight, for they had actually received Edward's safe-conduct, and were making ready to use it. Tudor, in shame and anger, had them both seized and securely held before he broke this bitter news to Llewelyn. Instead of riding into Chester with the king's letter, they were thrown into the prince's prison, and kicked their heels there in discontent for the rest of the year. So close did treason come.

It was then drawing near the day of the king's muster, his various companies already beginning to gather at Worcester. But as the term of feudal service is short, and he would have to revert afterwards to paid levies – though we had reason to believe that he preferred them – Llewelyn estimated that he would move north in arms from Worcester as quickly as possible, and make Chester his base, to strike at once at the prince's main stronghold. We were at Ruthin, with outriders stationed at intervals along the border to bring us early news of any movements, when a company of men rode in from the south, having travelled by way of Cymer and Bala, and the two young men who

led them were brought in to where Llewelyn sat with
Tudor and his captains in council. At sight of them he
rose with an astonished cry, quicker to recognise them
than were the rest of us, for they were stained and dusty
and unkempt with hard and hasty riding. The younger
flung himself first into the prince's arms, and then at his
feet, and clung to his hands and kissed them. And then
we saw that it was the youngest of the prince's nephews,
his namesake and godson, Llewelyn ap Rhys Fychan, and
the other was his brother Griffith.

'My lord,' blurted the boy, half in tears, and still with
his face pressed against Llewelyn's hands, 'we are come to
join you, to fight beside you. We have brought you all
the best we could gather. There's no other home or place
for us, now. The south's lost – Dynevor, Carreg Cennen,
Llandovery – all lost! The king's officers have taken them
to make another Carmarthen, a crown stronghold. And
our brother – our brother...' He was choked with tears
and swallowed fiercely to clear his throat of the grief that
strangled him, but for some moments could not get out a
word more.

Llewelyn freed his hands and took the boy by the fore-
arms and strongly raised him. 'Not dead?' he demanded
in alarm. 'Rhys is not killed?' He held the young man in
his arms, the dark head buried in his shoulder, and looked
across him at Griffith, who was fair, slender and quiet
after his father's fashion, and slow to anger or outcry.
'What has happened to him?'

'He is alive and well,' said Griffith. 'No harm has come
to him.'

'He has submitted!' cried the young Llewelyn, muffled
by his uncle's clasp but loud in accusation. 'He has surrendered his castles and gone with the king's men to
Worcester, to make his submission to Edward! So have
Griffith and Cynan ap Meredith of Cardigan, for themselves and their nephew. There is no one left of Deheu-
barth to keep faith with you, only we two.' And he wept

253

aloud for anger and shame. He was young, only twenty years old, and his uncle's worshipper from childhood.

Still Llewelyn eyed the older brother. 'They have all sued for grace,' said Griffith honestly but without excitement, 'and promised homage. We wanted no part of it. We are here. Those who would follow us we have brought with us.'

'And most welcome,' said Llewelyn, 'with or without your following.' He lifted the disconsolate boy away from him, and shook him gently between his hands. 'Never take it so hard, he is pressed in a way you cannot yet know, and he does but go after his kind. It is you who have learned something new. Though he has chosen a different way, that does not make your brother a villain.'

The boy lifted his head and blazed at his uncle with great, dark-blue eyes. 'He is not my brother,' he said with passionate bitterness. 'I have renounced him! I am done with him!'

Llewelyn's smile, though to my eyes somewhat grim and drear, nevertheless respected such rage and grief, and would not mock the boy's vehemence. He clapped him lightly on the shoulder, and laid an arm about him to bring him to a seat among the council.

'Don't write him out of your life too soon,' he said. 'Time will teach you – not too roughly, I pray God! – that brothers are not so easily done with!'

Thus we came to the beginning of July, with our powers drawn in upon themselves and shrunk to half the ground we had formerly held, with most of the south already occupied, and much of the border territory hacked away, leaving the king's approach to Gwynedd open but for our arms. It had been our invariable custom in the past to avoid great loss by withdrawal into our difficult mountain country, to keep our forces intact and deny all our resources to the enemy, while doing him all the injury we could, and then, when he was at length forced by pressure

254

of time and weather and want of funds to recoil and break off the engagement, to follow at every step, regaining the lost lands and harrying the retreating foe. Our speed of movement and our knowledge of the ground was our strength. And thus it had seemed right and wise to do yet again, rather than crash into pitched battle with immensely larger numbers than our own. Never before had we had cause to doubt these tactics, again and again they had served us well. Yet now, as I know, Llewelyn had moments of grave disquiet and self-searching, even self-blame, before he was shown cause.

'God forgive me,' he said to me once, as we rode along the river near Rhuddlan, and looked out broodingly towards Chester, in the summer calm that mocked our anxieties, 'God forgive me if I have misread the signs, and let him deceive me. How if this time it goes not as we are used to? If he has some new design? We have relinquished so much with hardly a fight. I know it has paid us time and again, but how if this time it was a mistake? Samson, year after year I have thought over the time before Evesham, and been shamed that I did not then have the courage to throw myself and all I had into Earl Simon's fight. Now it is on my heart that I may have made the same error again – that I should never have surrendered so much ground, but struck hard and risked all to break their concentrations as they formed, and keep them from ever moving far into Welsh ground.'

'You could not have done it,' I said. 'You could not have held together all those little chieftains in the south, kept fast hold of Bromfield, and fended off three armies, by your own strength alone. You were right, it is time that threatens us, the years you have not been granted to change men's minds and hearts.'

'Well,' he said, and set his jaw, 'we must work with what we have, fallible chieftains, a flawed prince, and brave but mortal men. I doubt it is not only poor Rhys Wyndod and his like who have erred in harking back to the past. I fear I may be just as guilty. Have I not loosed my hold of much of Wales to make Gwynedd into a fortress?'

In its way this was true, but also true that it was by far the soundest policy for us, for of all Wales the most unconquerable land was our sheer, silvered mountain country of Snowdon, and if half was to be sacrificed for a time to ensure an impregnable base from which all could be recovered, then that base could only be Gwynedd.

Upon this fortress of steely rock King Edward, in the first weeks of July, began his expected advance.

CHAPTER X

It is a strange thing that Welshmen should undo Wales,
but so it was. We were a society so inward and tribal, so
little disposed to look to a wider state, that as the chieftains in all the lands but Gwynedd fell away when
threatened, and made their peace one by one, hardly one
considering an association with his neighbours for a common resistance, so the ordinary men of those disputed and
ceded lands listened with interest when the king's men
came recruiting among them, and cheerfully contracted
to fight for the side that was able to arm and pay them.
Fighting was their business, and this was work and wages
offered, and it mattered nothing to them that they were
asked to fight against Wales. Wales was a word still, and
no more. They belonged to a village and a commote, not
to a nation, which was itself a conception out of their
knowledge. So great numbers of men born Welsh, speaking the Welsh tongue, took Edward's pay and went to
war for him against Llewelyn.

The prince was right. He had not had long enough to
reach hearts and minds, to teach a new generation how
the very air that nourished Wales was changed. It was his
grief that the hour came upon him so much too soon. It
was his glory that even in the short time he had, he had
won so many voices and minds, even if not enough. His
young namesake from Dynevor raged and ate out his
heart when he knew how many south Welsh archers had
accepted Edward's pay. But Llewelyn himself never cursed
them.

So far as I can recount King Edward's movements in

that campaign, he must have left Worcester about the tenth day of July, with some eight to nine hundred cavalry, and of foot soldiers, lancers, knifemen, archers and swordsmen, perhaps nearly two thousand five hundred, to be added to those already recruited in the three commands. He moved, for such a company very rapidly, through Shrewsbury to Chester, where he came on the fifteenth day of the month, and there he had also the men of the earl of Warwick, and David's two hundred and twenty troopers of his bodyguard, all in Edward's pay. Of archers and spearmen here, in the retinue of the various lords of those parts, there were perhaps two thousand, with large numbers of crossbowmen among them. The archers of Macclesfield were famous, and the muster included one hundred of them. It was no light army, and not lightly supported and provisioned. I tell you, we had never encountered so calculated and organised a force aimed at us. It was not easy to make the adjustment and see them coldly and truly.

About the same time that the host was moving up from Shrewsbury to Chester, we had word from our patrol boats, keeping watch off Anglesey, of the ships of the Cinque Ports navy being sighted rounding the island, holding well off from the land, and clearly sailing to rendezvous with Edward and lie at his orders in the estuary of the Dee. Gradually their numbers were reported, as they were sighted, to the number then of eighteen ships. Somewhat later others followed them, bringing the tally to twenty-seven, and one of them at least was French. The masters and sailors owed the king fifteen days of service without pay, from the day they came into effective action, and from the beginning of August he must have taken them into full pay, and very dear they would cost him. Our scouts also reported great numbers of men assembled at Chester who appeared to bear no arms, but to be workmen massed for some prodigious task, as though Edward intended extensive building, or something equally unusual in such a campaign. We began to see the full, daunting extent of his preparations, the like of which had never been used against Wales before, and I confess it chilled us.

'He is willing to beggar himself,' said Llewelyn, 'to break me.'

We had our line of outposts, the first defence, along the forest land above the Dee, and the mass of our northern forces well in cover inland, ready to act upon whatever word we received. The forest there was of great extent and very thick, a sturdy protection to us because we knew it well, and could penetrate it where we would with small, fast-moving raiding parties, while the royal army could not hope to operate well in such country, or bring us to open battle. It was our design to harry their every move by raids, and draw them as far into the forest as we could, where we could pick off any stragglers very easily, and hamper all their movements, especially since we expected them to be laden with all their baggage and supplies once they moved from Chester. And this was the first miscalculation, for they had now a large and powerful fleet lying in the estuary, and when they marched from Chester they marched almost as light as we, the ships carrying their supplies and keeping pace with them along the coast. Nor did Edward advance deep into the forest at all. He moved with method along the coast, his ships alongside, and all that great army of knights, troopers, archers and labourers went with him, north-westward towards the abbey of Basingwerk.

We in the forest moved with them, too, picking off any unwary enough to stray, and by night local knifemen silently stalked and killed such as they could of the sentries guarding the camps. But soon we saw how different this war was to be from any we had known. Edward's burdening himself with all those labourers was explained within two days, for they were felling trees ahead of the host, strongly guarded as they worked, and opening up a great swathe to make a road which an army could use. Unless we could prevent, we should be robbed of one of our greatest advantages, the difficulty the English always had in bringing up their supplies. Now they had the ships on one hand, and were tearing apart our forest to make a highroad on the other.

By day and by night we harried and raided them, and took heavy toll, but with our cover stripped in this wide swathe between us and them, and their picked companies of archers, more than three hundred of them, constantly on guard while the labourers worked, we had lost much of our sting. We tried every means of luring them into the thicker woods, but plainly Edward's plans were absolute and his orders were obeyed, and there were very few rash sallies, and only when we pressed them hard at some risk to ourselves. In ten days they had cut their way to within a few miles of the abbey of Basingwerk, where there was a great level plane of rock jutting out into the estuary, and there the main army made a strong camp, cleared about on every side so that we had no cover to approach them undetected. And there they stayed, so arraying their forces that it was clear they meant to fortify and hold that spot as a base. This rock we called the Flint.

An advance guard, strong in archers, still pushed on along the coastal edge of the forest with the woodsmen, who continued their felling, digging and levelling, and burned the underbrush as they went. Our scouts brought back word that the king had taken up residence at Basingwerk, and seemed prepared to stay some time, and that there was great activity at the main camp at the Flint. Several of his Cinque Ports ships were observed going back and forth to Chester, and bringing up and unloading cargoes of timber, while other materials, cords, wooden planking, lime, were already being carted along the new road in an endless chain of wagons. Within a few days we heard what was toward, though we had guessed it before.

Edward's labourers were building there a very large and strong base post, which would surely be well garrisoned even when the main army moved on.

This was the first time that Llewelyn turned to tactics the Welsh seldom used, and made one attack in force against the half-built stronghold. We did not then know it, but at that time Edward was not with his army, but had taken ship and crossed the estuary to return to Chester, partly to ensure that his transport lines in Cheshire were working properly, partly to meet his queen at a spot where he had decided to build a great abbey, to be called Vale Royal. This was the time he chose to see the foundations of that church laid, so confident and resolute was he, and such deserved trust did he place in his captains in the field, Warwick, Montalt, de Knovill, the warden of the Cinque Ports, who commanded the fleet, and many more. Yes, and David, too, for David was always close about his person and first among the defenders wherever we attacked. Thus it happened that in Edward's absence David with his own guard and other troops was in command of the defences of Flint the day the prince made his strongest bid to destroy the fences and walls they had raised. It was to be then or never, before too much work had been done, and too much ground cleared about it.

It was all timber, and might be fired if the wind was right. A wind driving up the estuary was what we wanted, for our best approach was from seaward, where the road was still in the making and less open, and with good fortune we might even fire any ships that happened then to be lying alongside, and destroy their landing-stage.

It was early in August that we got what we wanted, and in the early evening made our attack. Llewelyn had sent a company of archers ahead along the half-made road to make a feint at attacking the workmen there, and draw the guards to defend them, and by this means, though at some loss, for they never relaxed their watchfulness altogether, we did break through them and get across the road close to Flint, and drove down upon the palisades in strength. We had bowmen placed in cover as near as we dared, who loosed fire-arrows before us into the camp, and there was a good blaze within and a stir of wild activity before we reached the walls.

That fight was short and very fierce, and there were men killed on both sides, but they had such numbers that we never broke through to the ships. Surely we left much damage behind us when we withdrew, but not as great as we had hoped, for the traitor wind dropped with the gathering evening, instead of freshening as we had expected, and the blaze merely opened a large gap in the outer defences, and destroyed some supplies within. But what I chiefly remember of the clash is David marshalling the guard as they mounted in haste to meet and break our charge.

He was but lightly armed, and his face uncovered, and I saw him before he had discovered Llewelyn, and realised who led the attack. David's movements in action were always as sharp and cutting as lightning-stroke, but cold, if a kind of keen happiness can exist hand in hand with coldness. He was a born fighter, and could scent battle like a hound, but it was informed delight, not passion, that dictated what he did in battle. So he began this defence, very briskly and practically deploying his men and holding station with his line as they rode at us. Then he saw his brother. His face so changed, it might have been another man. Every line of his fine bones sharpened and burned deadly white, and the blue of his eyes dilated into a steely blaze, and from keeping his purposeful pace he suddenly spurred forth from the line, wrenching out his sword, leaned forward in the saddle and drove at the prince like a madman. So I had seen him do once before, very long before, on the field of Bryn Derwin, the field of his first treason. Now, as then, I saw in his blanched face and desperate eyes a terrible anguish of hate and love, and the more terrible hope of an end to it. Towards that

262

end he drove with all his might, and he might have achieved it, if the young Llewelyn ap Rhys Fychan, his nephew, had not deliberately wheeled in between them, with a defiant scream of anger, and confronted David with the younger, purer mirror-image of his own face, spitting generous rage.

I think he could have killed the boy very easily, and perhaps would have done, almost without thinking, but for that likeness between them, as if God had flung the fresh, sweet remembrance of his own youth in his face. He let his sword-arm fall, and checked so violently that his horse reared and swerved aside. And then his own ranks had overtaken his rush, and the two lines clashed and inter-mingled in a close, confined mêlée, in which the brothers were swept apart.

Twice thereafter, in the press, I caught glimpses of David's ice-pale face, straining towards Llewelyn, but the other Llewelyn kept always jealously close at his uncle's flank, and in any case, that fight was nearly over. Some-thing we had done, as yet at little loss. But if we did not draw off soon our losses would be great, for the camp was pouring out against us great numbers of reserves, and all surprise was over. Llewelyn signalled the withdrawal, and we massed and drew off in good order, gaining enough ground to wheel and storm across the road at speed, and so gain the shelter of the trees, where the advantage was ours. We put a mile or more between us and the borders of the Flint before we checked, but they did not pursue us into cover. They never did. Edward's will had decreed it, and they did his will with a confidence we could not but admire.

We left the stockade burning, but alas, it did not burn long. We also left a number of dead behind us, and took several wounded away, including the boy Llewelyn, who had a long gash in his forearm, of which he was proud, for he was exalted with the air of battle, and still enraged for his adored uncle.

'I hate traitors!' he said, quivering still when we bound him up in camp, and made him comfortable.

'So do we all, child,' said the prince sombrely, 'though not so sorely, perhaps, as they hate themselves. You had no call to fling this body of yours in between, very prettily as you did it, and much as I'm beholden to you for the thought. I could have satisfied him.'

And he praised and teased and soothed the excited young man into charmed quietness, and left him with the one brother he still acknowledged.

'We are beset by brothers, every one of us,' he said, when he came out to me by the camp-fire in our clearing, in the onset of the August night. 'It is the whole story of Wales, this blessing and curse of brotherhood, the spring of loyalty, of jealousy, of murder, of all the heroisms and the villainies of our history.' And he lay down on his belly in the rough grass, and gnawed on a spray of sorrel, with its hot, spicy taste, and pondered long on what we had both seen. 'In God's name,' he said, 'what is it he wants? To kill, or to be killed?'

I said: 'Either. He wants an end, it hardly matters which. He wants to offer you the chance you would not take at Bryn Derwin, or else to make an end of you, and so cut the knot that binds him. But he cannot do it, and you will not. I doubt his end is ordained otherwise.'

'And mine?' said Llewelyn, and smiled.

We never managed to destroy the base camp at Flint. They spent three weeks and more making it into a fortress. Edward came back from his pious labours at Vale Royal in mid-August, and by then the second part of his military road was extended well forward, for here the forest was less thick, and in parts they had only to fell and clear scattered trees, to open the field of fire for their defending archers. As soon as Edward came, the main army moved on. By the twentieth day of August it had reached Rhuddlan, from which our garrison withdrew into the hills, for Rhuddlan is among marshes on the right bank of the Clwyd, not far inland from the coast, a place tenable, perhaps, by an encroaching army moving in from the low land, but not by us who had to rely on the mountains for our heart-fortress. We did not forsake it gladly, for it covers two advances, one along the coast to Conway, one inland up the Clwyd towards Ruthin and Denbigh. But the dry season, not for the first time in our history, had laid it open to direct assault, instead of being inviolable behind marsh after marsh, and the truth is, we could not hold it.

We made Edward pay a high price both in men and money to get there. But we could not keep him out of it.

For the feudal host had been but the beginning of Edward's resources. By this time in August he had paid reinforcements coming in, in such numbers as we had never known, we reckoned nearly sixteen thousand foot at this time, and probably three hundred lances. Where he got the money to pay such numbers, and how deep he sank into debt, I cannot guess, but we cost him a great sum, that I know. The number of the crossbow quarrels that his arbalestiers loosed on us was beyond our reckoning, and must alone have cost a fortune.

Meantime, we also had a few strange reinforcements, deserters from Edward's army, a handful of foot soldiers and archers, but far more of his labourers on the roads. They grew weary of such hard work and peril of their lives, and fled into the woods, where we gathered and questioned them. Some wanted only to slip away and go home, being pressed men, some were Welsh, and desired to change sides, and we took them in gladly. God knows there were enough Welsh by that time shamelessly in Edward's pay. Welsh friendlies, the English called them. We had another name for them.

Still the military road unrolled mile by mile through the forest ahead of Edward's main host, while Reginald de Grey commanded the base camp at Flint, and a second

265

such strong garrison was established at Rhuddlan, thus protecting the king's rear and his supply lines. The detail that most surely opened our eyes to the gravity of our situation at that point was that the ships began to bring stone and other building materials as soon as the wooden fortifications were secure enough, and the workmen within the camp-sites began to dig foundations, both at Flint and Rhuddlan. This we beheld with deep disquiet. Neither the wide, cleared forest road nor this determined building accorded with our past experiences.

'This I do not like at all,' said Llewelyn. 'He would not go to so much trouble and expense if he meant to use these bases only for a season and then withdraw from them. Surely he cannot mean to man them through the winter? I do not believe he has the money or the supplies to feed two such garrisons and fight a winter war.'

A campaign continued through the winter was something we had never had to contend with before, for with long lines of communication and many mouths to feed it was impracticable in the mountains. But given two strong bases open to the sea, and a fleet of ships well able to cope with coastwise sailing even in wintry conditions, it began to look like a daunting possibility.

'Certainly,' said the prince, gnawing his lip over the threat, 'he seems to have plans for staying, even if he breaks off the fighting till the spring. No man cuts such a road or ships such loads of stone but to make a permanent stay.' And that meant this time we might be hard put to it to regain any part of what we had yielded. Either we must storm their camps and utterly destroy them, a terrible undertaking, or else they would hold what they had gained, and renew the advance when season and weather made it possible.

There was no sign of any slackening in their pressure on us, the road rolled on towards the Conway, clearly the king's objective, and moved with terrible speed. Nine days it took them to move their advanced base from

Rhuddlan to Degannwy, and short of hurling ourselves at them in pitched battle there was nothing we could do to prevent. We could and did make them pay heavily in men and supplies for every mile, but we could not stop the march of that road. All we could do was fall back before it, and withdraw beyond the Conway, on the granite heart of our land.

From Aberconway we could not so easily be shifted, having the great heights of Penmaenmawr at our backs, and all the complexities of Snowdon close at hand to shelter and hide us at need. So things stood at the end of August, Edward on the eastern side of the estuary, we on the western, and the ebb and flow of the tides between. But Edward had his ships, far too formidable for our smaller boats to tackle, and who has the mastery of the sea can cut off mainland from island, and draw a tight noose about such a prize as Anglesey.

It may be that we should have foreseen it, but even if we had I doubt if we could have prevented, for we had no such fleet to move an army across the strait, nor dared we detach half our force, and so weaken the garrison of our beleaguered Snowdonia. But Edward had the numbers, even though he had dismissed many of the Welsh levies at this time, and kept a smaller army to feed, but all of picked men, both the cavalry and the foot, and notably all the expert archers. At the beginning of September, very shortly after he reached Degannwy, he shipped a strong division across to the island, where the corn harvest was still standing. Fighting there must have been, but the companies we had there could not withstand such an army. On the heels of this invasion force Edward shipped also a large number of scythemen and reapers, and gathered our harvest, the chief grain supply of all north Wales, for the use of his own men. Those two weeks of September were the most desolate blow he dealt us, and the most irresistible. When the news reached us, we knew our case was desperate.

Llewelyn called a council in the mountains above Aber. We looked down from our crags to that best-loved court, and across Lavan sands to the island we had lost. A sombre gathering that was. There were some among his captains who were all for fighting to the end, but more who were not afraid to say what they saw, and what they saw, if we pushed this to the last, was the loss of all.

'At least we are not come to that yet,' said Tudor. 'But for Anglesey we hold all Gwynedd west of Conway, as we always did, and I cannot believe that Edward, however determined he may be, looks forward with any very high stomach to assaulting this eagles' nest in winter. It is possible it may suit him as well as us to talk terms for another ending.'

'It is true,' said Griffith ap Rhys Fychan, the elder of the two nephews, though with a very reluctant face. 'The lord prince still has enough bargaining power to be worth listening to. And the autumn begins to close in.'

His brother showed by the wryness of his face how bitter the thought of suing for terms was to him, but to do him justice, he kept his eyes fixed upon his uncle's face, and bit back whatever his passionate heart might have longed to say.

Llewelyn said with deliberation: 'We have contended on the wrong terms, yet I do not see what else we could have done. The one time when we might have upset the king's plans was at the beginning, by a total stroke against him before he could get his armies and his workmen into movement. But then we could not foresee so strange a war. No one has ever proceeded against Wales in this fashion. He has planned a march not merely to reach Degannwy, but to make a way which can be maintained and used again and again, and he has refused to be drawn into the hills and the forests after us, where we might have the advantage. He has left garrisons at all his bases, and patrols on the roads between, to ensure his lines, and he has taken our winter supplies from us, and added them to his own. And we had best realise that he has done more than snatch our granary from us in taking Anglesey. His next step, if we force him to continue, will be to put a fresh army ashore from Anglesey across the strait, and take us in a tightening cord from the west, and to send reinforcements up the Clwyd from Rhuddlan, and draw the noose about Snowdon from the east. But gradually and methodically as he does everything, because he may find it more practical to starve us out than attempt us by storm. I begin to see that it could be done. I would not have believed the day would come when one man could turn Snowdon into a single great castle under siege, to be starved into surrender.'

That was stark talking, and the more shocking because he weighed these considerations without rage, and without shutting his eyes to a single aspect of the grim truth. They looked at one another bleakly, and in their turn weighed his words.

'It comes to this,' he said, no less calmly. 'If we fight on, we may cost him very dear to take, but if he proceeds as heretofore, my judgment is that he can take us, and he will. If we ask for terms, we can stand fast on keeping everything we now hold, and what we still hold is the heart and source from which everything else has been won. And may be won again, some day, when time favours us, and we have learned how to make better use of our wits and our resources. It is not a matter of abject surrender. We know we are not come to that, and be sure Edward knows it every bit as well. If I am wide awake to our situation, so is he to his. I do not think he wants to drag this warfare on into the winter. I do think he may be very glad if we offer him the chance to avoid that labour and pain. And I think it may be wise to do so, for if we force him, he will certainly strike back, and strike hard. I begin to know him.'

I heard then in his voice, harsh and grim as it was, the note of something beyond knowledge. He liked what he knew. This is truth, that those two were on their best terms of respect and regard when they were at each other's throats in honourable battle. I would swear that those worse suspicions they had cherished, each of the other, had died and been burned to ash in the fire of that summer war. Neither of them any longer believed that the other had coldly planned murder or treason. They were two strong creatures who had crashed forehead to forehead like rams or rutting deer, and could not by their very natures yield ground once the horns were locked. There was a huge respect in their enmity that neither of them had been able to appreciate while they angled and argued, but only when they clashed in thunder.

'If we are to ask for truce and talk terms,' said Tudor with certainty, 'it must be at once, while we are still whole, and before he can even suppose that we are weakened by loss of the harvest. If the worst befalls, and we can get no honourable terms, we shall have lost nothing and committed ourselves to nothing, and gained time for the winter to close in on him as well as on us. We can still fight to the death if we must.'

'True,' said Llewelyn, 'but I will not even enter into negotiations but in good faith.' And when he had heard all that they had to say, he said: 'I will give myself this one night. Tomorrow I shall have decided.'

He took horse and rode out that night alone over the uplands of Moel Wnion, looking over the sea, and I went after him, unseen, to the rim of the camp and beyond, and sat on a hillock in the bleached autumn grass and watched him from far off. He walked the horse gently, riding slack and easy, in solitary thought, alone with the lofty rocks and immense skies of his Gwynedd, which he stood to keep or lose, according as he played this game aright. A bitter choice it was he had to make, but one many a good man had had to make before him, in conditions even more galling and grievous, though this was sorrow enough. I think the few scudding clouds above the sea spoke with him, and the wheeling falcons that hovered like black stars against the sunset, and the folds of the uplands under their long, seeding grasses, the colour of the stubble Edward's reapers had left on Anglesey. For if the south had crumbled and fallen away from him, and the marches shattered as soon as English hands tore at them, this pure rock of Gwynedd remained, and was still inviolate. It never yet had belonged to any but its own princes. And when it came to the last allegiance, Llewelyn was not only prince of Wales, but prince of Gwynedd, too, and prince of Gwynedd first, and if all else deserted him, Gwynedd would not, and he must not desert or imperil Gwynedd. So I think his decision was made before ever he came trotting gently home again into camp. He was never one to cast the load of choice, where it hung so heavy and hard to bear, upon other men.

But had there still been doubt, as I think there was none, it would not long have survived that return. For by then we had received into our camp one more deserter from among Edward's labourers, a forester from Hoyland, one of three hundred pressed men who had stubbornly sought their freedom throughout, so persistently that a force of cavalry was drafted to guard them at work. Edward's pressed labour, though well enough paid, was not popular, especially with married men who were forced to leave their wives and families This man wanted nothing more than to get home, but his only means of evasion at this stage was to take to the Welsh hills, and in expectation of probable questioning he had armed himself with all the information he could gather, as fair pay for our helping him on his way by a safe route.

When Llewelyn came back we were waiting to bring this man to him, and willingly he repeated what he had already told us.

'My lord, I've kept my eyes and ears open, and this was no secret about Degannwy. They say the king issued it in open letter. If he destroyed you, my lord, if you

271

were killed or dispossessed, he promised to divide a half of Snowdon and Anglesey and Penllyn between your two brothers, the Lord David and the Lord Owen – or the whole of Snowdon and Penllyn if he made up his mind to keep all Anglesey.'

'Did he so!' said Llewelyn, drawing in breath hard. 'Half to himself, and the other half between those two! When was this agreement made?'

'A good three weeks ago, my lord, when the king came back from Vale Royal.'

'And published, you say? Made letter patent?'

'So I heard it.'

'And upon what terms,' asked the prince quite gently, 'were my brothers to hold this land of mine?'

'Why, from the king, my lord. And to do him the service all his barons owe, and attend his parliament if he calls them.'

'So I supposed,' he said, as if to himself. 'Barons like any other barons, holding of the king in chief. And Gwynedd parted into a crown province and two diminished honours at Edward's good grace! No, there is no humiliation could be visited on me so bitter as that. Even if he had lavished all on David, and left it whole, that would have been more bearable. But it is the old story, divide and divide again, and part into fragments, the better to swallow all piecemeal.' He roused himself from his deep and grievous dream, and courteously thanked and rewarded the forester, and we gave the man shelter for the night, and fed him, and next morning set him safely on his way.

Llewelyn called his council that same night, for his mind was made up.

'You have heard,' he said, 'what Edward intends for Wales, to hack even its heart into two pieces, to take one for himself and again part the other between two lords. Never again would Gwynedd have any power to draw the fragmented princedoms of Wales into one. No, they shall not have it! I would rather go on my knees to Edward and offer him fealty and homage on his terms than let this thing happen. But we are not yet come to that. There is but one way to prevent the king from dealing as he has promised with Owen and David, and that is to force him still to deal with me. If I submit, he is at least robbed of his excuse for destroying me and turning this land into a mere appendage of his English shires. I can still bargain. If he asks too much, I can still fight, but that shall be my last resort, since it is the frailest hope. Tomorrow we'll send a flag of truce across the estuary to Degannwy, and ask the king to receive envoys and talk terms for peace.'

In mourne silence they accepted his decision. Only his young nephew and worshipper, mastering his quivering face and resolutely swallowing his tears, protested at the injustice, that his uncle should be forced to submit to indignity and humiliation in defence of what was his by right, for he feared King Edward's vengeful mind.

'It is what I do,' said the prince harshly, 'not what is done to me, that shows to my credit or my shame. There is only one man born who can humiliate me, and his name is Llewelyn ap Griffith. And I will see to it that he shall not.'

Before we slept he sent for me, and told me that if the king agreed to negotiate, and received his envoys, he wished me to go with them as one of their clerks, and be their messenger back and forth to him.

'For these will not be brief or easy bargainings,' he said, 'and though I know I must lose much of my state, I am resolved not to lose my honour. There are things I will not do, and things I will not forgo, and the chief of them I would rather not have written into any agreement or discussed as a bargaining counter publicly. It is enough if there is an understanding about it between Edward and me.'

I knew then of whom he was thinking, and I knew he chose me to be his voice because I already understood his mind. But I will not pretend I thought it an easy thing, or greatly to be desired, to approach Edward in my lord's name.

'Tudor's business,' said Llewelyn wryly, seeing my dutiful but dubious face, 'will be with the king's officers. Yours with the king. I will give you my personal letter to him and my small seal for a token. I do not think he will refuse to see you. I think it may even appease him if I advance a plea of my own, apart from the hard terms he may seek to impose. In view of the whip hand he holds, my condition – for it is a condition, and I stand fast on it – may seem light and easily granted now. It cannot threaten him any longer, or even seem to threaten.'

I said I would go to him, and do whatever was required of me.

'You know it already,' he said. 'I want his promise that my wife shall be restored to me. On every other point I will listen to him and meet him. But unless I have his word that Eleanor shall be released, there are no terms he can offer me that I will accept.'

In the morning following, Llewelyn with his court and his chief command returned to Aberconway, and the prince sent a boat with a herald across the estuary under flag of truce to Degannwy, and before the morning was over the herald returned with letters of safe-conduct from the king. We drew no hopeful conclusion from this promptness, for we had no proof yet that he felt any relief or satisfaction in being approached. But no sensible man turns aside what may well be the offer of what he wants, with less trouble, cost and loss to him than taking it by force. And his expenses to that point were extreme, though how much we had cost him we did not find out until much later, and would hardly have believed if anyone had told us the sum then.

The king, as soon and as decisively as he had replied

to our approach, at once retired to Rhuddlan, shortening his lines while leaving a working guard behind him, and took the opportunity to dismiss a great part of his foot soldiers, though he kept reasonable forces in Anglesey and at Rhuddlan, while Reginald de Grey continued as warden and commander at Flint. The fleet he kept with him until the end of the month. We knew it could easily be recalled, but his sending it home was a sign that he took the negotiations seriously and had cautious hopes of them.

Tudor was the prince's chief envoy, as was right and proper, and the high steward had with him a young lawyer and clerk who was then coming into prominence in Llewelyn's service, Goronwy ap Heilyn of Rhos, while on the king's side they had to deal with Brother William of Southampton, the prior provincial of the Dominicans in England, Robert Tybetot, who had been on crusade with Edward and was his close friend, and the king's clerk, Anthony Bek. All these were closeted together with their advisers for long and arduous hours of argument and bargaining at Aberconway, breaking off at intervals while messengers went back and forth, from mid-September to early November, and long before the end we were assured that an agreement would be hammered out, however bitterly, for it suited both parties, and neither was willing to break off and resume fighting but for the most grave and desperate reasons, which accordingly neither provided. Indeed, it grew clearer as we went that those two opponents, though they fought each other over every point as stoutly as in the field, and the fight was just as much in earnest, understood each other very well upon these terms of honourable enmity, and felt no remaining rancour, as though the encounter in battle had been an absolution.

As for me, I rode to Rhuddlan and sought an audience of the king on the second day, by which time he had surely been told that the envoys appeared to be sincere, and were not attempting delays for mere reasons of policy.

I presented my letter to his chamberlain, and showed the prince's seal, and after an hour of waiting in the ante-room I was summoned to Edward's presence. It no longer mattered that he might remember me, indeed the likelihood was but small, for it was a long time since last he had spoken to me at the parliament of Oxford, far longer still since I had been attendant on David when they were children together. And at Windsor, in Eleanor's retinue, he had never noticed me.

Nevertheless, when I went in to him and made my obeisance he looked at me hard and long, as though some corner of his memory retained a picture of which I was a faint reminder. But he did not pursue it. He was alone in the room when I entered. Possibly Llewelyn's letter had requested that the audience might be private, for he summoned no one while I was with him, and no one entered to trouble him with any other business. It seemed to me that even his giant body and great strength showed signs of wear and weariness. The droop of his eyelid was marked, but beneath it the brown eye glittered. He spoke to me very civilly but coldly, saying he was informed that I bore a private request from the prince of Wales, to be considered apart from the negotiations proceeding elsewhere, and giving me permission to expound the matter freely.

'It concerns,' I said, 'the lady who is close kinswoman to your Grace, and closer still to my prince. The princess of Wales is detained at your Grace's pleasure. The lord prince has no desire now to revive any complaint or ill-feeling upon that score, the time for such considerations being long past. But he bids me tell you that while he means and intends to come to terms of peace with you, and will do everything to that end, his wife's freedom and her right to join him are matters on which he cannot bargain, and should not be allowed to influence those issues which others are now debating. It is more fitting that her two kinsmen should behave with grace and consideration towards her, and towards each other. He asks, and I ask for him, that your Grace will promise that she shall be restored to her husband, when these talks have borne fruit and the peace is made.'

'I have yet to see,' said the king abruptly, 'how sincere the prince is in his wish to make and keep peace.'

'That,' I said, 'your Grace will see in due time. But I know it now. He is not asking that you shall make any concession until you are satisfied of his good faith. He is asking that this one most dear and most vital wish shall be granted as soon as you are satisfied.'

'And if I refuse to give him that assurance?' he asked, not angrily or arrogantly, rather as truthfully wishing to know.

'Then there will be no agreement. There are no other graces nor clemencies that can make any peace acceptable to him, if this is denied. Your Grace can say yes or no to peace and war in this one answer. Everything else is debatable. This is not.'

He accepted this from me as if Llewelyn had spoken it in person, gravely, even dourly, but quite without offence. He thought for a while, darkly and heavily, watching me but not seeing me. Then he said:

'And he wants, you say, only my word?'

'Yes. Your Grace's word is all.'

'And he will take my word? Unwritten, unsealed, without witness?'

'As he expects you to take his,' I said.

'The satisfaction I require,' said Edward, 'may not be short or easy. I have had good reason to withhold my countenance from this marriage, and I shall not be in haste to believe better of it. But if the lord prince makes treaty with me on terms acceptable, and shows by his keeping those terms faithfully that I no longer have reason to doubt him, then I give my word, the Lady Eleanor shall be delivered to him in marriage. The burden of proof lies upon him.'

277

'Your Grace will have your proof,' I said.

And that word I took back across the estuary to Llewelyn in Aberconway. And when I had delivered all, I asked him, for truly I was in need of being sure: 'And do you verily trust in his word? For so I swore to him, and for my life I do not know if I could swear the same upon my own account. I am not in two minds about him, I am in ten. He is a man I cannot reach, but the fault may well lie in me. He has given his promise. Not easily, not immediately, not warmly, not kindly, but he has given it. Do you trust in that word?'

Llewelyn was silent for some time before he answered me, but I could detect in his silence no disquiet at all, only a kind of probing wonder, as if he peered into his own mind as well as Edward's.

'Yes,' he said softly, like one reaching a hand delicately to touch an image in his mind that was still a source of astonishment to him, 'yes, I trust in that word.'

When, therefore, they clawed out from laborious hours of contention the terms of the treaty of Aberconway, one week into the month of November, Llewelyn at Aberconway considered them dispassionately, with an equable mind, endured what was injurious to his person and state, weighed what was hopeful for Wales, and rested content in Edward's word for the consummation of his love. On the ninth day of November he accepted the text agreed. On the following day, at Rhuddlan, King Edward did the same. Guardedly, and with mutual reservations, I think both were glad, and both, perhaps, with reason.

These were the main items of this agreement:

Item: The Prince submitted himself to the will and mercy of King Edward. Though stated as an absolute, it was well understood by both sides that this clause hung together with all the detailed conditions that followed, and was effective only when all were effective. The formula was necessary to Edward's position in relationship to his

278

own barons, and he was careful to insist upon it. As fine for the insurrection and damage done by himself and all his people, Llewelyn was required to pay to the king fifty thousand pounds sterling. But the understanding concerning Eleanor was not the only clause not stated in the text, for it was agreed beforehand that this great fine was merely a gesture to be recorded, and payment would be immediately remitted, as indeed it was. Edward was well in need of money – there never was a time when he was not – but even he knew he could not get it in that quantity from a prince he had just deprived of half his lands and a year's harvest.

Item: Llewelyn ceded to the king, for himself and his heirs, the whole of the Middle Country, those four cantrefs which once had nominally belonged to Edward as prince, with all the rights pertaining, and also conceded into his hands all those lands the royal forces had taken by conquest during the war, and now in fact held. But if any lands had been captured from the prince by others than the crown, and retained, then the king would entertain the prince's claims at law to those lands, and do him justice according to the laws and customs of those parts where they lay.

Item: The prince was to be absolved from his excommunication, and his lands freed from interdict, and when that was done he was to go to Rhuddlan in state to take the oath of fealty to the king, who would then appoint him a day to visit Westminster and do homage there formally.

Item: The prince was to release his eldest brother, Owen Goch, who had been many years his prisoner. But here Edward was careful and punctilious towards Llewelyn's honour and rights, for he did accept that Owen's imprisonment had begun when he rose treacherously against his brother, with whom he then shared the rule in Gwynedd, and sought to take all for himself. Therefore his release was hedged about with conditions. He was to be delivered to the king's commissioners, and would then have the choice between coming to definite terms of peace and settlement with Llewelyn by agreement, such agreement to be approved by the king, or else, if he stood on his birthright still, he could remain in royal custody until he had been tried for his insurrection by Welsh law, in the lands where the offence was committed. Then, if the judges found him blameless, he might pursue his claim to equal rights in Gwynedd, and the king would see that the legal process treated him fairly. In this matter I think the king did Llewelyn a good service, for the grievances of Owen Goch had troubled his peace for many years, and this was as good a way of disposing of the incubus as any, and bore the stamp of crown law as well as Welsh law.

Item: Other prisoners held because of their defection were to be released unconditionally, and many restored to their lands, such as Rhys ap Griffith ap Ednyfed, the high steward's nephew. This was natural practice after a peace. A victorious king could not well leave his adherents in captivity. Among those thus let out of prison was Owen ap Griffith ap Gwenwynwyn, none the worse for Llewelyn's usage, and soon hand in glove with his father in gloating over the prince's diminution, and doing everything possible in law to vex and harass him.

Item: The names of those Welsh princes, outside Gwynedd, whose homage was to be retained by Llewelyn were stated, and they were but five, Rhys ap Rhys ap Maelgwn of northern Cardigan, and four others, all kinsmen, in Edeyrnion, in Powys. Thus all the other chiefs of Powys and of the south became vassals holding their lands from the crown. And even these five were to be vassals of the prince of Wales only for Llewelyn's lifetime, afterwards reverting to the crown. And yet, though this reduction of his nominal state was very bitter, Llewelyn was left with vassals, and was given in the treaty, most markedly, the title of prince of Wales. Surely Tudor and Goronwy ap Heilyn stood firmly upon this point of courtesy, yet I think it was not at all displeasing to Edward to agree to it. I was and am in ten minds about him.

Item: All lands which had been occupied during the war because their lords had defected to the king were to be restored to them.

Item: The king gave over freely to Llewelyn all the lands David owned by hereditary right in Gwynedd, and would compensate David with equal lands elsewhere. But on the death of David or Llewelyn those lands were to revert to the crown. This, I think, was less at David's plea than at Edward's discretion, for he felt it easier and more prudent to keep those two brothers apart, and the simplest way was to remove David's interests and holdings completely from Gwynedd. Though in fact he was less wise when it came to allotting the lands concerned, for he gave him the two inland cantrefs of the Middle Country, and thus placed this divided creature, torn in two between England and Wales, in the marches between the two, where the dissension within could most desperately rend him.

Item: The king granted to the prince the whole of Anglesey, which was to be handed back to him by the royal army then in possession. Nominally he was to pay an annual rent for the island of a thousand marks, payable at Michaelmas, but this, again, was remitted. The clause was put in to assert formally the king's acquired right there.

Item: The holders of land in the Middle Country, and the other territories formerly Llewelyn's and now taken over by the king, were to continue undisturbed in their possession, and enjoy their liberties and customs as before, except for any among them who were regarded by Edward as malefactors, and refused such grace.

Item: Any legal contentions arising between the prince and any other person were to be determined and decided according to marcher law if they arose in the marches, and by Welsh law if they arose in Wales. So simple-sounding a clause ought not to give rise to complications and entanglements, but indeed matters of law and land are never simple, and here in these few lines endless troubles lay waiting to be hatched.

Item: Such lords as happened to hold lands both in those portions held by the king and those remaining with Llewelyn should do homage for the first to the king, for the second to the prince.

Item: The king confirmed to Llewelyn all the lands which the prince then held, without prejudice or threat, and to his heirs after him, except for Anglesey, which was confirmed to Llewelyn for life and afterwards only to the heirs of his body, no others.

Then followed the guarantees to ensure the keeping of the treaty. The prince was to hand over as hostages for his good faith ten of his noblemen, who would be honourably treated and need fear no penalties. The king promised an early release of these hostages if all went well, and he kept his word. Further, in every cantref held by the prince, twenty good men were to be guarantors annually of his good faith, and withdraw their fealty from him if he defaulted.

No question but this was a grievous constriction upon the prince's greatness, and bound him hand and foot to his dependence henceforth upon Edward, yet it still left him prince of Wales, not shorn of his right and title, not holding his land from Edward, but only, as before, under the power of the king of England. Had David been set up in his place, he would have held his lands directly from the king, and been a prince only by Edward's courtesy. Llewelyn was prince by right, and acknowledged right, that held good on both sides the borders. And though the terms and the safeguards were iron-hard, and meant to be, yet there was in all Edward's conduct of this submission a kind of harsh, unbending tenderness that spared to hurt or abase while he made all fast.

'I am back where I began,' said Llewelyn, facing the truth stonily. 'Well, I was not ashamed to be prince of half Gwynedd-beyond-Conway once, and now I am prince of the whole of it, and why should I be ashamed?'

For him there was no repining. He set himself to fill the place he had accepted open-eyed, and to maintain it, and for all his losses it was still a place any earl of England would have envied him.

Immediately on the sealing of the treaty he set to work to execute all the necessary deeds to put all its clauses into effect, and on the day of the ratification, the tenth day of November, Llewelyn rode in state to Rhuddlan to meet the king and take the oath of fealty. The king's plenipotentiaries, Robert Tybetot and Anthony Bek, with others of the king's council and the bishop of St Asaph, escorted him to within three miles of Rhuddlan, and there he was met by Edward's chancellor, that same Robert Burnell who had once brought the prince the homage of Meredith ap Rhys Gryg at Edward's request, and now came with all ceremony and honour to lead a prince to a king, rather than a vanquished man to the victor. With him came the earl of Lincoln, Henry de Lacy, who was as close a friend to the king as was Tybetot. And this noble escort was to be in attendance on the guest in Rhuddlan, and accompany him safely back to his own country afterwards.

Resolute and practical as he was, I knew well that not even Llewelyn could swallow so bitter a draught as this treaty without pain. To have half his lands hacked away from him, to lose all but five of his vassal princes and all his present hope for the Wales of his vision, was to be lopped of half his heart and drained of half his blood. The hurt of this coming ordeal might have been terrible indeed, had Edward been in a mood for vengeance. Instead, nothing could have been done that he did not do, to make it endurable. Whatever happened afterwards, whatever he did to others, I remember the Edward of that day with gratitude, for he was tender of Llewelyn's face as of his own, and paid him all the honour and deference due to an equal. Set it to the balance of his account in the judgment. To the end of my life I shall always be in more than one mind about Edward.

The king's hall at Rhuddlan was a great structure of timber then, but the stone foundations of his new castle were already in, and the walls beginning to rise. Edward's knights were gathered to welcome the prince's party, squires came to hold his stirrup and take his bridle. The earl of Lincoln and Bishop Burnell – for he was bishop of Bath and Wells as well as chancellor – ushered Llewelyn into the hall and into Edward's presence, and the glitter of that military court, spare and deprived of the grace of women, made a fitting setting for the meeting of those two men. War was the business that had brought them together, war lost and won, and soldiers know the fickleness of victory and defeat, and the narrowness of the gap between them. A man does not mock what may be his own fate tomorrow, or a year hence, at least, no wise man.

The king was seated in state, with his officers about him, when Llewelyn entered the hall. Edward was in rich, dark colours as always, very properly and carefully royal, and wearing a thin gold coronet, and at all points prepared to dominate, if not to daunt. His heavy-featured face, never given to smiling, remained aloof and stern throughout. Yet when Llewelyn advanced up the hall to him with his long, straight stride, weathered and brown and sombre, Edward suddenly rose from his seat and came to meet him those few paces that counted as a golden gift in my eyes, and astonished the prince into smiling. They stood a charmed moment face to face, quite still, each of them held. Edward was the taller by a head, but so he was among all those who surrounded and served him. And it disquieted Llewelyn not a whit that he must tilt back his head to look up at him, any more than it

284

awes a noble child, who must do as much for the meanest grown man.

'The lord prince is very welcome to our court,' said Edward, and gave him his hand, and Llewelyn bent the knee to him briefly, and kissed the hand. 'I hope this day,' said Edward, 'instead of an ending, may be counted as a new beginning between us.'

'That is my intent,' said Llewelyn. 'I have accepted these dues, and I shall pay them. The proof shall not be in words, but the first earnest well may.'

In due form before that assembled court he rehearsed the oath of fealty, in a loud, clear voice, and with wide-open, deep eyes upon Edward's face. And after that they sat down together, and went forward with the business of the day with due ceremony but briskly. There the king formally remitted the great fine, and the annual rent for Anglesey in perpetuity, and Llewelyn was left to pay only the residue of the old debt under the treaty of Montgomery, the money he had been withholding as a means of getting his grievances set right. Edward promised release for the hostages within half a year, which showed that he was relieved and reassured thus far in his meeting with his defeated enemy. And Llewelyn, seeing that the king, whatever his successes and prospects, was direly in need of ready money, paid two thousand marks of the money due from him on the spot, to the keeper of the royal wardrobe.

In such mutual considerations and such a strange but true accord did this half-dreaded meeting pass. Those two had met several times in old days, at conferences on the border, but briefly and upon precise business, and since Edward became king they had never met at all, and that was a strange metamorphosis, creating a new Edward. Now they came face to face, sat elbow to elbow at the board, and the enemies they had hated and confronted at distance were only illusions and dreams. At Rhuddlan they were new-born, each to the other. The business of the treaty, though heavy and grave and blotting out every-thing else until it was done, seemed but the veil that waited to be withdrawn from between them.

Afterwards they feasted the prince, and he was set at Edward's right hand at the high table, and they came to the open, easy talk of host and guest together. From my place lower in the hall I watched them, and marvelled, and yet did not marvel, for the world is full of exaltations and abasements, but men are men, and each is the man he is, and neither height nor depth changes the soul of a steadfast man. And what they said to each other I never knew, but for some few utterances that carried in a quietness.

'I never yet got a fair fall from a better lance,' said Llewelyn clearly, 'that I was not able to rise up, bruises and all, and give him credit for his skill. I might curse my own ill-judgment, but I should never grudge him his glory.'

The king turned to look at him with close attention, reserved of feature still, but with no droop to that tell-tale eyelid of his. And though I missed whatever he replied, it seemed to me that this forthright declaration gave him both satisfaction and thought.

I was seated at one of the side-tables, no great distance from them, but withdrawn into shadow near the curtained passage by which the squires and servers went in and out. I had not heard anyone enter and halt at my back, until a low voice said in my ear: 'If you are thinking, Samson, that his Grace the king could say as much, put it out of your head. He never took a fall from any man but it poisoned his life until he had paid it back with a ven-geance.'

I knew who was there, before I turned my head to see David leaning at my shoulder, with the small, devilish smile on his lips, and the hungry, mocking blue brightness in his eyes. He had a cloak slung on his shoulder, with a fine shimmer of rain upon it.

I said drily that the king had looked his approval, and should know his own mind.

'He does approve,' said David. 'He approves such chivalrous usage in every other man breathing, but it does not apply to Edward. Others may fall, and rise again without malice and without disgrace. Edward must not be felled, ever. Bear it in mind for my brother's sake. The price would be too high for paying.'

He drew up a stool at my elbow and leaned in the old familiar way upon my shoulder, and smiled to see me search his face in mortal doubt and distrust. 'And never think it was Edward who had the delicacy to find me duties to keep me out of sight at this feast. No, that was my doing. Doubtless we shall have to meet, before my brother goes back to Aberconway, but for tonight at least I can spare him the sight of me.' He said it as one quite without shame, merely making sensible dispositions to avoid embarrassment on either part. 'Well, we are both losers, are we not? He is back within the palisade of his mountains, and I am exiled.'

'Self-exiled,' I said, 'and to a fat barony.'

'Ah, but it was not a barony I wanted for my son! It was a kingdom. Will you teach me, Samson, how to take a fair fall as ungrudgingly as *he* does it?'

I said he had no choice but to be content, and resign himself to a lesser estate. And once begun I said much more, how it was he who had made this war, how he was his brother's curse and demon, undoing all that Llewelyn did, unmaking wantonly the Wales that Llewelyn had made, bringing down all that splendour into the dust, so that the work was all to do again, if not by Llewelyn by his son or his son's son, when an honourable way opened. For now the prince was bound by his word and faith, and the dues he had acknowledged he would pay in full. Very softly I said it, so that no other ear should hear, and truly there was nothing to be gained now by anger or denunciation. And he leaned upon my shoulder and

287

listened to all without resentment or defence, and though I could not bear to look at him then, I felt that all that time he was watching Llewelyn, and with what passion there was no guessing, but the ache of it was fierce and deep, and passed from his flesh into mine through the hand laid about my neck.

'Sweet my confessor,' he said, when I had done, in that soft voice that was music even in its malice, 'never labour to find me a penance extreme enough to pay all my score. I have already done that. A kingdom is not all I have lost!' And in a moment he said, lower yet: 'Do you hate me?'

'No,' I said, despairing. 'I would, but it is not in my power. As often as I come near to it, I meet you again, and though all is changed, nothing is changed.'

'Does *he*?' said David.

'God knows! He believes he does.'

'It would be something,' said David ruefully, 'even to be hated as is my due.' He gathered his cloak over his shoulder with a sigh, and drew back his stool, rising to return to his watch, or whatever duty it was he had appropriated to himself. 'I must be about my work. It was only to see you that I came.'

I knew better than that. It was to look at Llewelyn from afar, himself unseen, and to steel his heart before the ordeal of meeting face to face. Nor could I let him go like this, for my heart also had its needs. I caught at his arm and held him, before he could leave me. I said in entreaty: 'But one word more! For God's sake give me some news of Cristin! How is it with her now – with her and the child?' The word so stuck in my throat, it was no more than a croak, but it reached him. He was still in my grasp, eye to eye with me, shaken out of all pretences.

'The child!' he said, his lips forming the word without sound. 'Oh, Samson, I had forgotten,' he said with sharp compunction, 'how much you must have seen in Windsor

– and how little news of her can have reached you since. . . .'

'It must be a year old by now,' I said, labouring against the leaden weight on my heart. 'Is she well? Was it hard for her?'

'Cristin is well,' said David, with the swift, warm kindness I remembered in him from long ago, when he brought me the news of my mother's death, as now he sprang to ward off any dread of another death as dear. 'Safe and well with my wife in Chester, you need not fear for her. Neither Elizabeth nor I will ever willingly let harm come to her. But the child. . . . She miscarried, Samson. The child was born dead.'

CHAPTER XI

There was enough to be done, in that last month of the year, to keep us all from fretting over losses and deprivations. Llewelyn had a great deal of business with the royal officers concerning the release of both Welsh and English prisoners, the handing over of Anglesey, and other such matters, as well as the necessary adjustment of his own administration to his new and straitened boundaries and circumstances. There was no time for repining, for at Edward's invitation – he might have made it an order, and it was understood to have the force of one, but he used the more gracious term – the prince was to make his state visit to spend Christmas with the court at Westminster, and there perform his homage to Edward with all due ceremony, and before that visit it was expedient that he should be rid of his prisoners, have the matter of Owen Goch settled, and be ready to make a fresh start.

As for me, I had at least the peace David had granted me. I knew that Cristin was alive and well, and by a strange grief and a stranger grace delivered from her incubus, and that no guilt lay upon her, for the fault was not hers, only the peril and the suffering. And in London, God willing, I might see her and speak with her again. Of Godred I thought not at all, for there was no profit in it. I dreaded to think of him still pursuing her with his hatred, and trying to get her with child yet again, since this one poor imp had escaped him. I feared to consider the possibility that even Godred suffered, and could love a child of his own body, even one got for devilish purposes. In remembrance of my half-brother there was no comfort and no rest, nothing to benefit him or me, much less Cristin. My comfort was that she was dear to David, and David's loyalty, where it existed, was immutable. His own brother was not safe with David, but Cristin was safe. So I gave my mind and heart to helping Llewelyn in all that he had to do, to satisfy the terms of the treaty.

'At least,' he said, when he had sent for Owen Goch to be delivered out of Dolbadarn, 'perhaps I shall get peace from all my brothers now. David is a baron of England, and what small adjustments need to be made to him for the land rights he's quitting in Gwynedd can be made and sealed by the king, and let him quarrel with that arbitrator if he dare. The matter of Rhodri's quitclaim and its price is in Edward's hands, too, and Rhodri has a wealthy wife in England, and employment in the queen-mother's service, where he's surely more use than ever he was to me or to Edward in war. Now let's lean on Edward for help with Owen! Why not? I shall have some good out of the evil, after all. It is not I who must confront Owen with the choice before him.'

And that was truth, for as soon as Owen Goch was brought out of Dolbadarn and provided with a new wardrobe and household, he was handed over to the king's commissioners, in whose care he must have felt himself safe enough. So the choice put before him was not weighted either way, for it was the English who posed it. He could either be provided with a landed establishment agreed with Llewelyn and approved by the king, or else stand his trial for old treason by Welsh law, and bid for his whole birthright if he was acquitted. He chose to make peace with his brother, and let the law rest. It was no great wonder. Owen Goch was then fifty years old, and almost half his life had been spent in captivity. It is true that he could have gained his release long since, if he had been willing to accept the vassal status he was thankfully closing

291

with now, but he had been more stubborn and unbending then, and would not consider any such concession. He was growing more lethargic now, and less combative. He came out of Dolbadarn morose but subdued, after his fashion still a fine-looking man, large and in good health but for his corpulence, but pallid from confinement and indolence, and with his fiery-red hair and beard laced with grey. He was insistent on good attendance, quick to regain the imperious temper of a prince within his own household, but he no longer desired to challenge his brother at the risk of being adjudged traitor. I think Llewelyn heaved a great sigh of deliverance when Owen made his choice for a land settlement, and then to be let alone on his lands.

Llewelyn offered the whole cantref of Lleyn. Considering his own narrowed borders, I think it was generous, but he, also, was buying a measure of peace of mind. Owen jumped at the offer, astonished to be priced so high, after so many years. The king's commissioners solemnly considered and discussed, and came to the same decision. Owen was settled in Lleyn before the year ended, with Edward's officers to help him administer and rule while he was stiff from confinement still.

The night after this was achieved, and very shortly before we prepared for the departure to England, Llewelyn sent for me to his own chamber before he slept, and had me play to him for an hour or more. He lay in his bed and listened, and breathed long and deep. All the burden of his royal line and his royal struggle, unblessed by Welsh law, borne virtually alone, lay so heavy on his breast that he heaved sigh after deep sigh against it, and could not heave it off his heart.

When his breathing grew long and slow I ceased playing, thinking that he slept. But when I rose silently to steal out from him without disturbing his slumber, he made some small, involuntary movement among the furs of the brychan, and I stilled to listen, and knowing him awake,

292

asked if I should leave the candles for his chamberlain to snuff.

'No, quench them,' he said. And when I had snuffed out the last, and the dark closed on us, I heard the faintest thread of his voice breathe, I think to God rather than to me, and with such resignation and pleading: 'I am tired!' It was the saddest thing ever I heard from him, and the most solitary.

I went out from him as softly as I might, and drew to the door.

The next morning he arose refreshed and vigorous, and never again did I hear him utter word or sound to express the depth and desolation of his loss, or complain of the half-lifetime he had spent in building what was now razed almost to its foundations. He took up the simple daily burdens, bought in corn to replace the part of the harvest that had been consumed by the king's army or carried away, set trade moving again across the borders to bring in salt and cloth, and enable the monks of Aberconway to sell their wool. The king aided willingly in re-opening the channels of commerce and making it possible for Welsh goods to reach English border markets, for trade was of value to both sides. If there were any local raids and fights on these occasions, or any ill-usage of Welshmen venturing into Montgomery or Shrewsbury or Leominster at this time, it was the result of hot blood and high feeling so soon after the end of hostilities, and no fault of Edward's, and he gave strict orders to his officers to curb such offences and make amends where due.

Then we set out for London to keep Christmas with the king.

A great and glittering party that was, for we went more carefully splendid than usual, having a princely dignity to uphold in conditions possibly more difficult than at Rhuddlan. And I will say for him that Edward did his full part to make the visit outwardly royal, however hard the control he exercised behind the curtain. He sent a noble escort to meet the prince and conduct him to Westminster. Bishop Burnell led the party, and with him came the treasurer, who was the prior of the Hospital of St John of Jerusalem, Henry de Lacy, earl of Lincoln, and two of the greatest of the marcher lords, Roger Clifford and the prince's cousin Mortimer. Short of sending his own brother, the king could not have done the prince of Wales greater honour. Thus gloriously attended, we entered that island city of Westminster once again, on the eve of Christmas Eve, and were courteously received and splendidly lodged, Edward offering audience at once in greeting. And on Christmas Day in full court, before all the assembled nobility of England, Llewelyn was conducted ceremoniously into the king's presence, and did homage to him.

There were young lords there, and new officials, and many ladies, who saw the prince of Wales for the first time, though the chief officers of state knew him, even those who had never had direct dealings with him, from his visit at the translation of St Edward the Confessor. Thus many awaited their first glimpse of him as a defeated man, out-thought and out-fought and brought now to an act of submission he was held to have resisted for five years. And for once he had given some thought to his appearance in this hard role, for his pride could be stung by scorn, mockery or pity like any other man's, and he had the dignity of Wales in his hands, as well as his own. Yet he, who had never denied his defeat, or called it anything but what it was, would not stoop to arm himself with compensatory finery. He wore his best, and he wore jewellery, the polished mountain stones of his own Snowdon, but only as he would have decked himself at any feast to do honour to his host and the season. He chose to be dark, plain and without weapons, putting off even the ornamental dagger that would have passed muster well enough at his belt.

'Homage is homage,' he said, 'and I have incurred it and am bound by it. Unarmed is unarmed. There shall not be so much as a brooch on me that could prick his hand or my honour.'

But the talaith, the gold circlet of his rank, that he wore. For Wales, though shrunken to the bounds of Gwynedd-beyond-Conway, was still a distinct and separate princedom, not held from Edward, not subject to him. Thus the prince made plain his own reading of the relationship between them.

When the earl of Lincoln brought him into the king's great hall, every head craned to see him, and every eye fixed upon him, and that is a heavy ordeal when the necks stretch only from curiosity, not ardour, and the eyes are the eyes only of enemies or of those indifferent. The good opinions of individual men among them he had still to win, and did win, in the two weeks and more he was to be a guest in London. But he looked only at Edward, huge and grave and splendid in crown and state, and kept his eyes steadfast on the king's face as he walked the length of that great room to the steps of the throne.

Two of his brothers were among the crowd of lords and officers flanking the throne on either side, David close to Edward's shoulder, Rhodri withdrawn among the lesser men. The eldest was lording it happily in his new freedom on his lands in Lleyn. At his testing time, Llewelyn was brotherless. He had no one to lean on, and there was no one to let him fall. And better so.

He needed no one, he was prepared for this moment long before, and he was able to put away from him the circumstances in which it was required of him, and to perform it as directly and simply as if that first meeting planned at Shrewsbury had truly taken place. It was not he who paled and stiffened as he went on his knees on the steps of Edward's throne and lifted up his hands to the king, joined palm to palm, large, brown, able hands. Not he whose brows drew sharply together as in a spasm of pain, when Edward leaned and enclosed the prince's hands in his.

I was watching Llewelyn, but I was aware of David. Very handsome and fine he was in black and gold, and very confident and graceful at the king's side. Elizabeth among the queen's ladies might well glow with pride in him. But with every step that Llewelyn took towards his homage, those high, winged cheekbones of David's tightened and burned slowly into points of blazing white, and fine lines of pallor drew themselves along his jaw, until it seemed the bones would start through the gleaming skin. White as bone and smooth as bone, like an ivory carving of a face, he watched his brother kneel and lift up his hands. There was no contortion, no movement of that face, until the sharp, brief convulsion of his brows. Only his eyes were so desperate a blue that they looked like lapis lazuli inlaid under the high-arched lids. And I could not choose but wonder if he had suffered such pain when he paid his own homage for Rhufoniog and Duffryn Clwyd. I think not. Then he would have been graceful, easy and inwardly scornful, for he had shown Edward already, by his usage of this same brother, how lightly he held his troth, and it was Edward's fault if he paid no heed. But Llewelyn's troth was not light. A heavy load it was, and a tight shackle upon his freedom, yet he could bear it, and go his own way without discarding it. It was David, of all people in that great concourse, David, who found this joining of hands hard to bear.

There was a moment when it came into my mind that I might be seeing this the wrong way round, that it was Edward he grudged to Llewelyn, and not Llewelyn to Edward. And that was when the king very graciously clasped the hands he had been enclosing, and himself raised the prince to his feet, spoke some words of sudden, smiling condescension to him, and warmed from stone into human flesh. Until I looked again at David, and saw the blood flowing back easily into his cheeks, and his cool, bright eyes attentively studying Edward's face, flushed into content and benevolence at having got what he wanted at last, by force or fraud or no matter how. It hardly needed the slow curl of David's lip, aloof and disdainful, to set me right. It was not every man, Welsh or English, who had the hardihood to feel scorn for Edward.

The feast that Christmas night in Westminster was long, rich and splendid, and the prince of Wales was its guest of honour. No question but Edward was elated with his prize, and at his board and about his palace did everything to display him and show him favour. And gradually I began to understand the curl of David's lip as he beheld the first token of that favour. For I was present at many of those business meetings that took place during the last days of December, and the first two weeks of the new year twelve hundred and seventy-eight. Publicly in hall, feasting, dancing, out and about the city and on London river, wherever the queen and her ladies were, Edward showed his most friendly and beneficent face to the prince of Wales. But privately in conference, over the complex details of the treaty arrangements, his hold was tight and arbitrary, and his voice dry and commanding. The first great thing he had wanted, that he had got, and that was Llewelyn's fealty and homage. Everything else he sat down to exact in the same manner.

'For God's sake, what should we expect?' said Llewelyn, shrugging. 'He asks but what is due. He has not stepped one pace beyond what the treaty gives him.'

'Nor drawn one pace back,' said Goronwy ap Heilyn.

'Why should he? You and I, my friend,' said Llewelyn with good humour, 'both agreed to the terms as written. How can we complain now? He has not been ungenerous. He has put back a fair number of dispossessed young men into their lands, my nephews among them.'

'As vassals of the crown,' said Tudor sadly.

'According to treaty. And we know it, every man of us.'

It was true. Rhys Fychan's two young sons were installed once again as lords of Iscennen, along the Towy, as their elder brother had been allowed home again earlier, though not repossessed of his castle of Dynevor, which the crown intended to keep. Similarly several of Llewelyn's former tenants in the Middle Country were restored to their lands, but holding them from the crown. It pleased and comforted Llewelyn that these unfortunate young men should have protection still when he could not protect them. He had lost them, but they had not lost everything.

But though he was jealously aware of his duty to watch the interests even of the vassals who had been taken from him, since they were most of them loyal Welshmen, as deprived and repressed as he, the first thing he had sought on his own account was news of Eleanor, grace to meet her at last, and a firm promise that his proxy marriage with her would be allowed to be blessed finally in a more formal ceremony. It did not gall him to bend the knee and do homage to Edward, but it chafed him bitterly to have to ask grace of another to be allowed to visit his own wife. Nor was he spared the pain of waiting and watching at the Christmas feast, to allow Edward, if he so planned, to make the generous gesture of bringing her from Windsor of his own accord. He did not do it. Llewelyn was forced to make the approach. Nor was his request granted at once. Edward first desired to examine for himself the arrangements made, the nature and location of the dower lands the prince proposed to settle on his bride. The lady was the king's cousin, and in his care, and it was his duty to approve the proposals made for her future establishment, and to ensure that provision for her was adequate to her rank and needs.

I could not but remember, when this was said, that Amaury was also the king's cousin, and Amaury was still prisoner in Corfe castle, for no crime, however much Edward might dislike him, and still close-kept though two popes in succession had requested, urged and demanded his release. Some half-dozen of Eleanor's knights and officers were likewise in captivity, in spite of her pleas for them, for I was sure she had never ceased to protest at their detention, and to affirm that they had done nothing but their simple duty in serving and accompanying her.

Yet the manner in which Edward countered and delayed in the matter of Eleanor was not unfriendly, only cautious and austere, as though he still distrusted, and yet was disposed to give his blessing to the match. At the beginning of January he indicated to Llewelyn that he might send his proctors to Windsor to talk with the princess about her dower and her marriage settlement, and the constable would be instructed to allow the party free access, and leave to confer with her in private or with witnesses, according as they might desire. It was the first concession, and on the fourth day of January Goronwy ap Heilyn, with two others, paid that visit, and came back so deep in slavery to the lady that his face spoke for him. Llewelyn, starving, stooped to beg for what had not been offered. I think it was the one thing for which he came near hating Edward, that he had to ask what even a tyrant should have given freely. And strangely, Edward hovered half a day on the edge of refusal, though avoiding rather than speaking plainly, and then veered about and resolved to grant, and that with every mark of favour and approval, as if the idea had stemmed from him in the first place. He allowed the visit, he would himself accompany and present the prince to his bride.

They rode for Windsor handsomely escorted, but by none of Llewelyn's people, only a gay company of Edward's knights and squires. Either the king still did not quite trust in his hold over the prince, and wanted this meeting under his own eye to observe every word that passed, or else he was truly making an effort to convince us of his goodwill, and meant his patronage as an honour, an earnest of favour and familiarity to come if Llewelyn behaved well towards him and kept to terms. Llewelyn himself, though he would far rather have had the freedom of riding alone, took the king's attention at its open value, and was encouraged and reassured by it.

'I know well I am on probation,' he said to me, somewhat grimly, before they rode. 'Was there not some worthy in the Bible who served fourteen years for his chosen bride? I am like to run him close for mine.'

Being free of all duties while they were gone, on a fine wintry day without frost, I went out alone beyond the great church to the west gate, and so into the palace court, and crossed to the alley of St Stephen's, for David was lodged in one of the houses of the canonry with his family and his body-servants, the men of his following being at the Tower. All these days in Westminster I had half-hoped and half-dreaded to catch a glimpse of my dear in attendance on Elizabeth, but when that lady was in the queen's company Cristin was never with her, being left, as I guessed, to take care of the children. There were five of them now, as I had heard, and their mother placed absolute trust only in Cristin. So many of us, God knows, had learned to do that, too many leaned upon her. I was famished for the sight of her face and the sound of her voice, even if I might hope for no more, and this day I was resolved at least to walk by the house, and touch the walls within which she moved and breathed.

David himself had been sparing of his appearances, attending on the king only when he was summoned, and then remaining, as far as possible, apart from the Welsh guests. Not shame, but some manner of dire struggle with himself held him off. Edward, no doubt, thought he had only to issue his order, and himself behave as though no strains and stresses existed, and all men would fall into the pattern. But it is not so easy to take up and knit again threads torn from the heart, and truly Llewelyn had said, and meant, that he had been through David's to-and-fro once too often, and David was dead to him.

In the royal hall they had met and passed without words several times, but among so many who was to take particular note of how Llewelyn looked through his brother, as though he had not been there? They were not the only enemies of recent months now forced into proximity, and compelled to contain whatever hatred and enmity they still felt. They were only the two greatest of many like them.

The house where David's family was lodged was towards the further end of the alley, its upper windows looking over the Long Ditch where it flows down into the Thames. It had a garden and a courtyard, and its own stable, and when I drew near it I heard the voices of children shrilling in the yard, and my heart leaped, for if they were there, loosed out to play in the winter sunshine, then Cristin would be there, too, watching over them.

I could not forbear, I pushed open the narrow wicket in the yard-gate, and stepped through. Two little girls and a sturdy round boy were tossing a ball to one another round the courtyard, and a third girl-child, perhaps just turned two years old, was staggering in reckless runs between them to catch vainly at the flying toy as it soared well above her head. And on a stone bench against the stable wall Cristin sat wrapped in a blue cloak, holding in her lap the last-comer, still a month or two short of a year, a bright brown boy, with thick hair the colour of bracken, and large, bold, fearless eyes that lit on me as hers did, by that secret magic she had, the instant I passed the wicket, as though both she and the child had been waiting only for me.

Her hair, still raven-black and smooth, was down in a long braid over her shoulder, and her head was uncovered, for the hood of her blue cloak had slipped back and lay in folds at the nape of her neck. With her clear white face, oval and pure as pearl, framed in that deep blue, and the little boy thrusting his strong feet against her knees and raising himself in the circle of her arm, she brought

301

to mind all the fairest painting in manuscripts or stained glass of the mother of God holding her child, and she had in her eyes all the foreshowing and foreknowledge of sorrow beyond the brief experience of joy. But there was none of that sick despair and grievous loneliness I had seen in her at Windsor, only a white and stoic calm, and a resigned, unquenchable gentleness. She looked like one who has touched hands with death, and on the very threshold felt the hand disengage, and has turned back without complaint or question to take what pleasure she may in the living, and in quietness, and abandoning all self-seeking, finds there more pleasure than she thought for.

I stood unmoving to gaze at her, for she was beautiful as never before, finer drawn in every line, her lips, that smiled at sight of me, had regained their long, firm shaping, the white, arched lids of her eyes were smooth and clear. Thinner and older she was, worn away to pure spirit by that nine-months penance and the birth-death that ended it, but she was my Cristin in all her gallantry and force, unbroken.

She saw me look from her to the child on her knee, and her smile deepened. There was no shadow in her eyes and no constraint in her voice, as she said: 'Not mine! Only borrowed.'

'David told me,' I said, 'in Rhuddlan.' I could not say that I was sorry. Now that I saw her healed I could not be sorry, my heart in me was crying out defiant joy. 'Is this one David's?' I asked her.

'He is.' She knew already what was in my mind, and why I so stared at him. Beholding those big, fearless eyes, darker than peat water in the mountains but full of the sun, and that rich brown colouring, if only my lord's proxy marriage in Montargis had been a marriage completed I should never have thought to ask whose boy this was. He harked back three generations to his great-grandsire.

'This face he had from birth,' said Cristin, 'and this

colouring. And the name his father has given him,' she
said, 'is Llewelyn.'

I sat with her on the yard bench in the fair winter day,
watching the children play, we two together like well-
blessed parents taking pleasure in our young, we who had
nothing but our love, and that doomed never to bear fruit
in this world, or never earthly fruit. I told all that had
befallen me since she came to bring me word of deliverance in Windsor, and begged me to leave her for her sake.
And she told me of how it was in Chester, with David
active in war and frantic always to be of every party that
ventured an advanced guard, or planned a perilous raid,
all the more if it would take him face to face with his
brother in arms, and how he took always a high and
arrogant line with the king's officers, and would have a
prince's rights among them, yielding to none but Edward
himself. And how no word was ever spoken between them
concerning what he had done and what he had tried to
do, but never anything Edward could offer, no concession
in taking all his men into royal pay, no promise of
dominance in Wales after victory, no permission to retain
what booty he took, nothing ever was enough for him, so
high did he set the price of his treason. And that I understood, for the world was not enough to repay it. Only his
death or Llewelyn's could have satisfied him, and they
both lived on. And still there was not room in the world
for both, never short of a miracle, to cast them back once
for all into each other's arms.

Thus we talked of those two brothers, and of the
prodigies of creation and destruction they had wrought
between them. We sat, as it were, in the shell of a noble
castle not utterly ruined, but slighted by a passing enemy,
with years of labour to be spent on it before ever it could
be defensible again. But so have many castles been, time
after time on the same site, and yet risen again, and again
become seats of majesty.

But not one word did she say of her suffering, and her miscarriage, not one word of Godred. Of him we never spoke in the old days, but since Windsor I was afraid for her, and I needed to know.

'You have told me nothing,' I said, 'about yourself.'

'What should I say of myself?' said Cristin gently. 'You see me, you touch me, I am here beside you. There is nothing you need to know of me that you do not know.'

'There is,' I said. 'I need to know that you are safe from harm. That he no longer persecutes you.'

'I am free from him here,' said Cristin, measuring out words with care. 'He is at the Tower with David's officers and troopers. I have not seen him for nine days and more. But you need have no fear for me. There'll be no more such births and deaths, even when we are under the same roof again. Since I lost him his son he pesters me no more. If he comes to my bed at all, he lies far off from me. He holds it against me that the child died. He will always hold it against me.'

'He may try to harm you, then, in some other way,' I said, tormented, 'if he has turned so against you.'

'No,' she said, 'you need not fear it. He speaks to me as he would to a servant keeping his house, civilly but coldly. He shows no anger and no hatred, he never touches me. I have peace from him. Since his son died, I also am dead for him, being useless. I shall never conceive again.'

Her voice was low and meditative and tranquil, and her face serene and plaintive. My heart ached for her, because of the little ones still tossing their ball about the yard, and the baby boy half-asleep and crooning merrily to himself in her arm. But her heart was at rest.

'Never grieve for me,' she said. 'I do not grieve. I have what I prayed for. If it was a sin to pray for such a dark deliverance, I have sinned, and I will pay for it. But if ever I did Godred any wrong, it was in some way I could not help, not with my will, and it is not for me to apportion penance, only to bear it. It would have been a worse sin to bring his son into the world, when he wanted it only as the instrument of evil, against you, against me, against the innocent who is dead. True, he came to think of it with love before the end, and surely he would have loved it as well as he can love, but I think his love is a heavier curse than his hate. And now I am free of both, and so is the child.'

I said, trembling at this calm that passed so far beyond intensity: 'It sounds but a drear world for you. I wish to God I had the means to fill it with brightness and joy.'

'So you do!' said Cristin, her voice burning into sweet, warm passion, and she turned fully to me, with her great eyes glowing purple as irises under the high white brow, and laid her hand over mine. 'So you do, and will life-long, from the night I first met you in the snow to the day of my death. Oh, I have other joys,' she said, smiling. 'I have children, even if I must borrow them. I have friends. But above all I have this, that I love you and you love me, beyond change, and safe, utterly safe, from any betrayal. I would not change with any woman on earth.'

I folded both my hands about hers and held it, and it was warm and firm and steady. And I said to her all those things we had never said to each other but once, when we made our compact, and it was such strange bliss to get the words out of my heart and string them like pearls for her to wear.

As I reckoned the time of day afterwards, about this same hour that I sat clasping the hand of my love, so did Llewelyn at Windsor first see the face and touch the hand of Eleanor de Montfort.

We were still sitting thus, hand in hand, when the yard gate was flung open, and David rode in, flushed and vivid on a grey horse. The children heard, and dropped their ball to run and meet him, and the elder boy, approaching four years old then, reached up fearlessly to his father's stirrup. David leaned down and took the boy under the armpits, and hoisted him to the saddle before him, and

305

walked the horse gently into the stable with the three little girls clamouring after him. When he came out to cross to the house he had a girl by either hand, and the six-year-old Margaret trotting at his heels, but the boy had stayed to see the horse rubbed down and groomed. With all these blossoming creatures clinging about him, and himself glowing with exercise, David was like a fine tree bearing at the same time flowers and fruit.

He said a word in the ear of the eldest girl, and put the hands of both her sisters in hers, and sent them dancing before him into the house, and then he turned and came to us.

'My conscience and my confessor with their heads together!' he said. 'I tremble for the fate of my poor soul.' And smiling, he stooped and held out his arms for his younger son, and the boy crowed and went to him eagerly from Cristin's lap. 'Come away in with him, Cristin,' said David. 'You'll take cold sitting here so long, and I dare say Samson will condescend to accept a place by my fire and a seat at my table, now we've all made peace. Without prejudice to your loyalties,' he said to me, and filled a careless fist with my hair before he clapped me on the shoulder and walked away into the house, dancing his delighted son on his arm.

So we arose and followed them in, David who had plotted Llewelyn's death, and the boy who bore Llewelyn's face, and at David's wish had been given Llewelyn's name.

'Who is evil?' said Cristin, watching them. 'Who is good? It is too hard for me. All I can do is love where love is drawn from me. That cannot be wrong.'

So all that day I stayed with my dear, and it was the most I had ever had of her since our first journey together. But before I went back to await the prince's return, David prayed me to come and speak with him privately. He asked me of Llewelyn, for since he avoided a direct meeting he was in want of reliable news, and he was right in

306

saying that there was no placing any trust in the rumours of the court. I told him of the visit to Windsor, and of our cautious hopes that this was an indication of some unbending on Edward's part.

'I had heard of it,' said David, frowning and gnawing his lip. 'He was in two minds about it, so it seems. Some days ago he was bent on holding her in reserve, in case my brother needed a touch of the whip. Now he's graciously bringing them together. Well, it's another way of using his weapons.'

I said truthfully that though the king had taken good care of his own interests, and exacted what he could out of the peace, yet he had not been ungenerous, and Llewelyn well understood that he was still being tested, took Edward's suspicions and precautions with good grace, and appreciated his magnanimity in showing so much favour.

At that word David's smile turned very sour. 'Edward's favour is never magnanimity. For God's sake get that into my brother's head if you can. He spends favours to get his own ends, and he expects value for all. If he has graciously led Llewelyn to his wife, it means he has decided to take them over, both, to move them where he wants them, as he moves his other dolls, to place them under an unescapable obligation to him for life. Others give to give, Edward gives to get. It is a new kind of villeinage. Warn my brother so!'

I protested at this that the king had never attached any conditions to those concessions he had made previously, and none were attached to this.

'They are understood,' said David grimly. 'By Edward, at least, and they had better be understood by all those he takes under his wing. If he does not get value for his money he will take it, and with interest. It is better not to be in his favour. But if a man must, let him learn to fend for himself, and see to it that he sells nothing of himself in the process. Take what's given, by all means – since he
307

makes no conditions, force him to stand to that. But never think he'll be outbargained easily. It is Edward who makes the rules. We break them at our peril.'

'And you?' I said, for this was a man deep in Edward's debt now speaking, at least in the world's eyes and Edward's.

He smiled at me without resentment, though somewhat sombrely. 'I have not broken the rules – yet! If ever I do, it *will* be at my peril. All I have done as yet is to make my own rules in return, and stick to them. If he lavishes favours on me, I put up my price still higher. If he bestows a rich bride on me, and thinks to own the pair of us, we join hands and form a league of our own. He has bought neither of us. He has not enough resources to afford us.'

'Neither could he ever come near the price of Llewelyn or Eleanor,' I said with certainty. 'They are neither of them for sale. When they give, it is a gift, not a price. They expect the same dealing from him.'

'You know that, I know that,' said David readily, 'but Edward does not know it. By all means keep them in innocence and him in delusion, but watch over them, Samson.' He saw how I looked at him, and flinched, and as suddenly laughed, rising to herd me to the door with an arm about my shoulders. 'For God's sake go back where you belong. I do not know if I threaten your peace, but God knows you are perilous to mine. Go see as deep into Edward as you do into me, and Llewelyn may be safe, if there's any safety.'

At the doorway Cristin was waiting, and for her sake he relinquished me, clapped me loudly on the cheek by way of farewell, and left us together. We went without a word said. At the gate I took her hand and kissed it. 'God go with you, and God bring you back,' she said, and with that blessing I went from her.

Llewelyn came home with the onset of dark, but went

away again to the king's table, and I had no speech with him then. His face was bright but distant, like the face of a man who has seen the Sangrail of all legend, though he moved and spoke as briskly as ever, and went to the royal board as in duty bound. I thought then of all David had said, and wondered how true it was that in Edward's mind every motion of hospitality, every cup filled at that board, every gesture of friendliness, was scored as a debt, a link in a chain binding a slave.

To a Welshman the guest is holy, all that is in the house is his, he must not be questioned or prompted, when he leaves is his own concern. Blood feud, as of right, follows any violation of the sacred relationship. The home is not a spider's web, spinning gummy threads to bind and confine, but a hearth and a board open to guests and God.

When he came back from the meal in hall it was late, but he asked me to attend him for a while before he slept. It was the hour when we talked together most freely, and I think he wanted with all his heart then to talk of her, but he was so full of her that his wonder and gratitude and joy found no words fitting, and his voice would cease in the middle of speaking, and his mind go away from me silently, back to the chamber in Windsor castle, and the woman rising to come to meet him.

'I have lost and won,' he said. 'By God's goodness I see my gain outweigh my loss. Oh, Samson, I only half-believe this grace is meant for me.'

He told, though haltingly, how the king brought him in to her, and when they were formally made known to each other, left them together. It might be true that Edward, having decided to permit the marriage, had also decided to take possession of it and make it his own festival, but it was not true that he used no discretion or consideration in so arranging matters. I said nothing to the prince of what David had said to me, for mention of the very name would have darkened the brightness of that

309

healing evening. I resolved rather to watch how this thing developed, and speak out only if I must.

'He will not be in any haste to give her to me,' said Llewelyn, wryly smiling. 'I know I must prove my good faith, he takes no man's on trust. But now I am sure that in the end all will be well. No, all is well now! I have seen her, I have looked into her eyes, and seen Earl Simon's eyes looking through them, the same nobility, the same truth, and accepting me as generously as he did. She was glad, Samson! It was with her as it was with me. Now I have seen her look at me as sometimes I have seen Cristin look at you, and beyond that no man can go. Such a spirit, and in a vessel of so much beauty!'

Then in his rapture of humility and exaltation, so moved by his joy in her that he felt a saint's tenderness towards all things living, he bethought him of what he had said, and caught impulsively at my hand, reproaching himself for having so little regard for the deprivation I suffered, when he was promised such blessedness.

'God knows,' he said, 'I wish I could share with you, whose waiting has been longer even than mine, the happiness that is held out to me. If I could lay Cristin's hand in yours, by any means in my power, I would do it. I am learning how much the happy owe their fellows.'

'You need not grieve for me,' I said. 'We were born in the same night and under the same sky. All the while that you have been with Eleanor at Windsor, I have been with Cristin. I have seen her, and held her hand in mine. In the same hour! Our stars have not betrayed us.'

For all this hopeful beginning, and every indication on his part that the ending would be favourable, Edward made no haste, and offered no more such glimpses during that visit. Rather he concentrated on the stern business of preparing the administration of the Welsh lands he had taken into his own care, and though he expected Llewelyn to take part in all the conferences, and consulted

310

him freely, it was Edward's will that carried all before it. The lands being now taken out of his hands, the prince could but advise, and intercede where he thought not enough weight was being given to Welsh custom and feeling, pleading the cause of his lost vassals even when he could no longer affect their fate. Edward showed every sign of listening with care, and wishing to retain their peaceful adherence by treating them fairly, but what he and his officers best understood was their own system of shires and sheriffs, and they tended to believe it must necessarily be best even for the Welsh.

The prince, with Tudor, and Goronwy ap Heilyn and others, worked loyally with the king's men, and did what they could to ensure justice and peace. There were two judicial commissions set up during that month of January, to deal with all legal claims and cases in that part of Wales which was outside the principality, and therefore under the king's administration. One was to work in the eastern parts, the other in Cardigan and the west, and in both a balance was kept between English and Welsh members, for Edward declared his intent of appointing many men of Welsh birth to office in his new territories. Then there was also a third commission to be formed, to see to all the agreed restitution of lands and freeing of prisoners, to take the oaths of Llewelyn's guarantors, and receive his hostages, and even to view the lands he wished to bestow on Eleanor as her dower. With all this business the first two weeks of January passed very quickly, and the prince with his household prepared to set out for home.

Certainly everything seemed to be moving very fairly, according to the treaty, and Llewelyn received so much reassurance from the king's actions concerning the judicial commissions that any doubts he might still have felt were quieted.

'He is dealing honestly,' he said, 'and if his trust in me is slower to grow than mine in him, well, we are two men. It is for me to show him what he will not quite believe for the telling.' And he set himself to act steadfastly and honourably within his truncated state, and wait for his reward with patience.

I made occasion to seek out Cynan before we left for home, to let him know that his nephew was alive and well, and safe with us in Gwynedd.

'I begin to wish I had run with him,' said Cynan, sighing. 'And yet if ever sound Welshmen were needed here, it's from this on. Every man trusted enough to get office under the king has a duty now to take his pay and stand between him and the englishing of Wales, for with all the goodwill in the world it will come to that. There are those who have turned their backs on the old country already, and are busy doing the king's work for him before he knows he wants it done. Tell your lord to keep a close eye on Griffith ap Gwenwynwyn, and get used to thinking of him now as Griffith de la Pole, for that's the style he demands henceforth, and everything he does goes with it. And being a convert, he'll be more a marcher baron than Mortimer or Bohun, and lean harder on his Welsh neighbours to show his zeal. He's got a family settlement on the English plan already – the eldest son gets all.'

I said that Griffith had tended towards the marcher ways for many years, moving by short steps towards becoming an English baron.

'No short steps now,' said Cynan. 'Full tilt! De la Poles they'll be from now on, and even begin to believe in their Norman blood. And keep close watch when Griffith gets near the judicial commission, for he's bent on getting his revenge for the way the prince has always bested him. I judge he's already listing all the pleas he can bring for recovery of land, and in law there's endless mischief to be made.'

I took due note of it, for the possibilities ahead, in all the claims and counter-claims the turmoil of war leaves in its tracks, were already worrying our lawyers.

'Who knows?' said Cynan before I left, patting his growing paunch and stroking his grizzled dark hair. 'I may come and leave my bones in Wales, yet!'

I also went, in the twilight alone, to walk past the house in the canonry, and say farewell to Cristin. But it seemed that David also was contemplating a move from London, for the courtyard was full of a bustle of maidservants and grooms and knights, and through the open wicket I saw Godred among them, marshalling loads in readiness for the sumpter horses. He was as he had always been, fair and healthy and confident, as though time and even the long poison of jealousy and malice had no power over him. So I first thought, but when I looked longer and more narrowly I saw that all that comeliness and brightness of his seemed to have been clouded over with dust, as when a fair tree first shows the signs of drought. I waited a while, unseen, but he did not move into stable or house, and I was loth to go in and meet him, to goad either his anger or his misery. So I said my farewell unseen and unheard in the dimness of the winter evening, and went away.

The fair warning Cynan had given us soon began to show fruit. We had been home in Gwynedd no more than two weeks when at the very first sitting of the judicial commission for east Wales, at Oswestry on the ninth day of February, Griffith ap Gwenwynwyn entered several pleas for damages to his lands and castle at Pool against Llewelyn, and in particular entered a claim to those districts of Powys which Llewelyn had retained after the conspiracy against his life, when he returned the rest of Griffith's lands into his keeping.

Much of this land had come back into Griffith's hands during the war, but not all, and he sought to regain the rest, and to establish his title to all. Now it must be said of the parts in question, notably Arwystli, that they had belonged in old times to Gwynedd, not to Powys, and only during the last three generations had they been in dispute,

313

sometimes held by Powys, sometimes by Gwynedd, which was the reason the prince had kept them in his own hands when the chance offered. Though Arwystli was almost surrounded by the cantrefs of Powys, it belonged by tradition to the mountain lands of Snowdon, and though ringed on all sides by portions of the sees of St David's and St Asaph's, itself it belonged to the see of Bangor. Thus a case could be made upon both sides, but the prince's case rested upon longer history, and he felt strongly about this portion of his hereditary lands, as a matter of pride and principle. He resented in particular that it should go to the insolent renegade Griffith, who had turned his back upon his own people.

The prince had no intention of appearing in any court to the plea of Griffith, and therefore at a later sitting of the commission, in this same month of February, he had his attorneys take out a writ and proceed with a claim in his name to the whole of Arwystli. The head of the commission then was a certain Master Ralph Fremingham, but shortly afterwards he was removed, upon some suspicion of his own probity, which hardly promised well for his judgments. However, this first lodging of Llewelyn's writ was under Fremingham, and took place at Montgomery, to which place he considered he ought not to have been cited, Montgomery being a royal town, whereas the lands impleaded were wholly Welsh, and the treaty was precise in stating that pleas concerning Welsh land should be tried according to Welsh law, and that meant in the lands concerned, as well as by Welsh process. Llewelyn's case throughout rested on this, and he insisted on Welsh law, as was only right. However, in order to initiate his case at once, he allowed his attorneys to produce his writ at Montgomery, but also made a formal protest to the king against being cited there to a court in England.

King Edward replied reasonably that in cases concerning two magnates holding in chief of the crown it had always been usual, even where Welsh law was concerned, to hear them at fixed dates and places, appointed by the justices. There were already some differences in their reading of the treaty. Llewelyn held that the phrase 'according to the custom of those parts' was crystal clear, meaning Welsh law for Welsh lands, but the king was beginning to hedge it about with other phrases of his own choosing, such as 'as ought to be done of right, and according to the custom of those parts', or 'as was usual and accustomed in the times of his predecessors', as if what mattered was to adhere to the previous usage of King Henry and others before him in dealing with matters either Welsh or English.

'And who,' I said once to Tudor, 'is to be the judge of what ought to be done of right? Edward?' For if so, clearly that phrase might on occasion cancel out the treaty phrase, if he chose to consider that what Welsh law decreed did not fulfil his own notion of right.

However, the prince continued in his arduous but resolute patience and good humour, and therefore when the king himself appointed a day for the commission to hear the Arwystli plea at Oswestry, on the twenty-second day of July, the prince sent his attorneys, fully briefed, to present his formal claim against Griffith for the whole cantref of Arwystli.

Griffith ap Gwenwynwyn was a litigious person at all times, and well versed in all the tricks of delay, annoyance and obstruction. The commission was now headed by one Walter de Hopton, and the remaining three justices were all Welsh, and one of them our own Goronwy ap Heilyn, which on the face of it certainly argued that Edward's intent was to avoid bias and do right as well to Wales as to England. But the other two were Rhys ap Griffith ap Ednyfed, renegade from the prince's own trusted household, and another defector from the Welsh cause, Howel ap Meurig, both of them now in the king's service. Both were experienced justices, but their reputation was hardly calculated to give us confidence in their impartiality in such a cause. And in fact, with all the goodwill in the world, the commission, like its plaintiffs, was tied hand and foot by the difficulties of its task, for to disentangle Welsh, marcher and English interests and laws was then work for heroes or madmen.

Griffith began by challenging the credentials of the prince's attorneys. They produced Llewelyn's letter accrediting them, and firmly stating that the cause must be heard according to Welsh law. Griffith still refused to admit their authority, upon every technical point he could dredge out of his litigious memory, and on his plea the case was adjourned to the next sitting in September. Yet two days later, when Griffith brought up his own claim against the prince, and Llewelyn did not appear, as he had determined from the beginning, the court, seeing his attorneys present though silent, gave them instructions to notify him of the date he should appear in September, thus acknowledging that they were indeed his accredited representatives, though two days earlier they had allowed Griffith's objection to their status to cause the prince's case to be adjourned.

These are tedious matters, but they can ruin, madden and even kill, can undo good men and lay waste noble countries.

Letters and messengers went to and fro between the king and the prince, civil, dutiful but persistent on the prince's part, voluble and legalistic on the king's. Sometimes he used so many words, and they revolved clause within clause so artfully, that it was difficult to be sure of his real meaning, but always his professed meaning was to do even-handed justice, and that as rapidly as he could without risk to the rights of either party. He was then conducting cautious advances towards settling the details of the prince's marriage, but was in no hurry about it. Llewelyn shrugged, conceded the genuineness of the king's doubts, however vain they might be, and endured stubbornly, assured of the ending. And he was encouraged when Edward appointed a court session at Rhuddlan in September, over which he would preside in person, and hear both the Arwystli plea and also the case of Rhodri's final settlement, which was still pending, and had been committed to the king by both brothers.

That was a strange hearing, as it concerned Arwystli. Llewelyn had high hopes of it, for now he had Edward himself to deal with, and in our experience Edward was decisive and swift once he had facts before him. The attorneys put forward the claim, asked and were granted Welsh law, as was only right for lands deep in the heart of Wales, and produced their proofs. Griffith ap Gwenwyn-wyn appeared in rebuttal, and made his answer. By Welsh law the status of the land was clear, and no law but Welsh had ever run in that land. By Welsh law, all the formalities having been observed, and each party having had its say, it should not even have been possible to put off a judgment. Yet Edward, pondering long and attentively, in the presence of the lawful Welsh judges of Rhuddlan, who had been brought in to hear and pronounce, of his own will and on his own responsibility adjourned the case, putting it back into the competence of the Hopton commission.

'He was all too sure what the judges would decide,' said Tudor angrily, that evening, when we debated this set-back. A very severe shock it had been to Llewelyn, but he would not do less than justice to Edward.

'No,' he said, 'he is honest. I am sure of it. He has honest doubts about these procedures of ours, and whether they produce truth or not. He finds himself at sea in Welsh law as I do in English. He wants to examine further. It is galling, but we should not complain unless we have some-thing to hide, and I have nothing.'

So he accepted what desperately disappointed him, and made no ado. And the next day, in some measure, he had his reward. For that was the day when Rhodri appeared against him with a formal claim on his purparty of all the
317

lands of Gwynedd. This cause went forward readily enough, and with mutual consideration. Rhodri made his claim through his attorneys. Llewelyn through his produced in court Rhodri's quitclaim for those same rights, in consideration of the payment of a thousand marks. Rhodri acknowledged the quitclaim, but said he had not received the money payment. Llewelyn said and showed that he had made a first payment of fifty marks, and in his turn acknowledged that the balance was still due. Thus they came without dispute to a fair settlement. Rhodri agreed to renew his quitclaim, and Llewelyn acknowledged a debt to him of nine hundred and fifty marks, and not having the money ready to be paid immediately into the court, agreed to a date for its delivery, and that it should be distrained by the king's officers on his lands and chattels if he defaulted.

There were some among us who had doubts of this procedure, and thought it a dangerous precedent, for if once such an interference with his right was allowed in his own lands, it might be used against him in other causes. But he was positive that he could do no less, the debt being acknowledged, and further was disdainfully certain that he was risking nothing, since by meeting the obligation before the date assigned he could and would prevent a precedent from being created.

Then came the first check, and though it was delivered so reasonably and simply that Llewelyn himself attached no importance to it, and found in it no sting, yet I did, and so did at least one other. The king looked up mildly from under his drooping eyelid, and said: 'The sum being so great, I require another surety.'

Whatever the prince might have replied to that demand, through his attorneys, it was never needed or delivered. At the back of the hall there was a sudden movement, light and swift, as someone leaned and plucked at a sleeve before him, and I caught the blue-black sheen of David's hair. During all those sessions of the court he had of necessity been present in Edward's train, but he had kept out of sight, and refrained from troubling his brother even by appearing before him. Now he stooped his head to whisper in his law-clerk's ear, and in a moment the man stepped out free of the public ranks, and addressed the king.

'Your Grace, a further surety is forthcoming. The Lord David ap Griffith desires to be partner in the acknowledgement, and grants that the money shall also be levied on his lands and chattels in England or elsewhere.'

A stir went round the court at that. Llewelyn's eyes opened wide in astonished wonder, and he turned his head quickly to look for his brother, the first time, I swear, he had done so since David fled to England. Edward jerked up his head and sought him no less sharply. I will not say he was displeased, but he was startled, and whatever caused him surprise, or did not in every way behave as he expected, was in some degree offensive to him. However, he had no choice but to accept the proffer, which he did without comment, and had it enrolled in the records.

While the clerk was entering it, I saw Llewelyn's urgent gaze roving the ranks from which the attorney had stepped, and knew the moment when his eyes lit upon David, withdrawn as far as he could into the corner of the hall. The colour rose into David's face in a great wave, but knowing himself discovered he stood his ground, and looked back steadily at the prince, without by smile or frown or movement of any kind acknowledging how the meeting of eyes pierced and shook him. As for Llewelyn, he was lost in amazement, and stared as though by the very constancy of his regard he might penetrate this last of David's mysteries. But the width of the hall was between them, and there was no more he could do, until the king declared the case settled, the deed of quitclaim was delivered once again, and the court rose for that day.

Then, as soon as Edward made to withdraw, and all his magnates gathered about him, Llewelyn turned his back upon them, and thrust his way through the press towards the corner where David had stood. But David also had turned, as soon as he might with propriety, and stalked away towards the nearest door, and the tides of movement within the hall parting and crossing every way, we saw only the lofty flash of the light on his blue-black crest in the doorway, and then no more of him.

CHAPTER XII

Whatever Edward's intended stab, whatever David's impulsive generosity and resentment, in that session at Rhuddlan, both passed by without great significance, for Llewelyn paid his debt to Rhodri long before the day appointed, as was his habit, and that was the end of all Rhodri's claims in Gwynedd. Nor did Llewelyn pursue David to seek any explanation, but let him go his own way, and said no word of what had passed, even to me. In a little while it was as if it had never passed at all. David had made his gesture, which had cost him nothing, and which he had known, since he knew his brother, would cost him nothing. Nothing, that is, in money or goods. Edward had made his, drawing in the rein sharply to remind a spirited horse who was master, and Llewelyn, by reason of his free Welsh acceptance that he had no more privilege at law than any other man, had never even noticed the curb. And the irony was that Edward took that princely and proud humility for submission to himself, and was appeased and gratified by it, when no part of it belonged to him or did him any homage. And Llewelyn took the king's resultant benevolence for true and voluntary goodwill, and liked him the better for it. So they were both encouraged.

Within ten days after he left Rhuddlan, King Edward set free the hostages delivered to him under the treaty, and wrote appointing the day and the place of the marriage of his beloved kinswoman Eleanor de Montfort to his noble and well-loved vassal, Llewelyn, prince of Wales.

The day assigned was itself an omen, as was the king's appropriation of the right to assign it, and to order as his own pageant the marriage he had gone to such lengths to prevent. He had chosen to give his cousin in marriage with his own hand, upon the thirteenth day of October, the day of St Edward the Confessor, the special patron of his father and himself, and the place, appropriately, was the border town of Worcester, where Welsh and English could fitly meet, and where there was a noble cathedral. For the whole court was to remove there to grace the marriage day. And clearly the royal patron of the feast also intended to bear the whole expense himself.

'At least,' said Llewelyn, 'when he is at last satisfied that I approach treaties in good faith, he makes handsome acknowledgement, not grudgingly or by halves. He is doing me all the honour he can, and making a measure of amends to Eleanor. It would be churlish to resent even heavy-handed patronage, when it springs from goodwill and a wish for reconciliation all round.'

But for my part, though I understood his acceptance and pleasure, and his assumption that Edward's kindness meant what it purported to mean, I could not help remembering David's warning, and seeing the very choice of St Edward's day as the king's way of setting his seal upon bride and bridegroom alike, and marking them for his, and all the lavish gifts and giving as the price he was willing to pay to purchase them, a price for which he expected full value, and would exact it if he failed to get it. Try as I would, I could not get this view of the king's proceedings out of my mind, but neither could I reject Llewelyn's view. It seemed to me that both might be true. Edward would not be the first nor the last to assert possession and manipulate people like dolls, as David had said, without himself fully realising what his true purpose was. It did not necessarily mean that his professed friendship was false, or his motives all unworthy.

Llewelyn took the generous view because of his own

generosity, that knew no tethered giving, and scorned to buy and sell favours. But David, who could not rule his own life or find his own way, yet saw deeper into other men than did his brother.

It is true that there were other causes for disquiet concerning Edward's attitudes. He still had Amaury de Montfort in close imprisonment, together with several of the gentlemen of Eleanor's household, even now, when he was giving his blessing to the marriage which was the sole cause of their captivity. How could he justify himself? Llewelyn thought and said, and it may be truly, that Edward surely nursed some lingering suspicion that Amaury, even though he was not present, had contributed to the lasting hatred that brought about the death of Henry of Almain, and that was the cause of his lasting vindictiveness towards him. But what had those others done, knights and servants of Eleanor, and far removed from the crime at Viterbo? It was still some years before they all regained their liberty, after many, many prayers on their behalf.

'Take what's offered,' David had said, 'and since he makes no conditions, force him to stand to that.'

Llewelyn said: 'Let us take what he gives – all the more for fear it may be withdrawn – and then bid for what has not been offered us.'

In this they seemed not so far apart. Yet David spoke of putting up his own price, Llewelyn of pressing for the deliverance of others. There was not the meanest in Eleanor's service that he did not feel for as for his own. But the first consideration was the deliverance of Eleanor.

We rode for Worcester, by way of the border crossing at Oswestry, on the ninth day of October, the prince in full and careful state, with all his chief officers and councillors and an imposing retinue of noblemen and knights of the household. The autumn was fine and still, with a veiled sunlight most of the way, and every mile we rode brought back to me memories both sad and splendid. Here at the border crossing the Welsh envoys to Earl Simon's parliament at Oxford had been met by that other de Montfort, Peter of Beaudesert, unshakeably loyal from beginning to end, and dead at Evesham like his lord and friend. And when we approached the Welsh gate of Shrewsbury, and passed through that fair town to the English bridge and the abbey beyond, I beheld again the hall where I had first set eyes on King Henry of England, when this King Edward was but two years old.

As though he had been following the pilgrimage within my mind, Llewelyn beside me said: 'We have been a great journey, you and I, Samson, since first you came into Aber with Owen Goch, to ward off his dagger from my back.' We were riding a little ahead of his retinue, or he would not have spoken of that attempt. He had never said word of it to any but me. 'But I doubt we have but ridden a great circle,' he said, 'to come back to where we began.'

I said no. For he was still prince of Wales, still had vassals, still enjoyed the recognition of his right within his own land by the crown of England, none of which was true when we began. And then we journeyed with our faces set towards a battle, but now towards a wedding-feast.

'It is true,' he said, his face kindling. 'I have been taking too much upon myself. There is also a future, and a new generation comes with it. It may be my part will have been done, and my discharge honourably earned, when my son is born, out of the line of Gwynedd and out of that blood of hers, better than royal. Why should we try to rob those who come after us of their struggle and their glory? If I can hold what I still have, and hand it on to him undiminished for the ground of his own endeavour, that will be enough for me.'

In Worcester, which is a very gracious town on the bank of the Severn, and blessed with many noble houses, the king's court was established in the bishop's palace, and the attendants of his guard in the castle, while the prince was lodged in the guest-houses of the monastic college. As soon as we were installed there, Llewelyn went to attend the king, and I to see if by any chance I could get word whether David and his family were also come to grace the wedding-day. I thought it most likely that Edward would expect his attendance, and certainly frown upon his absence, for if it was the royal policy to pacify and reconcile Wales with England and brother with brother, he would not tolerate the frustration of his plans by one he considered so deep in his debt. The retort at Rhuddlan may have been a little too sharp, but at least it had accorded well enough with what Edward now seemed to intend. Too blatant a recoil in the other direction would not be so coolly accepted.

I went out into the court of the college, and sought for anyone I might know, going or coming about the palace, and walking in the cloister, a little fatter and a little greyer but always as smooth and neat as of old, I met Cynan.

There was seldom anything to be asked about the movements of the court and courtiers that Cynan could not answer. We went out into the garth, where there was some sunshine and little wind, and sat for a while together, while he told me all the gossip of the palace.

'Surely he's here,' he said, when I asked him of David. 'Who is not here? The prince will have enough noble witnesses. Not only Edward and his queen, but the king of Scots into the bargain, as well as all the officers of the realm. King Alexander is being wooed and urged to renew the homage he made to the English crown long ago. And doubtless he will, but only by way of putting himself under the roof of Edward's power, though his Grace would like more, and has a way of speaking of the act of homage as "for the kingdom of Scotland", as though Alexander held it from him and was his vassal-in-chief like any other magnate. At least he has not ventured to attempt so much

325

against the prince of Wales. Not yet! But bear it in mind, bear it in mind! Appetite grows with tasty food, and the larger the man, the more food he requires.'

I said even he might have some trouble swallowing the crags of Snowdon, but that, to do him justice, he seemed to have no ambitions now in that direction. His intentions had never seemed more reasonable and friendly.

'True,' said Cynan, spreading his palms over his firm round belly, 'but I have known more convincing doves. Still, speak as we find! He has other things on his mind to keep him busy. Archbishop Kilwardby was called to be cardinal-bishop of Porto in the summer, the king seized his opportunity to press Bishop Burnell's claims again, and this time the monks of Canterbury took good heed in what waters their best fish would be caught, and voted as he wanted them to vote, and he has sent a strong mission to Rome to urge his chancellor's case, but it seems that Pope Nicholas is in no hurry to commit himself. I judge the pontiff thinks they make a formidable enough team as they are, and all he has to enforce his own views here is this appointment to Canterbury. He'd be a fool to throw away his one weapon. Edward won't get his way.'

I asked if Burnell himself wanted the primacy, for able though he was, well capable of filling that post to good effect, he might find himself less free to act, and more directly responsible to Rome, than in his profitable double calling.

'Better hope for him to stay where he is,' said Cynan. 'If any man has influence on the king, he has, and he's well-disposed and shrewd, he could be a useful friend yet. But you were asking about David. He's lodged in the town with his lady, at St Wulstan's hospice, though himself he's usually about the king's presence. It's not far, down-hill from the gate and you'll find it.'

'He has the children with him?' I asked.

'The whole brood. He gets beautiful, vigorous children,'

326

said Cynan appreciatively. 'Strange how these things go! The king with all his health and strength fathers puny little creatures who sicken from birth. The girls survive, but the boys dwindle and die. He's lost two, and his third is a poor little wretch more often ill than well. And David's progeny come bursting into the world as pretty as flowers and as lusty as hound pups, and never look back.'

I left him still musing fatly in the cloister garth over the curious workings of providence, and went out into the town as he had directed me, to the old house Bishop Wulstan founded as a hospice for travellers. There were apartments there for many guests, and the courtyard and stables were full of comings and goings, and busy as a fair. Beyond, there was a small kitchen garden, and an enclosed court, and there I saw the three eldest of those same beautiful and lusty children playing with a half-grown cat belonging to the house, rolling a woollen ball for her to chase. But Cristin was not there, only a little nursemaid of sixteen years sat on the stone rim of the well sewing, and watching over the children.

I asked her if Cristin was within, but she said that she was gone with the Lady Elizabeth to hear vespers, and afterwards to make some small alterations in the veil of the head-dress the queen had purchased in the town as a gift to the princess of Wales. For the people of Worcester were known for the making of fine fabrics and stuffs, and the quality of their brocades, and so was Cristin for the delicacy of her needlework.

So I was disappointed, and yet I took heart even at knowing that she was well and valued, and close in Elizabeth's confidence as always. I turned back through the stable-yard to the gate, resigned to waiting until the morrow for a glimpse of her.

Llewelyn came from the king's audience, ate but very little and drank less and went in deep solemnity of mind to hear compline, and to spend some time in prayer after-

wards in the church. Now that he was come to the very
eve of the apotheosis of his life, so strangely linked with
the fall of his worldly fortunes, that balance hung in his
mind like the consummation of a long pilgrimage, at once
chastening and testing, and blissful reward. As he was
without personal vanity, though he had a hot and devoted
pride in his state and his land, so he accepted discipline
and loss as a part of his human due, and probably earned,
like the next man's. And as he possessed the true and
assured humility of those who respect themselves and
others, and ask no special favours, so the near approach of
great happiness astonished and awed him, as being beyond
his deserts, and demanding of him the utmost in generous
effort by way of acknowledgement.

He came back to his apartments silent, grave, immense
of eye, as though he had seen a great light, but was not
dazzled. And when all the remaining business in preparation for the morrow was done, and all his people dismissed, he kept me with him in his own chamber, and I
knew there was something he wanted, though still pondering the wisdom of proceeding with it, but still more the
impossibility of being at rest without it. Half I knew in my
heart what it was, even before he turned to me, all graven
in gold and bronze against sudden blanched white, for the
blood left his face, and the dark pools of his eyes, withdrawn deeper now, in his middle years, into the pure,
stark caverns of bone, burned from within with a fierce,
fixed light.

'Samson,' he said, 'my brother is here in this town, is he
not?'

At this depth he had, and always had had, but one
brother.

I said: 'Yes, he is here.'

'And you know where to find him?' he said, never
taking those deep eyes from me.

I said yes, I knew.

'Go to him, Samson,' said Llewelyn, not ordering but

entreating, 'and ask him, of his grace, to come to me.' He saw how I gazed, pondering the meaning of such a plea, when he was able to command if he would. 'I have a great need in me,' he said, low-voiced, 'to be reconciled with all men, but most with one I have loved most, and smarted against most fiercely. The deeper the wrongs between us, whether mine or his, the more need I have of mutual forgiveness. If I am to go to her tomorrow with a quiet mind, I must have peace and absolution all about me. There is no other way of approaching perfection. I cannot touch her hand while I still have an ill thought in me. Once in a life comes this moment, I will not let it be defaced.'

I was more than willing, but I thought of David burning in defiance of his own chivalry and striding away out of the court at Rhuddlan, and I dreaded his obduracy. I said: 'What if he will not come?'

'I cannot call him on his fealty,' said Llewelyn, 'he no longer owes me any, he has given his fealty elsewhere. I am not his lord, and he is not my vassal. So much the better. I can only ask him, out of old kindness. The rest lies with him.' And in a moment, when I was already at the door, he said, quite softly and certainly: 'But he will come.'

I went down through the town to St Wulstan's hospice, and it was clear dark, and all the sky above me was a moony stillness, hushed and windless. I had barely reached the doorway of the guest-hall when I met Godred in the passage, and at sight of me he stood squarely in my path, and made to halt me with the pretence of his particular love and friendship, which still he kept up as of old, though every last vestige of goodwill in it was long since turned to gall. I saw then, in the torchlight, that the flaxen gold of his hair was dusted over, as it were with ash, and his comeliness dried and withered with malice, but still he liked his comfort and his finery, and took good care of his body, which was youthful still.

'Samson!' he cried in high, glad tones of welcome. 'They tell me you were here earlier in the day, looking for Cristin. A pity you should miss her! But why did you not come and spend an hour or two with me, brotherly as in the old days? We could have passed the time very pleasantly, you and I, talking of old friends. We all grow older year by year – even Cristin! You know we lost our child? And that she'll have no more?'

Once he would have been handling me before this, but now he did not come within touch, only stood blocking my path with his smiling face like a mask, and his eyes gazing from far within his skull, like fine, furtive beasts peering out of ambush. He no longer cared even to trick or trap me into Cristin's arms, no longer grudged us the anguished triumph of our virtuous love, or lusted after the victory of dragging us down to his level, where we could be despised and forgotten, perhaps even forgiven. He had gone beyond that, into pure and perfect hatred of us both, but now that she had lost him his son, the child of his revenge, she had become as it were both holy and an abomination to him, and could not be touched, and all that immense hatred turned towards me.

All this was in his face, like the growing shadow of deadly sickness. And him I could not hate. He was his own torment, and his own poison. I was sorry for him.

'Not now!' I said. 'I am here on the prince's business. Stand out of my way, or, better, bring me to your lord.'

'Endlessly dutiful, and never time for dalliance,' said Godred, sighing, and turned and led me to the room where David was. 'Some day,' he said to me, with his hand at the door and his glance sliding along his shoulder to my face, 'you and I will reach that quiet hour or two together that time has never given us, with no one else by to come between – not even Cristin.' And he went away and left me to go in to David.

Cristin and Elizabeth were sitting at a small inlaid

330

board playing at tables. David was watching them moodily over his wine, his face in repose but not at ease, the black, winged brows drawn down into a tight line above half-closed eyes. They all looked up when I entered, surprised and enquiring, for the hour was getting late.

'My lord,' I said, 'your brother sends me to ask you, of your grace, to come to him.' It was my whole message, I saw no need to add one word.

'Now?' said David, and drew his feet in under him and sat sharply forward in his chair, astonished. 'Of my grace?' he said, and the contortion of a smile came and went on his lips in an instant, like a flash of stormy light.

'Now?' said Elizabeth, echoing him, startled and distrustful, and reaching, as always, to stand between David and anything that might shape into a threat. 'So late? Can it not wait until tomorrow?'

'Hush, love!' said David, with quite another smile. 'Who knows whether tomorrow comes for him? And think how full tomorrow is to be. It may well be tonight or never.' And he looked at me, and through me, and very far beyond, perhaps back, perhaps forward, I could not tell. 'My brother!' he said. 'Not the prince?'

'Your brother. Not the prince.'

'I will come,' said David.

We went uphill through the streets with two of his attendants to light us with torches, and I brought him into the room where Llewelyn sat alone. The prince rose as soon as the door opened, but did not come to meet us, and when I would have stepped back and left them together, David laid a hand quickly and imperiously upon my arm. With his eyes on his brother's face he said: 'Stay with me! God knows I may need my confessor.'

'Stay with us,' said Llewelyn, echoing and amending. 'We may both need a witness, we could not have a better. What is there you do not know already about us both?'

So I remained in the room with them, standing apart,

and what passed that night I know, and none other knows it now in this world.

'You sent for me,' said David as the silence grew long. 'I am come.'

'That was kind, and I am grateful,' said Llewelyn. 'David, of all the needs I have now, the greatest is to be at peace with you. I am going to a new beginning and a great happiness, and I cannot go without an act of purification, and the peace of absolution. While I am in enmity with you I am not whole. For my part, I ask pardon for all I have done amiss towards you, for too much preoccupation with other things and too little regard to your wants, for failures of understanding and of kindness. I ask your forgiveness. Will you take my hand, and be my brother again?'

The candles were low and dim in the room, the twilight kind to those two, but even so I watched the colour drain away out of David's face until he burned whiter than the puny flames, and the blue of his eyes was both bright and blind, as though he looked equally at Llewelyn and deep into his own being. But his voice was even and low as he said: 'It is generous in you to make the first move, but beware of being too hasty.'

'I have not made the first move,' said Llewelyn, and smiled. 'You did that, at Rhuddlan, when you would not let me seem, even for an instant, to be without a guarantor.'

The first ease of blood returning came faintly into David's face. 'I dislike insolence,' he said, 'in underlings, but hate it in kings. You would be justified in believing that was done against Edward rather than for you.'

'So I might,' said Llewelyn, 'if you had not fled me so resolutely when I came looking for you. I am ashamed that I did not do then what I am doing now, and pursue you until I had you safe in hold. Well? May I have an answer?'

'Not yet!' said David, recoiling. 'There is much I have to say before I let you take me back into your favour.

332

Forgive me if I rehearse again what you already know, but if you will not call it to mind, I must. Have you forgotten Bryn Derwin? The first time I played you false? It was I who stirred up Owen to play my game for me, I who put the arguments into his mouth, and when that came to nothing, the sword into his hand and the treason into his mind. I told you then you would do well to kill me, while you could, before I did worse to you, but you would not do it. Within the year you took me back into your grace, mistaking me for the innocent tool. You gave me land and office, and trusted me, and I took and took from you all that you offered. But I had warned you! Why would you not be warned?'

'This is foolish,' said Llewelyn gently. 'I have not asked you for any promises or any recantations. There are no conditions. Let the past alone, we have all been at fault.'

'No!' said David. 'Let me speak. If you have needs, before you can go clean and whole to Eleanor's love, so have I before I re-enter into yours. I have not finished yet. There was a second time – do you remember? When you went to keep the border for Earl Simon, and called me on my fealty, and because of some high words between us, and because of my will to take them in the worst meaning possible, I withdrew myself and my best men from you, and went over to the king's side. Have you forgotten that? Samson will not have forgotten! He tried to bring me back to my duty, and I all but slew him and left him lying. The second treason! No, wait!' he said in a sharp, wrung cry when Llewelyn would again have hushed him. 'I have not finished yet. There was a third betrayal, the worst. I cannot claim I hatched that plot myself, it took a woman to do that. But when Owen ap Griffith came to me with the bait, I swallowed it. There was I with children, and you barren and unwed, and Wales to be won for the son I was sure of getting. We planned your death! Have you forgotten so soon? But for the floods we should have accomplished it.'

333

All this he said without any visible pride or shame, without any expression of regret or plea for pardon, without one word of excuse or explanation, without dwelling on or hastening past loathsome details. For him the healing was in uttering these things and laying them open without conceal. But even then I could not be certain, nor, I think, could he, whether he would ever have let it come to the proof, that night in the February storms, whether it was success or failure he prayed for in the chapel at Aber.

'Leave this!' said Llewelyn. 'It is too grievous. And I have not asked you anything of all this, and feel no need to hear it.'

'But I need to say it, and to be sure that you have it well in mind. I am what I am! I make no pretence to show better or worse. I *know* what I am. And if you want to make peace with me, it must be with open eyes, without any promises or pledges of amendment. God may amend me! I doubt if I can.'

'One question, then, I will ask, and only one,' said Llewelyn. 'Do you not *want* to be reconciled with me?'

Very mildly and simply he said it, and David writhed, and tried three times to answer, and each time withdrew and swallowed the words, unable to get out the severing lie, unwilling to pour out the aching truth, because if once he showed his longing he knew it would be supplied out of hand. Shamelessly he had taken from both Llewelyn and Edward whatever was offered, as I think despising Edward for welcoming and making use of a traitor, and even in some degree disdaining Llewelyn for so rashly forgiving and harbouring one to his own danger. Shamelessly he had taken, and acknowledged no debt in return, but this one thing, and on this one night, he could not accept without feeling himself bound for its full price. The sweat stood on his forehead and lip, and he was mute. And Llewelyn read him rightly for once, and smiled.

'There have been others,' he said mildly, 'have betrayed
334

three times, and yet in the end died for the cause they betrayed.'

'But, by your leave,' said David, wrestling with his devils, 'you are not yet the son of God, only of Griffith, like me. And it will be some while yet to cock-crow. True,' he said, with a tormented grin that was like a contortion of pain, 'I am come by night and with torches to salute you – worse than Saint Peter! Would you not do well, even yet, to avoid and denounce while you may? After the kiss it will be too late!'

For answer, Llewelyn took three long strides across the room, certain now of his victory, gripped his brother by the shoulders, and kissed him, first on the right cheek, then on the left. In his grasp David shook terribly, like a beast in a fever. But at the second touch he heaved a great groan out of him, and caught Llewelyn fiercely into his arms, and returned the kiss with passion.

A moment they clung thus, supporting each other. Then David slid from between the steadying hands, crumpling like an empty gown at his brother's feet, and with long palms clasping the prince's knees, broke into a storm of desperate and blissful weeping.

I went out with him when he left us, an hour later, flushed with assuaged grief, hushed with weariness and wonder, for a brief while purged of all ills, and docile and biddable as a child. A long while they had sat and talked together after that third peace was made, not of any great things, not disposing of old grudges or making more of penitence, but very simply, as memories stirred or thoughts blew them, like severed friends discovering each other afresh after long absence. In the autumn night the moon was still high, whiter and better than his servants' torches, and silvered his face in such daunting purity, as if he had just been born into a man's prime without sin.

'No, come no further,' he said, when I had brought him

335

out as far as the gate. 'I am confessed and shriven clean, I need my confessor no more tonight. Only pray for me, that I have heart for my penance, for this time it will be a life-long penance. I never shall quit him again, Samson. For what I am worth, he has won me. I only pray I may not do him worse injury with my love and loyalty than ever I did with my treason. I am two-edged, Samson! I dread I need not even turn in a man's hand to cut him to the heart.'

So he said, and the moonlight that blanched him was overcast for a moment by a drift of cloud, and shadow passed across his face. But when it was gone, and the light came again, he was tranquil as before, and if he moved like a man exhausted, it was the exhaustion of happiness.

'Go and get your rest,' I said, 'if you mean to attend him in his glory at the church door tomorrow.' The prince had not asked it, nor thought of it, but I knew it would make him glad, and it kindled David's eyes into pale blue flames, as though I had lighted a lamp.

'Well thought of!' he said. 'So I will, and be splendid enough to do him credit, too. I shall be the one gift of his marriage day that Edward cannot claim to have given him.'

And he laughed, with devilry in his laughter again, and by way of sealing the ceremonies of the night kissed me, too, in parting, and went away down through the town to his bed and his Elizabeth.

The next day, therefore, when Llewelyn's groomsmen assembled before the hour at the great door of Worcester cathedral, one among them came unexpectedly, and he the finest and most glittering of all. And if some among the younger princes, notably Llewelyn ap Rhys Fychan of Iscennen, received him with dubious and offended faces and unflattering astonishment, Tudor and the elders were quick to grasp the meaning of his presence, and be thankful for it. One enmity the less, and one so close and

336

damaging, was wedding gift enough. And when Llewelyn himself came to take his stand before them at the door, and the look those two exchanged made their reconciliation and their joy in it plain to be seen, even the young nephews, jealous for the prince's rights and burning with resentment of his wrongs, melted in the warmth of his high contentment, and were tamed.

A fresh, bright day it was, after that clear night, with mild sunlight and a breeze blowing, and a fair scene that was, above the green meadows and the winding river. Before the great porch of the church the knot of glittering gallants waited, with Llewelyn standing alone at their head. That day he was all russet and gold and burning red, and on his hair the gold talaith, the crown of Wales. for he still had a principality to bring to his bride, and held it not from Edward but of hereditary right, and so would assert, for her sake even more than for his own, but most of all for the sake of his sons unborn, whose inalienable heritage it was. David glowed and smiled when he saw it, approving.

Then came the court guests, a very splendid company, led by the queen and her noblewomen. This Spanish Eleanor was a slender lady, tall and fair, and in her manner very gentle, quiet and gracious, not beautiful or of assertive character, but in her own fashion steadfast and brave, as they say she had proved herself again and again in the crusade. After her party came the great officials of state, Robert Burnell, bishop and chancellor, the justiciar of Chester, the wardens of the marches, Mortimer, Clifford, Bohun, even William of Valence, the king's uncle and lord of Pembroke, and Gilbert de Clare of Gloucester. King Alexander of Scotland also came, a widower at that time after the death of King Edward's sister, Margaret. A fine man in the prime of life he was, and handsome. All the nobility of the land flocked into the cathedral of Worcester to do honour to the prince of Wales, and after them the lesser people of the court, and the attendants, until the vast church was full of colour and light and brilliance.

I saw Elizabeth go by in the queen's train, and saw the look she exchanged with David as she passed, so full of pride and delight in him, and he of tenderness towards her, that their love was plain for all to see. And I thought again of the warning David had expressed only to me, and would not cast as a shadow, however slight, upon Llewelyn's day of happiness. These two Edward had joined in marriage, and though they seemed to move as free of him as the birds in the sky, how if he had never yet needed to collect the debt he conceived they owed him? And what if some day he did call in the bond they did not acknowledge, and demand payment in full for all his outlay?

I was thinking of it still when the king came crossing the green from the palace, with Earl Simon's daughter on his arm.

Beside his huge figure she looked tiny, fragile and delicate, for the crown of her head came well short of his shoulder, and she had to reach up to lay her hand upon his arm. Beside his magnificence of black and scarlet and ermine she walked like a pale candle-flame carried very steadily, for she was all ivory and gold from head to foot. Those who had not seen her before, for she had been kept in virtual retirement still, drew breath deep and long as they set eyes on her, for the beauty she always had, which was indeed excelling, was doubled in this deliverance, and made of her a blinding light that dazzled the eyes. To watch them come, at distance, you would have said she was an exquisite image he had bought, and could have been carried aloft on the palm of his hand. But to look closely into her face, as she fixed her eyes upon Llewelyn and advanced towards him, looking neither right nor left, as to a lodestar, was to see her larger than Edward's grandeur, and more durable than his majesty, and to know that he had not money nor jewels enough in his treasury,

338

nor lands enough in all his dominions, to buy the jewel that she was.

They mounted the steps towards us, and came to Llewelyn. And there before the doorway the king laid Eleanor's hand in Llewelyn's hand, and I wondered if he saw as he did it that neither the one nor the other gave ever an eye to him, or was any longer aware of his great shadow falling across their joined hands. They had eyes only for each other, the prince's deep and dark and full of secret light, and Eleanor's wide and clear in gold-flecked green, like sunlight in spring forests. Their faces were pale and serene, the one as rapt as the other, and they did not cease to gaze upon each other thus in wonder and bliss as they turned together, and went hand in hand into the cool dimness of the church, to their second marriage.

That was not the end of the king's favours. At the steps of the altar, before they were blessed, he laid his own personal gift upon the open pages of Llewelyn's prayer-book, a bookmark of woven gold and silk, intricately made. And over their marriage-feast, that night in the bishop's palace, he himself presided, in vast good humour, and bore the expense of all. And I saw the small curl of David's lip, and knew that he was reckoning how lavish the sum laid out to buy what could not be bought, and saw, too, the stern, straight line of his black brows over aloof and critical eyes, and knew he resented the very suggestion of such a purchase, where for himself he had merely shrugged and despised, taken all and conceded nothing. But Llewelyn, I am sure, saw nothing but somewhat possessive kindness, and a desire to seal the peace with promise of a friendly future, and for the sake of Wales that was a good omen.

When the long evening ended, they brought bride and groom in procession to the prince's apartment, where the bedchamber was decked for them, and the candles lighted. And there the bridal pair said their thanks and their goodnight, with that same rapt composure that had

339

possessed them ever since their hands touched, but with such authority that even the king accepted it as dismissal, and drew off his retinue and left those two together.

When the door was closed upon them and all was quiet, I went out into the cloister and walked in the cool of the night, and saw the last candle go out in their chamber, and thought of Cristin, who had been left behind with the children. All that day I had not seen her, but now my heart was the lighter because David was reunited with his brother, and would surely join his household with Llewelyn's on the morrow, and ride to Oswestry in the wedding company.

So my lord came at once to an ending and a beginning, and the loss he had sustained was compensated with as great a gain. And I, too, sat alone in the night, weary but cautiously content, measuring my own losses and gains, and found a good hope in the omens of that day.

But the best and strangest omen was yet to come. For when I had been alone there in the silence a great while, and was about to rise and go in from the chill of the air, suddenly I heard from the window above me the paired murmur of two voices, in words too soft to be distinguished, and needing no interpreter, two threads of sound that interwove and caressed like the strands of a song. And then the deeper voice pealed out in a cascade of exultant bronze laughter, and over it the other soared like a silver fountain of sparkling drops. And I sat lost in amazement and giving thanks to God, as I listened to the sweetest sound ever I heard, the prince and princess of Wales laughing aloud together for joy, and in each other's arms at last.